Praise for Relics:

'An impressive debut,
colourful personalities a
S er, *Sunday Telegraph*

'Pip Vaughan-Hughes has given us a monk, a corpse, a sinister Templar and a terrific adventure that romps across medieval Christendom. A great read!'
Bernard Cornwell

'An audacious plot . . . suffused with intelligent writing . . . a satisfying read'   *Book & Magazine Collector*

'A debut that will hopefully spawn many sequels . . . a rattling yarn from an author who knows his history, *Relics* is high entertainment people will relish'
Waterstone's Books Quarterly

'*Relics* is a great fix . . . it packs power, fear, rage and revenge into a fine 13th-century thriller . . . it's the answer to your prayers'   *Ladsmag*

Pip Vaughan-Hughes grew up in South Devon. He studied medieval history at London University and later worked as a reader for a literary agency when he wasn't dabbling as a bike messenger, food critic, gardener and restaurant owner. He now lives in Vermont with his wife and daughter. *Relics* is Pip's first novel and he is currently at work on a second.

RELICS

Pip Vaughan-Hughes

An Orion paperback

First published in Great Britain in 2006
by Orion
This paperback edition published in 2007
by Orion Books Ltd,
Orion House, 5 Upper St Martin's Lane,
London, WC2H 9EA

3 5 7 9 10 8 6 4 2

A CIP catalogue record for this book is
available from the British Library.

ISBN-13 978-0-7528-8124-9

Typeset at The Spartan Press Ltd,
Lymington, Hants

Printed and bound in Great Britain by
Clays Ltd, St Ives plc

The Orion Publishing Group's policy is to use papers
that are natural, renewable and recyclable products and
made from wood grown in sustainable forests. The logging
and manufacturing processes are expected to conform to
the environmental regulations of the country of origin.

www.orionbooks.co.uk

For Tara

Acknowledgements

My thanks go to Tara, for always being right; Christopher Little, for his dogged persistence and encouragement, and for his friendship; to Jon Wood; to Emma Schlesinger; and to my family, for their certainty and support and, quite frankly, for just putting up with me.

Chapter One

Every drunk is a magician. Or rather, there is a brief moment within drunkenness when magic is a hair's breadth from reach. As I leaned on the rough sandstone of the bridge and stared at the dark river below, I knew that, with one more effort, I could transport myself from this dismal valley to the warm riverbank of my home. A three-quarter moon rising over my shoulder picked out the sinews of the water. I squeezed my eyes shut, and in the same moment knew that I had lost my chance. The magic had gone. These things are a matter of timing. I have still to get it right.

I opened my eyes to find that, indeed, I was still in the wretched city. A northerly breeze blew cold, marshy air around my neck and ankles, and I gathered the thick worsted of my robe hard against my body. But the hiss and gurgle of the river beneath me and the moonlight overhead combined agreeably with the ale in my stomach, and for a drowsy moment I fancied I could hear the spheres of heaven turn and ring somewhere in the distance.

Enough. There was ale to be drunk, and warmth to be enjoyed. I walked to the far end of the bridge, took a couple of steps down the bank and pissed long and hard into the flood, my little stream arching over in a pretty silver thread. Arranging my robes, I made my way back towards the tavern where I had left my friends.

The Crozier, if it still stands, is a small, mean building from the outside. Its cob walls are melting back into the ground like cheese left in a hot sun. The innkeeper, whose sallow skull-face turned many would-be clients away at first sight but who was in fact a cheerful soul, once told me that an ancestor of his had built the place in the time of the last Danish king. Given the cheesy nature of the walls and the toadstools springing lavishly from the eaves, I was inclined to believe him. But once past the door – big rusting iron studs keeping warped planks in some sort of order – the brave or foolish found a big room warmed by a fire that takes up most of one wall, long benches polished into dark mirrors by countless arses, sweet herbs among the clean rushes on the floor stones and two huge butts of strong, sweet beer. This was – and for the sake of that dismal city, I pray it still is – the finest brew in the Bishop's domain.

The Crozier's beer was the best I have ever tasted. It had . . . but no. One man's favourite drink is another's pond-water. If I could have tasted every drop described to me by thirsty bores far from home (or just far from drink) I would be drunk for all my life and half way through the life to come. Sufficient that this was honey-sweet and strong as sunlight, with a lingering something of heather in the taste.

The breeze picked up a notch and all of a sudden I was chilled. I turned into Crozier Lane and there was the tavern, just a few yards away. At that moment, the door opened and yellow light poured into the alley, along with raised voices. Three figures lurched out. By the way they staggered around each other, arms plucking at clothing and heads lifted, a fight was obviously about to happen. Cold, homesick and thirsty, the last thing I wanted at that moment was to push through a brawl, and so I turned left up the narrow passage that sep-arated the tavern from its neighbours, keeping my feet wide apart to avoid the runnel of night-water that trickled down the middle. A right turn, and I was at the side door.

The Crozier's side entrance was a stone archway over an old iron-bound door, behind which a short, stone-floored corridor led to the tap-room. As the door squeaked shut behind me, I noticed something peculiar about the old straw that lay on the flagstones. Something was reflecting back the light from the reed spill that burned in the one wall-sconce, something bright and golden. I bent down to get a closer look.

It really was gold. Sharp-cornered pieces that had been cut from bigger coins. There were a lot of them, scattered over the rotting straw, which, now that my nose was closer, stank of mould and nameless fluids. Without thinking, I reached out to the piece nearest to me, but something made me stop. Looking back, I like to think that I was prompted by divine guidance or my own sharp senses, but in fact I had realised that the floor was alive with lice that skipped over the straw and coins like fat jumping in a hot pan. So instead, I straightened up.

The next moment I felt someone grab me from behind and the weight of a body slam me against the wall, knocking the air from my lungs. Then I was spun round. A hand clamped itself over my mouth.

'This is how you kill someone quickly and efficiently. Knife forward, your thumb on the blade. Strike upwards under the ribs and keep pushing upwards.' The voice was like wind seething across frozen snow. 'If your man is against a wall, put your hand over his mouth until he stops moving. That way, he will not cough blood into your face.'

I felt the man's breath flutter across my own face as he spoke. My eyes were so tightly shut that I was seeing stars. Somewhere in the back of my skull a small, calm voice seemed to be telling me to open them, that I was going to die anyway and that I might as well find out how and why. And so I did.

And found myself looking into a long, thin face. Copper skin stretched tight over angular bones. Thick black hair cut to wear under a helmet. A jutting beard, and dark eyebrows arching over shining slate-grey eyes. A slash of a mouth, which began to laugh. The hand left my face.

'How now, my little monk! Still alive?'

3

'Yes,' I squeaked with the air that remained in my chest.

'Well, well. And are you wondering why?'

I could only manage a nod.

'The reason, priestlet, is that you kept your delicate fingers away from my gold. That told me what a wonderful little fellow you must be.'

I tried to say something. I felt the sudden need to tell this man how grateful I was to him, and at the same time to stand up for myself. A word formed itself on my dry tongue.

'Fuck,' I croaked.

The dark man roared with laughter. He let me go, and my knees almost gave out beneath me. Hardly daring to look, I nevertheless saw that my attacker was tall and slim, and wore clothes of some fine green damask. Then I noticed his right hand. It held a very long, narrow and sharply pointed knife. Seeing my eyes flick down, the man whipped his blade up, holding it a finger's length from the tip of my nose. At this unwelcome distance I could see that the blade was finely chased with swirling patterns in silver, and that the handle was some pale green substance, inlaid with red stones.

'Pretty, isn't she?' said the man. 'Her name is Shauk. She and I were playing a game.'

'A game? What sort of fucking game?' I did not feel this brave. It just came out.

'A game to find the greedy people.'

'I'm not greedy.'

'No indeed. You were blind to temptation. A veritable Saint Anthony!' The man laughed coldly. 'Shauk means "Thorn" in the Mussulman tongue. She can be a sharp little thing.'

And he pressed the tip of his thumb down onto the point of the blade. It came away with a bead of blood already welling from it. He raised his hand and flicked the blood at me. I felt warm drops spatter my face.

'Now it is time for you to run along, *Brother Petroc*.'

He hissed the last two words. I hesitated for a moment,

trapped by his dead blue glare, then turned and ran, kicking up straw and gold as I stumbled up the corridor, heaved open the tap-room door and burst inside.

It was like stepping into another world. Later that night, when my humours had settled into something like their normal configurations, I decided that it had felt like a story my mother used to tell, about a young man called Tom. Young Tom was a tinner, and had dug into one of the mounds that cropped up on the brown and windy slopes of Dartmoor. Deeper and deeper went Tom until his spade struck empty air. He wriggled into the hole, and tumbled into a great hall where the faery court was feasting. In the story, roguish Tom had been welcomed, given a comely faery lass to wed, and returned to the moors after a happy day underground, only to find that the seasons had turned twelve times in his absence. But here in the Crozier, no one had missed me. An eternity had passed outside, and inside time had taken its usual slovenly pace as beer levels crept down, logs turned quietly to ash, and dirty laughter faded in the rafters like smoke. This world was the same, but like Tom the tin miner I had been changed, although I did not know it then. The sparkle of gold and the wave of the steel thorn had worked on me as surely as any faery glamour, and would go on working like slow poison until the old Petroc became merely the person telling his story, a world away in distance and an age away in time.

But now I hung in the doorway like a dead crow on a gibbet, panting, waiting for my heart to burst out through my ears. Then I remembered there was a sharp knife and an open door at my back. The slam turned a few ruddy faces in my direction. I reeled over to the bench where my friends sat. Welsh Owen glanced over his shoulder, and shifted his bum over to make room for me. I sank down next to him. Suddenly I was very angry. I slammed the palm of my hand down on the table. That got the company's attention. William of Morpeth turned his pox-marked face to me.

5

'Where in the name of Saint Agatha's dugs did you get to?' he asked.

My friends were staring at me now. My five friends: Welsh Owen, Cornish Owen, William, Alfred and Martin de Gallis.

'Someone get me a beer,' I said. 'Then I'll tell you.'

Chapter Two

B ut more than one mugful of the Crozier's delectable beer nestled in my belly before I turned to my friends at last.

'Well, get on with it!' demanded Martin de Gallis.

I reached for yet another mug, and saw that my hand was shaking a little less.

'A little respect, by your leave, for one who has looked into the eyes of Death,' I said. Now I had their attention.

'I went down to the river for a piss,' I continued, 'and when I got back some drunkards were scuffling in front of the door, so I took the back entrance. I walked in and saw gold all over the floor, and then someone jumped on me.'

'Who jumped on you?' said William.

'What sort of gold?' said Alfred.

'Gold,' I said. 'Real gold. A great amount. And then that madman . . .' I paused. The man must really have been mad. I shivered. 'He pulled out a knife and put it to my throat – said he was waiting for the greedy people.'

'Like us!' shouted Cornish Owen. I ignored him.

'He cut his own finger and flicked blood in my face,' I said. 'Then I ran.'

William of Morpeth leaned over and stared at me.

'You do have blood on you,' he said. 'What did he look like, Patch?'

Patch was my nickname. I was christened Petroc, but as I left my mother the midwife blacked my eye with a fat finger, and I was Patch from that day forth. Although the mark faded as I grew, the name remained, and while to most folk I was

Brother Petroc, to my friends I was Patch – and Will was my greatest friend. I took a long drink and described the man.

'I believe I've seen him,' said William, scowling. 'Going in and out of the Bishop's palace – I thought he looked like a man-at-arms.'

'Well for God's sake keep away from him,' I snapped. 'He has evil about him. And he has a Moorish knife,' I added, remembering.

My companions were gawping at me. All at once I felt sick inside, and sick of them. I stood up.

'I'm going,' I said.

I glanced back as I walked unsteadily to the door. They were still open-mouthed, apart from Cornish Owen, who was reaching for my beer. Outside, the air had got chillier. The moon had set, and a sky full of stars blazed above me. My lodgings were across the river, and I set out for the bridge. The streets were empty. I realised that sweat had soaked though my underclothes, and the cold was biting clammily at my goose-bumped skin. I heard quick footfalls behind me, and a hand clapped to my shoulder as I turned, my heart jumping madly for the second time that night.

'Hold up, Petroc,' said William of Morpeth.

I stared at him blindly for a long instant, while my blood cooled and drained from my throbbing head. And so we stood, each with a handful of each other's clothes, until I found my voice.

'By Christ and his virgin mother, Will! Cut my throat and have done, if I must spend the rest of my life pissing in my robes from fear.'

William gave my shoulder a hard squeeze and released me. There was worry in his pox-eaten visage, and now that my fright had passed I was glad of his company.

'You are my bait, Patch – I wish to see this Moorish knife-man for myself,' he said, linking arms with me. We started off again, towards the bridge.

As I have said, Will was my closest friend. The rest were hangers-on; friends of convenience, useful to pass the time with (and in the case of Martin de Gallis, a courtier's bastard, useful for an occasional loan), but Will was the only one with any depth. In their beer-blurred and half-formed minds the others resented this bond a little, probably because they too were not particularly fond of each other, and made sport with us at times. They called us The Tups, in honour of our sheep-rearing origins, and would sometimes bleat at us by way of greeting, which we ignored. They were not, I confess, inherently wicked in any way, but more like children who stir the bottom of clear puddles merely to see the water muddy and spoiled. I have no doubt that each of them attained fat parishes and are lording it to this day, raising the skirts of their parishioners' ripe wives and guzzling down the fruits of other folk's honest labour. Go to, my friends, go to: I wish you joy.

Will, though, pursued his pleasures single-mindedly and without regard for the strictures of canon law. We were cut from very different cloth, he and I, he the knowing one, myself the innocent – although that is untrue. Will, in his way, was an innocent too, and threw himself into his drinking, whoring and fighting with the passion of a child, not of a fallen man. Perhaps that was why we were friends. For he never attempted to draw me into his wicked ways, and I, for my part, could not find it in my heart to scold him or even, truly, disapprove.

But nevertheless we were very different. And I had felt that difference keenly this very day. It was my habit to call on Will at his lodgings and find out from him what the evening's entertainment was likely to be – another telling indication of my own rather pious nature, that I was happier to go along with another's plans than admit to my own – and around sunset I had knocked on his door in the mean lodging house that stood rather too near the tanneries for comfort. He had bid me enter, and I strode in, to find him sitting on the edge of his pallet, arm around a girl.

9

I knew that Will made free with the city's whores – 'courtesans,' he delighted in calling them – but it was a shock to find one of these creatures sitting in front of me, close enough for me to smell her, a warm waft of vetiver and sweat. She was young, no older than me, with the round, pink face of a country girl, a tangled mass of yellow hair piled on top of her head in a comically inept attempt to ape the courtly fashion of the day. She was plump, and her bosom was straining the threadbare linen of her tunic.

'This is Clarissa,' said Will. 'Clarissa, this fine personage is Petroc, my brother in Jesus.'

'Come in, Petroc,' said Clarissa, with a giggle that was almost coy. Her voice confirmed that she was indeed a local girl from some outlying village. I stepped into the room and closed the door hurriedly.

'What ho, Will,' I stammered, trying but failing to sound like a man of the world.

'What ho, yourself,' he replied. 'Are we away to the Crozier?'

'I hope,' said I.

'Well then,' he said to the girl, 'I will take my leave of you, dearest.'

'You've kept me too long as it is,' she pouted, and pinched him lightly on the earlobe.

I saw then that Clarissa was arranging her clothes. So I had at least blundered in on the end of their business, not the beginning. She stood, plucked something from the top of Will's clothes-chest. I saw the flash of metal as she wound it into a fold of her skirt. Then she was standing before me, and regarding me pertly, her head cocked to one side. I found myself searching her face for the marks of sin, but all I saw was a pretty, tired country girl.

'You're a big boy, brother Petroc,' she said, and pouted again. I realised that she was searching my face in turn. 'Do you need anything?'

'Nothing,' I blurted.

'Petroc really is good,' said Will from the pallet. 'But not in a bad way,' he added. 'Time to be off, Clarissa.' I caught a warning note in his voice.

But the girl stood before me, as if trying to decide some small but niggling problem. Then she gave a lopsided smile and hooked her thumbs into the top of her unlaced tunic. She jerked it down, and her breasts came spilling out. They were large and round, and very white. As a sea of mortification flooded over me, burning and freezing every inch of my body, I saw blue veins and brown nipples. She shook them slightly, and they juddered. Then I saw that there were flecks of white on the puckered teats. Clarissa was nursing. I tore my eyes away and glanced at Will. He sat there with a rather confused grin on his pitted face. I had never before seen him blush.

'Clarissa . . .' he said again.

The girl shrugged, and tucked herself back into her ridiculously small bodice. She put her forefinger against her thumb to make a little circle. It would not be the only time I saw that odd little gesture tonight.

'It don't cost nothing to look,' she whispered to me, and, reaching down, flicked me in the crotch with her finger. Then she was gone. I heard the door grind open and thud shut again.

It hurt between my legs where she had flicked me. Her aim had been true – my pitifully weak flesh had risen proudly to meet her. I gazed dumbly around the room. Something had changed, although what it was I could not tell. Then I understood. It was I who had changed. Something had been broken or damaged. I was like a new knife that, used carelessly for the first time, picks up a nick or a tiny twist to the blade and never fits so smoothly into its sheath again.

'Oh no,' I breathed.

'They weren't that bad,' said Will, who had stepped to my side. 'Anyway, you didn't touch anything, so you should be safe. Soul-wise,' he added. He grabbed me round the shoulders and shook me. 'Come on, boy. Don't tell me that's the first pair of bubbies you've clapped eyes on.'

But it was – save nursing women glimpsed and hurriedly turned away from in the streets. Clarissa, too, was a mother, and yet Will . . . I shook my head to clear it. How easy damnation crept upon one. How simple, and how sweet. Oh, Christ. I thumped myself in the groin, and my flesh howled in protest.

'Easy, brother,' said Will. 'You need that for pissing.'

Then he was pulling me from the room and out into the dreary Balecester dusk, and we made our way to the Crozier, and I found Clarissa's breasts all too easy, after a brace of beers, to forgive, if not quite to forget.

Now Will was worrying about me yet again. 'Those oafs care for nothing but drink and women, and as they cannot lay their nasty mitts on the one, they must perforce concentrate on the other,' he was saying. 'And they are as greedy as swine: no sooner were you gone than Owen and Alfred rushed to look for the gold, but the passage was empty. Now they have returned to their slothful chatter, and I for one am tired of it. Besides, this is evidently a dangerous night to be walking about alone.'

'What kind of a man plays games with knives and gold, Will?' I said. 'Who do you suppose he is?'

'If he is the man I have seen near the palace, I would say that he is a knight returned from the Holy Land. He has been under a hot sun, and he has a fighter's look. Besides, his clothes are foreign.' I remembered the man's green cloak: it had looked like rich, patterned silk.

'He was French, I think,' I said.

'Or Norman,' said Will. 'The French are small – this fellow is tall, and his lip curls like a Norman.' He spat.

Will had no love for the Normans. His father's grandfather, or the grandfather's grandfather, was a thegne who had died in

King Harold's shield-wall at Hastings. The family lost their lands and had become wool-merchants instead, growing quite rich again and building a fine house in Morpeth, a town in the far north which my friend described as 'a whorehouse for Scots and drovers, but lacking the whores'. Will, the bright third son, had been packed off to Balecester 'to become a bishop', Will would say ruefully. 'A burgher's fat soul needs a bishop in the family if it is to squeeze into heaven. My father is about as pious as his sheep. But the Lord is a shepherd, and Pater trades in wool, so the old monster feels a certain kinship with his Redeemer' – and here he would wink at me – 'but he knows you can fleece men as well as lambkins: he longs to see me with crozier in one hand, shears in the other, and my holy bum on a golden woolsack.'

As we turned up Ox Lane, the street where I made my lodgings, the curfew bell sounded in the distance, and as always I strained to hear the scurrying of feet which I always imagined must follow. In my experience, bells were rung for a purpose: to summon, to warn and to drive away storms. Here in the town, no one took much notice, until the Sheriff's men came at them with their knobbled staves. We students were meant to fight these dullards, it was expected of us, and Will boasted a long scar that divided his tonsure almost from ear to ear. Sophisticate that I was, I felt inclined to be at home and abed whilst these rumpuses took place. And now, as my landlady's door came into view, I turned and caught that twinkle in my companion's eye that meant his night was not yet over.

We reached the threshold of my lodgings. Will tapped me on the chest with a loose fist. He was grinning like a hungry fox.

'Bar your door tonight, brother, in case your crusader comes a-knocking.'

'My crusader, Will? You are more than welcome to him yourself,' I replied. I was tired now, although it was not late, and sleep seemed the most desirable thing in the world.

'Keep safe, brother,' I said. 'Don't go picking up stray coins.'

'My eyes will be on the heavens, Patch, as always.'

And he turned and loped away into the moon-shadows. I climbed the narrow, creaking stairs to my lodgings under the roof. The latch stuck, as always, and then the usual smell of mildewed thatch greeted me. I lit a candle stub and let the warm tallow reek fight off the roof's stale breath – I had decided, soon after taking up residence, that the thatch was so damp that I was unlikely to set it on fire. My pallet, too, was damp and I shivered for a while, my sheepskin mantle tight around me. The candlelight flickered yellow along the rafters and over the bilious straw. Sleep was near, and the bedbugs were hungry. I could hear their little guts rumble as I snuffed out the flame.

Chapter Three

The next morning brought rain. It woke me in the near-dawn before matins, filtering through the decay of the thatch, drip-dripping onto the end of my nose and down into my open mouth. I carried the taste with me as I sloshed through the puddles, my robes hitched up like an alewife, and as I dozed through the morning service. Only when my head drooped and my jaw hit the pew in front with a hollow clunk did the savour of blood drive it away. I had bitten my tongue, but I was awake.

The rest of the morning passed in an unpleasant haze. My head throbbed slightly from the evening's beer, and my tongue throbbed where my teeth had pinched it. I had volunteered – always the eager one – to copy out a lengthy gloss of Origen for one of the masters, and the effort of keeping the quill steady left me exhausted by lunchtime. I found Will in the refectory. He looked sour and twisted, like a hawk with an excess of bile, and like a hawk he croaked and baited when I enquired about his nocturnal activities. He cheered somewhat when I insisted he drink my share of the small-beer provided. In the afternoon I would have to endure a lecture on Roman law, and I needed to keep a clear head. Any unfortunate who dropped off while Magister Jens Tribonensis lectured would be woken by the fat German's stave across his shoulders, and a verbal flaying thereafter. Master Jens might look like a jovial, red-faced buffoon, but he took his Cicero very seriously indeed.

Will squinted at me through red eyes. 'Sweet dreams, brother Patch?' he enquired.

'The pure of heart never dream, as you well know.' I lied. A dream of sorts had returned again and again. Cornish Owen pelted me with gold coins in a stinking tavern room, and I knew that, in a chamber above us, a man in a green cloak admired his knife. I heard my name, a whisper that slid down the staircase in the corner of the room. As I scrabbled at the door, which of course would not open, Owen burbled a mindlessly filthy ditty behind me.

'You, on the other hand, have not put the purity of your own heart to the test lately, Will. Your eyes look as if they need peeling.'

'Strange, my dearest brother, for they were peeled all last night, looking for your dagger-man.'

'I earnestly want to forget that bastard.'

'Well, of course. But as I said, I'm sure I have seen him before. So I sniffed around the palace—'

Before I knew it I had grabbed Will's sleeve.

'Please, brother. Let us forget last night.'

We both looked down. My knuckles stood out white against the dark cloth.

'Softly, Patch,' my friend said. 'I'm sorry. I just wanted to warn you. Your friend – your acquaintance – is the Bishop's Steward. Or at least I am fairly sure he is.'

'What is a madman like that doing in the Bishop's service?' I asked, curious despite everything.

'I don't know. Making enough money to throw about the place, for one thing.' Will patted my hand soothingly. 'Don't worry, Patch. I'm sure he's forgotten all about you. On the other hand, according to my sources, he is a really unpleasant creature. Likes tying up girls and tickling them with his knife.'

'Oh yes? So your enquiries involved looking up skirts as well as around corners.' I was feeling a little better.

Will ignored me. 'He isn't a Norman: he's Breton. He has not long arrived from the Holy Land, it seems, and the Bishop keeps him as a strong-man of some kind. From what I gathered, his duties are of an—' He paused, and cleared his throat. '—An executive nature.'

'What do you mean?'

'I mean if someone is tardy with their debts, your man pays a visit. But I understand he is also employed in more complex matters. He tracks down heretics, apparently, and keeps an eye on anyone who strays from the true path.'

'He didn't look much like a scourge of the ungodly last night. More like a dandy with nasty Eastern habits.'

'Oh, yes,' Will added, taking a pull at my beer. 'He is, or rather was, a Templar Knight. Got kicked out over an affair of honour in Jerusalem.'

'Templars are monks first and soldiers second, I thought. They don't go in for affairs of honour.'

'As I said, he was kicked out.'

I spent the afternoon in the company of Aristotle, gazing at text, but thinking instead about the mad Templar. I knew about the Templars, of course: knights who served only the Lord, monks in armour who were the soul of honour and the scourge of the Infidel. Will's information explained the exotic dress and the sun-touched skin, not to mention the Moorish knife. It did not seem surprising that such a man would have found himself unsuited to life in an ascetic order. But now to be involved in Church matters? I suddenly remembered a nasty fact: he had known my name. How? How would a heretic-finder know the name of a lowly student, and, more importantly, why?

I was no heretic. I was plainly and honestly orthodox. Looking back, I can see that my spirituality had all the refinement of the tonsured rustics who taught me. I had an enquiring spirit, to be sure, but not in matters religious. I knew the beliefs of the moorland people, but those were nasty, odd superstitions. I was aware, of course, that the Mahometans and Jews followed a different path from ours, and had heard the uneducated slanders about idols and child sacrifice, which I did not believe. I knew that there were Christians who picked quarrels with Holy Writ, but I had little interest in that. In truth I cared little about doctrinal niceties. I fancied myself a historian, with a touch of the botanist to relieve all the dust and dead bones.

If anything, I felt a little safer now. I had sacrificed no children, after all. It was a coincidence, a malicious joke, a mistake. I began to shrug the encounter off along with my hangover.

And so I stayed at my books until evening, in that kind of near-trance that spidery writing, old pages and guttering tallow-light often conjures, much to the detriment of scholarship. It is now, when eyelids droop and the mind substitutes its own text for that on the vellum, that Satan reaches for ripe monastic souls. To my mind, bigger windows and a liberal expenditure on candles would keep more clerics on the strait path than a lifetime of hair shirts and midnight prayers. But forgive these maunderings. For the purposes of my story, however, they will perhaps deflect your attention from the boredom of that life, and from the fact that I have forgotten some of the smaller events of those days. Enough, I hope, to say that at some time after vespers I was walking past the great west doors of the cathedral, on my way, I suppose, to my lodgings. Balecester cathedral stands on the crown of a low but steep hill that rises out of a bend in the river. It is surrounded by a pretty, paved space, the Cathedral Yard. Shops and fine dwelling-places bound the Yard on three sides, and on the north side stands the great stone pile of the Bishop's Palace, more a fortress than a palace and guarded day and night by armed men bearing the crest of Bishop Ranulph: a yellow crozier and a white hound on a sky-blue field. The grim palace, such a contrast to the soaring, airy (if stone can be airy) presence of the cathedral itself, was the object of the towns-people's muttered resentment. If it was true to say that the

Normans had replaced the ancient cathedral with a far more beautiful and majestic building, it was also true that the Bishop's palace was bald proof of the conquerors' power. But tonight my thoughts were still with the long-dead Romans and their legal tussles, and I heard nothing until a sudden rustle of clothing behind me broke into my reverie. I spun around, knowing as I did so that my tormentor had found me again.

There was a stronger moon tonight. It shone into the stranger's dark face, lighting the white crescents of his eyes, which stared unblinking into mine. I stood like a pillar of ice, all my fears, driven out by the boredom of the day, flocking about me like starlings returning to their roost. The man was dressed in the same green damask he had worn last night, but now a short surcoat of a darker green covered his body. Upon it I saw two long bones, embroidered in silver thread, forming an upright cross. Around it were four stars with long wavy arms, also in silver. The man put out his hand and, as my sinews clenched, laid it gently upon my shoulder. A smile appeared on his lips. My terror only grew.

'Well met, brother Petroc,' I heard. The voice was soft, nothing like the cold hiss I remembered from last night.

The man bent slightly and peered into my face. 'Petroc!' he said again, and shook me gently. 'Have you turned into a mooncalf, my young friend?'

I felt the power of speech return. My mouth was arid, but words began to form.

'Who are you?' I managed. Not the most well-chosen words, I grant you. But the creature grinned. He gave my shoulder another companionable shake.

'Your friend, Petroc, your friend – but you are still afflicted by last night.' Now there was concern in his voice as well. 'A game, truly, as I said it was. I would no more have cut you than . . .' his smile became rueful. 'Let us become friends, then? It is the least I can offer after curdling your wits like that. For which I beg your forgiveness.'

The advice of any sane man would be to mistrust anyone who calls you friend more than once in a single breath, but I was little more than a boy with country mud on his boots. God help me, I dropped my guard, and smiled.

'Last night was taken as no more than a game, sir. I struggle even to recall it.' Such a poor attempt at urbanity, but greater fates are sealed by less.

'I am happy for it, brother Petroc!' And with that, he linked his arm through mine and began to stroll. 'As to who I am, my name is Sir Hugh de Kervezey, knight of Monmouthshire and Brittany, late of Outremer and now Steward to his Excellency Bishop Ranulph.'

And so I found myself strolling in the cathedral precinct with the Bishop's Steward, too startled to resist – and who, indeed, would have resisted? This man was powerful. He had the Bishop's ear, and he was a crusader, as my own father had been. I was just worldly enough to know that fortunes turned on just such acts of chance. Patronage – I hardly knew what it meant, but it almost made me forget the knife that had gleamed in front of my nose so recently. Fortunes had been decided by a chance meeting; why not my own? Perhaps, I now thought – young idiot that I was – the knight's behaviour had been nothing more than some test well known to worldly men, which I had passed. In any event, no harm was likely to befall me in the shadow of the cathedral.

We walked thus, in companionable silence, until we had crossed the Cathedral Yard and the walls of the Bishop's palace rose in front of us. Then Sir Hugh stiffened, as if struck by a sudden thought.

'Would you like a look inside the palace, brother?' he asked, turning to me. 'I must speak to the Bishop, but it will be a matter of a few minutes. Why not wait for me inside? A promising young man like you might well be spending time there soon enough, and it will be my pleasure to show you around.'

This was my daydream of power made reality. I nodded like a simpleton. 'Yes please!' I gushed.

'Wonderful!' said the knight.

The guards at the palace gate bowed their heads respectfully to Sir Hugh, and let me past without question. Now we were inside, my companion became more talkative.

'A little while ago you were staring at my surcoat, Petroc,' he said.

'Forgive me, sir, but it is striking,' I said carefully.

To my relief, Sir Hugh laughed. 'Yes, it certainly is that,' he said. 'And there is a noble tale behind it. You shall hear it.' And not waiting for my reply, he continued.

'My grandfather went to the Holy Land with His Majesty King Philip of France,' he began. 'He was a knight in the service of the Duke of Morlaix – that is in Brittany – and when the Duke was killed near Aleppo, Grandfather was at his side.' He glanced down to where I scurried along beside him trying to keep up and listen at the same time. 'The Duke's dying wish was for his bones to rest in Brittany, and his heart in Jerusalem,' the knight continued. 'Grandfather saw to it that his lord's bones were boiled in wine, and then he carried bones and heart towards the Holy City. But his party were ambushed by the Saracens, and things went ill for them. A young page who lay hidden behind a great stone saw Grandfather fight to his last breath. When they found him later, he was lying on a hill of dead Mahometans. His sword was broken at the hilt, but in each hand he held one of the Duke's leg-bones, all smeared with the blood of the Infidel.' He sighed. 'The King gave us the crossed bones for our crest, and Grandfather lies buried near his lord's heart in Jerusalem.'

'Have you been there, sir – Jerusalem, I mean?' I said.

'Indeed I have,' he replied. 'And to Jaffa, Aleppo, Homs – strange and wonderful places.' He fell silent, and a certain wistfulness played across his face, softening it for a brief moment. We walked on a few paces, and then he seemed to shrug off his mood.

'How old are you, Petroc? Nineteen, twenty?' The voice was brisk and purposeful.

'Eighteen, sir.'

'And where are you from?'

'Dartmoor. Which is in Devon.'

'Devon.' Something in his voice hinted that his question might have been rhetorical. But how could he know my origins? Absurd misgivings, I told myself.

'Well, that moorland air has served you well – you seem older.'

'Thank you, sir,' I said, extremely flattered.

'And here we are,' said Sir Hugh. Talking, we had strolled through a long stone-paved corridor, its walls hung with rather drab tapestries, then climbed a narrow spiral stair that seemed cut out of the thickness of the palace walls. At the top was another, wider passage, and the tapestries that hung here were finer and brighter. Rush torches burned in finely wrought wall-sconces. The door Sir Hugh was now leading me towards was flanked by two great iron candelabras, festooned with heavy swathes of dried wax like frozen honey. An armed man and a page, both in the Bishop's livery of white hounds rearing on a blue field, stood in the shadows.

'The Bishop's quarters. I'm afraid you will have to stay out here, my friend. But Tom—' and he gestured towards the page, who stiffened, then scurried over to us, '—will bring you a little refreshment. Won't you, Tommy?'

'At once, Steward,' said Tom. The poor boy – younger than me anyway, I supposed – looked terrified.

'Thank you,' I said, embarrassed. Being waited upon by liveried servants was a new experience, and I wasn't sure if I liked it.

'Sit, brother,' the page offered, pointing to a wooden bench just beyond the light of the candles. 'I will return in a minute.' And he set off running.

Meanwhile, the guard had opened the door. A warm glow, of candles and firelight, ebbed out. Sir Hugh patted my shoulder gently.

'I will be a little while. Then, perhaps, you will be my guest for dinner? I have yet to make amends for last night.'

I was speechless yet again, and managed an idiot's nod.

'Very well, then. Tom will take care of you in the meanwhile.' And with that he stalked into the Bishop's chambers, and the guard pulled the door shut behind him.

And so I spent a pleasant half-hour in a corridor of the Bishop's palace, eating cold fowl from a silver plate and sipping at a goblet of some rich, garnet-red wine. The page, Tom, presented these delights to me with a nervous bow and then retreated to his place in the shadows by the door, from where he watched me like a timid owl. The wine's smoky fumes reached into my head like the roots of a tree that sends tendrils creeping into every tiny crevice of the rock on which it grows – and indeed I fell to thinking of the moor, and of a hot day in August when I had laid down to rest on a tor high above my home. I had dozed and woken to find a little adder asleep in the curve of my neck. I gasped in fright and it opened a yellow eye, gazed at me with surprise, and disappeared into a fold in the stone. I had been taught to fear the glossy brown vipers, short and stocky with a black zigzag running the length of their backs, but this little creature had been gentle and as afraid of me as I had been of it. Perhaps Sir Hugh is that sort of viper, I thought idly, picking at a chicken wing. But on the whole, I doubted it.

Finally the door to the Bishop's chambers swung open and Sir Hugh strode out. A smaller, wider man followed him to the threshold, and I recognised Bishop Ranulph. I had sprung to my feet as soon as I heard the creak of the door, and was surreptitiously wiping chicken grease from my fingers onto my habit when Sir Hugh beckoned to me.

'Brother Petroc,' he said, 'come.'

Ducking my head in dismay, I did as I was bid.

'I have commended you to His Excellency,' said the knight. 'You are greatly honoured.'

I looked up, and found myself looking at the Bishop's outstretched hand. Upon the fourth finger squatted an immense ring of gold and carnelian. I knelt and kissed it, shooting a moment's glance upward as I did so. Perhaps my daydream of the moors had not quite faded, for I realised that Bishop Ranulph, whom I had only ever seen from a distance, looked like a buzzard. A thick shock of grey hair fell close around a face that held close-set, slate-grey eyes either side of a hawkish nose, below which was a thin, curving mouth. The man even held his head cocked bird-like to one side as he looked down at me beadily and, I thought, hungrily. I had seen buzzards rip the guts from baby rabbits with just such an air of concentration, and I hurriedly dropped my eyes.

'You are a constant surprise to me, Hugh,' I heard him say. 'I hardly thought you'd be one for protégés.' The Bishop's voice was deep, flat, and every word had an inflection of finality. This was not a man who expected to be questioned.

'Hardly a protégé, Excellency,' Sir Hugh replied casually. 'Of mine, anyhow. Brother Petroc is a thinker. I merely wished to demonstrate some of the promising material the University is nurturing.'

'Thinker, eh?' the flat voice said. 'Make sure he's thinking the right thoughts, then, Hugh.' There was a sort of laughter, a rustle of fabric, and the grumble of a closing door. Sir Hugh tapped my tonsure.

'Unfreeze yourself, brother. Let us find some dinner.'

And so we retraced our steps through the stony anatomy of the palace, Sir Hugh wrapped, seemingly, in his thoughts and I in mine. Chief of these concerned my introduction to the Bishop, and my sense that I had acquitted myself rather poorly. The man was quite terrifying, and kneeling on the flagstones between him and Sir Hugh I had felt like a frog caught between two sharp-beaked herons. But now the Bishop knew my name and face. What a stroke of fortune – an introduction to Bishop Ranulph! 'Wait and see,' I told myself. 'Wait and see.'

By now we were back in Cathedral Yard. Sir Hugh was still preoccupied, and although ignored I reasoned I had been invited to dinner, so I kept close to his side. Then, to my surprise, Sir Hugh steered me towards the great west door of the cathedral.

'Forgive my silence, Petroc. The cares of work. And I'm afraid I have an errand to perform,' said Sir Hugh. 'A small matter of the Bishop's business. It will take but a few minutes. In fact—' and he turned to me as if a new thought had struck him, '—you can be of some help . . . that is, if you don't mind?'

And although I was too surprised – not to say worried – to reply, he cuffed my arm companionably. 'Splendid. That is, unless you have made other plans for your evening?'

'No, no,' I managed, unable for the life of me to imagine how I could help this strange and intimidating man.

'It is simply that, as a cleric, you are the appropriate person for this task, which will assist me and please His Excellency the Bishop,' said the knight, as if reading my thoughts.

After that, how could I resist? Besides, we were now at the cathedral door. It was unlocked at this hour, and Sir Hugh gestured me inside with a courtly flourish.

I had always loved Balecester cathedral, although love is too easy a word. It is a titanic cave of stone, and yet the artisans who made it shaped that stone as if it had been wood, or wax. It was always cool and silent, except during Mass and on feast days and festivals, when it blazed with candles, buzzed with humanity and was filled with billows of incense from huge censers. Just a few weeks back, a great Mass had been held in the presence of the Pope's own legate, one Otto, and it seemed as if the entire city had craned its neck to catch a glimpse of this exotic plenipotentiary from Rome. Tonight it was empty, and lit only by the candles that burned in its chapels and before the altar. As we walked through the transept and reached the nave, I looked up, as I always did here. Columns of stone soared up and away, and met far over our heads in a filigree of arcs and leafy bosses, some carved as clusters of leaves, others as heraldic designs or grotesque beasts and men. It was like being inside a stone forest, and now, although the ceiling was deep in shadow, I felt tiny, awe-struck and insignificant compared to this mighty work honouring a mightier God.

If Sir Hugh felt such things, he did not show it. While I made a full genuflection towards the high altar, the knight gave a curt bow and crossed himself briskly. Then he strolled on up the nave, and I hurried along behind him, trying to keep up. I was surprised when we passed under the rood screen and into the chancel. Sir Hugh was a layman – a knight, of course, and an erstwhile Templar – but he was also the Bishop's man, and so maybe had some kind of dispensation that allowed him access to the sanctuary. The rood screen itself always made me shiver. I saw it as a colossal web of stonework that held seemingly hundreds of statues, of kings, noblemen, bishops and saints, guarding the altar. So much holiness – and so much weight, supported as if by a miracle. But if I felt the fear of the pious, Sir Hugh was immune. Or was he? Now he hesitated, dropped quickly to one knee and, taking my arm, led us back into the nave.

'I will have to ask forgiveness for that,' he said, and I thought his voice sounded strained. 'But I used to be in orders myself, and the training never leaves one.' The poise and presence of the man seemed to have left him all of a sudden. I was intrigued. He was human after all. Will had mentioned the Templars, and I was about to say something, when Sir Hugh continued.

'As the Bishop's Steward I have the right to approach the altar, but I do not like to do so,' he said. 'Which is how you can be of service, Petroc. The Bishop has asked me to bring him a certain holy relic that is kept there,' and he pointed to the altar. 'It would be right and fitting if you were to carry it, brother.'

I felt a glow of pride. 'Of course,' I said.

'Excellent!' said Sir Hugh. His spirits seemed to have revived a little. 'The Bishop has need of the hand of St Euphemia. It is held in a reliquary shaped like a hand, thus,' and he raised his own hand in imitation of querulous, feminine benediction. It was startling in its precision, and faintly mocking: an actor's gesture. It was also deeply out of place, somehow: like the polished, tightly coiled knight himself, with his white eyes and evil little knife. I heard, somewhere in the back of my mind, a gasp of outrage from the stone worthies in the rood screen. But the sense I had of Sir Hugh's otherness, his utter remoteness from anything or anyone in my experience, only tightened his hold over me. I had no familiarity with power. For all I knew, this was how it manifested itself to lesser persons like myself.

So it was against my better judgement, indeed almost against my will, that I turned and entered the chancel once more. The floor here was made of richly coloured tiles, which were quieter than the flagstones of the nave. The tiered pews of the choir rose on either side of me, and at any other time I would have paused to admire the dense carving that rambled over every surface. The misericords – the hinged seats that folded up against the pew-backs – each had a face or a beast under them, some obvious caricatures of real people, others leaf-haired wood-woses or green men. They were cheerful things that brought a spark of fun to the serious business of Mass, but tonight the thought of all those odd faces made me

27

uncomfortable. Like the statues in the screen, I felt their eyes upon me.

But now I had reached the altar. I climbed the three steps slowly; the inlaid marble of different hues and patterns that made the treads glow in the light was smooth and slippery under the leather of my soles. The great stone table before me was laden with candles, and the flames winked and slid over the gold and jewels of the tall crucifix, the covers of the Bible and Psalter, the chalice and pyx. I saw a casket of figured ivory; the stand for a crystal globe which held a single tooth of St Matthew suspended within it like the iris of a grotesque eye; a small cross of filigreed gold and garnets that I knew guarded a splinter from the True Cross. And there, almost hidden by the Psalter, slim golden fingers rose to catch the tiniest beads of candlelight on their tips. The reliquary. Catching my breath, I gathered up my right sleeve so as not to brush the altar or the gems that studded the Psalter's cover, reached across and took the hand of St Euphemia.

It was cool, not cold, to my touch, a thin hand smaller than my own, and finely boned – not unlike my mother's, I thought suddenly. It rose from a richly patterned sleeve that formed a base. The Saint had seemingly lost her hand three or four inches below the wrist. I held the thing reverently. Although I had heard of St Euphemia, a Roman woman of Balecester who had been chopped into pieces by the soldiers of Diocletian, and knew that her powers of healing were revered by country women, I had never given her much consideration. My favourite saint had always been St Christopher, whose image my father wore always and whom I could imagine striding across the moors, carrying Our Lord across brook and mire. St Euphemia had lived and died in Balecester, and her cult was here in a city I neither liked nor wished to remain in. Nevertheless, holding this thing, a thin skin of gold separating my flesh from the flesh of the long-dead woman, I felt a tingle of power coming through the metal. I closed my eyes and offered up a prayer to her, and again, the image of my mother came unbidden to my mind. Feeling oddly comforted, I turned from the altar and found myself face-to-face with a man whose pinched face twitched with shock and outrage.

'What have you done?' he said in a strangled voice. 'How dare you – how dare you!'

I was terrified. The man was clearly a deacon, and quite young. He must have been in the vestry and heard Sir Hugh and I talking. I had been so preoccupied that I had not heard him come stealthily up behind me. For all he knew I was a common thief and the worst sort of impious blasphemer. But then I remembered why I was here.

'I am doing the Bishop's bidding,' I stammered.

'The Bishop? What have you to do with the Bishop, boy?' The deacon had merely been shocked before: now he was angry as well.

'I am with Sir Hugh de Kervezey, Steward to the Bishop. He asked me to fetch the hand of St Euphemia. The Bishop requires it.'

'I see no Steward,' said the deacon. And, looking past his shoulder, neither did I. From where we stood, the body of the cathedral beyond the rood screen was in shadow. Sir Hugh must be sitting in a pew out of sight, I thought.

'He did not wish to approach the altar, although he has permission,' I said, desperately. 'The Bishop wants the hand. I am Petroc of Auneford, late of Buckfast in Devon and now studying here at the Cathedral School. Please,' I added, feeling close to childish tears, 'I mean no harm. Sir Hugh will speak for me.'

'Sir Hugh be damned, boy,' spat the deacon. 'Give me the hand.'

'Please, sir, it is true,' I pleaded.

'Give me the hand, and then I will call the Watch. You should not have drawn the Bishop into your poisonous lies, boy. You will surely suffer for what you have done.'

I was about to give up the reliquary, but a flash of something in the nave caught my eye. And there was Sir Hugh leaning against the rood screen, his arm raised casually.

'Come, Petroc, the Bishop is waiting for us,' he called.

I looked at the deacon in triumph. 'Sir Hugh,' I told him. The man glared at me. 'I see an accomplice, and a bold one,' he said. 'Come with me.' And he grabbed a fistful of my cowl and began to drag me down the aisle.

We were about half-way across the chancel when I felt his grip loosen, and we halted. The deacon turned to me, and his face had changed. Rage had fled, to be replaced with doubt.

'That is Sir Hugh de Kervezey,' he informed me. I nodded.

'I know,' I said. 'Please talk to him, then you will see I was telling the truth.'

And now I followed the deacon as he strode across the tiles. He was quite a tall man, and perhaps ten years older than me. Now that he had regained some composure, I saw that his face was not unkind, although he looked very tired. Long hours in this cold building, I thought, and who knows what battles he fought in prayer? I began to feel less ill-inclined towards him.

Sir Hugh was waiting for us, a tight smile on his lips. After the glittering majesty of the altar, the green damask of his clothes looked drab, but his face was almost as noble – and as unreadable – as one of the stone images that regarded us from all sides. His eyes, as they followed the deacon and me, did not blink. As we approached, he drew himself upright.

'Master deacon,' he said, ignoring me completely, 'I see you know me.'

'Yes, my lord,' said the man at my side. Now it was his turn to stammer. 'I found this boy taking things from the altar, and thought I had caught a thief. Now I see he told me the truth, and I am sorry for thinking ill of him.'

'No matter, no matter,' said Sir Hugh, and treated us to a wide, white smile. 'I have the honour of addressing Jean de Nointot, I believe? Your uncle fought at Hattin.'

'Yes, yes, my lord. That is so. I am amazed that you know of my family.'

'Brother Jean, remember that I am the Bishop's man. Now, has my young friend Petroc given offence?'

'In no way, my lord,' said the deacon, laying his hand on my shoulder. 'Although I fear I have terrified him. I certainly did not wish to interfere with the Bishop's affairs.'

Sir Hugh laughed. 'Terror seems to be Petroc's lot,' he said. 'But of course he will forgive you. Besides, I believe his fortunes are about to change.'

While this exchange went on, I stood between these two men, still clutching the golden hand. I was pleased that Jean the deacon had more or less apologised for frightening me half to death, and as he seemed a likeable man I was all too ready to forgive him, although I wished Sir Hugh had not done so for me. But what did he mean about my fortunes changing?

The knight and the deacon were now talking freely, Sir Hugh asking little questions about cathedral life, Jean de Nointot answering him happily. Then it seemed Sir Hugh noticed me again. 'But we are keeping you, and the Bishop is waiting,' he said. 'Will you walk us to the door?'

'Gladly,' said the deacon, and then paused. 'It is none of my affair, but I am cursed with an enquiring nature,' he said, with a shy grin. 'But would you tell me why St Euphemia's hand is needed at the palace? I might also have to explain its absence to the Dean.'

'Nothing simpler,' said Sir Hugh. He reached out a friendly hand to the deacon, whose smile grew broader as he waited to be drawn into the confidence of the Steward.

Instead, Sir Hugh grabbed the front of his habit and pulled the deacon towards him so fast that the man's head jerked backwards. He yelped as Sir Hugh's knee came up between his legs and slammed into his groin. He began to crumple, but Sir Hugh's left arm snaked around him, spinning him to face me as I stood petrified, the world around our little group erased by this dreamlike flash of violence. Jean de Nointot hung from Sir Hugh's grip, choking and gasping for air. The knight looked past the twitching head and our eyes met. It was like falling through ice. Then I saw that the long blade of Thorn was in his right hand. He let the deacon slip down until the man's chin was under his left forearm, the throat stretched long and pallid. Quick as a kingfisher's beak piercing water, he stabbed Thorn deep into the side of the deacon's neck and cut forward.

There was a ghastly whistling sound, and then the deacon's blood burst from his neck in a thick roiling jet that hit me full in the chest. I staggered back, burning liquid in my eyes, in my hair, my mouth, running down inside my habit. There was a full-bodied reek of salt and iron and I gagged, spinning away in my soaking robes, the hot gore seething against my skin as it trickled down my back, under my arms and into the hair between my legs. The dead man in Sir Hugh's arms whistled once more, an empty squeak that ended in a forlorn burble. I could see, as if through a red gauze, Sir Hugh still holding the deacon under the chin so that the weight of the corpse dragged its slashed throat apart into a vast wound in which secret things were revealed, white, yellow, red, like the inlaid patterns in the altar steps. I thought I saw the flap between head and torso stretch like dough in a baker's hands, then I was running down the nave half-blind, blood squelching between my toes at every step. Behind me I could hear Sir Hugh's voice echoing in the cavernous shadows. He was laughing, a great, warm laugh full of ease and pleasure. 'Stop,' he called, happily. 'Come back, Petroc! What a mess you've made! What on earth made you do such a thing?'

Chapter Four

My eyes were raw with the salt of the deacon's blood and my own blood was roaring in my ears as I threw myself out of the west door and onto the pavement of the Cathedral Yard. It was not late, and people were still abroad, clerics bent on some errand, strollers arm in arm with friends or sweethearts. My mind was empty of any thought save that of escape, and I ran towards the nearest figure, waving my arms and yelling for help at the top of my voice. But the man, a merchant, stared at me for a moment, his mouth open in a parody of shock that would have been at home on a misericord. Then he turned and ran from me, shouting incoherently as he went.

'Wait, wait,' I called after him. 'Deacon Jean is dead! Sir Hugh killed him! Help me!'

Now the other people in the Yard were staring. A woman screeched once and fell to her knees. I was still running, but seeing the horror on the faces before me I slowed to a stagger.

'Good people, fetch the Watch! There is a murderer in the cathedral! Fetch the Watch now!' I was hardly aware of my own voice: it sounded thin and reedy. Stretching my arms out to the kneeling woman and her escort, a stocky man in livery, I caught sight of myself.

Jean de Nointot's blood, still hot, was steaming in the freezing air. The sleeves of my habit hung, soaked and heavy, and my hands were dark and shiny. I found I was still holding the hand of St Euphemia, and the bright gold was goresplattered. Then another voice, loud and full of authority, rang behind me.

'Stop that man! In the name of Bishop Ranulph, stop him! Murderer and thief – hold him fast!'

It was Sir Hugh, and he was not laughing now. I glanced back. He stood under the arch of the west door, tall and commanding, pointing a long white finger. He started to walk towards me. I turned again. People were beginning to edge forward, forming a loose crescent that was closing slowly.

'He is the murderer! He's a butcher,' I pleaded. 'He is bloody. He has a knife!'

'Poor Deacon Jean caught him stealing the hand of St Euphemia,' Sir Hugh shouted. 'See, he has it. Beware, he is possessed! He cut at the deacon like a beast. I saw him tear at his guts with his teeth!'

The fine lady toppled forward in a dead faint. Some of the men had drawn blades. But I was far more terrified of the man behind me than of the frightened folk ahead. I bolted, running straight at the stocky man-at-arms who knelt by his fallen lady. His eyes bulged with fright and he threw himself out of my way. The people nearest scattered too. Legs pumping, I was across the Yard in an instant, and ran up the first street that opened before me. I was lucky: this was Silver Street, a narrow thoroughfare that led away from the cathedral precinct and the Bishop's palace. Unlike the Yard, the street was empty, and I raced down the cobbles unhindered. I heard angry shouting behind me, but no one seemed to be following. But as the street began to curve, following the contours of the hill, I turned into a narrow alley that sloped steeply down towards the river. I dimly remembered that it came out not far from the Crozier. If I had a thought in my head other than escape, it was to wash myself of the foul, clinging blood that clung to me and chafed me as I ran. At that moment I knew I was doomed, but I did not wish to meet my end fouled with the stink of another man's death.

My steep and precipitous descent soon had my legs scissoring in wider and wider strides, and my arms flailed as I tried to keep my balance on the slippery cobbles. Before I knew what was happening I had catapulted from the mouth of the alley and was running headlong across Long Reach, the wide street that bordered the river on this side. There was a yell, a clatter of hooves and the high whinny of a frightened horse, and I found myself sprawled next to a high-sided cart. The horse, a big old beast, was lunging in its traces and regarding me sidelong with one bloodshot eye. A man was standing on the front of the cart, yanking on the reins and almost doubled over with the effort of shrieking curses at me.

In a blind panic I wriggled away from the crazed man and his horse, scrambled to my feet and fled down Long Reach towards the bridge, a dim, crook-backed shadow perhaps fifty paces away. There were other people on the street. This was a busy place of commerce by day, but after dark was trawled by bawds and harlots, and a few of them now watched me with vague interest as I hurtled past, a young cleric in wet robes, carrying some sort of artificial hand.

The hand. I had forgotten what I was clutching, but now I felt the weight of all that gold. Something rattled slightly within it. I stuffed it down my habit. As I ran, it began to slip down between my skin and the woollen undershirt I was wearing, leaving an icy trail, as if a huge slug were crawling down my body. Finally it came to rest on my stomach, held in place by the rope belt cinched round my waist. I felt its fingers cupping my belly, cold and reproachful.

Here was the bridge. I slowed down: there were more people here, people who might know me. Many students lived, like me, in the shabbier districts on the east side of the river, and their taverns were here on this side. I stopped, and leaned, panting, on the end of one of the bridge's stone parapets. I could smell myself: fresh blood, horse-shit and refuse from the street, and the sharp tang of fright. Touching my face, I felt a scabby crust of congealed gore. Thus masked, my friends would not recognise me, I thought now. But recognisable or not, I looked like a fiend escaped from hell. No safety lay in this disguise.

My mind, frozen by shock and the panic of flight, began to thaw. Like blood returning to numb limbs, reality crept back, painfully. I found myself taking stock of the situation. There had been a murder. I was to blame. No, that wasn't right. I had been blamed. The knight was the killer, but was leading the hunt for me. Because the hunt must be on. I had escaped so far. I had to explain what had really happened . . . No. Ridiculous. My word against the Steward. I was dead. No! I was alive, and perhaps I could remain so.

This debate with myself took mere seconds, but already people were stopping, staring in my direction. With no plan but a growing desire for life, I took a deep breath and set off across the bridge. I looked neither left nor right, and tried to keep my steps regular and slow. If I could reach my lodgings I would have clean clothes, a little money. But perhaps that wasn't a good idea. Sir Hugh had known my name – why not my lodgings? I shook my head, trying to clear it of the returning hum of panic.

It would take me two or three minutes to reach Ox Lane. For some reason there was no hue and cry behind me: through some quirk of good fortune I seemed to have eluded pursuit. Perhaps Sir Hugh had led the chase the full length of Silver Street, thinking I was making for the tannery district and the water-meadows beyond. But as I dithered, my steps less sure now, the great bells of the cathedral began to toll. The sound, pure and deep, rolled out across the town. This was no call to prayer, no striking of the hour. It was a death-knell, and an alarm. St Euphemia's hand stroked my guts like a baleful premonition.

I had no time to think now, only to act. I sprinted the few paces to where Ox Lane cut across Bridge Street, stopped short of the corner and peered round. The lane was dark and seemed empty, so I ran for the door to my lodgings. Opening it cautiously, I saw nobody in the hall. Taking the stairs two at a time I reached the top landing, badly out of breath. Panting and smarting from a stitch in my side, I pushed open the door – there was no lock – and stepped into the dark room.

Except that the room was not dark. A candle was burning in the pewter holder by my pallet. And on the pallet sat a man.

My heart lurched. I could actually hear it bang against my ribs, so quiet was the room. Fright had mastered thought, and I leaped backwards, only to meet the edge of the door, which had swung half-closed behind me. Now my weight slammed it shut and I was trapped on the wrong side, fumbling with the old latch, which as usual had seized for want of the dab of tallow I always meant to give it, but never did. My back was to the figure on the bed, but part of me waited numbly for the blow to fall, glad not to be facing my death.

'I have been waiting for you,' said the presence behind me.

My hand stopped its convulsive scrabbling. Everything was suddenly very still and silent. I inhaled the mildew reek of the thatch, felt a stinging in my face where I had mashed it against the splintery pine of the door. Very slowly I turned around and edged to one side, until I had my back to the wall.

'If you don't breathe soon, your eyes will pop out of your head, pop, pop.' I knew that voice, and it was not Sir Hugh. It was Will.

And I did breathe, a horrible, ragged gasp. Another breath, and I was choking, down on all fours with Will pounding my back. I had been sick, and my room smelled worse now, if that were possible. Little points of coloured light were dancing before my eyes. There was a cold, heavy sensation in the pit of my stomach and I ducked my head for another heave. But it was only St Euphemia's hand. I crawled over to my pallet and lay still.

'Jesus, Patch! You're hurt!' Will was kneeling beside me, running his hands over my robe. He was muttering in his haste. 'All this blood. I thought you'd fallen in the river. Where are you wounded, Patch? Come on!'

I sat up, and brushed him away.

'It isn't my blood, Will. Get off me. What the hell are you doing here?'

'Well then, for fuck's sake whose blood is it?' said Will, ignoring me.

All at once I had to be free of my gory habit. I jumped up and began tearing at the knot in my belt. The cord was soaked and had tightened, and my thumbnail broke before the thing came undone. I pulled it away, and with a clank the golden hand dropped from between my legs like some grotesque birth. Will gasped and I saw his face go white as he backed away down the pallet.

'Mother of God!' he whispered.

Meanwhile I had struggled out of my habit, which settled on the floor in stiff folds as if some part of me were still wearing it. Throwing open the lid of my trunk, I grabbed a dirty flaxen shirt that I had stuffed there some weeks earlier and began scrubbing myself. There was water in a clay jug on the floor, and I poured it over my head, hardly noticing that it was freezing cold. I scrubbed some more, Will staring with great round eyes at the naked madman who had recently been his good friend Petroc. Then I attacked the trunk again, flinging clothes over my shoulder until I had what I needed.

I soon had myself dressed in a pair of baggy grey woollen britches, a linen undershirt and a brown fustian tunic. The small bag of coins I kept hidden in the thatch I tied into a corner of the shirt and tucked it down around my groin. At the bottom of the trunk was my old sheepskin jerkin, very worn and moth-eaten and only packed for sentimental reasons. I had outgrown it a little, but pulled it on anyway: it would be warm, at least. I had my sandals. Now all I required were garters, and I had none. So I tore another dirty shirt into strips and began to bind my calves with them.

In the meantime Will had been watching me, his intelligent face frozen in a mask of confusion. He was owed an explanation, and so, while I wound the makeshift garters up my legs, I tried to give one.

'The Steward found me again,' I began.

'Sweet Christ! He attacked you!' Will broke in.

'No, not me. He took me to the palace, and then to the cathedral. He told me the Bishop wanted St Euphemia's hand for something—' and I touched the thing with my foot, '—and told me to fetch it from the altar. Then Deacon Jean caught me.' A sob rose with my gorge. I gulped it back. 'Deacon Jean caught me, and Sir Hugh killed him. Cut his throat like a lamb. Pretended I'd done it. Made me run.'

'Wait a minute, Patch,' said Will, carefully. 'Sir Hugh killed a deacon? Why?'

'God's guts, Will! Why? He's a madman – there is no "why"! He killed the poor priest, and he's killed me, too. I'm running, but there's no fucking point, is there?'

'And there's the hand,' Will said, his calm cutting across my growing panic. 'You kept the hand.'

'I did.' I sat down on the bed. 'I found it in my own hand when I reached the bridge. I thought of chucking it in the water, but that would have been a sin.' I laughed mirthlessly. 'There's no room for a bigger stain on my soul, brother.'

To my surprise, Will rose, picked up the relic and, using the wet and bloody shirt I had used to wash myself, began to rub the stains from the golden fingers. 'It's very beautiful,' he said, softly. 'He told you the Bishop wanted it?'

I nodded. 'And the deacon refused?' he asked.

'No, no.' I shuddered, a spasm that caught me off guard and set my teeth chattering. 'He was happy for Sir Hugh to have it. He was friendly. All he did was ask what the Bishop needed it for. And then . . .' I saw again the fountain of blood, and retched.

'Softly, Patch. Did he try to kill you as well?'

'No.' It was true. The Steward had not lifted a finger against me. 'I ran, and he laughed at me, mocked me. Told me I'd made a terrible mess.' I fought down another dry heave. 'I got outside, and tried to raise the alarm. Then he appeared and accused me. He was spotless – you saw what I looked like. So they turned on me, and I ran.'

Will had finished polishing. He held the hand up to the candlelight, and it gleamed warmly, as benign a thing as it had been on the altar. 'I don't think the Steward is mad. He is playing a game, as he did before. What happened in the palace, Patch?'

'Nothing. The Steward had business with the Bishop. He presented me to him.'

'You met the Bishop, Patch?' Will was incredulous.

'Yes. He looked like a buzzard. Has a nasty laugh.'

'I know what he looks like,' said Will. 'You've stumbled into something, my dear old friend. God knows what, but you've got to get away right now.' And with that he hauled me to my feet. 'Do you know where you'll go?' he asked, looking me hard in the face. I blinked.

'I'm going home,' I said.

I don't really remember the next few minutes. I know that I tried to leave the hand – I felt it might go better for me if I made some effort to return it, perhaps through Will. 'Terrible idea,' he said. 'There is a trade in such trinkets – there's a fortune in gold and gems here. And the relic . . . what price the hand of a martyr?' I was to keep the relic, to sell or to bargain with. It was priceless, after all, but its value as gold bullion alone would probably be enough to buy all of Dartmoor. He bound it to my chest with a linen scarf, which my mother had given to me when I became a novice. St Euphemia's touch was oddly comforting, but the metal dug into me in awkward places. It would be maddening, I knew, but there was no time to think of that now.

Will's plan, if it could be called such, was simple. I would leave Balecester dressed as I was, a peasant to any curious eyes. Once I had put a day between the city and myself, I would put on my habit and be a monk once more. Monks were revered or reviled by country folk: in any event, they generally left us alone. It was the best protection I could hope for. My tonsure was a problem, however, and Will paced for a moment. Then he picked up my water jug and held the base over the candle's flame for a minute. The clay was soon coated with a layer of lampblack, and Will wiped this off with one hand and, before I could protest, began smearing it on my shaven pate.

'Lucky you went to the barber last week, my boy,' he said. 'Your hair is no more than black fuzz, and this will look like more of the same, I hope. Don't forget to wipe it off.'

I was not about to put my habit back on, though. 'There's more blood in that thing than I have in my own body,' I told him.

'Well, you'd better have mine, brother,' Will replied, and he pulled off his robe and rolled it long-ways, binding the ends together to make a great, heavy ring. I hung it across my body. It was bulky and hot over my rough clothes, but I said nothing. Meanwhile my friend was standing in his tunic and breech-clout. 'If you could loan me a pair of britches, I'd be eternally grateful,' he said. I gestured at the trunk. He rummaged, and found a tattered thing that nonetheless proved to fit. It was strange to see Will dressed like a layman, and seeing my expression, he winked at me. 'I feel like a real person again, Patch,' he said. 'That sack may be good for the soul, but it lacks grace.'

Then he blew out the candle and pushed me from the room. The stairs were still empty as we crept down them. Will stopped me at the door with a look, opened it and peered out. 'No one about,' he breathed. Then we were in the street and walking, arm in arm, two friends out for a stroll. We headed away from Bridge Street, towards the wall, beyond which a smear of tumble-down houses faded into hovels and then into the patchwork fields that stretched for miles out into the flat lands to the south and east. I would head south, skirting the city, and then turn west, into the wooded hills. It would mean crossing the river, but upstream where it was more narrow.

The cathedral bell had ceased its tolling, and there was no sign of a manhunt in these poor streets. 'They've forgotten about me,' I muttered to Will. 'I expect they realised they were making a fuss about nothing.' The thin joke tasted like ashes in my mouth, and I wished I'd kept silent.

'Well, next time kill the Bishop,' said Will. I looked at him in surprise, and he grinned back. There was something alert and wolfish in his scarred face that I had not noticed before.

'You're enjoying this, aren't you?' I said.

The grin disappeared. 'I'm enjoying your company, brother, because I fear it will be the last time I shall do so,' he answered. 'And I have the feeling that we're spoiling someone's nasty plan, and I'm enjoying that as well. But if that hog of a Steward catches us, we're fucked. I'm not going back either, Patch. Christ knows I'm a sorry excuse for a cleric, but I won't serve a master who has knife-men and lunatics in its pay. I've seen things in this city. I've been up and about while you dreamed of Cicero.'

'What are you talking about? What things, Will?'

'The Bishop's men running here and there, up to no good. Don't tell me you've noticed nothing.'

I shook my head miserably. 'Not a thing,' I admitted.

'Christ, Patch, you dreamer.' There was no rancour in his voice. 'You've been living inside your bloody books, man. Now you've bumbled right into the heart of something. Listen.' He paused, and lowered his voice even further.

'Surely you've heard that His Holiness is demanding one-fifth of the English Church's tithes?' I nodded. 'Good,' he continued. 'And you can probably guess that the bishops aren't too happy.' I shrugged: politics didn't interest me in the least, especially now that my neck was practically in the noose. 'But listen, Patch. Even that share of the tithes is an ocean of gold. You met the Bishop tonight. He's no priest, he's a lord, and a rich one. Interests, brother. They need to be protected. By people like the Steward.'

He still had hold of my arm, and must have felt my flesh shrink at the mention of Sir Hugh.

'Don't be afraid, now,' he said gently. 'You'll be safe. Once we're over the wall, we'll disappear.'

'Why are you telling me all this, about His Holiness and gold?'

'Because I've heard the name of Deacon Jean de Nointot before. He was cosy with Legate Otto. It seems that Otto was cultivating allies within the diocese, and de Nointot's loyalties were to Rome.'

'So what?'

'So it's an open secret that Otto has been promising advancement to those who take the Pope's side against the bishops – not just here, but all over the kingdom. De Nointot is – was – young and ambitious. He was a viper in the Bishop's bosom.'

The thought of the Bishop's bosom made me chuckle despite myself.

'You're laughing. Excellent. But what I'm telling you isn't so far-fetched. De Nointot is out of the palace's way, his blood is on the hands of a young nobody – sorry, Patch, but do you disagree? – and the Bishop has a witness, to wit, his own Steward. Quite a pretty story, with all its ends tied up tight.'

'But the hand, Will – what about the hand?'

'Motive, you thickhead. They catch you soaked in gore, with the hand on you. No need for questions.'

'But why me?'

'You told me yourself – he was looking for greedy people last night.'

'But I wasn't greedy.'

43

'Absolutely. You were trustworthy. A lamb, not a wolf. No room for two wolves in Kervezey's plan.'

We walked in silence after that. My feet felt like two stones, and my heart made a third. I could find no argument against Will's theory. I was a dupe, and a scapegoat. All the thoughts I'd had in the palace, about power and favour, and how I'd been singled out for advancement, came back to me, and I almost moaned aloud at the horror of it all, but most of all at my own stupidity. I had let pride blind me and make me ignore my instincts about Sir Hugh. And after all, how could I have put myself in the hands of such a man? I was in no manner worldly, but I was not a babe in arms. And now Will had been caught in the smoke of my damnation.

He was by no means a perfect cleric, or a model student, but his wit was the sharpest I had ever encountered, and he soaked up learning without any effort at all. Granted, he was addicted to nocturnal escapades of one sort or another, and no stranger to the bawdy-houses I had so recently dashed past on Long Reach. He had precious few illusions about anything, but I had always thought he would find quick advancement in the Church – a bishop by thirty, as we would sometimes joke. Now he was slinking away from all that, at the side of someone the whole country would soon know of as the foulest murderer of the age. I paused and grabbed his sleeve.

'You've done nothing, brother,' I said. 'No one need ever find out you met me tonight. Let me give you back your habit – and then please leave me. I will not be responsible for your destruction as well as my own.'

But Will only laughed again, a little hollowly. 'You haven't been listening, Patch. This is about popes and bishops, but mostly about money. We're gnats. We don't count at all. I'm your best friend: if Kervezey doesn't know it yet, which I'm sure he does, he'll know it by tomorrow. My life in the Church is over, and probably my life on this earth if I stay here. It's not your fault. You just used the Crozier's back door when you should have used the front.'

'But you would have been a bishop by thirty!' I burst out.

'Haven't you noticed that I've been less than diligent of late, even by my standards? I have been fighting with myself. My faith never was very strong – I'm sure you knew that – and now I fear it has completely left me. I'm a sinner; it's in my bones. And I hate this bloodless life, brother – hate it. I was no more born to this than to lord it over bales of wool like my God-bothering dad.'

'You mean you'll break your vows?'

'Aye.'

'And do what? Christ, Will, they'll cut your ears off just for that, let alone for helping me.'

'I'm heading north. Perhaps I'll tap my dad for some money on the way – perhaps not. But I've been planning for a while, and the plan is to seek my fortune. I'll find a free company to join, and then away to France and the wars.'

'Jesus Christ!' My voice rose, and my companion cautioned me with a look. 'A soldier? You? You're a cleric, brother. What in hell's name do you know of soldiering?'

'More than you.' That at least was true. Will loved to fight, had spent his childhood scrapping and brawling through the streets of Morpeth and was a well-known hellion here in the city.

'You won't be finding dozy drovers and fat watchmen over in France, you know,' I went on. 'They'll chop you to bits quicker than a lamb at Easter.'

'Better than the death-in-life I've been leading.' He paused. 'I could never be a priest. I might have made a scholar. But the Cathedral School is finished anyway, Patch.'

'What do you mean, finished?'

'The Masters are packing up. They're moving to Oxford. Have you really not heard any of this? Magister Jens, all of them. There's a real school starting up there.'

'That's just gossip.' I knew about it, of course. Scholars were drifting together all over Christendom. Our teachers had told us of the new places of learning at Paris and Bologna, and the same thing was rumoured to be happening at Oxford. And we were just a school, constrained by the Church and firmly under the Bishop's thumb. He could make it comfortable for teachers and students as long as it suited him, but schools like ours came and went according to the whims of the mighty. I had dreamed of going on to Paris, or Bologna, or even Oxford. That dream was dead now. But if Will was right, perhaps our days in Balecester had been numbered anyway.

'It feels as if it's all falling to pieces behind us,' I muttered.

'Perhaps we were the only things holding it up,' Will agreed. After that, there didn't seem to be anything else to say.

But now the city walls were in sight, rising up to block our way. Ox Lane ended just ahead, and there was no gate. Fortunately for us it had been years since Balecester had been threatened by war, and the walls were neglected. They were high, but sheds, lean-tos and the odd house had been built against them, they were crumbling in places, and there weren't enough Watch-men to patrol their whole length. I had often wandered this way, and I knew that it would be simple to get up to the parapet. The other side was more of a problem: a sheer drop four times the height of a man. But the shanty-town that spread out from the city on the south had crept up to the walls, and there were plenty of refuse piles and rotten roofs to break a fall.

We ran the last few yards, more from bravado than anything else – there were still no signs of a hunt behind us. In the moonlight the wall's dilapidation was obvious: the Roman bricks that made up its lower courses were crumbling and the mortar was gone, the dressed stone from the Conqueror's time was no longer smooth and straight, and vertical cracks shot up every few feet where the foundations were sinking. I steered Will to the left.

'There's a woodpile along here somewhere,' I told him, and sure enough, a big stack of split logs appeared around a curve, stacked against a buttress. We threw ourselves at the wood, scrambled up without much difficulty, and found that the slope of the buttress made a convenient ramp to the top of the wall. Up on the parapet, the crenellations stretched away toothily on each side. We crept along, keeping our heads down, peering over every few feet to find a soft landing place.

'See anything?' said Will.

'All I can see is the easy way to a broken neck,' I muttered in reply. Then I caught sight of something far off along the wall to the east.

'Lights, man! On the wall!' Will had seen them too.

And now there were sounds from behind us. Feet on cobblestones. Torches flickered at the distant end of Ox Lane. They seemed to drift slowly in our direction.

We scuttled along the battlements like a pair of rats, bobbing up to look for a place to jump, ducking down and running. We both sensed that we could be seen against the moon-washed sky, and the mob in Ox Lane was near enough for us to hear voices. Or perhaps it was other hunters in other streets. There seemed to be nothing near the foot of the wall on the outside: maybe the city had been pulling down houses, or one of the fires that seethed through the squatters' shacks had cleared away the rotting shelters that usually huddled right up to the bricks. We would have to jump now, and take our chances. I hunkered down to let Will catch up with me, but as I leaned against the chilly stone my nose caught a whiff of something unpleasant. I peeped over, and there below me rose a dark mass, rising up to the height of a tall man against the wall and spreading out on all sides. Will appeared at my side.

'Look there, man,' I croaked. 'Dunghill.'

Will peered in his turn. When he turned back, he was grinning. 'Just look at that great big pile of shit,' he said. I stared at him for a second, and then we were both cramped with laughter, trying to stifle it with hands stuffed into mouths, pounding each other and the stone battlement. We laughed as only those who have a choice between the gallows and a long fall into ripe shit can laugh. Then we jumped.

It felt like a long way down. I noticed air hissing past my ears, and a griping tingle of expectation in my feet. Then I landed, and sank to my knees in soft, warm, sucking matter. An instant later, Will arrived beside me. The stench was unbearable down here. We were imbedded in a monstrous heap of dung, kitchen rubbish, offal from butchered animals – the mound was like a towering carbuncle on the face of the shanty town, filled to bursting with all the poisons and fetor of that filthy place. From the miasma that rose around us, I gathered that human as well as pig, cow and horse-shit had a place here. My legs were becoming unpleasantly warm – hot, even – and I tried to drag myself out. It felt like quicksand below me, drawing me down into the pile, and I braced myself for another try. Will was cursing and struggling. I felt hot slime ooze between my toes. Something was trying to wiggle between my sandal and the sole of my foot. I yelped, and threw myself forward. My hand struck something sharp. Now I was hanging forward over the pile. For a second I thought I was still trapped, and then the weight of my body dragged me downwards and out, and the front of the mound gave away. Will and I tumbled head-first down the slope, clods of horror bouncing around us, until a thick wall of brambles and last year's nettle stalks caught us at the bottom. I found I was still clutching something: a pig's jaw. I flung it away. Will reared to his feet, and I followed.

'Patch, oh Patch,' he rasped, and hawked mightily. 'I think I kissed a dead cat.'

'That must be what Purgatory feels like,' I said. 'But the Devil himself would leave us alone in this state.'

We were in a dark, stinking bower formed by the skeleton of a large apple tree which had fallen onto the roof of a dilapidated shanty. Years of live and dead briars, goose-grass, nettles and bindweed had grown up and died back, forming a dismal, snarled wall. We pushed our way through as best we could, squeezing ourselves along the crumbling side of the shanty where the thick lattice of dead apple boughs was thinnest. Will was through and I had almost fought clear when footfalls sounded high above us on the wall, and then the gabble of angry, frustrated men. I froze. A torch appeared between two battlements, then another and another, the guttering orange light skittering down the dunghill towards me. I pressed myself into the rotten wood, and the light fluttered past me. I was in the deep shadow of the apple's trunk, just out of reach of the trembling, searching fingers of torchlight.

'Move on, Jack. That's a neckbreaker, down there.'

'Didn't I fucking tell you? He'll have got down onto one of them tannery roofs further along.'

The light went out as suddenly as it had appeared. I waited until the hunters' voices were a faint snarl in the distance, then pushed through to join Will on the other side. His eyes were very wide and white in the gloom.

'That lot are off to the tanneries,' he said, pulling pieces of bramble from his arms. 'If we skirt along to the right for a bit, we'll get to the river upstream of town. That puts the whole city between us and them.'

'They chased me down Silver Street,' I agreed. 'Maybe Sir Hugh believes I made for the water-meadows.'

'So we'll follow the river upstream. It will lead us to the Fosse Way. Watling Street cuts across it and will take you to London. I'll go with you as far as the crossroads, then go north. Coming?'

I shrugged. 'You'll be safer there, at least,' Will pointed out. 'Hide in the crowds. Then find a ship and go abroad: Flanders, perhaps. Yes, indeed, Flanders!' His voice held a little warmth now. 'My father has business partners there. They will help you. A plan, Patch, a plan! Trala!' And he slapped me lightly across the shoulders.

'Save yourself, Will,' I told him. 'What would I do in Flanders?' At that moment, as the dunghill stench crept around me with the memory of how I had shrunk, like vermin, from the torchlight, I felt myself at the end. 'I'll give myself up. Perhaps the courts will believe my story – it is, after all, the truth. Anyway, they'll hang me quick, and Sir Hugh will be cheated of his fun.'

'You are no coward, Petroc,' he snapped back. 'So move yourself. Now!'

There were shadows all around us, darkness that gave forth the stink of death and decay. Death was behind – death was surely all around. But ahead?

'I don't speak Flemish,' I muttered.

'Don't worry. I'll teach you all the necessary profanities,' said my friend, and headed off into the night. I followed: there was nowhere else to go.

We were in some sort of street, lined with low huts which, judging by the lumpy shapes picked out by the moonlight, were built of cob or perhaps just mud. There was no one about, and no lights showed in the dwellings around us. The mud beneath us was thick with rubbish and shit: animal and human, judging by the smell. We had started off at a quick walk, but soon we were running, trying to keep from the puddles and little streams that seemed to criss-cross our path. Once we surprised a herd of pigs that were sleeping in the middle of the street. Will saw them first and swerved, but I had no choice and leaped, the fear of landing on an enraged hog driving, for an instant, every other fear from my mind. We left their resentful squeals behind, and soon enough the huts thinned, and we were among fields. The moon shone on the rows of winter vegetables and the first green shoots of spring, and the air grew sweeter. Ahead I could make out a line of trees, great spreading shapes that must be the willows lining the river's banks.

The street, such as it had been, had narrowed to a track between the raised fields. I remembered how the land had a slow roll here, some gentle dips and ridges, unlike the water-meadows downstream, which were as flat as a counter-pane. It was friendly country. My breathing began to slow a little. We slowed to a trot, then a walk. By and by the track dipped and we saw the river before us. A few paces from the bank another track crossed ours and we took it, heading upstream.

'There's a road up ahead about three miles,' said Will. 'It'll take us to the Fosse.'

I did not like the idea of the Fosse Way. The great road, built by the Romans many ages past and still the main route from west to east, would be crammed with traffic of all kinds. We would have to travel by night, of course, unless we cobbled together some sort of disguise. But I did not feel capable of deceiving anyone. Again my thoughts turned to surrender, but the night air smelled sweetly of cow-parsley and wild garlic and I said to myself: 'Not yet, not yet.'

The first hint of morning showed on the horizon as we reached the road Will had described. It was a wide, well-surfaced trackway, hedged on both sides. We came upon it through a gap in the hedge and scrambled up onto it over a wall of neatly cut stones. I glanced down and noticed a number, XI, carved sharply into one block, clear in the last light of the sinking moon. So the Romans had built this road too. What odd people they must have been, numbering and ordering the world. But their neat lives had been no more immune to chaos than mine.

A fox ambled away from us up the way, and we followed. The moon fell abruptly behind the thick wall of oaks that had replaced the hedge to left and right. It was suddenly very dark, but there was a faint glow overhead. We walked fast in grim silence until the sky had lightened to the colour of ash, that strange time the instant before dawn when everything is dead and cold, and the magic that conjures a new day out of the void of night seems to have failed. We were visible now. I saw that Will's face was drawn and set. A few paces on, and he paused and pointed.

'See there. That's the Fosse.'

I looked, and saw a break in the tree line, perhaps half a mile distant. Beyond, the land opened out, and I saw patches of fields and woods. In places a faint dark streak was visible against the rolling land: the great road. It seemed dreadfully exposed.

'We'll get to the end of the trees, and see who's abroad,' said Will.

'But they will be scouring all the roads, man,' I said.

'This far from the city any men will be on horseback,' said Will. 'There won't be many of them, and we'll hear them coming. We'll stay out of sight today, though – but wouldn't you like a bite to eat?'

In truth I had not considered hunger. My stomach felt like a cobblestone in my chest, and the thought of swallowing food made me queasy. Will, however, was made of even stronger stuff than I had imagined, for he began to ramble on about breakfasts. Salt pork and smoked fish, small-beer and hot bread appeared in the air before me as he spoke, and despite myself I smacked my lips. My belly rumbled and came to life. Soon we were both cackling like schoolboys, rubbing our guts as ever more furious gurglings rang out in the lane. It was time for the birds to awaken, and it was easy enough to believe it was our hungry bellies that had roused them from their nests. I wondered, for a moment, whether the past night had not been a foul dream, and I was now awake.

I was about to suggest that we jump into the river to wash away the grisly reek of the dung-heap when all of a sudden I stopped dead. Something was amiss. It was as if we had stepped through an invisible door into a silent room. The birds, pouring out their songs in front and behind us, were silent on each side. The river had looped back on itself and to our right the lane touched upon the outside edge of a deep, lazy curve of water. To the left, a line of old oaks and may trees stretched ahead to where the land opened up and the lane met the Fosse Way, a few hundred yards off. Will looked about him, all laughter vanished from his face. I dropped to one knee, following some deep-hidden instinct. Then the sky filled with beating wings and the may trees burst open and flung a great horse out into the lane. With the horrible clarity of deep nightmare, Sir Hugh de Kervezey's pale face seemed to float above the gigantic, plunging beast. I felt no glimmer of surprise. As in the nightmare that returns again and again in the same form, so I felt not fright but a horrible resignation.

The man's right arm whipped round. As I saw that he held a flail, the iron bar on the end of its chain struck Will, who seemed frozen in mid-flight, catching him across the back of his neck. I heard his skull burst and he dropped like a sack of bones and meat. He was gone, I knew, even before the shock of it took me. I blinked as if moonstruck as huge hooves danced over his body; then the horse was above me. Sir Hugh stared down at me, his mouth drawn back in a skull's white grin.

'Do you surrender, Petroc?' He swung the flail before my face, a faceted rod of iron that shone dully. 'I hope not. Better dead than alive, eh, boy? Eh? Eh?' And with each barked word he urged his mount a nervous, high-stepping pace nearer to me. Behind me was the river. I could see Will's lifeless, muddy feet framed by the legs and belly of the horse. Closer and closer swung the flail as Sir Hugh jabbed his spurs, one evil graze at a time, into the lathered flanks. I made a desperate grab for the flail, felt the smooth metal slide through my hand and lurched forward, off balance. Suddenly my nose was against the knight's leg and I clutched at it, sliding down the cloth until I was hanging from his stirrup. I must have turned his foot, for I saw the spur, a sharp gilded beak, open a deep gore in the horse's side. The beast gave a shriek and reared, spun and reared again. Sir Hugh shouted a curse and tried to shake me loose, digging his spur again into the spurting wound. The horse shrieked again and bucked. I felt Sir Hugh slip in his saddle, then I was under the horse and I was tangled, for an instant, in its back legs. It was like being caught between two living millstones. The breath was forced from my chest and I was sure every bone inside me would be ground to dust.

Then the horse, no doubt panicked to feel himself wounded and now hobbled, gave a last shriek and threw his bulk sideways. But the grass of the roadway had run out, and the three of us, a writhing puzzle of men and beast, plunged abruptly into the freezing river.

A dark swirl of water, bubbles and limbs surrounded me, seemed to chew me up like a vast mouth. Blind, I breathed water and choked. An implacable weight was pinning me against stones, crushing my breast, and I knew that I was dying. Sadness rushed into me, became the river. I was drowning in regret. The weight vanished and I floated in blackness. As my life guttered out, my last, absurd, thought was of an old, one-eyed sheepdog I had loved as a child, barking and barking, begging me to play.

Chapter Five

It was dark and cold, and a dog barked in my ear. I floated, caressed by the cold which tugged at my fingertips and my feet. I was lying on my back, and found I could see stars through the branches of a tree. Then I understood. I was floating in the river, held somehow against the current. I felt about carefully, and found that my rolled habit had snagged on some part of a dead tree. Then I panicked, struggled, and almost drowned a second time. It was agony to twist myself around and grope with frozen hands until I had a firm hold on the branch and could pull myself close enough to it to free the cloth. Spiderwebs of pain shot across my chest, and the memory of the horse's terrible weight pinning me down came to me in a flash.

I do not remember how I dragged myself up the bank. Much later I awoke in a nest of dry grass and rushes. The dog was barking again, very loud, and I opened my eyes to find a wet snout a hand's breadth from my face.

'Hello, dog,' I said, and fell back into darkness.

It was night again, or late evening. I sat up, and the pain rippled over my chest again, not nearly so bad this time. My clothes had dried, at least the front of them, so I must have slept through a sunny day. There was no dog to be seen, and I wondered if I had dreamed him. I got up and staggered away from the water. I was in flat country, that much I could tell in the fading light. I was in a swale of bulrushes that lay in a crook of the river, but all around me stretched fields, and I could see the dim shapes of cattle standing about, hear the soft scrunch of chewed cud. Away upstream a darker mass flecked with faint lights hunkered across the skyline. I was in the water-meadows.

I shook my head, trying to clear it. Pain clanged inside my skull and I began to understand. Dead to the world, I had floated right through the city and out the other side. How far – two miles? Four? Why had I not drowned? Now I remembered, in tiny, tattered rags of memory, a sensation of weightlessness, of flying, water dragging through my fingers. Some instinct had kept me on my back. Then I remembered my burden, and felt for the golden hand. It was still bound to me, but it had slipped, knocked in the fight, I supposed, and was now hanging against the small of my back. So there was part of the answer: St Euphemia's hand had been my ballast, my keel, keeping me face-up and arse-down. I rebound it tightly to my chest, but could not bring myself to look at the thing and recoiled from the oily coldness of the metal. I felt a sudden and overwhelming urge to tear it from me and throw it far out into the river, but Will's voice came back to me. 'It's all you have, Patch,' he'd said as he wiped the blood from the gold.

Sound advice as ever, dear friend, I thought. And then I remembered: Will was dead, lying in a ditch away on the other side of the city. A new pain flared in my breast, as if some part of my vitals had been torn away as I slept: the raw, bloody void was filling with grief and with an awful, bitter guilt. No more beer or whores for Will, no more laughter or warmth. He would never see Flanders now, and I would not see his crooked smile again in this world. I fell forward into the wet grass and his face swam before my mind's eye, slack and lifeless as it had been the instant after Sir Hugh's flail had caught him. I had killed Will as surely as if my hand had struck the blow: Death had followed me from the cathedral. And Sir Hugh himself? I seemed to recall the horse rolling over him as we went into the river. Dead as well, I supposed, the madman undone by his own madness, his game finished too. And the end of any hope for me. I had no doubt that these new corpses would be laid to my account. Night was coming in, and I felt Death, like an old friend, settle down beside me to keep the long vigil until dawn.

The water-meadows were ravishingly lovely in the dawn. They wore a shimmering silver cloak, dew clinging to festoons of spiders' webs, bright points of colour glowing through the sweet grass. The big red cattle grazed oblivious as they waded through the spectral veil. I must have slept: the spiders had woven me a glimmering winding-sheet of my own. The city was close: much less than a mile lay between me and the last hovel of the tannery quarter.

Still, the black mood of last night had lifted a little, and I no longer felt brim-full of despair. It might be worth living a little while longer, perhaps, if for no other reason than to give Will's death some meaning. I had been skulking here for too long already. I took stock of myself. I had the golden hand, and the clothes I stood up in, which were dryish but by no means magnificent. Save for my tonsure, I looked like a farmer who had taken to sleeping in hedgerows – and there I had it. I was a farmer's son, sent up to one of the Midlands fairs with a load of wool, on my way home. I had fallen among thieves, and must needs go on foot. So it seemed I was going home – or at least towards it. I found I did not have the stomach for London now. Some linen torn from my gaiters made a passable head-cloth, and as I covered up my shaven scalp it came to me. There was one person left in the world who could help me. I turned to the west and set out on the long road back to Brother Adric.

There was much country between us. The Mendips, Sedgemoor, the Blackdown Hills. I travelled by starlight when there were people about, by day when I moved through empty country. It was a long journey, and a hard one, but there is little to tell of it. I ate berries, fish from streams, small beasts I could trap. I was a Dartmoor child – I would not go hungry outdoors. And luck paid me a visit in the guise of a halfwit carter who let me ride on his rickety old wain amongst a load of oakum bound for the shipyards of Plymouth. The man did not want money, which was fortunate. Carrying superstition about him like heavy armour, he took me for a wandering demon, I believe, and helped me in order to forestall any mischief I might work on him. We met at a crossroads outside Cullompton, and he carried me almost to the threshold of my destination.

So I was alone with my thoughts for the two weeks it took me to cross Somerset and half of Devon. I had little I wished to dwell upon from the immediate past, but still I worked the nightmare over in my mind endlessly until the colours and the horror had receded a little. It seemed as though not a minute passed when I did not think of Will, and how we should be sharing this adventure – although there was nothing adventurous about my condition now – and every such thought was a knife thrust. His death, and I suppose the likelihood of my own, followed me like ragged shadow and brought with it the chill of the grave. To escape it I thought about the past. I was a young man who, out of the blue, had lost his future, had been stripped of the life he knew. I had nothing left but my story, and I told it to myself, for it gave me comfort when hope felt stretched as thin as spider-webs wafting in the mist of an uncertain dawn.

The young man in this story is myself, but then again, he is as different from myself as the worm is to the butterfly. Although what I am today – worm or butterfly – is not so clear to me. Enough. The eyes, squeezed shut against the summer sun, preserve an image of the world that lasts for an instant and then changes, becomes grotesque, a shifting field of darkness and glowing patterns that mock reality. I wish to preserve that first moment, before the grotesqueries of the present blot out my past.

I was born in the twelve-hundred and seventeenth year of Our Lord, the second year of the reign of Henry Plantagenet, in the village of Auneford on the southern foot of Dartmoor. I was named Petroc for the village saint and for my grandfather. My father, like his before him, was a yeoman sheep-farmer, and grazed his flocks on the high moorland common that rose up behind our house. The house itself was long and low, built of granite the colour of a fox's tail, and stood on a south-facing slope a bow-shot from the village proper. A brook ran past the left wall, and below the river Aune flowed amongst smooth boulders and great oak trees. The water was clear and brown, and full of gold-green trout that hid under its rocks when I tried to grab them, and sometimes big salmon that would splash and flop in the shallows when night fell.

Lowland people are frightened of hills. Mountains and moors, which perhaps they have never even seen from a distance, are empty wastes where monsters play and set snares for feckless travellers. But our moor was anything but empty. Sheep wandered the high grassland, and the valleys and folds of the landscape swarmed with the works of man. Tin, copper and arsenic lay in the stream-beds, and Auneford men dug out the ore as they had done since the beginning of time, or at the very least since the Flood. Our village lay in the demesne of the abbey of Buckfast, but had never known a lord, and so formed a refuge for landless people, those with a past that needed escaping, or a future that did not include serfdom or fealty. As a result, the villagers were taciturn, rabidly independent and as turned in on themselves as any closed monkish order. Those who did not farm the valley bottom or run sheep over the moor worked the tinning pits, and they were the toughest of all.

My father was a big man who talked little but laughed more, a kind man who had spent too much time wandering the moors to be very adept with words. Although his sheep had made him quite wealthy – certainly the richest man in

Auneford, if not exactly a second Midas – he preferred to live the life of an ordinary shepherd, roaming with his flocks with only his two dogs for companionship. When I got older, I would trespass on his happy solitude. We would hardly ever speak, but he taught me every inch of his grazing land. Green Hill, Old Hill, Gripper's Hill, Heap of Sinners, Redstairs, Black Tor Mires – remembering these names is the only way I can recall his voice. He would show me larks' nests, and how to tickle the little trout parr – speckled red and marked with blue thumb-prints along their flanks – that swarmed in the brooks. We would build a fire amongst the boulders and toast them on blackthorn twigs. We watched ravens soar and tumble, and picked bilberries until our hands and mouths were stained dark purple.

My grandfather, whom I never knew, was a man of energy. As a youth he had performed some service for the Abbot of Buckfast, and as a result enjoyed the abbey's special favour. God alone knows what that service was – something to do with boundary stones that left him with a game leg, Father once let slip – but Grandfather was able to sell his wool for the highest price and pay the lowest tithes of anyone in the Aune valley. He built our stone house, and must have had some status, as well as money, for my father married above his station. My mother was the daughter of a minor knight, Guy de Rosel, who held lands in the South Hams, that broken, hidden country that lies between the moors and the sea. Life had reduced my maternal grandparents to genteel wrecks. Taxes, obligations and the workings of fate had paupered them, and their manor, more wood and mud than stone, was falling down. The match was brokered by, of course, the abbey, and the old knight jumped at the chance. My mother was, I think, happy to leave the priory where she had been sent and find the pure air of the hill-country. I truly believe that she loved my father, and I know that she loved me. She was beauty itself to me, and words and laughter where my father was touches and secret smiles. She was tall for a woman, straight-backed, long of neck. Her hair was the colour of candlelight through amber, and her eyes were green.

Perhaps my father was not quite what my mother's family had in mind, but in the event he proved an excellent choice. The abbey, of course, obtained the promise of the de Rosel lands in return – generous as the abbot was, the aggrandise-ment of a yeoman sheep-farmer would have been out of the question. But it was a fine match even so. Mam gained the freedom of the high places, and a quietly adoring man. Father found, I think, an anchor for his soul.

And I learned to read. The priory had managed to teach Mam her letters – Latin and French – and infected her with a passion for them besides. She had no luck with Father, who, while he did not have the rustic's usual fear of books, felt that he would be an unworthy student, that in some way his shepherd's attentions would corrupt the written word. But he would sit by the fire for hours and watch my mother at work over the lives of the saints or holy martyrs. It was a sight that seemed to enthral and comfort him.

The little scholar soon came to the attention of the abbey, like a branded man is noticed by bailiffs. In my innocence I presumed that I would be a shepherd like my father, but in reality I had been chosen for a loftier destiny. And if I had suspected what that destiny was to be, how I would have savoured every single moment of my simple and ordinary life. I would have walked every hill, picked every flower and thrown a stone into every pool. But, to trim my tale a little, I did not. Instead, in my tenth year I became a novice monk.

Mam and Father must have been sure that they would have other children to offer up their only child so willingly. But a year after I left home they fell sick with a brain fever and died within a day of each other. My mother's parents having also been carried off by old age, I was left with no other family but my brothers in the abbey, but because a religious community is in itself a family I did not feel the shock of my parents' passing at the time. It was a slow, creeping bereavement, and I am still surprised by how deeply it cuts me even now. But I still loved the hills, and would slip away from the abbey whenever I could to walk through Holne Chase or beside the river Dart where it runs through the forest of Hembury. At the age of seventeen I left that paradise, to study under the scholars who in those days had formed a college in the cathedral city of Balecester, a day's ride east of Bristol. The abbey itself remains with me as nothing more than a medley of smells: candle-wax, boiling cabbage, spilt beer, old parchment and leather. I made only one friend, and a peculiar one at that.

Brother Adric was the abbey librarian. He was tall and sepulchurally thin, with the sharp nose and sunken eyes of a gargoyle. He was interested in me, I think, because I was interested in his precious books and had a wolfish appetite for knowledge. I do not believe that Adric had taken orders to be closer to God, or to atone for any grave sin. He simply wished to be as near as possible to books and learning. One day, soon after I joined the school, he found me peering through the library keyhole and, instead of sending me away with a clout, as I had expected, opened the door and let me look around. After that, I came to rely on the library and Adric – whose ghoulish looks hid a sweet soul – as an escape from the monotony of monkish life. But Adric was not tied to his books like some librarians I have known: the pallid creatures whose skins gleam like fish from underground caves (I have seen such monsters) and who guard their lairs like basilisks guard treasure. My friend liked to wander the villages and fields, talking to the people he met there about their customs, old stories, odd beliefs, and soon I was accompanying him on these 'investigations', as he called them. He was a collector of strange facts, which he noted down in a vast ledger that no one else was allowed to read. And what fascinated him most of all were the numberless ruins that dot the moor: the circles and rows of stone, the mounds and cairns that hang above the valleys and crown most hilltops. I, of course, had learned of these from my father, something which made Adric value my company as something more than simple friendship.

As far as I knew, the stones had been put there by the faery folk – except, that is, for the ones that were the work of the Devil himself. Adric, however, had another idea. He believed that the moor had been settled by the Trojans who, led by Aeneas, had escaped from their burning city as the Greeks put it to the sword. One of the Trojans, Brutus, had founded the city of Totnes – that was a well-known fact. But Adric theorised that, after Brutus had defeated Gogmagog (one of the terrible giants who, as any schoolboy knows, once guarded Britain), the grateful people had given him the moors upon which to build a new Troy. I think that Adric wanted to prove this theory so that he could rewrite the history of our islands. He would be a new Geoffrey of Monmouth, and put Devon in its rightful place at the centre of the world, which he, I and everyone else I knew believed to be the case anyway.

This picking through the past reminds me of two apes I once saw, sitting on a prince's throne and sifting through each other's fur in search of tasty fleas. When one beast found a particularly toothsome morsel he would pop it between his jaws and chew ecstatically, and then give his fellow ape a little pat, as if to thank him for harbouring such a flavoursome insect. The prince and his courtiers watched this spectacle in fits of laughter, pointing and cheering whenever the little ritual of thanks was played out. The world regards historians thus, I have found: the spectacle of the poor, half-blind bookworms seeking out tasty nuggets of fact is far more amusing than the finds themselves. I am neither ape nor scholar, but mine is a long story and there is a single flea that I would bid you chew upon before I continue.

It was the spring of my last year at school. I was in the

library, trying to concentrate on a gloss of Augustine, when Adric hurried in, looking excited.

'Petroc, I would like your company, if you please,' he said.

I need no persuasion to leave my studies, and followed him to the stables, where one of the grooms was holding two saddled ponies.

'Where are we going, brother?' I asked.

'Vennor,' he said. Then, seeing my concern: 'Mount. I shall explain as we ride.'

Vennor is a mean little hamlet about five miles to the north-west of Buckfast. I had been there once with my father to look at some breeding stock, and could not imagine what the present excitement could be about. Nevertheless I obeyed, and we set off at a lively trot.

The sunken lanes of Devon make for pleasant riding. Their high, tree-lined banks are shady, and in places the way has been worn down so much that one could almost be passing through green tunnels. Adric and I rode side by side. I had accompanied him on his investigations before, but this was obviously something special, and he was not able to contain himself for long.

'A pack-train passed through early this morning,' he began, 'and the drover had a message for me. A peasant called Beda has cleared a patch of waste-ground and when he ploughed it yesterday, he turned up an ancient grave.' He glanced at me, knowing very well that I was almost as passionate about the long-gone moor-dwellers as was he.

'I was not able to gather much from the drover, but evidently this Beda assumes whatever he has found to be the work of Satan, refuses to go near it, and has summoned me to prevent or remove the inevitable curse he has stumbled upon.' Adric chuckled happily.

'What do you think we will find?' I asked.

'Whatever it is, it will not be the work of the faery folk—' and here Adric shot me a look '—or the Devil. But perhaps we might find something of the people of Troy. Maybe Brutus himself?' The laugh that followed told me that my companion fervently wished that this could indeed be so, despite his self-mockery.

And so we rode, through the fly-buzzing lanes, until the land started to rise. The lane became a track through a wind-sculpted oak copse, then we splashed through the Vennor Brook and into Vennor itself. The hamlet was a group of five houses – little more, in truth, than cob huts – around which fowl, dogs and a couple of mat-haired, snot-faced children chased one another joylessly. It was, like many another moor-land village, a hard place where the people worked so savagely to extract a pittance of livelihood from the land that they became almost savage themselves. We dismounted, Adric rather monkishly choosing a dung-free spot to plant his sandals, and called out to the children, who wandered over to us looking sullen and frightened. Adric asked for Beda, and after a little coaxing one child, possibly a little girl, was induced to point directions.

We found the peasant on the edge of a newly turned patch of ground. The field – more of a clearing in the surrounding jumble of bracken and boulders – was three-quarters ploughed, and the farthest ridge came to an abrupt end a good fifteen paces shorter than its fellows. The plough was still there, a marker to whatever it was the ploughman had found. After a brisk conversation with Beda, who looked scared out of his wits by the librarian's ghoulish visage, Adric beckoned me, and we picked our way over the broken earth.

The plough had struck the edge of a stone chest which was made up of separate granite slabs, crudely worked so as to fit together. The lid, a bigger slab, was askew.

'Aha,' Adric muttered. 'The man must have taken a look inside – not so frightened, then.'

I saw my friend could hardly contain himself. 'Give me a hand with this, Petroc,' he said, already tugging at the lid. I bent down beside him and together we heaved the flat rock up and dropped it to one side. At first we saw nothing but loose earth. Adric reached in and grabbed a handful: it was very fine, almost like dust. I joined him, and together we ladled the dust out with cupped hands. I was the first to find something: a round bead, as big as a sheep's eyeball and covered in a sort of hard ash. Adric grabbed it from me with a most unmonkish haste.

'What have we here? Eh, my lad?' The monk spat on the bead and polished it on the rough wool of his robe. The ash came away and amber glowed dully at us.

After that we fell upon the stone chest, digging inside it in a frenzy. I dread to imagine what poor Beda made of the sight of two monks kneeling over the work of Satan he had found, gibbering to each other and hurling fistfuls of earth around and about us. Soon our scrabbling fingers found other prizes. I felt something rough, hard and rounded, and dug out a small clay pot, about the size of a beer mug. It was a sandy colour, and when I brushed off the dirt that clung to it, I saw it was covered in patterns, bands made up of myriad tiny impressions in the clay. I turned it upside down and shook, and amongst the dust that fell out I saw more beads. I heard Adric suck his breath in sharply. He tugged, and suddenly he was holding up a skull, two fingers crooked into the eye-sockets. There was a muffled shriek from where the peasant stood, and I turned to see him on his knees, crossing himself like a man trying to beat out a flaming smock.

Adric thrust the skull at me. In his urgency he misjudged his aim and the bony lump hit me on the nose, hard enough to numb it and for the taste of blood to come into my throat. I smelt damp soil and crushed lobworms. The librarian was prattling at me as I rubbed my bruised snout.

'Ancient, Petroc, ancient! Mark me, we have found our Trojan. Stop picking your nose and help me dig, for God's sake.'

Our frenzy continued until the stone chest was empty. On the flattened earth in front of us lay a heap of bones, stained almost chestnut by their peaty grave, a handful of beads, three axe-heads made of polished stone, and a few other lumps of dirt that might or might not be treasure in disguise. Adric's face was flushed with joy – for a few moments his true character displaced the gargoyle mask he was fated to wear.

'Look at these axes, my son,' he gushed. 'See how dark and smooth the stone is, and flecked with red. This is not Devon stone, nor Cornish or Dorset either.'

The stone was indeed beautiful, but I suddenly felt uncomfortable as I realised what it looked like: the liver of a freshly slaughtered hog. I dropped the axe I was holding, and started to polish an amber bead instead. Adric did not notice my discomfort. He was rubbing the dirt from one of the encrusted lumps, jabbering away to me, or to himself, about Brutus, Aeneas and a score of the other wondrous facts on which his mind so often dwelt. A tiny arrowhead emerged between his fingers, tanged and with a wicked-looking point. It was of chipped flint, and very beautiful. I was about to tell the librarian that at last I recognised something, that this was a faery arrow, and that my father had found several on the moor and brought them home for us to wonder at, when I realised that he had fallen silent, and was staring over my shoulder. I turned as well.

The peasant Beda had been joined by a gaggle of other wretched-looking men. I counted eight in all, and they were all carrying scythes, pitchforks or billhooks. One man was hefting a long and gnarled club of bog-oak. They were staring at us and our finds and I fancied that I could actually feel the terror and hatred they held for us. Fear rose in my chest like a bubble rising from a marsh, and I coughed, a pathetic little sound that nonetheless broke Adric's trance. He blinked at me, and I saw that the gargoyle had returned. He hissed at me under his breath.

'Petroc, my son, do you mark them?' I nodded, and he went on: 'They see devils doing the Devil's work, there is no doubt.' He bit his lip. 'Follow me, and by Christ, say nothing.'

He gathered up the front of his robe and began shovelling the grave-goods into the pouch thus formed. He motioned me to do the same. When everything, bones and all, were gathered in bundles, we stood. The thought came to me that we must look ridiculous, not frightening, like goodwives out mushrooming, but one look at the gaunt librarian, with his death's-head visage perched atop a great cloth belly full of bones, put that idea to flight. He began to lope towards the peasants, and I could but follow. All at once I realised that, in all likelihood, I was about to be rendered as dead as our jumbled Trojan.

But Adric did not falter as he marched up to the little mob and came to a halt in front of Beda. There was a moment of silence. The peasants' faces were like the faces of the damned in the painted hell above the altar of our church, I noticed absently. Then the monk spoke.

'Beda of Vennor, and you good men: you are witness to a miracle today,' he said, and his voice fairly rang out across the field. 'Your plough was guided by Divine Grace, for it has discovered the tomb of a Holy Martyr, one whom I have sought for years, and who will rain down innumerable blessings upon this fortunate place.' Beda gasped, and the group all took a step back as Adric reached into the bundle at his waist and drew out the skull. He held it up to the men and with it made the sign of the cross, as if he were blessing a congregation. I saw the man with the club drop his weapon, and then a scythe and two billhooks wavered and were slowly laid down.

'These are the bones of the martyr Ælfsige of Frome, who brought the Scriptures to the ungodly Briton before the time of great King Alfred. On your knees, lucky men!' he boomed, then turned his head for a moment: 'You too, Petroc,' he murmured.

I fell to the soft, ploughed earth, and my loot clattered as I did so. To my amazement, Beda and his companions were on the ground as well, genuflecting and praying. Some wept. Adric's sermon rolled on above us.

'The very air is tinctured with the scent of holiness – these bones might be a meadow of sweet flowers! Smell, and know that you are blessed.' I recalled the aroma of blood and worms, and shuddered, but the club-carrier and one of the billhookers were snuffling like otterhounds, rapture lighting up their pinched features. But now Adric was drawing matters to a close.

'I will take these relics with me and place them before the Abbot. We will go to the Bishop himself, and you will have a church for Vennor, my sons.'

With this he grabbed my cowl and hauled me to my feet. I followed him at that pace which is a walk trying not to be a run, and together we hurried back to where our ponies were tethered. Adric did not pause and, thrusting the hem of his robe between his teeth, fairly leaped into the saddle. I followed suit, trying not to spill my own cargo of bones and beads. Looking round, I saw that the peasants had followed us at a distance and were gazing at us like rabbits tranced by a weasel. As Adric kicked his mount into life, and as we took off down the path and splashed through the ford, I heard the men cry out behind us: 'God keep you, Father!'

We were soon out of sight and earshot of the hamlet, and Adric reined his pony to a halt. His face was filmed with sweat, and was as white as his robe, but he was smiling a wide, skull-like grin, and his eyes sparkled. He pulled the cloth from his mouth.

'God forgive me,' he said, with no trace of repentance. 'In one day I have discovered a Trojan warrior and created a martyr. Hold up, Petroc, and help me squirrel our treasure away.'

We busied ourselves with the saddlebags, taking care not to

break the beautiful pot, then dusted the russet soil from our habits as best we could. I could not contain myself any longer.

'Brother Adric,' I quavered, 'who was Saint Elfseed?'

'Ælfsige,' he corrected me cheerfully. 'I have no idea. Now he's the pride of Vennor, of course, but a new church will do their muddy souls no harm.'

'Do you mean that we invented a saint, just to save our hides?' I suddenly felt the hot breath of damnation.

'Perhaps Ælfsige indeed saved our hides,' said the librarian. 'Do not be concerned, my son. The Abbot will understand. And besides, you saw those men. They truly felt the miraculous, and that can only be God's work. That, I do believe' – and he fixed me with those shining eyes – 'and so must you.'

'But . . .' I began. Adric waved the skull in my direction to silence me, and the empty sockets dried the words on my tongue.

'People of that sort believe many things that I, the Bishop, the Pope himself know to be rank paganism,' he said. 'Devils, imps, sprites and the old gods are as real to them as the lice that bite their flesh. If it will comfort you, look upon our work today as a mission to the Infidel. Do not worry, Petroc. It was a little harmless trickery that may bring forth much good.'

I was as eager to believe this as the men of Vennor had been eager to believe in our new saint, but I still hesitated. Adric read my face.

'Have you ever been bitten by a viper?' he asked. I thought of the little adder that had nestled in the crook of my neck that afternoon on Black Tor. I shook my head.

'I have,' he went on. 'I was a little older than you, picking bilberries on the heath near my home. The snake bit my hand. I knew I was going to die, but my father sucked out the venom and told me not to despair. "Grown men should not die from snakebite," he said, "only young children and the very old. But men do die, because they believe that they must." So he said, and I trusted him, because he was my father. And indeed, I

70

had a day's sickness, a week's stiffness of the arm and no more pain than from a hornet's sting.'

'I was taught to fear adders,' I said.

'As you were taught to fear the saints,' Adric said. 'But the saints cannot harm us. Their greatest gift is the good they allow us to bring to the credulous and ignorant. If the Church can use that good, then that is pleasing to the Lord. The people of Vennor would die if an adder bit them, because they believe it to be evil, and that is how the Devil works amongst men. What we have done is use the Devil's methods against him, nothing more.'

I admit that even then I was somewhat baffled by Adric's argument, but it had the ring of conviction to it, and besides, was not the librarian a good and learned man? I felt my doubt and my guilt lift and vanish in the summer air. As we tied up our saddlebags and climbed back on our ponies, however, I wished to know more.

'Father, what made you say those things? Was there any truth at all in what you said?' I finally asked.

'Well, Ælfsige was a name in an old ledger that stayed in my mind. I have been reading Gildas on the English invasions – *De Excidio et Conquestu Britanniae*, a fascinating work, Petroc, you should glance at it – but of course the poor old Britons were as Christian as you or I, and not given to killing bishops. I am afraid the desperation of the moment wrought a convenient alchemy and brought forth our saint.'

'And why Frome?' I persisted.

'Where I was born, my son!' And with that the cadaverous librarian spurred his pony on down the track, and I followed him down through the deep green lanes, a dead man's bones in my pack, a miracle behind me and a monk's laughter leading me home.

Chapter Six

I had been awake for hours when the wain juddered to a halt, and it felt as if I had not slept at all. I heard the carter curse his stiff joints, and then he was pummelling me through the burlap.

Clambering down, I mumbled my thanks as he jumped back onto the wain with ungainly speed. He stirred the old nag on its way with a slap of the reins. I heard him spit and make devil's horns with his fingers. So now I was something to ward off. Feeling more like a sack of turnips than a demon, I tottered to the ditch for a piss, then took my bearings.

I was on the Exeter Road, and just ahead was the old bridge over the river Dart. It was as dark outside as it had been under the burlap, and there was no one about, so I crossed the bridge and started up the track to the abbey. Passing the mill and the outlying barns, I saw something white loom ahead of me. I jumped into the shadows, then saw what had scared me: a may tree in full bloom. I could smell its rank sweetness in the damp breeze.

The air was almost warm, and full of the scent of wet earth. I was home. Feeling more alive than I had for long days, I decided to find a place to spend the rest of the night. From my days as a mischievous young monk I knew all the hidden ways in and out of the abbey precinct, and now I followed the mill's north wall down to the river, climbed down the bank and splashed into the shallow water. It was cold, fresh from the high moor. As I sloshed upstream, hauling myself along the willow roots, a bell in the abbey sounded vespers. Here the riverbank was choked with old straw and reeked of wet dung. I pulled myself up onto a shelf of granite and scrambled up the bank and over a low wall. There before me was the door to the abbey stable. I lifted the latch and slipped inside.

The stable was filled with the warm fug of horses. Although I could not see a thing, I could hear the animals shift in their stalls. They did not sound very interested in me, and I was glad not to have roused them. I had a few hours of darkness left for sleep. A lighter patch in the darkness seemed to show a window, and I groped towards it. I did not want to be discovered by the stable-hands, and I hoped the dawn would wake me in time. I found the wall, kicked some straw into a rough pallet and lay down. Sleep descended like a blow.

Something furry, with sharp little claws, scuttled across my face. I flinched and opened my eyes. A pale light was filtering into the stable. I muttered my thanks to the mouse that had woken me: the watery dawn would have let me sleep. Outside the window the abbey was still, although the mumble of early Mass came from the direction of the church. I thought I would give the brothers time to settle in to their daily tasks before seeking out Adric, whom I thought would be the best person to hear my woes. He would surely know what I should do next, and I devoutly hoped he would take my side. Meanwhile I picked the straw from my robe as I wandered around the stable. The horses and ponies snorted at me as I passed their stalls, and I patted their great long heads. Some of the beasts I knew: here was the little black pony that had carried me on many a trip over the moors. He nickered as I rubbed his velvet nose. In the next stall stood a great chestnut horse, more magnificent than any I had seen in my years at the abbey. I wondered if the Abbot had acquired a new mount as I held a bunch of hay for the creature to nibble. Then I noticed the tack hanging from the stall's door. It was rich, caparisoned with fine silver. It was too fancy for the Abbot, I thought absently, as I bent to take a closer look. There were symbols on the bridle, and in the growing daylight I saw what they were. One medallion carried a crozier and a hound; on another two long bones crossed between four blazing stars. The arms of the Bishop of Balecester and his seneschal. Sir Hugh de Kervezey's charger bit my hand.

I lurched backwards, tripped over a leather bucket and stumbled against the wall. The shock felt like Sir Hugh's knife twisting in my belly. So my escape, those days of lonely misery and terror, were for nothing. Kervezey still lived, and I had been outwitted, as if my wits would be a challenge to a man of Sir Hugh's nature. How could I have ever dreamed of escaping? My pursuer was a hunter of men. And I had walked blindly into his net. I sat on the floor, nursing my bitten hand. The horse had nipped the web between thumb and first finger, but not hard. The pain was enough, however, to prove that I was not dead yet. Until my throat was cut, I could still run. And so I did, bolting from the stable by the back door and darting behind the chicken coops. From there I crawled past the swine-fold and into the patch of long grass and nettles that spread down to the river, a little wasteland where old wagons, broken ploughs and other wreckage was allowed to crumble into the brambles. I found a heap of wheels and boards that had once been a hay-wain, and wormed underneath. Young nettles, always nastier than grown-ups, stung my hands and face. But I was hidden. I had gone to ground, I thought grimly. But few people came this way. And I could just see a corner of the stable-yard. Perhaps Sir Hugh would lose patience and go home. I rubbed my bite and my stings and settled down to wait.

It was really quite pleasant under the hay-wain. Honeysuckle and a dog-rose had grown over the old boards, and the sweet pink flowers were so bright and innocent that I began to feel, if not safe, then at least protected in some way by the sheer force

of nature around me. Green shoots were everywhere. Perhaps
it is strange for a man who has seen many wonders to think
this, but there are few sights more awe-inspiring than a stand
of young nettles in the first flush of their growth. They are
greener than emeralds, and strain towards the sun with such
vigour that one can almost see the life-force working within
them. And their stings are a reminder that the mystery of
creation may be approached, but not grasped. Now, watching
the green spears soak up the light, listening to the bees at work
in the roses, my fears began to subside.

I found some dock-leaves to soothe the nettle rash and
began to plan once more. If I could find Adric, I would at
least have an ally. I wondered what day this was. If it were
Sunday, I would wait all day. Monday he would spend in the
library. Tuesday was the day he liked to saddle a pony and go
in search of oddities in the countryside. I prayed it was a
Tuesday. From my cave under the roses I could see, beyond
the stable, part of the main abbey and the physic garden.
Monks were beginning to show themselves, walking to their
appointed tasks with the calm of a sheltered existence and an
assured afterlife. Unfortunately I seemed to have abandoned
both luxuries. But their presence meant that at least it could
not be Sunday. I lay there, sucking the honey from the tiny
funnels of the honeysuckle flowers, and reflected that I was
looking at my life, as it had been, from outside. I had been one
of those calm figures just two years ago. But the filthy outlaw
lurking in the weeds was a lifetime removed from them now. I
realised that I could not go back to that life, that I despised
their calm now. I had an urge to reveal myself, to let them see
that everything was illusion, that they could fall through the
flimsy walls of their world in the wink of an eye, into the
wasteland outside.

As I lay there thinking these gloomy and uncharitable
thoughts, I noticed a commotion over by the stable. Some
monks weeding the garden dropped their hoes and started

running towards the stables. Voices were raised, in surprise or anger – it was hard to tell from my distance. Then there was an almighty crash and a clatter of hooves, and from the stable burst a huge horse. The rider was dressed in dark green, and I saw it was Sir Hugh. The knight held something in his right hand, a long black bundle which dangled a few inches from the ground. As I watched, Sir Hugh raised the bundle to his face, shook it and flung it from him. It tumbled away, and I saw it was another man, a very tall, thin man in black robes. Sir Hugh wheeled the horse and seemed to make it dance for the monks who were watching the scene from a safe distance. Then horse and rider grew calm and trotted serenely from my view.

The monks rushed towards the man, who had been thrown into the weeds by the pigsty. 'Adric,' they were calling, 'Adric!' I could only lie in my hole and watch as they picked my friend from the ground and held him, tottering, between them. At least he was still alive and, it seemed, unhurt. But he allowed himself to be led to a sunny bench in the physic garden and waved the other monks away. There he sat, his head in his hands, like an old raven, while the smaller brown birds twittered around him. Finally they let him be and went back to their tasks, shaking their heads and, I guessed, chattering like old women.

This might be my one opportunity to talk to Adric. I eased myself out between the briars and slithered towards the pigsty. It was obvious that Sir Hugh had found out that I had been friends with the librarian, and that he had been trying to shake some information from him. I hoped he was satisfied that Adric knew nothing, and that he had left the abbey for good. But the horse had not been loaded for a journey, and Sir Hugh had worn no cloak. He would be back within the day. As I crept closer, I thought how terrified my friend must have been, and that it was all my fault. I flushed with shame. The news of my disgrace must be all over the abbey now, of course. It would be fatal to be seen by anyone else but Adric. I hoped with all my heart that he, of all people, would not betray me.

The monks were giving Adric a wide berth now. I suspected that was because they saw the librarian as a lightning-rod for the wrath of Sir Hugh. They clustered at the far end of the garden, over by the beehives, and busied themselves with pruning the rose-bushes and trimming the low box-hedges – all tasks that allowed them to keep their backs to Adric. Out of sight, out of mind, I thought bitterly. But it suited my purposes very well. Adric's bench sat alongside a hedge of pruned beeches, just beginning to leaf out, planted in front of a high stone wall. Between it and the pigsty was a further swath of waste-ground, a cobbled track and a stand of yew trees cut into broad, flat-topped skittles of green. Between the yews apothecary roses had been planted in a thick line, forming another hedge about three feet high that met the beeches at a right-angle. If I could reach the roses unseen, they would screen me until I slipped between the beech-trees and the wall. But from where I lay peering out round the angle of the piggery's fence, the low grass and track might as well be a mile. I would be in full view of gardeners and, God forbid, the mad knight who might gallop back at any moment.

Snorting and munching sounded through the thick wooden fence beside me. The pigs should be out foraging, so I guessed I could hear the old boar, who was far too cantankerous to roam free. Many a novice monk had been bitten by the huge old beast, and I had been charged by him once, coming too close with the slop-bucket. He was a gross, bristly brute with beady eyes and jagged yellow tusks, and I was glad of a wall between us. Then it struck me. Without stopping to think, I hauled myself up and over the fence and dropped into the stinking, churned-up mud inside the sty. The hog was over in a corner rooting away, and he raised his red-rimmed eyes and stared at me with undisguised malice. Not giving him time to act, or myself time to have second thoughts, I rushed to the gate and, with three hard kicks, had it open. Then I charged the boar.

The hideous old creature had never faced such insubordination, and he panicked, as I had desperately hoped he would. Instead of disembowelling me on the spot, he gave an undignified shriek and bolted away. Waving my arms, I chased him out of the sty, then climbed back over the wall. The monks in the garden had heard the door being kicked open, and the boar's surprised squeal. Now they watched in horror as the beast, free at last, hurried around in widening circles, squealing in rage or perhaps delight. One of the burlier monks began to walk gingerly towards him, carrying his hoe like a lance. The others began to follow, and I almost laughed out loud as the boar bolted off towards the stable. The monks, running and yelling now, set off in pursuit, and the jolly cavalcade was soon out of sight. Meanwhile, Adric had barely glanced at the cavorting beast and yelling fools before dropping his face into his hands once more. I leaped up and dashed towards the roses. If anyone had seen me, they would have assumed I was running to find reinforcements for the boar-hunt. Sprinting over the cobbles, I threw myself down behind the nearest yew-tree, and crawled fast along the line of rose-bushes. In another few seconds I had squeezed into the narrow, dank passageway between beech hedge and wall.

I needed to catch my breath. Hunkered down with my back to the cold stone, I wondered what had possessed me just now. The old boar had for years been a tenant of my nightmares, and could easily have maimed or even killed me. But somehow I had known what to do. It was nothing to do with bravery, I thought now: more the instinct of a hunted animal. In any case the creature had proved more coward than monster. I would offer up a prayer for him the next time I sat down to a meal of pork – if there was a next time.

Adric's black outline was just visible through the beech twigs. I edged along until I was directly behind him.

'Adric,' I whispered. 'Don't turn around, but it's me, Petroc.'
The tall shadow in front of me made no movement.

'Adric!' I hissed again, a little louder. 'I'm here, behind the . . .'

'Quiet!' the librarian croaked back. Sir Hugh's grip had been tight around the poor man's throat: he sounded half-strangled. 'If that really is you, Brother Petroc, and not that perfumed assassin, what in Jesus' name are you doing here?' There was an ugly rattle as he cleared his throat, and then: 'You are a murderer, a thief and a blasphemer. You are dead, to the abbey, and to me.'

I felt myself collapse inside like a punctured wine-skin. What had I expected? This was what I deserved. My ears burning with shame, I began to move away, when Adric's croak came again.

'That being said, I shall sit here in the sun and say a quiet Mass for the soul of a dead friend, I think. We believe our prayers are heard, do we not? Then listen now.'

I crouched in the damp shade, hardly daring to breathe.

'I have missed your company, young brother. And as a writer of letters you are not diligent. When the Sieur de Kervezey arrived here a week ago with his tale of butchery and theft, it was more news of you than I wished to hear. Kervezey tells a fine story and acts the courtier's part well enough to turn country heads, but I could smell lies on him like rotting meat. I did not believe his account, although the others were quick enough to damn you.'

I began to protest, but Adric cut me off.

'Whatever happened, he is a devil. He knows that we were friends. Sweet as honey he was at first, flattering me with his "Master Librarian". Then he revealed his mission. You were my pupil, as he put it, and he represented the Church in their interest in discovering how a young monk had in reality been a murdering apostate − a living devil, as he would have it. Officially you are dead, dear boy, but Sir Hugh seems to have reasons of his own to think that untrue . . . and so just now he dragged me from the library and promised me extreme pain if I did not give you up. But,' and he coughed, as if feeling hands around his throat, 'he may now think that you truly are not here.' Adric chuckled, never a pretty sound.

'And you are not here, are you?' he continued. 'You must not show even a sliver of your shadow. I do not know what your plans might be, but they should involve getting as far from this place as you can.'

I could stand this one-sided dialogue no longer. 'I have just been there, and it did me no good,' I muttered, bitterly. 'My dear friend Will is dead and I am the cause of it. I am not far behind him, Adric. If I am to die, it may as well be at home.'

There was silence from beyond the hedge. I could see the black outline of my friend, and he was leaning forward, head in hands once more.

'This is *not* your home now!' he hissed. 'The abbey believes you are dead – I am sorry, but you must have thought of that. The news has been all over the county – monks are worse than fishwives for gossip, as you know. You would not wish the brothers under Sir Hugh's suspicion, I think . . . I am sorry. Truly sorry, my son.'

I felt myself growing empty inside. As I cowered beneath the hedge I felt my old life cut from me with a finality that might as well be that of death. I had lost my past as I had lost Will. I raised my hands to pray but no words formed, and instead I watched a party of ants overwhelm a squirming caterpillar on a beech twig. The brothers were shouting again, a long way away.

But I was young, and found that a tiny spark of indignation still burned in my hollow guts. 'I am an innocent man,' I said at last, as loudly as I dared. 'Sir Hugh played a game with me. He killed Will and the deacon before my eyes. He did it as easily as you would open a book.' I stopped, sickened by the memory of the hot blood on my face.

Adric's shadow straightened suddenly. 'Yes, yes. You are no killer, Petroc. A dreamer, perhaps.'

'Will thought the deacon was killed for being in league with the Papal Legate, Adric. How . . . how did I come to be tangled with such things?'

'The Papal Legate? No, no. Kervezey is a hunter, but you are not the quarry.'

'How can you say that?'

'Because it is the truth. We have no more time for explanations, but believe me when I say that you are blameless. Sir Hugh's wickedness . . . This was no chance. He killed your friend, not you, he let you go – and he knew where you were going.'

He must have heard my sigh of miserable confusion, for he continued: 'Trust me, lad – I'm afraid that you have no choice. Now listen, because I think there may be a chance for you to save yourself. We should have a little more time before those fools catch that hog, so please, pay attention.'

'There is a man,' he began. 'He is a Frenchman, and yet he belongs to no country. He is a traveller and a merchant of sorts. He keeps a small stock of curios of the kind I am interested in, and we meet, every now and then, when he puts into Dartmouth. This Frenchman owes allegiance to no one, and he hates the Hugh Kervezeys of this world. I have had word that he is in Dartmouth now, and wants me to meet him there. He has something for me, doubtless some ancient wonder that I cannot afford and that will make me commit countless sins of covetousness. But he will be at the White Swan tavern this week. Ask for him there. His name is Jean de Sol. I assume you still have the reliquary you stole.' I spluttered audibly.

'That is good,' said Adric, to my great surprise. 'Show your loot to Monsieur de Sol. It is the kind of thing he likes. He might be persuaded to carry you abroad. This island is too small to hide you now. You will leave tonight. I will bring you food and clothing – I can smell you through the hedge, Petroc – and a little coin if I can muster it.'

I murmured my thanks. This was like confession, I realised, and Adric had just granted me absolution of the most wonderful kind. 'I will be out in the long grass, under the old wagon with the rose growing through it,' I told him.

'I will not risk your life or mine that way,' he replied. 'Kervezey will be keeping me under his gaze, I am sure. No, you will find a bag outside the privy, the one that faces the river, after the evening service. I will drop it from the window. It should land in the willows. If you find nothing, leave anyway. Eat roots if you have to. Follow the river. And find the Frenchman.'

He stood up then, and knelt, facing me. I could see the shape of his face through the branches, although I doubt he could see mine. 'I can hear the brothers,' he said. 'They are wrestling with the pig, by the sound of it. You must go. But Petroc,' he began, and paused. 'Go safely, my son. I will pray for you, of course. I believe the Holy Martyr Saint Ælfsige of Frome may intercede in a case such as yours.' He laughed his dry laugh. 'Remember him? Perhaps I will light a candle in front of his skull tonight.' He sighed. 'But a long life to you, Petroc,' he said, in his true voice. 'I am glad we were friends. Now go.' He sat down on the bench and bent his head once more.

I felt truly abandoned then. I was no longer a cleric. Adric had surely told me that. In helping me escape he was releasing me, in his way, from my vows. I was an outsider. Tears were streaming down my face as I crawled back down the green tunnel. I could hear the monks away behind the barn, clamouring in triumph. Sobbing, I hurled myself across the track and into the weeds. I dragged myself through the rough grass and thistles, hardly caring if I was discovered. Adric of all people had been caught up in my nightmare, and now his life was in as much danger as mine. I was like contagion, infecting everyone around me. I should never have come back. As I regained the pathetic refuge of the wain, I wished Sir Hugh had skewered me in the cathedral. Death must be better than this half-life. Guilt, fear and uncertainty pecked at me like crows worrying a corpse. I pulled my cowl over my head and cried as I had never cried before.

The rest of the day passed. That is all I can say on the subject. The shadows grew long, it turned to evening, then night. I do not wish to remember my part in that day. There was a pile of rotten wood, and under it a filthy vagrant dozed, and woke, and cursed, and wept. Or perhaps it was another sort of creature that lay there, writhing in pain as he shed his old skin and suffered the pangs of transformation into an entirely different form.

But night came at last, and the evening hours were rung. I left my shelter for the last time and sloped across the wasteland to the stable and the river beyond. The refectory was to my right. Warm light and the happy sounds of eating came from it. I slipped down the bank and followed my nose to the privy, a lean-to that clung to the abbey wall and hung precariously above the river. Willows and other plants grew thickly underneath with the sinister vigour of things that feed on dirt and decay. The stench was bad, but in the cool of evening not too intense. I ducked behind a tree and settled down to wait as the moon rose behind me.

I had sat there for perhaps half an hour when the little window showed the dim light of a candle. A shadow reared briefly, and a dark shape flew through the air, hit the bank a few yards in front of me and began to roll towards the river. I leapt from my hiding place and threw myself at the bundle, managed to catch it before it reached the water, and found myself holding a leather satchel, its strap wound and knotted tightly around it. Looking up at the privy I might have glimpsed a pale face at the window, but more likely I imagined it. In any case it was time to be gone. I turned and scrambled along the bank, heading downstream. Soon I was past the mill and saw the outline of the bridge in the distance.

Chapter Seven

Under the bridge it was cold, and water dripped from the shadows above onto my head. My tonsure had almost grown out, and it was odd to feel the drops land on hair, not bare skin. Adric's package contained a silver florin, half a dozen wizened apples, a chunk of ham and a gourd of small beer, wrapped in a pair of rough woollen breeches, a linen tunic and a monk's robe. My own robe was a disgusting web of worn and torn cloth encrusted with dirt, and I gladly threw it off. When I unwrapped the bindings that held the hand to my body I found a belt of angry skin beneath. I walked into the river with my sandals still on, and sat down on the smooth granite stones, letting the icy water play around me for as long as I could bear it. Then I grabbed a handful of river sand and scrubbed myself quickly all over, ducked down again to rinse off, and ran up the bank, my body burning with cold. But despite the pain I felt new hope as I bound the hand back in place, pulled on the breeches and tunic, and let the clean robe fall about me. Now I looked like a monk of the abbey again, at least for a little while longer. I sat and ate the ham – muttering my thanks to the old abbey boar – and two apples, chewy and wrinkled from their winter in an abbey cellar, until I felt ready to begin my next journey.

The moon was nearly full, and it was easy to pick my way along the river. The Dart runs fast over stones between Buckfast and Staverton, and for the first hour the gurgle of water kept me company. It was not cold, and although my feet were wet from fording the little streams that crossed my path, I was as happy as I had been since leaving Balecester. I stopped once to wrap my old robe round a boulder and drop it into a deep salmon-hole under the bank. Before long the stone bridge at Staverton came into view, and I slipped under one of its arches. I knew that there were fat sea-trout – peel, we called them – lying in the dark water. I had often leaned on the bridge and watched them hold their own against the current with just the lazy flicking of their tails.

Below the bridge are the water-meadows of Hood, and beyond the woods of Dartington. I followed a well-worn path, clambering over the high wall of the Lord of Dartington's deer park and following the river that now flowed deep and quiet. In another hour I was in the King's Meadow, and the mound of Totnes Castle crouched ahead of me in the moonlight. I kept to the riverbank, slipped past the mill and under Totnes bridge. I was in luck: even on such a bright night there were no fishermen about, checking eel traps or setting illicit nets for peel. I did not want to disturb any poachers. But the meadows were empty, although I could hear big fish jumping, and silver ripples appeared on the silver water. The river was tidal now, and there was a salty, muddy smell in the air. I made good time to the hill at Sharpham and, skirting it, struck inland. A sunken track led south and west, so I followed it gladly, the packed earth a pleasant change from dew-soaked grass.

As I hoped, the track led to the little hump-backed bridge over the Harbourne at Tuckenhay. The Dart, like other rivers of the West Country, spreads itself out into a long, deep estuary with many fingers that jut into the hills. These fingers are themselves deep, wooded estuaries, and I was at the head of one of them, where the Harbourne, a little stream that rose close to my home, flowed into the main river. Downstream the Dart widened and meandered, and following its banks would take far too long. I would have to head inland and find a shorter route to the port. It would have to be across country. Farmers would be awake soon, and I did not intend to meet anyone.

Adric's advice had been to cross the bridge and leave the track, heading south-east. My way would be across the ridge to Capton, then on to Dartmouth. Adric knew the country well. He loved to poke around in old churches and had visited even the tiniest, amassing reams of esoteric information that he would share with me. Upstream from where I stood now, I remembered, Harbertonford church had a font carved in the Byzantine style, though Adric had been less sure about what a Greek stonemason had been doing in Devon. There were old burial mounds on the coast as well, and the librarian was irresistibly drawn to such things. He also had a fine memory for landscapes and directions, and I knew his map, though rough, was sure to be true. And in any case my mother had grown up here, and her childhood home was just four miles from this bridge, so this was familiar ground. I was in the South Hams, a land of secrets, hidden folds and ancient tracks. I would have a hard scramble up through woods to a long ridge of rough pasture before I came to the steep hill above Dartmouth. It would take me another day, at least. I ate another apple, tightened the wet thongs of my sandals and set off once more.

A couple of dogs barked as I made my way through the tiny gaggle of thatched huts that was the hamlet of Tuckenhay, but their owners, and everyone else, slept on. The track rose and turned right, but I scrambled up the bank on my left, crushing the yellow primroses that covered it, and jumped down into the wood beyond. The oak-trees grew thickly, but the ground between the trunks had been cleared by foraging hogs and the going was easy. The moon was setting, but a thin light still trickled through the branches overhead. It was a hard climb, but soon enough I reached the top of the hill and the ground sloped down in front of me. My legs were glad of the respite, but after a few minutes I was climbing again. The land was folded into troughs and crests that the trees hid, and the constant climb and descent were exhausting. The local hogs had apparently thought so too, as their rooting had been lazy here. Brambles and thorn bushes had begun to sprout, and as the dawn began to glow away to my left I was becoming scratched and worn out.

But I reckoned I had made good time, and a rest was in order. I pushed on through the undergrowth, looking for a clear patch to sleep on, or perhaps a tree with a crotch wide enough to support me. I must have stumbled around like this for nearly an hour when the brambles suddenly cleared and I found myself on the brink of a small precipice. It was nearly light now, and I saw smooth stone below me. I had come upon an old lime quarry, long deserted judging by the thicket of elder that filled it. A perfect place to lie low for a few hours. I made my way around the rim of the quarry until I found a place where I could scramble down. The dark grey stone was damp with dew and almost greasy to my fingers as I lowered myself from ledge to ledge. It was only a few feet to the bottom, but a twisted ankle now would be the end of me, so I moved like an old man, slowly and gingerly, finally stepping down onto the mossy floor of the pit. The elder thicket was low but dense. I forced my way inside. As I had thought, there was a hollow space in the middle where the older trees had grown tall, and I dropped down and stretched myself out. The ground here was dry and chalky, the refuse from many tons of burnt and powdered lime. Moss grew thinly, but there did not seem to be any nettles, for which I was thankful. The sharp, sour smell of elder leaves was strong here, and mixed with it was the rank musk of a fox or badger. I lay for a while staring at the trunk of the nearest tree, following the path of a tiny black and white spider as she hunted amongst the furrows of the bark.

When I awoke the day was almost over. Luckily for me the

sun had not quite set, and its last rays showed me in which direction west lay. I stood up and shook away the aches of sleeping rough. Munching an apple and sipping at the stale beer in the gourd, I pushed through the bushes and out into the quarry. As I had thought, it had been scooped out of a hillside, and the way out was downhill and to the south. The old lime-diggers had worn a deep path that was still quite clear, and it went in my direction. I set off whistling.

Everything went well at first. The path was good and straight. The light was fading, but I hoped I would soon be out in open country. Through the trees the sky was a wonderful pink, the oak branches with their clusters of new leaf sharp and black in contrast. A few early stars were beginning to shine. Somewhere to my left a rookery was settling down for the night, and a few birds, late to bed, cawed above me. The moon was coming up, and I was looking forward to another good night's walk when the moonlight all of a sudden went out. A wall of cloud was sweeping across the sky, and in another minute there was pitch darkness. Not knowing what else to do I sat down in the middle of the path. Then I heard rain swishing towards me. I could see nothing, but the sound of water on leaves and branches was growing into a roar, and then the storm was all around, huge raindrops pounding me until my skin stung under my clothes. I cowered in the roaring darkness. And then the storm passed as quickly as it had come, just a squall blown in from the sea that had vented its rage, so I imagined, on the first living thing it had encountered on land: me. The moon came out again, and I was in a world that seemed drowned in quicksilver. Light glinted from every tree, and the path stretched away like a stream of white fire. The vision faded in a moment as the dry earth sucked up the water, and I felt a thrust of utter dejection. I was alone in the wilderness, and everything, even the sky, was against me.

The night air chilled my wet robes until I shook with cold. My wet sandals chafed against my feet and ankles. The path had become a mire and after another mile faded into a mass of blackthorn. I tried to find a way around, but the thicket seemed to be interminable so I began to fight my way through. The branches, each armed with a hundred inch-long thorns, were as unyielding as iron, and I had to turn around and push my way along backwards, taking the slashes and stabs of the thorns on my cowl, back and, worse, my bare ankles. Adric's satchel became hopelessly entangled and in near-panic I struggled free of it, abandoning my last apple and the dregs of beer. I was crying with pain and frustration by the time I burst through the last tangle and fell over into moonlight on open ground. I was in an overgrown meadow mounded with dead bracken. A stone wall stood ahead, and I waded through the crackling foliage, climbed the wall and looked around.

I had reached the high ridge. The sea was a dark blue line to my left. To my right, the South Hams rolled away eastwards. I turned and saw, away in the distance, the dark wall of the moors, the great hump of Ugborough Beacon with its topknot of boulders standing out before the line of higher, more distant hills. Under that hill was my home. My father and mother rested in the churchyard there. The image of a peat fire, burned down to a handful of bright jewels in the hearth, flashed before my eyes so strongly that I could all but feel its heat on my face. But it was an illusion that only served to make my freezing robes more cold, and my loneliness even deeper. Then I remembered Adric's words, and found some glimmer of comfort, enough at least to warm me for what I must do next. There was a grim walk still ahead, and no welcome, no safety in sight.

So I turned my back to the moors, and did not look behind me again, although I could feel their presence there. I crept along now, picking my way through the bracken and gorse. The moon was sinking. Somewhere on the path I had exchanged my confidence for a nagging fear, and my ears were constantly pricked for the least sound. I was not alone in the night, of course. Other creatures were abroad. Bats piped above me. Things rustled in the bracken. I thought I heard voices and saw, over a low ridge, a farmhouse some way off. There was a light burning in a low shed – someone woken up for some nocturnal task and cursing it. I gave the farm a wide berth and had left it behind when from somewhere in front of me came a horrifying shriek. High and empty, it trembled for a second and died, only to come again as a deathly, sobbing wail. I threw myself to the ground. Behind me, the farm dogs began to bay. Face-down in the grass, I realised that the sound was not murder or rape, or some blood-drinking phantom. It was foxes in heat, a sound I had heard often as a boy. Picking myself up again I almost laughed to think what a town-man I had become, not to know the night-song of the fox. But it is a bitter, human noise, and it mocked me as I tramped on towards the sea.

My footsteps were heavy now, driven by fear again. But fear drives one as fast as hope, and before long I had crossed the track that led from Capton to Downton – at least I hoped it was Capton church that I could see over to my right. Now I was walking through pastures, and sheep scattered before me like white clouds in the night. It was almost dawn when I came to the steep slope that dropped down to the town. The track fell away into darkness. The air was still, and the world seemed to be gathering its powers for sunrise and trembling in anticipation. Above and before me the sky was the deepest blue. This was my sky. The morning star, an ember of pale fire on the horizon, had bid me good morrow every day of my childhood. The air was full of the sweet musty scent of the moors. Then a bat whirred around my head, squeaking like a tiny lost soul for whom the dawn held no relief. I stumbled on down the Dartmouth road.

It is a pretty place, this nest of rogues and pirates. The wharves line one long bank of the river, and fine houses look out over the broad estuary towards the little village of Kingswear, a tumble of cob on the far side. There is a castle to guard the river's mouth, and a rich church in which thieves and fishermen can salve their consciences. I had been there once before, on the Abbot's business, keeping Treasurer Ivo company as he took delivery of some embroidered hangings from Quimper. Then I had hovered around the quay, watching men unload fish, chests and bales from the boats. As I stood absorbing all the sights and sounds, a fisherman yelled something and tossed a fat, glistening lump at my feet. I looked down into the face of a gargoyle: a great slash of jagged-edged mouth, bulging eyes and a tangle of horns and spines. 'There's a demon to play with, young master!' the man cackled, and I looked again, shocked, to see a fish, just a fish. A monstrous one, to be sure, but – ''tis a *monk*-fish, boy! Grey and ugly all right, but the flesh is sweet . . .' He smacked his lips in a lewd, fishy kiss. Furious, I lashed out with my foot, booting the horrible thing, which tumbled in the air and caught the man on the temple, knocking him over into the hold of his boat. Then there was much cursing and laughter from the other boats, and Ivo chose that moment to drag me back to our wagon, his slender money-counting fingers twisting my ear.

But now I crept past the sleeping watchman at the gate and into the steep alleys that led down to the waterside. Only the fat wharfside cats noticed me. The church loomed up on my right. I glanced up at the turret and the motion set my head whirling. Slumped against the churchyard wall, dead-tired and bone-hungry, I saw what the future held if I gave up now. The watch would find me, drag me to gaol and throw me into the stocks as a vagrant. The townsmen would have their fun, then Sir Hugh would cut my throat.

Food was just a wish, so sleep would have to do. I managed to scramble up and over the churchyard wall, scraping my hands, and fell in a heap on the other side. I crawled through the grass and nettles towards the dark pavilion of a yew-tree whose branches drooped to the ground around it. Brushing through the sweet-smelling leaves and into the little space beyond, I crumpled onto the litter of twigs and moss and was asleep in a moment.

It was day when I woke. The sun was trying to shine through a curtain of drizzle. Drops of water were rolling down a branch above me and falling onto my robe. A big patch on my chest was soaked. I was well rested, and wondered how long I'd been asleep. Given the weather, I reckoned I'd been out for a whole day and night. I peered out between the yew fronds, and jerked back in surprise. Two men were standing a few yards away from my hiding place, and as I watched they hefted shovels and began to dig. I cursed silently. I was trapped, at least for a while, and I was starving. To make matters worse a big earthenware jug and a leather satchel sat on the ground next to the gravediggers. I began to imagine their contents. Beer, and salt pork? Oatcakes? Pasties, perhaps? It was unbearable. My belly growled, then roared. I stuffed a corner of my soggy robe into my mouth and chewed.

The men were hard at work, and the ground must have been soft, as they made good progress. They began to sink down amongst the grave-mounds. First their knees, then their thighs, then their belts disappeared from view. I knew what I was going to do. It seemed to take an age, but at last the gravediggers were deep enough that when they bent, they bobbed out of sight. I blessed the person whose grave this was. He must have been important, or else his grave would not be so deep. And the men were reaching the six-foot mark. All I could see were the shovel blades as they flung earth out of the hole. Now was my moment. I bolted out from under the tree, grabbed flagon and satchel and hurled myself up and over the wall.

Luck was keeping an eye out for fools that day. As I landed on the wet cobbles I realised I had leaped before looking, but now I was in a deep, narrow alley and no one was about. I could hear the faint sounds of shovel-work behind me, so the theft hadn't been noticed. But it would be soon enough. I shoved the flagon into the satchel, which I tucked up under my robe. The leather strap I pulled through the collar and looped around my neck. Now boasting a fine beer-gut, I crept to the mouth of the alley.

I looked out onto one of the broader streets that sloped down to the river. People were about, but the drizzle was keeping their heads down. I decided to take a risk: hopefully my appearance, filthy, unshaven and starved as I was, would be disguise enough. I hurried down the street until I reached the bottom of the hill, then took a right turn. I was now in a busy thoroughfare that ran parallel to the river. It led to the castle, I figured, and to the rocky, deserted shore beyond. Cowl pulled down, hands clutching my stolen prize, I trotted on.

At last the street ended. I was beyond the town. Some fishermen sat around mending nets, looking wet and dejected. They did not notice me as I passed, and soon I was amongst the rocks in the lee of the castle. The tide was out, and the river was a narrow ribbon winding between wide plains of rippled sand. I found a jutting tusk of stone to hide behind, just beyond the tide line. The gravediggers' lunch turned out to be a great hunk of yellow cheese the colour of the skin on an old man's heel, but tasty and powerfully strong. There were two raw onions still in their skins, and two slabs of black bread clamped around a slice of salted pork fat. In the flagon was scrumpy, fresh and fine, as sour as death. I took a bite of onion, then a bite of cheese, then a swig of scrumpy, chewing all to a pulp in my mouth which I savoured until every morsel was swallowed, then began all over again. I finished an onion, most of the cheese and enough of the cider to feel it in my head and limbs. Then I stuffed the remains back into the satchel, which I used as a pillow while I took a long, deep and dreamless nap. The gulls woke me to bright sunshine. It seemed to be about three hours after noon. The tide was in and boats were bobbing on the water. A couple of big sea-going craft were edging towards the wharves, and a gaggle of fishing boats were sailing out to sea. A few yards off shore, a little rowing cob rode at anchor while its occupant jigged a hand-line up and down in the water. The fisherman looked up to see me watching him. Feeling suddenly exposed, I waved a hand, not knowing what else to do. The man waved a languid hand in return, and went back to his jigging. To him I was no one important. That felt good, so I had a few more swigs of scrumpy and a corner of bread and pork. I would have to wait until dark before going back into town to find Adric's Frenchman, so I settled myself against the warm rock with the flagon between my legs and watched the gulls wheel overhead.

There were fewer people in the darkened streets, but the wharves were still busy. Fishing boats were putting out and coming in. Catches were being piled up and inspected by lantern-light. Sailors were coming and going from the bigger ships as well. I wondered which of those belonged to Monsieur de Sol. I had slipped back into the town just after dusk, not wanting to risk being caught by the Watch. It was still too early, I thought, to look for the inn, so I made my way back to the church and slipped into the graveyard. I noted that the grave had been filled in and was strewn with flowers. There was a wooden marker, but I could not make out the name carved upon it. I gave silent thanks to the unknown soul who had inadvertently supplied me with lunch, and returned to my nest under the yew-tree.

There I waited. It was pitch-dark in my leafy cave, but I was too anxious to sleep. Instead I went back over the past few days, reliving them in my mind: the meeting and parting with Adric; the Dart in the moonlight, the foxes. It is strange how quickly the human spirit adapts to change, for I was already putting behind me the pain of leaving my old life. Wounds as deep as those do not ever entirely heal, perhaps – and I could no longer bear to let my mind linger for even an instant on Will, for the pain would come at once like hot iron pressed on flesh – but they were closing now, and I could half-smile as I remembered how the old boar had stared at me, indignation and terror in his piggy eyes. My heart sank again as I thought of Adric, who might even now be suffering the anger of Sir Hugh. But I had seen unsuspected depths in my friend, and a strength and goodness that someone like the Sieur de Kervezey could never understand or dominate. Somehow I knew that the coming summer would see Adric back on his pony, seeking out new wonders to delight his voracious mind and filthy, old and grisly artefacts to horrify his brother monks. I toasted him with the scrumpy, and grew a little more calm. An owl landed in the tree somewhere far above me and hooted softly to itself. In a little while I heard the watchman calling out ten of the clock. It was time to go in search of the White Swan.

But first I finished the scrumpy, needing the courage and not wishing to be weighed down by the empty flagon. I took off my robe and wedged it into a bole of the tree. Now I would look like any country boy, so long as no one looked too closely at my scalp. I left the flagon on the new grave-mound as a puzzle for the diggers, and made my way out into the streets. Not knowing anything of Dartmouth's inns, and being too afraid of drawing attention to myself to ask directions, I would have to search the town, and do it quickly. I had not passed the White Swan so far, so I could rule out two big streets. I decided to investigate the wharves first.

The waterfront was as busy as before, and no one paid me any mind. Dartmouth stretches out along the river, and it took me some time to walk the full length of the docks. There was no White Swan inn, although there were a number of other noisy hostelries and I was tempted to step inside more than one of them for a beer and some company. Finally I was back on the outskirts of town and turned back. I would have to search the alleys that ran back from the river first, then take to the back streets. I walked into a couple of empty courts. The third sheltered a sailor and his whore, hard at work against the wall of an old house. I slipped out of sight before they noticed me, but the woman's groans, and the cider that still warmed my guts, began to give me a warm glow inside, and not one that a cleric should be feeling. I began to feel my blood heat up – began, perhaps, to feel like a hunted fox, and not like the fox's future dinner.

The fourth alley I tried was not a dead end, but turned sharply to the right. I followed it, passing through a narrow opening where the houses leaned so close together that they formed a kind of tunnel. Then the alley turned again, and I was in a small court, blocked at the far end by a tall house from which poured lamplight and the sound of a hurdy-gurdy. The front of the building was plaster between wooden beams carved with laughing, leering faces and animals scurrying amongst oak leaves, and from a jutting post hung a great white-painted swan, a crown around its neck. I looked back down the alley, but saw only darkness. Time, then, to take my new road, be it short or long. Better to go on, and to get matters over with for good and all.

Chapter Eight

Stepping over the threshold of the White Swan was like walking into the heart of a vast bonfire. Candles and lanterns hung from the ceiling, burned in sconces on the walls, rose in great mountains of wax from the tables. At one end of the long, low room logs crackled in a big stone fireplace. Meat and birds roasted on spits or hung from slowly revolving strings in front of it, and kettles steamed merrily on the hearth. I had been living in a world of cold and shadows for so long that my senses faltered. The carved swan over the door outside and the light inside merged, and I truly believed for a moment that I had been enfolded in the wings of a great bird of fire, whose feathers were flames that did not burn but fluttered softly against my face. Coming back to reality, I discovered that I had walked right over to the fireplace and was staring into it, standing there like a statue.

I looked around me, horrified that I had dropped my guard so recklessly, but it seemed no one had noticed. I was just another customer warming himself before he ordered food and drink. And after all, I was just that, in part at least. Looking neither left nor right, I marched to the bar and put down my florin.

'Your pleasure?' asked the innkeeper. He was a tall, thickset man with a round face and a nose broken so badly in the past that it sprawled to one side, the tip pointing towards his left ear. But despite looking somewhat demonic he had friendly eyes, and I decided I could probably trust him. But not quite yet. I ordered a mug of ale, and gulped off half of it the moment it appeared before me. It was cool from the cellar, light and fragrant. I had not had strong beer since that night at the Crozier, and this was nothing like that rich elixir. Instead it reminded me of a moorland stream and the taste water has after running over oak roots and moss. I finished the mug and called for another.

And another. I asked for food, and a pewter dish of roast meat was brought, with a hunk of bread to soak up the bloody gravy. By this time I was starting to relax; indeed, the food and drink – especially the drink – was giving me little choice in the matter. The fire that the sight of the rutting couple had roused in my blood was flaring, and I began to look around the room. I had no idea, of course, whom it was I was searching for. The place was full. There were many men whom I took to be sailors by their dress, and others were plainly merchants, wealthy ones at that. There were many foreign voices in the general hubbub, holding forth in tongues I did not know, some of them outlandish to my ears. And there were dark faces, sallow faces, pointed black beards and white-blond hair. Women lounged here and there. I assumed they were whores from their bright clothes and brazen laughter, and the way they wrapped themselves around their chosen men. But some of them were young and sweet-looking, and the thought that I was nothing more than an ordinary man made me pause and turn back to my beer. 'Concupiscence,' I thought, rolling the fleshy word on my tongue. How wonderful the religious life was for providing men with rich words to describe things they would never experience. Well, I reflected, I was free to put actions to those words now, but I was unlikely to live that long. Finding survival still upwards in my mind, I decided that time was wasting.

I caught the innkeeper's eye and motioned him over.

'Another beer, my boy?' he asked. It occurred to me that he probably did not serve many young peasant lads who spent silver coin, but was treating me as well as any other customer.

It was then that I decided to put my trust in him, although I was not overly furnished with choices in the matter.

'In a minute, yes, please,' I said. 'In the meantime I am looking for a friend of mine. Do you perhaps know Monsieur Jean de Sol?'

If the man was surprised, he did not show it, although I thought I saw a new alertness in his eyes, and that ruined nose suddenly seemed more hawk-like than comical.

'Perhaps,' he agreed, and turned to serve another patron. Now that I had played my hand, I was terrified. What now? I supposed I would have to wait and see. I was grateful when the man brought me another beer, but his silence and sharp gaze unsettled me still more.

The next few minutes were agony. I drank quickly, although tension made my stomach, full for once, feel as if someone were squeezing it in a huge fist. I felt sick. At last the beer was gone, and I signed to the man that I wished to settle up. He cocked his head at me in surprise and was about to say something, but then with a shrug he took up my florin, grabbed a pair of large iron shears from beneath the bar and snipped the coin into quarters, three of which he handed back to me. As I turned away I felt his eyes on my back. I glanced around, but I was as unnoticed as before, and I made my way through the tables towards the door. I was almost there when a tall man stepped in front of me, barring the way. He placed a large hand lightly on my chest.

'You have some business with Jean de Sol, I think.' It was a statement, not a question. The voice was low and distinctly foreign.

I almost denied everything and was bracing myself to spring away from the stranger when I saw that his sunburned face, though serious, was not menacing. A few faces were turned towards us now. In any case I was all too aware that the man's hand must be feeling the reliquary through my tunic. I swallowed. 'Indeed,' I said hoarsely.

At once the man smiled. It was a good smile. 'This way,' he said, and without waiting, stalked off through the spilt drink and outstretched legs. I followed him to a door I had not noticed, in the shadows to the side of the fireplace. Behind the door was a staircase, which led to a long, narrow corridor flanked with many doors that seemed to run the full length of the building. The man selected the second door on the left, knocked once and muttered something through the keyhole. It opened, and I was waved inside with a gently mocking flourish.

The room was larger than I expected. Most of it was taken up by an enormous bed with carved pillars and heavy drapes of some once-rich cloth that had seen better days and a great many moths. A cluster of candles burned on a high stand in one corner. By the shuttered window was a low table, and a man sat there, his back to the door. He seemed to be writing in a ledger. Another man, the one who had let us in, stood by the bed. I saw that a short-sword hung at his belt and his hand rested on the hilt, although he was smiling. He too gestured, in that mock-courtly way, towards the figure at the table. Not knowing what else to do, I stepped into the room, made my best bow towards the seated man and cleared my throat. The lock clicked behind me.

'Monsieur de Sol, I bring you greetings from Adric of St Mary's abbey. I am called Petroc of Auneford, and I have . . .'

The seated man turned and stood up. I saw that he was dressed in the French fashion, and that the cloth was expensive. A dagger hung from his crimson leather belt. He had long black hair and a sharply pointed black beard, and his eyes were quick and bright. His two colleagues were laughing quietly. I straightened, blushing wildly. What was I doing wrong? What was the right way to sell a stolen relic, in God's name? But the Frenchman saw my confusion and gestured to his chair.

'Sit, please. We are not polite, I think. My apologies.' His accent was heavy, but his manners were as good as any

Englishman, I thought, sitting down carefully and feeling like a plump mouse in a room full of cats. The three foreigners sat on the bed facing me. They seemed to be appraising me carefully, and I thought even more strongly of cats.

'Monsieur de Sol,' I began again. 'Brother Adric of St Mary's abbey at Buckfast advised me to seek you out. I need to find passage to the Continent, and I have the means to pay my way.' Perched on the low stool and facing my inscrutable hosts I felt like a schoolboy under examination. I was certain I sounded like a scared child.

I ploughed on. 'Brother Adric thought that you might be interested in acquiring something in my possession.' There was no reaction from my three examiners. 'It came to me by accident, but I have no way to return it to its rightful owner . . . I mean, I am its owner.' This was horrible. 'My good sirs, I do not want this thing! I pray that you do.' Silence. 'Please, you must help me. I have carried the hand of St Euphemia with me all the way from Balecester. A man was killed for it, but I was not the murderer. There is a man who is hunting for both of us, me and the hand. He killed the verger and then my dearest friend Will, but I was blamed, and now Sir Hugh will kill me and take the hand.' Whatever had loosened my tongue, it was not in my control. 'I walked here from Buckfast, through wood and briar, and death has followed in my footsteps. Adric is my friend. He said you would help me. If you will not help me, take the cursed relic and let me go to my death with a clean conscience.'

Telling my story to these strangers made me almost light-headed. In a fury I ripped open my tunic and began to scrabble at the silk that held the reliquary. At once the Frenchman was on his knees in front of me, holding my wrists and murmuring as if to soothe a frightened animal.

'Be still, be still, young sir,' he was saying. 'We will help you. Do not worry. We will help.'

But I had pulled the binding free, and the reliquary tumbled to my lap and onto the floor, where it lay, palm up, slender golden fingers glowing softly in the candlelight. Everyone gasped, including me. The disembodied thing on the floor seemed to offer a blessing to the room.

'Heavens above,' said the Frenchman, unnecessarily.

After that, everything changed. The swordsman wrapped me in a fur robe from the bed. The man from downstairs, who seemed to be called Rassoul, poured a goblet of wine and made me drink. All the while, the Frenchman turned the golden hand in his own two hands, holding it up to the light, seeing how the gems on the rings sparkled, examining the workmanship. Finally he shook it. Drawing his dagger, he deftly inserted the point at the base of St Euphemia's wrist and turned it. With a faint pop the casing opened, and a black thing fell out onto his palm. He held it up to me.

It was frightful, a little wizened claw like a bunch of old blackthorn twigs. St Euphemia must have been very small, for her hand was no bigger than a young child's, though the reliquary had seemed to shelter that of an adult. The Frenchman was holding it between thumb and forefinger.

'Look at what a sad little thing you have been carrying,' he said, and his voice was full of some emotion I could not place. 'Dead flesh and gold. What power they have over the living.'

Tenderly, he slipped the claw back into its golden glove and sealed the end once more. He passed the reliquary to the swordsman, who placed it carefully on the table behind me. I was glad I did not have to look at it any more. I could feel the fingers still pressing into me and, looking down, I saw that the outline of a hand stood out red above my breastbone. Sweat, dirt and chafing had branded me with St Euphemia's mark. I wondered if it would ever fade.

'Now, Master Petroc, I am afraid we have deceived you,' said the Frenchman. My heart stopped. So this is what happened to fools who meddled in matters beyond their understanding. I waited for the swordsman.

My face was hiding nothing tonight. 'No, no, no,' the Frenchman went on quickly. 'You are safe with us. But I am not Monsieur de Sol.'

'But who are you?' I managed. 'And where is he?'

'I am Gilles de Peyrolles, his lieutenant. He is aboard our ship. He does not often come on land these days. We will take you to him.'

I must have looked unconvinced, because he laughed and went on: 'We have not heard such a tale since—' and he looked at his companions '—since we told our own stories. I know Adric. He is an odd man, but very wise, and always welcome amongst us. If you have his friendship, you have ours. As to your burden, we will be happy to purchase it, but it is worth far more than your passage to France. The captain will know, and he will not cheat you.'

The Lieutenant helped me to my feet. 'Now it is time to go. We were going to stay another night or two, but now we had better catch the tide.'

The other men moved through the room quickly and soundlessly, gathering up the ledger, quill and ink and throwing clothes into drawstring sacks. The Lieutenant wrapped the reliquary in a damask handkerchief and hid it inside his robe. The swordsman handed me a tunic of fine, supple broadcloth, deep blue and woven with tiny silver circles. 'Put this on,' he said. I obeyed. It was the finest piece of clothing I had ever worn, and it fitted me well enough.

'It suits you,' said the swordsman. 'Now keep your back straight and your wits about you. Come along.'

Someone blew out the candles, and then we were in the corridor. We hurried down the stairs and into the tap-room, emptier now but still loud and bright. I thought I saw a signal, no more than a look, pass between Gilles de Peyrolles and the innkeeper. My three new companions ducked their heads together for a brief moment. The door opened, and we left the White Swan.

Outside, the Lieutenant held the wrapped hand out to me. 'Would you carry this just a little further?' he asked. It was the last thing I wished to do, but I took the bundle and tucked it inside my new doublet. We set off again, hurrying down the crooked alley. I noticed with a lurch that the men were gripping the hilts of their weapons. We passed through the tunnel and I could see a narrow strip of moonlight twinkling on water, framed by the narrow mouth of the passageway. We were almost at the entrance when the moonlight vanished. Shadows blocked our way. The Lieutenant cursed and barked something to his colleagues. I did not catch his words, but suddenly Rassoul had me by the arms.

'There will be trouble. I will carry you through – it will be safer for all of us, and you are all bones and air. Do not let go. And do exactly what I tell you,' he hissed, then he swung me across his shoulders as easily as if I were made out of straw. Guessing what he meant me to do, I wrapped my legs around his waist and my arms around his neck. He drew his sword, and we were charging the shadows.

In an instant there was a crash and thud as bodies collided. A staff swung by my head. I saw the swordsman leap up and it seemed he stood for a moment on a man's shoulders before they both tumbled. The Lieutenant ran full tilt at another figure, ignoring a falchion that swung too soon. His left elbow smashed into the man's neck, and as the figure lurched backwards, I saw de Peyrolles' dagger punch into his belly, three or four stuttering thrusts almost too quick to follow. The stave whistled past my head again. Then my bearer flicked his sword and the stave went spinning away. Something hot splashed my arms and I felt my grip loosening. But now we were clear of the alley and on the broad wharfside. In the dim light two figures lay on the cobblestone, one kicking its legs like a crushed frog, the other still. I heard moaning from back in the shadows. There was a shout from the right, and four more figures were rushing at us. The Lieutenant shouted something.

Rassoul handed his weapon to the swordsman and turned, but he had gone only a few steps when a stave thwacked across his shins and we sprawled. I landed on my shoulder and rolled, my left ear mashing against the stones. Then Rassoul was up with a knife in his hand.

'Big boat, serpent on the bows,' he gasped at me. 'Fifty paces upstream. Go!'

I ran for it. Not from fear – there had not been time for that. But the swordsman's voice held the power of command. These people knew their business, and I did not. So I sped away up the wharf. The madness of a fight fills a man with energy that he must release somehow, and that energy carried me along now. I barely felt my feet on the uneven cobbles.

It was surely fifty paces by now, I thought, slowing down a little and trying to see the boats tied up beside me. I thought I saw a bigger vessel just ahead, then was sure: a great, ocean-going ship with lights burning on deck. My breath was coming in gasps now, and my mouth filled with a bitter metallic taste. Head down, I ran for the gangplank.

But at that moment a flash of white flame spurted deep in my skull, and then I was lying with my face to the dock, breathing a stench of old fish guts and my own blood. A voice muttered above me, and then my ears stopped ringing and I heard more clearly. It was a voice I recognised, and one that I expected.

'Got you, Petroc!' hissed Sir Hugh de Kervezey, kneeling down upon me. His knee dug into the small of my back and I gasped with the pain.

'What a tough little priest you turned out to be,' he said, and flicked my head down onto the stone. I felt something pop in my nose and blood gushed down the back of my throat and poured onto the ground. 'I knew you would come home, of course,' the silky voice continued. 'And your old librarian fooled me for a while. But your other . . . *erstwhile* brothers are not so gristly as Brother Adric, and they watch and spy on their fellows. A plump one – Thomas? Tobias? – let slip that Adric had met, from time to time, with a certain French collector of curios at the Sign of the Swan in Dartmouth. A collector, an outlaw and a stolen relic – all became clear. It is but a morning's ride, through such pretty country, and so here I am.' He smacked my left ear with a cupped hand and a frightening pain blossomed. 'And now I want the hand.' He smacked my other ear, the bruised one.

'Give it to me. I'm going to kill you anyway, but if you make me grope in your filthy clothes I'll cut off your balls and make you eat them first.'

'Don't!' was all I could say. The hand was digging into the pit of my stomach, winding me. Then: 'Turn me over. I have it!'

He jerked me onto my back. 'Hurry up, boy!' he said, calmly, squatting astride me. 'Bring it out.' He passed his hands before my face and I saw he had drawn his knife, which I half-remembered had had a name. The sheath he dropped carelessly to one side. Now he rested the tip of the blade against my belly and held it upright, balancing it loosely with the palm of his hand. I dared not breath, in case the point slipped into my guts. Slowly, slowly I reached into my doublet and grasped the bundle. Then I remembered the forlorn little claw inside its golden coffin. Sadness welled up inside me.

'Why did you choose me, Sir Hugh?' I asked him, blowing little bubbles of blood as I did so. 'Why did you scatter the coins under my feet?'

He leaned closer and pressed a little on the knife. 'Everything has to mean something, doesn't it, Petroc? All those prayers, all that sacrifice? But we are bags of blood and bones, and what we do to each other matters not one little bit. Perhaps you understand now. Even if you don't, you will in just a little while.'

'But why?' I croaked through the blood.

'Oh Christ! You fucking little *scholar*. I wanted to see if you would run when the time came, or if your little legs would fold under you. Like choosing a horse, or a dog. Now keep still, little boy. I will hurt you more if you struggle.'

Seeing his face above me, his smooth skin shining, his mouth stretched in a half-smile, I saw what I would do next. It would be wonderful for a moment. After that, I would not care. St Euphemia's hand had come free of its wrappings. I closed my own hands around its cold wrist and thrust upwards at the face of the knight. The golden fingers, rigid in their frozen moment of benediction, caught Sir Hugh on bridge of his nose and slipped sideways into his right eye. I felt the eyeball resist for a moment and burst, then the tip of St Euphemia's index finger ground against bone.

The Sieur de Kervezey howled. It was a worse sound than the foxes above Capton, more empty, more despairing, more devoid of humanity. His back arched convulsively, and he jerked backwards. I waved the hand feebly. '*Te absolvo,*' I told him. I tried to roll away, but the knight's knife-hand was flailing at me and I felt an icy needle bury itself in my shoulder. As the street began to open beneath me and suck me I saw him rise to his knees. His good eye blazed from a welter of blood. He shrieked again and I heard him stagger away as the darkness closed over me.

Chapter Nine

The heat of the sun on my face woke me at last – not the awakening that comes from a good night of sleep, but a sudden rushing-in of the world: one moment oblivion; the next, noise, smell, heat and dazzle. I lay on my back; beneath me was something soft. I was gazing up at a sky of the purest blue, and my first thought was that I had overslept by hours, and that there would be hell to pay at college. Then I noticed that everything was heaving, and although my head was spinning as if from the foulest hangover, the sickening lurches and plunges I felt were outside, as well as inside me. I started to look around, but a sharp pain in my neck made me hesitate. I gritted my teeth and turned a little further. Something came into view. I was looking at a tree-trunk festooned with ropes. Not a tree, exactly, but a high stout pole, supporting a great sheet of dirty cloth that ballooned out in the breeze. I was looking at a sail. With that revelation I jerked upright, and my body rebelled with a swarm of aches, pains, stings and twinges. I yelled, feebly. But I was still alive, apparently, so I steeled myself for another look around.

I was indeed aboard a ship. The only water-craft I had ever been on were the little coracles that the Dart fishermen used. Imagine, then, my utter confusion now. It seemed as though I were on a floating island of wood. I lay on a thick pile of sheepskins, which I now noticed still smelled strongly of the tanners. The ship stretched away in front of me for several yards, rising up to a stubby point. Beyond, the sea rose and fell from view. Behind me, the deck ended in a wall that rose up into the glare of the sun. As my senses returned to their usual state I saw that men were working all around, heaving on ropes, moving barrels and sacks, scrubbing the deck. The wind hissed in the sail, and water hissed somewhere below.

My head and face hurt. I explored with cautious fingers. My ears felt hot and swollen, but I could still hear. My forehead carried a lump the size of a hen's egg. My nose felt both numb and extraordinarily painful, numb when I breathed and raw when I tried to wrinkle it. I touched it very carefully, but it still seemed roughly in its rightful shape, although there was a big bump on the bridge, and as I felt a tiny scrape of bone on bone the silver mist of a faint poured over me. Then a hand was forcing my head down between my knees. I gagged, and then the world regained colour and form.

'So you are alive, Master Petroc. I am so very happy – but not happy enough to welcome any more puke on my boots. Welcome aboard the *Cormaran*.'

The voice was clear, but strange. There was an accent – almost French, but not quite. I had heard it before, I thought, but as to where . . .

'Drink this.' A flask appeared under my nose and, not really having any choice, I took a sip. The liquid was thick and strong, like mead but fiery and full of tastes I did not recognise. I took a longer pull. The man above me laughed.

'You like it? Drink deep. You need it.'

The mead was already buzzing in my blood, and I felt better. A great deal better, apparently, as I found myself staring into the face of the man with the odd voice.

The sun was behind him, and at first I could make out only a halo of curly hair. It was dark brown, and later I would see that it was shot through with silver. The curls framed a dark, lined face, clean-shaven, in which shone a pair of slate-grey eyes that seemed to pin me to the deck. The man had an eagle's nose, but his mouth was wide and he was smiling. His teeth were very white against his tanned face.

It was the smile – the first I had seen in a great age – that brought me fully to my senses. I was alive, possibly without serious damage, and in the hands of someone who smiled, laughed and dispensed strong drink. A rush of pure joy surged through me from toes to fading tonsure. I clambered to my unsteady feet, and tried to stretch my arms. Pain erupted in my neck, and the man with the white teeth grabbed my right arm and held me steady.

'Keep still, master. I am sorry – that arm should be in a sling.'

'My arm? It is not my arm that hurts,' I said.

'You took a knife-thrust, lad.' He touched me gently on my left shoulder, where the muscle rose towards my neck. 'It went through here. Very lucky. A little lower and it would have been in a lung. A little to the side . . .' And he moved his hand to my neck, where I could feel my blood pulse strongly. 'But the knife was very sharp and thin, and made a clean wound. Keep it still and you will knit together in a few days.'

'Are you Adric's friend?' I asked suddenly.

'Michel de Montalhac, sometimes called the Frenchman, also Jean de Sol. I'm honoured to meet you, Master Petroc. Gilles has told me something of your adventure.'

Then everything came back to me, and I sat down heavily on the sheepskins. De Montalhac knelt beside me.

'Do not call it an adventure, sir, please. I have lived in hell for . . . I don't remember. But I have pulled others down with me. My friend Will, and Adric. And Gilles: was he killed?'

'Do not worry about Gilles. He is extremely good at looking after himself, as are Rassoul and Pavlos.'

'Did they bring me here?' I asked.

'No, I found you myself. The . . .' he hesitated for an instant. 'You were brought down almost at our gangplank. I reached you just in time. Although you seemed to have given quite an account of yourself without my assistance.'

'What about Sir Hugh – the man who attacked me?' I asked.

'Aha. It seems you put out one of his eyes. I would have run him down and cut his throat—' and I flinched as he drew his hand sharply across his own neck '—had not Gilles and the boys come up then with the Watch at their heels. But in any case he may well be dead. I confess that I have been on fire with curiosity these last three days—' de Montalhac saw my surprise, and went on: 'You did not come aboard last night. We have been at sea for two whole days and nights, Petroc. You were unconscious at first, and we worried, but then it seemed that you were just asleep, and we did not wish to wake you before you were ready.'

I shook my head in amazement. The longest, finest sleep I had had in who knew how long, and I had taken it on board a ship, surrounded by strangers. But something in what the man had just said made me look at him more closely.

'Do you know something of Sir Hugh de Kervezey, sir?' I enquired carefully.

'Know of him? More than that. I know him very well, in some ways at least. But we are not friends. Or were not.'

My face must have betrayed the horror that the thought of Sir Hugh brought back to me. The fragrant flask was again at my lips. I took a draught. The man was speaking to me gently.

'The sun is shining. You are safe. He cannot follow.' He patted my shoulder. 'Let me show you my ship. Then we will eat, and talk some more.'

A little later, I was dressed in clean clothes and seated in a leather-backed chair in de Montalhac's cabin. My beautiful tunic, caked in blood and other things, had been given to one of the sailors, who expressed doubts that it could be rescued. Then de Montalhac had shown me below. Under the main deck was a long, dimly lit space where men slept in hammocks. It was ripe with sweat and old cooking, but not dismal. At one end a cloth had been hung, forming a private space where I found a pitcher of water and a large bowl. There were clean clothes: loose, ankle-length breeches of sailcloth, a sailor's tunic and a sleeveless sheepskin surcoat. I was left to wash myself. The water in the pitcher was perfumed with some kind of oil which smelled of roses. I hesitated before using it. 'Is this for washing or for drinking?' I called out. There was laughter from behind the sheet.

'This is no monastery, Petroc,' de Montalhac replied. 'On this ship we keep our bodies clean, as well as our souls.' He was chuckling. 'Roses will not hurt you. Do not take offence, but we would all rather smell the scent of a rose than that of a dead horse. Give thanks that you could not smell yourself.'

I had never thought about washing in these terms, and I confess I was shocked. The only person I knew who smelled like anything other than the day's sweat had been Sir Hugh, although as I thought longer I remembered that Gilles, Rassoul and the swordsman had also seemed faintly perfumed. But, I reflected, I was certainly damned in so many other ways that one more aberration would not harm me now. I rinsed myself stiffly, trying not to jostle my wounded shoulder. Then I dressed and found de Montalhac waiting for me. He held out a pair of low boots made from supple deep-red leather. 'Spanish,' he told me. 'Good boots. But you would do better to go barefoot on deck. Less slippery.' He gave me a belt in richly tooled leather that matched the boots. I thought it was a curious choice to go with my sailor garb, but de Montalhac anticipated my question.

'You need something to hold this,' he said, holding out his hand to me. In his palm lay something long and narrow. A knife in a sheath of some green material. I took it gingerly. The sheath was rough to the touch. I rubbed it experimentally with my thumb.

'Shagreen,' said de Montalhac. 'The skin of a sting-ray. Do you recognise it?'

I did not. The knife had a hilt of a cool green stone, and

where the stone widened to form a pommel, two red gems twinkled. I drew the blade, and almost dropped it in shock. I was looking at the cold, slender steel of Thorn.

'A prince once owned that knife,' de Montalhac was saying. 'It was made in Damascus a century and more ago. There are plenty of men on this ship who will be delighted to teach you its proper use.' Seeing my pale face and shaking hands, he added, 'Now put it away before you cut yourself.'

He said it in such a solemn, parental voice that Thorn's spell was broken. I laughed out loud as I slipped her back into the green sheath.

'How . . .' I stuttered.

'It was buried in your shoulder when I found you. And now,' said de Montalhac, 'let us eat.'

He showed me to his cabin, where Gilles de Peyrolles, who was delighted to see me up and about, and who seemed unmarked by his brawl on the Dartmouth waterfront, was waiting. The room was small and low. An arched doorway gave out onto the main deck, and I had been lying next to it on my pile of sheepskins – which I noticed had now disappeared. Opposite the door was a line of three windows that looked out on the ship's wake. I had stuck my head through one of them on first entering the cabin and found myself looking down – quite a long way down, I thought – on the green water that boiled and foamed out from under the stern. Gulls were following us, swooping and sometimes hovering low over our white trail. It was then that I realised I did not feel in the least bit seasick; one of the few things I knew about boats was that they made land-folk feel terrible, but I was fine. Perhaps, I reflected, I had come to terms with the ship's heaving while I was dead to the world. Whatever the reason, though, I was famished, and was delighted to find, when I pulled my head back into the room, that a great cold ham was waiting for us on the little round table that took up most of the centre of the room. Sitting down, I was reaching for Thorn with my good arm – the other was now in a sling and strapped tight across my chest – when the captain laid a hand on my arm.

'Do not ask a Moslem blade to cut pork if you wish her to serve you well,' he said gravely and handed me a plain, wooden-handled knife. 'You can keep this one,' he said. 'It is an apostate and won't care what you carve.'

Gilles gave a snort of rueful amusement from across the table. 'I'm sure that our guest is too hungry to give the faith of his cutlery much thought,' he said.

He was right. The food was plain but good, and I ate a great deal of it, and drank all the wine that Gilles poured into my pewter goblet. When at last I was full, and fell back in my chair with a barely stifled belch, I realised that my hosts had been silent the whole time. They had eaten too, but less ravenously than I, and they had taken care to keep my plate well stocked. But now de Montalhac spoke.

'Gilles called you our guest,' he said, 'but that is not strictly true. No, you are not our prisoner,' he added quickly. 'But you cannot return to England, as you know, and we will not be making landfall anywhere that you would wish to stay, not for a very long time. So—' and he glanced at Gilles, who nodded gravely, '—I propose to take you on as one of my crew.'

'Where are we going?' I asked, suddenly uncomfortable. My mouth was perhaps a little behind my mind, or else I would have been more worried about my sudden transformation from cleric to seaman.

The two men laughed. They seemed pleased. 'North. Far, far to the north, where the Skraelings live,' said the captain. 'And then, with a little luck, south.' Seeing I was ready with another question, he held up a hand.

'Don't worry, Petroc. We won't make you climb the mast if you don't want to. Your head will be more use to us than your muscles, although they will not go amiss. No, you have a quick wit and a strong spirit. Anyone, boy or man, who could keep one step ahead of a wolf like Kervezey – such a man has skill enough to find honour on this ship.'

'And now is the time to tell your story, before the wine sends you to sleep for another three days,' Gilles said, filling our goblets once more.

And so I told them. Beginning with Sir Hugh's golden trap at the Crozier and the next evening's horror in the cathedral, I let the tale unfold. And indeed, now that I was looking back on things and not living them, I found that it all seemed like invention, more a tale than reality. The memory of the deacon's blood made me pause. The knife that had killed him was now at my belt, and I wondered at the grim circles that fate drew with men's lives. I hastened over Will's death, but then I was explaining my escape, and my long days of travel, and finally my return to the abbey. De Montalhac interrupted to ask about Adric, but Gilles silenced him with a raised finger. I glossed over the final stretch of my journey. In those early days I was filled with a confusion of emotions: sorrow for my lost future; mourning for Will; burning regret; and a creeping sense of shame at my flight. My body would knit fast, but these other hurts would be long in the healing. So now I hastened on to my stay under the graveyard tree, and my audience had the good grace to laugh at how the gravediggers provided me with lunch. 'And the rest you know,' I finished.

'That is by no means true,' said the Captain. 'But you are tired. We have overtaxed you already. Sleep will heal your wounds and spread a little balm over past horrors.'

And indeed, I had not realised the depth of my fatigue. I made to stand, but my legs had no strength and I would have collapsed onto the table if Gilles had not caught me round the waist. To my great embarrassment, he swung me over his shoulder and carried me from the cabin as a hunter carries a fresh-killed deer. But there was no censure in the Captain's eyes as he watched us leave the cabin, only concern – or perhaps sadness. And then we were on deck, in the strong salt of the wind. It was late in the afternoon, and low clouds were scudding across a pale sky. The great sail was full and straining, and sailors were passing to and fro, attending to their mysterious duties and sparing us not even a glance. Gilles carried me below. A pallet had been laid out in the sharp angle of the bow. Eyes closed, I sank into the sweet, fresh straw and barely felt Gilles cover me with a soft and heavy blanket. For a minute or so I felt the ship heave and fidget under me and felt myself speeding along, head first, like a seabird over the water. Then came sleep, and no dreams.

Chapter Ten

I awoke to dim light, the rushing of water beneath me and a crushing weight on my chest. Opening my eyes, I found another pair of eyes staring back at me. They were large and golden, and set rather close together. I realised I was pinned down by a gigantic cat. Judging by the cosy warmth of our two bodies, and the contented look upon its furry face, it had been there for some time. The creature was truly enormous. It was covered in long, grey-golden hair, which fanned out around its head. Its ears were pointed and topped by long tufts of hair. In amongst all this fur, the animal's face seemed oddly small, and its close-set eyes above a small black nose gave it a sweetly intelligent look, like a quizzical monkey. I raised a cautious hand to stroke its head, and a great paw stretched out and touched me gently on the chin. I rubbed behind the tufted ears and it began to purr. I could feel the vibrations right down to my liver.

'Good morning,' I ventured.

The beast yawned, and its whiskers tickled my neck. 'Who might you be?' I persisted. The cat stood up and stretched, unfurling its plumed tail. It leaned down and butted my face in a friendly sort of way, turned and picked its way down my body, and trotted off into the gloom, still purring.

I rose and, following the cat, climbed up on deck. The sun was bright and the air, cold and damp, blew away the last rags of sleep. As always, men were hard at work all around, scrubbing the decks, mending sails and doing all manner of other things that looked completely baffling. No one greeted me, or even looked my way, so I decided to have a look around. Yesterday had passed in a blur, but now the ship began to form itself as a definite presence around me.

It was a great, wide thing. From where I stood under the mast, which reared up in what seemed to be the dead centre of the deck, the ship seemed to curve up both front and back. In front, the deck rose and met in a sharp point, and above this stood a kind of large wooden hut, sturdily built and topped with a circlet of crenellations. Beyond this jutted a short mast that pointed our way through the green and white sea. Behind me the deck ended in a wooden wall, in which was set the door to the Captain's cabin. Above this was another, smaller deck, surmounted again by crenellations. I confess that I, a landsman used to stone walls, found the effect of all these slightly ridiculous. A little castle, made of wood. A little wooden castle afloat on the sea. Even the mast was topped with a fortress in miniature, a turret the size of a big half-barrel. Then I looked about some more and noticed weapons stacked neatly here and there: pikes and ugly, wicked-looking halberds that sprouted notched hooks like talons; big, gnarled grappling irons. And the crew: they were all shapes and sizes, some fair, some dark. All were burned by the sun, and all seemed grim. Any one of them looked ready to take up one of those savage halberds and split heads apart like firewood. I shuddered, but then the ship gave a lurch, the sail flapped and snapped overhead, and everyone looked up from their tasks, alert and ready. Then I saw that I had mistaken grimness for concentration, that these were men who lived in a world encompassed by these wooden walls and who had mastered their world completely. This really was a fortress and would be defended to the last drop of blood.

The wind seemed to have shifted slightly. Commands were passed to and fro, and ropes were hauled on until the great square of cloth filled once more. I was in the way, although I might have been a lifeless piece of cargo for all the attention the crew gave me. Dodging between them, I made my way to the back of the ship, where a kind of ladder led up to the little fortress atop the Captain's cabin. I climbed up and found myself in a small, enclosed space. The wooden battlements were much more formidable close-to: thick, scarred and as high as my head. And there in the middle of the deck stood a figure, legs braced wide, seemingly bonded to a great spar that quivered and jerked in his grasp. The sun was behind him, and in my eyes. I had exchanged the frenzy below for an audience with a shadowed giant. Turning back to the ladder, I collided with the Captain, who fended me off, laughing.

'Awake and about, Petroc? How did you sleep?'

I told him my night had been dark and dreamless. 'But who,' I added, 'was the monstrous creature who woke me?'

De Montalhac frowned. 'Monstrous, you say – not Dimitri, the master-at-arms?'

Now it was my turn to laugh. 'No human creature, sir. This one had four legs, lion's teeth and a tail like a fox. Unless that was indeed your Dimitri.'

'Aha. Fafner found you. Bigger than the master-at-arms, although not as fierce. He is a *skaukatt*, one of those cats that live in the forests of Norway, that mate with the wild lynx. We had him as a runty kitten. Rassoul took him off a market-woman in Trondheim who was set on his drowning. Sweet as a baby and clever as an ape. I've seen him swallow a rat in one gulp.'

'I believe he could have done the same to my head.'

'Like as not. But I see you are curious about our ship. That is good. What have you noticed?'

'I have seen sailors who look like warriors, wooden castles and . . .' I lowered my voice and motioned over my shoulder to the figure behind me, 'and that one.'

'You mean Nizam,' said the Captain. 'Another giant, but he must be, to handle the tiller. Come, let us meet him.' And before I could decline, he was leading me up the sloping deck.

Without the sun in my eyes, I saw that Nizam was human after all, bigger than myself or the Captain and powerful, but no monster. And he was a Moor, the first I had seen. I was face to face with one of the Infidel demons loosed upon the world, devourers of children, worshipers of the idols of Mahomet, defilers of the Holy Places. I had seen their images on tavern signs and the like: coal-black gargoyles with red eyes and sharp, white teeth. Here, though, was a man with light brown skin, almond eyes, a strong, curved nose and ordinary-sized teeth. His hair was short and black, a small ruby hung from each ear, and he wore a close-cropped beard that came to a point below his chin. We were introduced, and he nodded solemnly and touched his right hand lightly to his chest, his lips and then his forehead.

'Peace be with you,' he said.

'The same to you, sir,' I replied. To my horror, the man barked with laughter, leaned over the tiller and slapped my good arm.

'My dear young fellow, you must have a Moslem soul,' he cried. '*Salaam aleikum* is our greeting – the reply is *wa'aleikum salaam* . . . "and with you" . . . Where did you find this prodigal?' he asked the Captain. 'The usual Frankish dolt would have thanked me or invoked his Christ or some other nonsense. This one thinks. I like him.'

'No talk of souls until after the noon bell, old friend,' said de Montalhac. 'As to where I found Master Petroc, the truth is he found me. And looked death in the face to do it.'

'I have heard a little of your story, my young friend,' Nizam said, turning to me, 'but perhaps you can tell it yourself.' Seeing my face fall, he quickly added, 'In a few days, of course – after you are a little more at home. These long watches are lonely. Your company would place me in your debt.'

'I will gladly keep you company, sir, and no more talk of debts,' I said.

'Gallant, very gallant,' said the Captain. 'But beware, lad –

you have fallen into a nest of storytellers. My advice is to demand a tale before you part with your own. Most of them are wild and bloody, but you will find that yours will hold its own with the wildest.'

He turned and made his way back down to the main deck, and I murmured a farewell to Nizam and tripped down the ladder at the Captain's heels. I cannot deny that my new home, with its armed, scowling denizens, was beginning to fill me with misgivings, especially as I could see that what I assumed to be dry land was but a long blue blur on the horizon. De Montalhac, Gilles and Rassoul I counted as allies, and Nizam was by no means the ogre I had at first taken him to be, but I was painfully aware that I was more or less alone, hurt, in surroundings that at the very least were unfamiliar and in fact downright outlandish. Even the ship's cat seemed a furry titan. My best chance for survival, then, must be to keep a tight hold on the hem of the Captain's cloak.

That morning, however, de Montalhac had, unbidden, appointed himself my guide and protector. One by one he introduced me to his crew, each man seemingly happy to turn away from whatever task occupied him to make my acquaintance. At first I felt myself shrinking back behind the Captain, but to my great surprise I soon found that the crew were by no means as menacing as their countenances might suggest. Each gravely bowed to me, some taking my hand, others saluting me in the manner of their own country. Several favoured me with the gesture which Nizam had used, although, strange as it seemed to me then, there were no other blackamoors aboard.

The next introduction was the most terrifying. The Captain had mentioned Dimitri, the monstrous master-at-arms, and now he led me towards the odd little fortress that sprang from the front of the ship – 'She is a ship, Petroc, never a boat,' he told me firmly – where a hulking figure was sharpening halberds on a stone wheel, sending sparks flying in the scant shade of the wooden wall. I saw that he was passing the sharpened blades to another man, who packed them into rough wooden chests filled with what looked like tallow.

Hearing the Captain call his name, the man at the wheel looked up from his work, showing me a face that seemed a jumble of bumps and crags, as if sharp pebbles had been worked into dough. Smallpox had ravaged it, and one cheek had been sliced flat to leave a shining plane of scar-thickened flesh. The fleshy nose had been broken high up between the eyes, which were small and brown. The man's close-cropped hair was iron-grey. As he turned towards us, I saw that the razor-keen blade which had removed his cheek had also carried away his right ear.

'This is Dimitri the Bulgar, who carries us all upon his shoulders,' said the Captain. The monster shrugged and fixed his gaze on me. It was bright and alive, and stabbed like an awl.

'This is Petroc. I'd be delighted if you could put him under your eye,' the Captain went on. 'I would have him learn our ways and the ways of the ship. You will find him promising, I think.'

'Petroc?' said Dimitri. His voice was hoarse, and his accent guttural. He leered, and I realised that this was how a grin appeared on a face that lacked a cheek. I took his proffered hand, as big as one of his halberds, and as hard. 'I have seen you.'

That was all. My presence noted, Dimitri went back to his whetstone. I glanced at the Captain for an explanation, but he was already introducing me to the man packing the blades in grease, a thin, sunburned man whose blue eyes twinkled as he told me his name was Istvan, from the island of Split in Dalmatia, and that he was overjoyed to make my acquaintance, a stream of words which poured out in barely intelligible English in an accent close to, yet oddly different from that of Dimitri. I stammered and bowed in return, and Istvan winked, holding out a tallow-daubed hand to me and cackling when I hesitated to take it in my own. I blushed furiously.

'A smart one, this one, Captain,' the man laughed. 'Looks out for tricks. I like him.'

I bade Dimitri and Istvan farewell, and the Captain led me towards a group of men sitting cross-legged on the deck, sewing patches into a great expanse of sailcloth. 'It is well that you are in favour with those two,' he murmured. 'Dimitri looks fierce, does he not? And he is even fiercer than his countenance promises. But Istvan too is a great warrior. Those two fear nothing, but are clever enough to keep blood and breath in their bodies. Listen to what they tell you, be grateful if they teach you a little of what they know and stay close to them in a fight – should occasion arise,' he added quickly, seeing the look I darted at him.

And thus we spent the morning, de Montalhac taking care that I met every man aboard the *Cormaran*. I learned that not all – indeed almost none – of the evil-visaged crew were as forbidding as they appeared, but were happy or at least curious to make my acquaintance, knowing that I came to them trailing dark clouds of some sort and so, in that way at least, already one of them. I still remember every face and every name, although there is no time in my story to dwell on all of them. Men like Zianni the Venetian; Horst the German, who had been no less than a knight of the Teutonic Order; Isaac the surgeon and his friend the poet and cook Abu, Jews of Valencia; and Pavlos, the swordsman from the White Swan at Dartmouth, who had been a guard of the Despot of Epirus – a Greek princeling of whom I had never heard, to my embarrassment – but had run foul of a palace intrigue and been lucky to escape with his life. Then there were Elia and Panayoti, brothers from Crete, Rassoul, who was a Sicilian Moor; Snørri the Dane and Guthlaf the dour ship's carpenter, also a Dane; and scores more besides, from every nook and corner of Christendom and many places beyond.

In all, the crew of the *Cormaran* was a strange stew of vagabonds, men of faith and of the sword, scholars and minstrels. These men, who almost without exception had found themselves unable to live in the everyday world, here worked together, lived together, died together. Quarrels were rare. Fights were rarer, and quickly over: although every man aboard knew war and death as well as they knew the lines of their own hands, I believe that very few of them loved violence for its own sake. And if some of the crew had little regard for each other, they were all joined in their devotion to the Captain.

And now here I was, an erstwhile monk who had been nothing but blamessly orthodox, fallen amongst Moors, Jews, Schismatics, heretics. And those where the ones who professed their faiths. Behind many others I detected closely guarded secrets. The truth was that I had fallen amongst men upon whom religion had been turned like a weapon. Yes, there were rogues like Zianni who had placed themselves beyond the laws of men and God by ill-fortune or simple choice, and men of war who knew no other life than that of violence. But perhaps the greater number of crewmen would find persecution or even death if they practised their beliefs in any country other than their own – and many were condemned out of hand in their own lands too. The only home they had, the only church or temple, was the ship. Chief among these were the group of men closest to the Captain, former subjects, like him, of the Duke of Provence. They spoke their own language, which they called Occitan, and which sounded like French and Latin stirred with honey and warm sunshine. To a man they carried some secret burden of the soul, a great anger and greater sadness within them. These men of Provence had suffered some fearful wrong, and de Montalhac, judging by their deference to him, had suffered most of all. I had heard of the dreadful wars that had afflicted their land – I was a cleric, after all, and knew of the Cathar heretics and their blasphemous, idolatrous ways – and remembered, dimly, when the news came to my abbey that the great heretic castle of Montsegur had fallen. It had meant little to a twelve-year-old novice monk, and now I wished I had paid more attention to news from the wider world. There was nothing monstrous about the Captain and his companions, though, and I confess I was filled with curiosity, although I did not have the nerve ever to enquire further.

So we made our way northwards through the Irish Sea. We had calm seas and light winds, and the land drifted by, a distant bruise on the starboard side. At first I was more or less ignored as I wandered about the ship, and I quickly found a place for myself in a corner of the forecastle where I was unlikely to interfere with anyone else's business. This suited me. My whole arm had swelled, and it ached and throbbed as if it were a sausage stuffed with tiny demons trying to find their way out. It was almost impossible to turn my head. Isaac the surgeon changed my bandages daily, prodded my shoulder, and assured me I was healing well. It did not feel so to me, and the pungent, slightly nauseating balm he pasted over the wound failed to work its magic on my spirit, although it had great effect upon my body. Within a week I could look stiffly from left to right, and the demons under my skin were beginning to lose heart. But meanwhile I felt like a cripple and a useless mouth in a place where no food, no motion appeared to be wasted. Unlike the quiet regime of my monastery, I had been thrust into a community defined by constant activity. If a man was awake, he was mending, painting, trimming the sails, steering, navigating. Even the Captain and Gilles, who to my way of thinking were the lords of the ship, never seemed to take their ease, unless it were at the supper table. But even here they were frugal, eating with one ear cocked to the sounds of the crew and the wind in the sail.

One day – it must have been our sixth day at sea, although I stopped counting soon afterwards – Fafner woke me in his usual fashion, taking my nose whole into his mouth and giving it the gentlest of nips with his great white teeth. His breath was as foul as his nature was sweet, and banished the last mists of sleep like a splash of cold water. I lay for a while, stroking the cat, until he slipped away to other entertainments and I rose and went on deck.

For the first time since leaving Dartmouth, land was clear on our starboard bow. I saw dark, low hills in a line fading to the north. Looking around, I noticed that the crew were paying little attention to the shore. But I was curious, and instead of climbing forward to my spot in the forecastle, I went aft and joined Nizam on the bridge. I had exchanged no more than a nod with the helmsman since our meeting, but he greeted me with a smile. I remembered his odd gesture of welcome and made it now, a quick touch of my fingertips to breast, mouth, forehead. He returned it with great solemnity, then roared with laughter, so much so that I feared the ship would career off course.

'Master Nizam,' I began, cautiously, 'I see land over yonder. Do you know where we are?'

'I would be a poor helmsman if I did not,' he replied. 'Those hills are the Rinns of Galloway. We are in the North Channel – Scotland is to starboard, and Ireland will show to larboard soon. If it stays clear, you shall see the Mountains of Antrim on one side, and the Mull of Kintyre on the other. We shall clear the Channel today, and perhaps tomorrow, perhaps the day after we will be in the Minches between the Western Isles and Skye. From there, it is due north to the Faroes, and Iceland beyond.'

This was more information than I had dared to expect, and so I sought some more. 'Is this ice-land where the Skraelings dwell?' I ventured.

'No, no. Iceland is – well, it is indeed a land of ice, but that is also its name. To the north-west of Iceland is Greenland, which is more of an ice-land than Iceland – if you follow me – and still further west are Aelluland, Markland, Vineland and

Skraelingeland. I see you have never heard that such places lie beyond the setting sun, but men have visited their shores for centuries – nay, men – your Skraelings are men like you and I – have lived there time out of mind. There: I have told you the last great secret of the world. But this time we go to trade with the folk of Greenland.'

'Are they not Skraelings?'

'They are Norse folk. Their forefathers were Vikings out of Iceland. They tell us that in the Viking days, Greenland was indeed green. Now it is becoming pitiful: winter has crept down on them from the north, and allows them but a grudging summer. With the ice and snow come the Inuit, Skraelings who cover their bodies in seal fat and furs, and eat their meat raw. They kill the Greenlanders whenever they can, and in return are slaughtered like vermin. But their numbers grow, while the Greenlanders grow thin and weary. We trade warm cloth for their walrus ivory, and they are horribly grateful, poor wretches.'

'Is that what the Captain does? Trade with the Norsemen?'

'Yes, among other things. We are traders, it is true. But we prefer to keep our arrangements – what is your word? Ah, yes: informal. Where we are going, it is the King of Norway who holds the monopoly on trade. Bergen is where he holds court, but Bergen is far out of our way. And we would not bother the King with trivial matters. The poor man has quite enough to worry about.'

It dawned on me. 'So you are smugglers,' I said, half to myself. Realising what I had let slip, I jerked my head down in panic, wrenching the wound in my shoulder and sending a ghastly spasm of pain down my left side. Gasping, I regarded Nizam through eyes misty with tears, sure that the giant would toss me overboard like a piece of carrion for my hasty words. But instead he reached a hand across the tiller and steadied me.

'We are traders who keep no accounts but our own,' said

another voice. 'We respect no borders other than the walls of this ship, pay neither toll nor tax save to our own consciences, and as for kings, each man of us is king unto himself.' It was the Captain; I had not heard him climb up to us. 'Fancy words. Smugglers – yes, you cut through to the quick. Does the thought trouble you?'

I tried to think above the waves of misery flowing from my wound. 'No,' I said at last. 'No. Truly it does not.'

'I am glad – truly. But whatever your feelings, you are safe with us. I will put you ashore in some safe port, if you wish. That has always been my intention. Or . . .'

The thought of the world beyond the *Cormaran* filled me with sudden dread. Dry land – it looked so peaceful, drifting far off in a haze of blue and purple, but it held only death for me now. Then I patted Thorn where she lay against my tunic. I was safe out here on the sea, in this strange company that seemed to have adopted me. Laying my good hand on the smooth wood of the tiller, I followed Nizam's gaze to the far horizon, where sky and ocean met in a perfect silver line.

'I wish to stay,' I said.

Chapter Eleven

North and north we sailed, until I was sure we would brest the top of the world and fall down the other side into oblivion. But then we reached the Faroe Isles, and I wondered whether we had not already sailed out of the familiar world. This place of looming cliffs and smooth green grass was unearthly. Myriad seabirds wheeled and shrieked about the crags, and waves boomed and rang in the caves below. The beaches were desolate, and the inhabitants avoided us, although we passed one of their villages, the low houses thatched with living turf so that the place looked like nothing so much as a colony of ant-hills. There seemed to be as many sheep as seabirds. White shapes against the blue sky above, and the green grass below.

We put in to a sheltered cove on a little island to take on water. My wound having healed in the salt air and Isaac's bastings, I went ashore in the long-boat with the watering party, and after the casks were filled at a little stream that ran clear as diamonds down to the sea, I wandered among the tussocky grass for a while, marvelling at the odd birds that squatted and scurried about everywhere on bright red feet, creatures the size of ducks with grotesque wedge-shaped beaks that seemed to bear all the colours of the rainbow. In the air they whizzed about like crossbow bolts. 'Puffins,' Horst called them. 'Funny, are they not? You will be cursing them before long.' I wondered what he meant: the stubby, self-important creatures looked good-natured and harmless. I stored Horst's remark away in the overflowing sea-chest of my mind with all the other odd lore I had heard on board. 'Ask about puffins,' I told myself. A shout came from the long-boat: time to be off. I forgot all about birds as I ran back down to the shore, horrified at the prospect of being marooned in this desolate place.

We put in for half a day at Tórshavn, a little town of turf-roofed houses that Nizam told me was the most important place hereabouts. Tough, salt-wizened men with bleached out hair and eyes unloaded a few dark bales from our hold, and loaded on a few more casks and bottles, some bundles of seal-skins, and many sacks of wool. The Captain went ashore, and I saw him deep in conversation with a small but important-looking islander. They nodded back and forth, then the Captain roared with laughter while the other grinned gap-toothed at him. They embraced, and the Captain strolled back to the ship.

'These are good people,' he told me later. We were standing on the bridge, the Captain, Nizam, Gilles and myself, watching Tórshavn dwindle to a blur behind us. 'Sheep and whales are all they know, but although they are farmers, they have pirate blood in their veins.'

'They look as tough as old ox-hide,' I said. 'I would not live there, not for all the spices of India.'

Gilles grunted pleasantly. 'It is lucky you did not wish to be put ashore in a safe port, Master Petroc,' he said. 'I can think of no safer port than Tórshavn.'

'What did we take on board?' I asked, to change the subject. 'I saw woolsacks.'

'We trade wool for skins,' answered the Captain. 'Bear, wolf, simple stuff. The fur is as welcome as gold, and we will trade the wool in Greenland.'

'And where do we sail now? To Iceland?' I shivered. Further north, towards the abyss. I could feel the loneliness of the islands with me still, as if it lingered around the ship like mist. I dreaded to think what awaited us next.

'Aye. We'll stop for water and provisions, but no trade, I

think, this trip. Sturri – the man I was talking to, a councillor – warned us off. King Haakon has men in Reykjavík, to smother unlawful business. A shame. You would like the Icelanders. Odd folk, but friendly. They are all related to each other, you see. Vikings, every one.'

'And the Greenlanders?'

'You will see for yourself. A sad place, too near the world's edge for people to settle comfortably. In times past it was safe and green, but this age of the world is turning cold, and they freeze, little by little, year by year. It is . . . you will see.'

With that, the subject was closed, and we stood quietly and watched the petrels skim our wake as the islands dropped below the edge of the world. The horizon was wide and desolate, and the water was fretful. Away ahead of us, sea and sky merged in a dark green haze. Nizam hunched his shoulders for an instant, as if settling a heavy load upon his back.

'The Sea of Darkness,' he murmured.

A steady south wind eased our crossing to Iceland, although the sea was black and troubled, and we were followed by dark sea birds that swooped and scudded across our wake. Leagues and leagues from any shore they wandered, never alighting, not even on our masts, which to me seemed incredible; but these creatures were wedded to the air as men are bound to the land: even on the oceans we create little landscapes of wood on which we can firmly set our feet. When I was not working – and I now had my share of chores with the rest of the crew – I would climb to the bridge and stand with Nizam, looking out at the little birds that were so close and yet so unknowable.

Iceland appeared as a stern grey line one late afternoon. We found landfall at Hofn, a small port on the south-eastern coast, a dour place that huddled on a flat shore behind which mountains rose and beyond them, so the Captain told me, the great ice-fields of Vatnajökull spread out in a frigid hell, many days travel of desolation in any direction. As in the Faroes, some business was conducted on the wharfside, and we carried many small but heavy barrels aboard. As the Captain had said, we did no trade, but he and Gilles spent half a day in conference with some of the town's important men. We took to sea again, stopped for water and set a western course.

The southern wind blew for a week or so longer, and we skipped and rolled crosswise over a steady swell, although I began to notice a deeper mood in the motion of the ship, a faint, almost imperceptible roll at odds with the action of the waves. I asked Nizam, who had become my oracle in all things relating to the sea and the ship, about it.

'It is the swell of the deep ocean,' he told me. 'Though the winds shift all about the compass, yet steadily all weather comes from the world's edge in the far west, and always the oceans feel it and are driven by it − perhaps there are great storms far, far away that whip the seas into mountains of water, and this swell is a faint memory of that. No one knows, but I have heard that on the western shores of Ireland the waves can top the highest cliffs, and that after a great storm sea monsters have been dragged up out of the abyss and thrown onto the beaches. We had an Irishman aboard for a while − Colm, his name was − who swore he had seen such a creature. A great pale serpent bigger than a forest tree and as thick around; when he approached, it yelped at him in a language he did not understand and writhed away back to the water.'

This was not likely to comfort someone new to the life of a deep-water sailor. My dreams became invaded by writhing tangles of colossal serpents that seethed far below me like the eels that I had seen in the river at Balecester, feasting in the shallows on dead cats and dogs.

That night in the Captain's cabin each diner wore the same look of tense excitement I had seen on the crew's faces all day. The talk was quieter, the banter a little more restrained than usual. Nizam was there, and Horst and the ship's carpenter, Guthlaf, a pale Dane who generally kept to himself. Tonight, however, he was almost garrulous, deep in a conversation with Nizam about the northern seas. I chatted idly to Horst, who had been teaching me the complexities of knot-tying.

Just as my stomach began to gurgle audibly, the door was flung open, and Jacques entered. I had become inured to *skerpikjot*, the dried, smoked mutton of the Faroes that the rest of the crew loathed, indeed almost looked forward to its appearance even though we had been lucky at fishing and had often enjoyed fat cod and herring since leaving Iceland. Wordlessly he set down a great trencher piled with a brown, dried meat. 'Aha,' said Horst at my side. The rest of the party eyed the dish in silence. Finally, Gilles cleared his throat.

'My friends, the time has come again to give thanks for that special blessing of northern seas, the bounty that comes from above and stints not.'

'Amen.' The word rippled around the table.

'To our youngest, newest brother goes the serving of honour,' continued Gilles in the same sepulchral tones. The Captain speared a portion of meat and flicked it onto my wooden plate.

'Eat, and join us in the brotherhood of the Whale Road,' he murmured.

I prodded the stuff, and glanced up. All eyes were upon me. I sawed off a corner and cautiously slipped it into my mouth. To my surprise, it was not at all bad, something like very well-aged and smoked venison. It was a little oily, and left a hint, after it had gone down, of the bottom of the herring barrel, but in all it seemed to me to be manna indeed. I said so.

Gales of laughter. Horst slapped my back so hard I thought for a moment he had dislocated my shoulder. 'Welcome, brother,' he hooted. 'Welcome, welcome,' carolled the rest. I blushed and took another, bigger bite. Even tastier this time.

'What is this?' I asked through a full mouth.

'Puffin. Smoked, cured puffin, prepared by those witches in Iceland,' said Horst. 'Do you truly like it?' I nodded. 'Churning bowels of Christ! Truly? Captain – do you hear it? The English are hard folk, to be sure.'

'Why do you make such a to-do about this food?' I asked.

'Lad, this is your first – your second, Mary's tears! – but the rest of us must have eaten a hundred score each of the damned painted imps. By the end of this voyage our feet will all be turning orange, mark me well.'

Then the Captain slapped the table to get our attention. 'Brothers, friends,' he said, 'late tomorrow or the next day, we will be sighting Greenland. The folk in Hofn gave me news that I find worrying, however. It seems the western settlement at Godthåb is all but abandoned, and on the east coast Eric's Brattahild is no more. The chill is creeping over the land, and the Skraelings come with it. It was but four years since we were there last, and in so short a time the lives of those poor wretches have come quite undone.'

'How could things be worse there, Captain?' asked Horst. 'It was no paradise, to say the least, that we found on our last visit.'

'That is what I dread to find out,' replied de Montalhac. 'But we will be at Gardar in a short time, and you may have your answer then.' After that the subject seemed to be closed, although the rest of the meal passed under something of a cloud.

We sighted land mid-morning two days later. It was a grim-looking country, and I wondered why anyone had chosen it as a home to begin with. Dark mountains streaked with snow fell to a rocky coast. Here and there a clutch of pallid green fields clung to flatter areas of land, and smoke rose from tiny stone houses that were very few and far between. By evening we had rounded a sombre headland and were approaching the little port of Gardar. It was almost dark by the time we bumped against what passed for a wharf, and though the Captain, Gilles and Rassoul went ashore to seek the harbourmaster, the rest of the crew stayed aboard.

I gazed across at the meagre little town and marvelled once again at the tenacity of folk who lived in these northern lands. The Faroes were a land of milk and honey compared to this place; even barren Iceland seemed almost comfortable. It was cold, of course, a bitter cold that spoke of desolation and death. The wind that plucked at the rigging came, I was certain, from some awful wilderness where only spirits of ice and snow dwelt. Dim lights flickered in the long, low houses, but other than the lap of the sea and the rustling wind there was silence. No one was about, not even a dog. This, I thought, is truly the edge of the world.

The next morning it was raining when I awoke. Water came down in thick ropes that struck so hard that a thin mist hovered at ankle height above the deck. The bilges gurgled. In Hofn I had acquired, on Snørri's advice, a sailcloth cape that had been soaked in seal blubber to make it waterproof. I stared glumly out from under the hood, upon which raindrops exploded like fat on a hot pan, at the water cascading from the roofs of Gardar's houses. The streets were empty, and now that every window was shadowed it seemed as if the town was deserted. Then I saw a swaddled figure dash from one building to another. There was life here after all.

Fortunately the rain stopped around midday, and we went ashore to see what, if anything, Greenland had to offer. The answer to that was, it soon emerged, precious little. Over half of the crew had been here before on the *Cormaran*'s last northern voyage, and they shook their heads and clucked their tongues at the changes the intervening four years had wrought. I gathered from Horst that Gardar had come down in the world, which to me seemed hardly possible. It was a clutch of Viking longhouses whose gable ends, crossed and jutting above the roof line, were carved in the likeness of dragon heads. Looming over all was a colossal stone barn, which turned out to be the cathedral, and a high but clumsy bell tower. Instinctively, I threw the hood of my cape over my head and drew it tight – even though I knew that this was a far country, indeed the farthest country in the whole world, I had a sudden dread of being in the company of churchmen. Only when a skinny deacon passed us and gave a haunted, distant smile did I concede that I was just another stranger to these folk. I wondered who the bishop was, and what he had done to earn such a demesne.

Some of the men remembered a whorehouse, but could not find it. There were a couple of taverns, and we repaired to the first we came to. It was dark and reeked of smoke and wet straw, but the beer was drinkable. The tavern-keeper was a burly, red-bearded fellow who recognised Snørri and a few others and made us tolerably welcome. His wife, a skinny haint with blond hair and a red nose, watched us with suspicion in her smoke-reddened eyes as she ladled out some manner of lamb soup into wooden bowls. In their turn, the crewmen regarded her with ill-concealed lust while her husband glowered. I thought of a circle of dogs each chasing the tail of the beast in front, and supped my beer, feeling left out and not particularly sorry for that. After sucking down a good few mugs I tottered outside for a piss.

The cold, damp breeze felt better than the stale fug of the tavern, and I chose not to rejoin my friends for the moment. Instead, I wandered back in the direction of the cathedral, the first house of God I had seen since leaving the graveyard in Dartmouth. There was a broad patch of grass before it, and from a distance I had thought that sheep grazed there, but as I drew closer I saw that what I had taken for sheep were bones, great white skulls from which tusks as long as my legs jutted, their empty eye sockets regarding my trespass balefully. Guarding the door were still stranger wonders, and I would have most likely fainted in amazement had not one of the crew already told me of the narwhal, the strange fish of the deep ocean from whose forehead sprouts a twisted unicorn's horn. A small forest of these things were clustered on either side of the path, and even though I knew what they were they left me with a sense of the unearthly which, in those surroundings, was not pleasant. I hesitated at the towering door of time-bleached wood. The last time I had been inside a cathedral . . . Perhaps it was partly to exorcise the image of Deacon Jean's eyes as they bulged with pain and terror, and the memory of scalding blood streaming over my skin, that I turned the big iron handle and stepped inside.

It was like stepping into a cave, a cave with wooden pews and candles burning dimly at the farthest end. The smell of incense mingled queasily with the ranker scents of mildew and burning tallow, and shadows fluttered moth-like across the rafters. As my eyes accustomed themselves to the gloom, I saw that every wooden surface – pews, rafters, beams – was carved into fluid, rippling forms. I ran my hand over the nearest pew. Dragons writhed and chased one another through flowering branches, and other monstrous beasts chased them in their turn. The work had the mad energy of a fever dream, and there was a kind of desperation in the urgent repetition. The beer and the heavy air of this place were making me feel slightly sick. I advanced reluctantly up the aisle.

What, exactly, was I doing here? I asked myself as I approached the altar. A pale Christ, carved from ivory, hung from a golden cross. It reminded me of suet, the thick fat from around an ox's kidneys, hanging on a butcher's stall. Why was I, a churchman, a servant of Our Lord, for whom churches and monasteries had been home since I was a child, suddenly thinking of carcasses and the squalor of death in this holy place? With a start, I realised that I had not been thinking about my soul of late, that, in fact, I had all but sloughed off my monkish skin on the long voyage north from Dartmouth. I sank down onto the nearest pew. Holy Mother! I had not talked of God with another person for months, not read a sacred text – I had not even prayed since that long night in the marshes outside Balecester. My faith had shattered like the frailest eggshell, and what had emerged? An unwashed, uncouth boy, the pet of a boat-load of heathen cutthroats.

I had had enough of this place. Turning my back on the altar, I left the strange cathedral to its damp and dragon-fretted dreams. I could not even bring myself to genuflect. I hurried outside, looking neither left nor right to avoid the ghastly sentinels of bone, and almost ran full-tilt into the Captain himself. Wrapped in a thick woollen cloak and with a bulbous satchel slung across his body, he almost looked ordinary, until I met his gimlet gaze.

'Hello, Petroc,' he said with a tight grin. 'Did you find what you sought?'

'I found something; but what I was in search of, I do not know,' I replied, honestly enough.

The Captain chuckled, the same odd grin on his face. He looked wolfish, I thought.

'In your experience of cathedrals, how did you find this one?' he asked.

'It is too big,' I said carefully. 'And full of strange carvings. I do not care for it very much, to speak the truth.'

'And what of the trappings? Is it rich, would you say?'

'I would say it is tolerably poor, at that. There is little gold. The crucifix is ivory, there is an ivory pyx, and some silver candlesticks with dragons on them.'

'In a place as poor as this, even the Church goes hungry,' said the Captain. He gave a snort, as if in response to some wry inner jest.

'Were you looking for me?' I asked.

'For you? No, lad. My business is with the Bishop. I am not happy inside such places . . .' and he waved at the cathedral door. 'So I hoped to catch him as he went amongst his flock.' Abruptly he bent at the waist so that his head was below mine, and stared upwards into my eyes. His look was so fierce I could almost feel my eyebrows singe. 'Did your soul pull you hence,

Petroc? Do you still feel the pull of duty? Are there some ties that have yet to be broken?'

'Nothing like that,' I answered, stung. 'I went in from curiosity, and because, as you say, I felt the tug of long years' habit. But sitting before the altar I could think of nothing but the tales of my crewmates. I had tried to picture Our Lord's passion, but all I could see were the hidden workings of Deacon Jean's throat. My soul is dead within me, it seems.' I spoke sharply, but at my words the man's face softened, and he smiled his familiar smile.

'Your pardon, lad,' he said. 'I did not mean to put you to the question. I fear that this place works its misery upon me. Whatever you keep close to your heart is your own affair. I have not kept a crew like mine together by prying. And now, let us find somewhere warm, you and I, and pass the time before the wretched Bishop shows himself again.'

The Captain led me through muddy streets to Gardar's other tavern, which looked a good deal worse than the one I had left earlier. The innkeeper wore a leather skullcap and had a squint, and his guests, for the most part, seemed to be on the verge of death. There were no women to be seen. The Captain seemed to be known, however: the squinter greeted us warmly and we were ushered to the rear of the longhouse and behind a thick hide curtain, which concealed a private room of sorts, complete with a crackling fire. There were three high-backed chairs of dark wood, carved all over with more dragons and nightmare-beasts, as I noted with a private shudder.

When we were seated and our feet were before the fire, the Captain reached into his satchel and brought out a large clay bottle sealed with red wax. The innkeeper bustled in with two drinking cups and a trencher full of roasted mutton – fresh mutton, by God! I had not smelled anything so savoury for many a sea-tossed day. As I gnawed a rib-bone, the Captain opened his bottle and filled our cups with wine, red wine so dark it was almost black.

'Drink, my friend,' he said and took a slow pull himself. His eyes closed. 'The wine of my country,' he said. I sipped. The taste was heavy, almost sweet but with a hard edge. I thought of wild marjoram and sun-baked stone, and sighed.

'A sigh! Ah, Petroc! You are a lucky find,' the Captain laughed, and slapped my knee. 'For me, this wine is almost like a bottled sigh. I knew these very grape-vines when I was a boy. I have pressed their grapes with my own feet. That was long ago, and other feet press them now, but no matter. I keep a secret hoard on the *Cormaran* for just such dismal landfalls as this. I could not set foot in Gardar without it, I swear!'

We talked thus for the time it took to drain a cup or two and finish the mutton. I told him about my own home, the sights and smells of the moor. I dwelt a little on my mother, which made me sad, and on my father, which cheered me. And then in his turn the Captain told me a little of his childhood, and I listened as one listens to the words of a famous teacher, aware that mysteries were on the verge of being revealed. I learned that he was the first son of a noble family who held lands in the western part of the Duchy of Provence. His home had been a castle, a place of rose-coloured stone that perched upon a thyme-scented crag. Goat-bells had lulled him to sleep at night. His father had been a warrior but also, wonderful as this sounded to me, a poet – a troubadour, as the Captain said – who was famous in the land for his songs and fine playing on the lute. He had raised his son to be the same, although the Captain waved his hand in refusal when I asked for a song. Fearing I had spoken out of place I begged his pardon, but he laughed away my apology. 'My voice would scare a raven now, and besides, the songs of that sunny place would sound a strange note here, I think.'

The mutton gone, we settled back in our chairs. The fire

spat and sparked, and burning birch-wood filled the room with its tart, spicy smell.

'So, are you curious as to my business with the Bishop?' the Captain asked. I confessed that I was. He reached into his satchel once more and pulled forth two small packages wrapped in oiled cloth. Untying one, he held it out to me. I reached in, touched something hard and drew it out.

And blushed furiously. I was holding an exquisite ivory carving as long as my hand. Or rather, two carvings that fitted together. Two figures, a man and a woman, represented in every particular by a master craftsman. They were naked, the man stretched out with his arms bent at the elbow, the woman crouching. The man's – how would I have described it then? His *membrum virile*? His shame? – stuck out as plain as a pikestaff. There was a crease between the woman's thighs that deepened into a little hole. With shaking hands I moved the strange dolls together. The man fitted perfectly into his mate, and they clung together, their little ivory faces scrunched up in a simulacrum of ecstasy. I laid them down carefully upon the table, not daring to look at the Captain. The couple rocked together. Very slowly, I breathed out.

'Exquisite, are they not?' said the Captain. I managed a nod. 'Look in the other parcel,' he murmured.

It was about the size of my fist and bound tightly. I untied the soft leather cords and unwrapped the oil-cloth. Inside was another bundle of deep crimson silk. I found an end and began unwinding. Three feet of silk later, I was holding a simple wooden box, plain and unadorned and yet giving off a feeling of great age. I swallowed and opened it.

Instead of the obscenity I had been expecting, I gazed down at a black, wrinkled lump. 'It's a prune,' I blurted in relief.

'Show some deference, boy!' the Captain barked. I flinched in surprise. 'You hold the only true heart of St Cosmas in your impious hands.'

Holy Mother! I dropped the relic onto the table as if it were a piece of white-hot iron. 'I beg your pardon,' I gibbered. 'I had no idea that . . .'

The Captain's laughter drowned my words. At last I dared to look at him. Rich red wine was dribbling down his chin and neck. He thumped the table, and the carven beast with two backs jumped and clacked.

'I am truly sorry, Petroc,' he croaked, when the breath had returned to his body. 'But I could not resist . . . Pick it up again. Pick up the heart.'

I hesitated, then remembered my feelings earlier in the cathedral, my Saviour as so much tortured meat hung up for my adoration. What was this poor man's heart to me except meat, dry meat? I picked up the box, and felt nothing: no tingle, no flicker of the Other such as I had received from the hand of St Euphemia. I looked closer. The thing did indeed resemble a very large prune, although as I examined it, coal also came to my mind. I glanced at the Captain, who had just pulled a second wine flask from his satchel.

'How does this come to be here?' I asked.

He tapped his nose with a long finger, refilled our cups and raised his in a toast. I did the same, if only because I suddenly needed to feel strong liquor in my veins.

'To heart's ease,' said the Captain, and drank deeply. I followed suit.

'How did you come by St Cosmas' heart?' I asked again, the strong wine making me bolder. 'Did you steal it?'

He regarded me gravely, his eyes unreadable, almost blank. Reaching between us, he picked up the wizened heart and held it up to his face, turning it with his fingertips like a usurer examining a precious bauble. 'Steal it?' he echoed. 'Steal it?' His eyes flicked back to mine, and held them. 'And what do you think *it* is?'

'The heart of St Cosmas,' I said, stupidly. The Captain just stared. 'So it is not the Saint's heart?' I ventured. He gave his head a minute shake. 'But it is a heart, and it is very old,' I ploughed on. 'Whose is it, then?'

'It is very old – older than St Cosmas, whoever he really was,' said the Captain. Suddenly he was holding the thing an inch from my face. 'Smell it,' he said. With infinite reluctance I sniffed, and smelt dust – dust, and something else: the faintest suggestion of something astringent, spicy. Then the Captain was slipping the grisly lump back inside its silken wrappings. 'I found it in Egypt,' he said. 'While this is indubitably *not* a portion of St Cosmas, it is a heart, the heart of, I believe, a woman from the time of Pharaoh, or one of the pharaohs, as the Egyptians say that there were many. The ancient ones used unguents and spices to preserve their dead, which is what you might have scented.'

'Egypt!' I marvelled.

'Perhaps we will go there together,' the Captain said. 'I make it a point to stop there as often as I can. The markets of Cairo are rich hunting grounds for me. And now I see you require some explanations.' He refilled our cups, threw another log onto the fire, and began.

'I once told you that we were traders. Insightful as you are, you guessed that we are really smugglers. The truth is a little of both, but stranger yet than either. Yes, we trade. We trade in the strange, the odd, the difficult, the dangerous and, as you saw just now, the holy and the sinful. We bring sheepskins and wine to these sad Greenlanders, which we trade for white bear skins and walrus ivory that will find an eager market in Germany and further south. We have even brought back Gyrfalcons – great white hawks – that many a prince would knife his best friend to possess. From the land of the Skraelings we bring beaver, fox and sable pelts. We will sell Baltic amber to the Saracens, and Saracen rosewater to the dignitaries of Hamburg. Because we are fierce and strong we pay no heed to charters or customs. So in that way we are smugglers, and that is no great thing. But our true calling, Petroc, is deeper. We procure items for those who desire them – powerful patrons with tastes broadened by experience and, perhaps, happy or malign humours. Such a man is the Bishop of Gardar. You wonder how a man could find himself exiled to such a place as this. The answer to that lies in those ivory toys you admired so well – at home in Denmark he played with living mannequins, of course, but here he must content himself with make-believe. He asks me to find him trinkets and books to keep his weak flame alight, and I am happy to oblige. That toy, by the by, I found in Cairo. It is Chinese – do you even know where China is? East from India; further, even, than the lands of Prester John. Judging by their works, the people of China and India are positively roiling in what the Bishop knows as sin. I have promised that I will find out for myself one day. In any case, there are things in our hold that would have made Mary Magdalene blush.

'But that was not all that the good Bishop requested of me. He has his cathedral, but it is lacking in a crucial respect – there is no important relic. A cathedral needs relics, as you know, like a fire needs wood: something for the faithful to warm their hands against. In Gardar they have a few wisps of cloth from the habit of some nun no one has heard of, and an old nail from St Andrew's cross that no one believes in – quite rightly so, as it probably came from some unlucky fishing boat. The Bishop wanted a relic, and so he entrusted the search to me. For that is my trade, my true calling. I deal in relics. I sell them to any man, woman, abbot, bishop, king or queen who can pay for them. I find relics. When I cannot buy them, I steal them. What cannot be stolen, I make myself. The Bishop of Gardar is paying me much of what lies in the cathedral's muniments room for a true relic of the oldest ages of man, although instead of a saint's heart he will be enshrining part of a woman who worshipped animal-headed demons and had as much inkling of divine grace as the shores of Greenland have of date-palms. He will never know – how can a holy relic be verified? The spices of Egypt provide the requisite odour of sanctity, the thing is as old as the hills, and he has my word on the matter. And besides, I know he has paid for the *other* trifle – and other less pretty ones – with the hard-won pennies of these pitiful Greenlanders, so he will be very, very careful not to annoy me. As far as my usual business goes, this will be an easy transaction.

'Think of the hand of St Euphemia that you bore in so much terror. A poor old shrivelled thing it was, was it not, inside its precious glove? But you believed, Petroc, and for all I know you believe still. I can tell you this: it was a human hand, all right, but St Euphemia? Perhaps. I know that a corpse lying around in a damp place like Balecester will moulder and rot, and I'd lay my fortune that Euphemia herself has been dust for a thousand years. The precious claw was bought or made – I said human, but I would not have been surprised to find the paw of an ape. Credulity and greed will blind most men – that is the truth that keeps the *Cormaran* afloat. I can show you much, my good friend, but I fear it will tear the guts from your faith and trample them into the mud. It was easy for me – I never had any faith, at least not in the way you understand it. But for you . . . think for a while.'

I paused. There was one more question to be answered, and I hardly dared ask it. But ask I must.

'Captain,' I began hesitantly, 'You, Gilles and the others from . . . from Provence: forgive me, but are you what I would call Cathars?'

To my immense relief he smiled, the weariest smile I had ever seen. 'There is nothing to forgive, my boy. We are indeed *cathari* – Cathars. Was it such a hard guess?'

'No,' I said, and he chuckled. 'Then we are not as mysterious as we suppose ourselves to be,' he said. 'We are *credenti* – believers, the least of our kind, but there are few of us now indeed, and perhaps . . .' he shook his head. 'You do not fear us, at least, and I do not think you even judge us.'

'I do not,' I interrupted.

'That is good. And what *do* you think?'

'I can guess what became of the grapes you tended as a boy,' I said quietly. 'News reached us even down in Devon, and so I heard of the war against your people from my friend Adric. For the Cathars, I am sure you know what nonsense they teach boys: cat-worship and blasphemy. I have also heard that you believe the Devil created the earth, and that Christ is a ghost, and that you swear no oaths, for there is no one above you save God himself.' I paused. 'In my present mood, and at this point where I find myself, I am no friend to my Church, and when I look for faith I find myself as empty as a new-dug grave. I mean that I can find no fault in your people's beliefs.'

The Captain gazed at me for a long silent moment. 'You are . . . indeed you are the very first man I have heard such words from. I know the turmoil of your soul, and I will not press you further. But I will say one more thing, and then we are done with this matter: if you would know more – and there is much to learn – we will be glad to teach you. I believe you will know when the time is right.'

He reached for a mutton-bone, took a small bite and tossed it into the hearth. The deep glow from the flame-caressed embers had lent his profile a sombre, brooding edge, and his grey eyes held splinters of fire. He ran his thumb along the lip of his wine-cup again and again.

'Master,' I said, feeling as I did so the sensation of falling, so strongly that I reached out and grabbed the table's edge, 'you have given answers to all my questions, and I have given none to yours. Here is my answer: I will join you. My head is glad, but my heart is empty. If you will have a soul that is beyond care and a spirit that has lost its footing in the darkness, I will serve you. My love of Mother Church has curdled, and I see only rottenness where I once saw salvation. If you can use someone like me, I am yours.' So saying, I took a great gulp of the wine, and met the Captain's level gaze.

'Done,' said de Montalhac, and grasped my hand. 'I have the better bargain, Master Petroc of Auneford. Your heart is not empty: it is full and strong, and your soul is but dull and sooty with the smoke of false ritual. It will shine once more. You are one of us now. You are right: my people do not swear oaths, so you come with us of your own free will, and you may leave when and where you wish.'

We drank again, and slowly the night's edges softened once more until we were nothing but two friends enjoying wine, warmth and each other's company. But I was not the same as I had been before. My faith was gone: I knew it for a certainty.

Chapter Twelve

We left Greenland two days later. I had not seen much of the Captain, as I was busy about the ship and he was away in town conducting business – and I will admit that, now I had a clear notion of what that business was, I dwelt upon his affairs with a much enlivened interest.

I was on deck on the afternoon of the day that followed our strange night at the inn, lashing water barrels in place. The Captain swept up the gangplank, vexation clearly written on his face. He went straight to his cabin and slammed the door behind him, and I heard his voice and that of Gilles raised in some heated debate. Then all of a sudden there was laughter, and the Captain swept out again, this time with a big grin. He trotted back down the plank and off into the sorry huddle of Gardar.

Late the next day, as the sun – which had honoured us with a watery light since noon – was going down behind the mountainous promontory in the west, there was a sudden hubbub on the wharf. I was sitting in the forecastle, mending rope. Peering over the side, I saw a gang of the crew, led by the Captain and Pavlos, struggling with three long bundles, each around six feet long, knobbled and bulky and wrapped in black tarred canvas. The cloth looked slippery, or perhaps the bundles were very heavy, for the men were having a difficult time keeping a grip. I skipped down the ladder and called out to offer my help, but Pavlos waved me away. Finally, grunting and cursing in the most livid tones, the men hoisted each bundle onto their shoulders and bore them on board. They were manhandled down into the hold, where more muffled oaths told me that, in the cramped space below decks, the burdens were even more awkward. At last Pavlos emerged, dusty and bleeding slightly from a banged temple.

'What the devil was all that?' I asked him.

He spat and rubbed his wound. 'Jesus, Mary Madonna and every one of the fucking saints. Whalebone! A wonderful idea, wouldn't you say? Enough whalebone to build a sister-fucking elephant. Or a bastard whale.' He stamped away and vanished into the Captain's cabin.

I couldn't help laughing as I went back to my frayed rope. A whalebone elephant, perhaps. Or a hundred, a thousand fornicating dolls, one for every bishop in Christendom. Ha! I spat in my turn, feeling uncommonly happy to be alive.

We cast off before dawn the next day. Our return from Gardar is not a memory I often dwell upon. Almost from the minute we left the pathetic harbour at the edge of the world we were forging through an endless expanse of clear green waves that towered on all sides. Sometimes, when the wind came less fiercely, they loomed like smooth hills, so that I imagined we were in a kind of watery downland, the chalk hills of England turned to liquid on some devil's whim. But when the gales blew – and they blew, day in, day out, for two weeks – the hills became mountains that reared above us, their sharp peaks and ridges trembling like monstrous green flames, spume flying from them like smoke.

I was on deck now as often as any crewman – indeed I was a sailor now for all intents and purposes. It had happened on the crossing from Iceland: although no one had ordered me to work, I fell into it naturally, and soon I was mending sail and hauling ropes alongside the rest of them. At first my soft scholar's hands rebelled and I spent two or three days with them salved and bound while the salt-inflamed blisters dried. But soon my fingers and palms grew tough and hide-like, a transformation that I found obscurely pleasing. Before sleep I would feel each callous with a kind of modest pride. I suppose they were a symbol of my greater transformation, although then I thought only that they reminded me of when I worked alongside my father, building stone walls and wrestling sheep at shearing-time. The long passage of time between then and now, my long sleep, as it seemed, at the abbey and then in Balecester, was starting to fade a little, like a well-remembered dream.

Another transformation had taken place. It had been months since I had even thought about the language we all used aboard. It was the *lingua franca*, a traders' simple tongue, bastard child of Occitan and the many dialects spoken by the folk of Italy and Spain with scraps borrowed from Arabic, Greek, Ladino and a hundred other languages of the world. I had limped along for the first month on a smattering of French, ancient Greek, Latin of course, and a few shards of German. But without really knowing how, I had learned the *lingua franca*, and at the same time I found I had begun to know Occitan, the native tongue of the Captain, Gilles and perhaps a quarter of the crew. I grew to love its gentleness and poetry, so much at odds with the harsh, matter-of-fact life aboard a ship sailing the deep ocean.

But I had but little time for poetry as the *Cormaran* creaked and lurched through the cold ocean. Sleep was impossible when the weather was evil, as it so often was, and when things were calmer, my exhaustion dropped me into a slumber that was only a little less deep and dark than death itself. When we left Iceland I had moved from my cosy berth in the bow, feeling that it set me apart, something I dearly wished to avoid. And now that nook was hidden behind a wall of sailcloth, home to the great bundles of whalebone, and furs that must be kept from the damp, Pavlos explained. The days passed in a fever of morbid anticipation, and the night watches were worse. With every jump over a wave-crest or swoop into the deep troughs between, the planking would groan like a thousand souls in purgatory, and I was certain the hull would burst apart and send us plummeting down through the green water. For me, the misery was made worse by Fafner's desertion. I rarely saw him now: he had found himself a cosy cave amongst the whalebone and fur, I supposed, for that was where his great tail would be vanishing those few times I caught sight of him.

We were avoiding Iceland this time. The danger from the King's revenue men was too great. Nizam had plotted a course that would drop us down the face of the world in a slow curve until we landed on the top of Ireland. A slow curve it sounded in his descriptions, but our progress, as marked obsessively on the Captain's charts (parchments that he gave more reverence to than any holy text I had ever encountered), seemed more like the weavings of a drunken spider: short leaps in one direction, crazy crabbing zigzags in another, but all the while, undeniably, edging us towards the south and east. We were bound for Dublin, and it seemed we were in some hurry to get there.

At last we caught a screeching gale from the west, and for endless days we flew on a broad reach, every man on deck for an eternity, working with frost-numbed hands. And then one day I felt a rope slacken in my grasp, and we all paused and looked aloft. The sail had relaxed, so slightly that I could have imagined it. A petrel whizzed past the crow's nest. Then the ship bucked again and the moment was past.

But the next morning I woke – suddenly, with no transition between sleep and absolute wakefulness, as I had begun to do lately – to see a washed-out blue sky above, some harmless-seeming clouds and a white bird. The wind had gone; we were tacking across a fresh southerly breeze, and soon the bird was joined by others, a wheeling, screeching party of gulls. Not petrels or the solitary albatrosses that had tracked us through the empty seas, but big seagulls like the ones that would swarm over the newly ploughed fields back home. The men began to smile and talk a little more easily, and in truth we had all been a little subdued of late. The relentless diet of puffin had taken its toll, and something else was weakening us. My mouth had swollen and my tongue with it. Eating was a chore, and if a piece of dry meat should slip between my teeth there would be agony and blood in worrying amounts. My legs were always stiff and they were becoming speckled with dark spots. Many of the others were spitting blood and complaining of swollen joints. Horst had lost two back teeth, and Zianni nearly choked on one of his that dropped out as he slept. And our breaths all had the same sour, tomb-like reek. 'It is the scorbutus,' said Isaac, but he could offer no cure. 'We must wait for dry land and another food than this cursed puffin,' he said, and we had to believe him. But indeed we could smell land in the warm breeze: wet earth, a ghost of something green. The ship seemed to wake from a long fever dream.

We were three days from Ireland. Our mad spider's course had brought us back to the Scottish isles, and that day we passed St Kilda, a tiny hermit's perch where countless gulls wheeled like bees around a hive. Nizam was aiming us at the North Channel, and Dublin – and some measure of civiliza-tion – had begun to occupy a large part of my waking mind. Streets, bustle, inns, beer! We talked of little else. Women, too, although that subject I tried to avoid as discreetly as I could. Will had often talked of the city whores he had enjoyed – to him such fleshly transactions were as natural as breathing. But the whores had scared me with their leering faces and heaving, sweat-streaked bosoms. There lay mortal sin, and of course I was also somewhat timid by nature.

Oddly, though, the only naked female bodies I had seen were in church, the painted ones in the hell that covered the west wall of Saints Sergius and Bacchus, a holy place much frequented by Balecester students. Here, women complete with round, turnip-like breasts, little bellies and black stains between their thighs were herded by serpentine devils who fondled them lewdly and prodded their heavy buttocks with eel spears. I had often lain awake in my mean little room in Ox Lane with those pale figures writhing before me, my own flesh rebelling from my control. I would try to focus on the devils, to imagine their spears stabbing at my own flesh, but those breasts and the dark patches below the bellies that sagged ever so gently . . . I would have to get out of bed and pray, kneeling until the hard floor hurt me enough to drive the foul visions away. Sometimes I would have to leave my room and wander the streets until dawn, saying my rosary and muttering to myself like, I daresay, a simpleton. It was on such a night that I had found the way onto the city walls.

Now, I supposed, I was no longer bound by the Church and its strictures, and the lewd and often frankly bizarre tales that seemingly every crewman now found time to share with me seemed, if anything, a little more terrifying because of the knowledge that I could now have such adventures of my own, should I so choose. Meanwhile my dreams grew lurid: patchworks of flesh, scraps and fragments of the day's talk. It was on the second morning past St Kilda that I awoke from the dream of a painful tangle of limbs (an Egyptian gypsy and her snake, courtesy of Zianni, had befriended Elia's Finnish twin sisters and an obese but talented Genoese, as described by Horst), to find that we were putting in to land. A long beach of white sand lay ahead, lying like spilled milk below crag-topped moors.

It was one of the Western Isles, lonely and uninhabited save for the wild sheep that grazed it, abandoned by settlers in time out of mind. There was a spring of sweet water above the beach, and we would fill our barrels here. Fresh water, and fresh mutton! The *Cormaran* preferred secrecy wherever possible, given the nature of its business. When we put into a populated harbour the traffic was one way: we brought our business to the land, and not the other way around. When it came to provisions and repairs, the Captain chose small, friendly villages or, even better, the privacy of a deserted shore. We were almost out of water, and although we had enough to bring us to Dublin, Gilles explained to me that the sharp and insatiable curiosity of the traders of that town was something to be deflected at all costs. And Guthlaf the carpenter was keen to repair a sprung plank and right some other ills inflicted by our dash across the Sea of Darkness.

The tide was half out, and Nizam ran the ship up into a shallow gulley carved out by the stream that ran down off the moors. It would hold the *Cormaran* while Guthlaf went about his work and let us float off again at high water. In an hour we were high and dry, and I was swarming over the side with the rest of the crew. It was high summer, I realised with a shock as my feet sank into the warm, wet sand. I could smell the heather, and knew that the moorland would be alive with bees storing up their wealth for the dead times. So, after I had helped fill the butts at a place where the stream poured over a granite lip and down onto the sand, and rolled them back to the ship, and spent a gentle hour gathering sea kale with Abu (how wonderful the thick, green stems felt to the touch, and even more wonderful was the sharp juice that stung my destroyed gums), I slipped away and, turning my back on the sea, set off to follow the stream up the hill towards the lowering crags. It led at first through a field of scattered boulders. The orange and grey lichens that clung to the rock were the same ones that grew in Devon, I noticed. The stream picked a narrow way through two great tumbled slabs, and beyond them lay a small, deep, sedge-rimmed pool fed at one end by a little waterfall that gurgled over a ledge thickly padded with moss. It reminded me of a pool I used to bathe in on the Red Brook near my home, and so without thinking I shed my clothes and slipped into the water.

It was icy cold and the peat made my white skin seem golden beneath the surface. I took a deep breath and ducked my head under, the chill gripping my skull like a helmet of ice.

But it was wonderful after so long in damp, salt-stiff clothes and as I watched the tiny trout weave in and out of the smooth granite cobbles I soon felt myself warming up. The waterfall beckoned, and I clambered up and sat on its lip, cushioned by the deep moss, letting the water play under and around me. The sunny air fluttered across my back. And then I thought I heard someone laugh. It was a low, rich sound, but soft, so soft that it had to be some trick of the breeze among the stones. People who often wander alone in waste places are alive to the fancies of solitude: I had heard things on the wind before, and felt my flesh crawl under the gaze of eyes that were not there. The country people call it the work of faeries or demons, and I do not quarrel with that, but often it is the power of the land itself, and so I was not really surprised now. I took it as a greeting from the island. But I realised that time was slipping away, and so I dragged my clothing back on and set out upstream.

I strolled for perhaps an hour, although I was lost in a cloud of moorland incense: heather flowers, bilberries, moss, sheep-shit and peat. I am home, I thought again and again. This path will lead me to my father's house and the tumbling brown waters of the Aune. My soul felt at ease here. Pausing to cram another handful of warm, bursting bilberries into my purple-stained mouth, I found that there was a stillness within me that I had not felt for many, many days. Since the Deacon's murder, I had been quivering inside like a plucked harp string, but now there was calm.

It was an easy climb to the base of the crag, and though I had not intended even to come this far, I was soon scrambling up the coarse, fissured granite. It was far less terrifying close up, this great dark cliff, and I had spent my boyhood scaling Dartmoor tors and scrabbling about on scree slopes. So it took me little time to reach the top. Standing on the wide platform, the warm wind ruffling my clothes, I looked back for the first time since leaving the beach.

The boat was a little black crumb on the white sand, the crew a sprinkling of soot around it. Beyond, the sea was an impossible blue-green, like no colour I had ever seen. It stretched away, darkening, as far as I could see to north, south and west. To the east, some low shadows could have been land, or more islands, or just cloud shadows on the water. I was on the pinnacle of the island. Turning, I saw that our beach made up perhaps one quarter of the shoreline. There was another beach on the opposite side. To the north, the high ground met the sea in a great swooping curve of cliff. To the south, the moors petered out in a tumbled, stony puzzle of coves and rocky spits. To the east, a skewed grid of old dry-stone walls pushed inland from the beach. The grass was greener here, and here and there among the walls stood the remains of stone dwellings, their roofs long since tumbled in. Who had made this place their home? People like me, I supposed. I would be happy here, a little crumb of Dartmoor all my own, with no one to bother me. I gazed down at the boat, ugly as a dead fly on the perfect white of the sand. Perhaps I would stay up here. I sat down on a clump of thrift. Would they come looking for me? Would they bother?

All at once I heard another laugh. I leaped up. I was alone on the rock, but it had been real, this time. So I had been followed after all. I cursed, loudly. We had been cooped up, a pack of starving madmen, on a tiny ship for God knew how many weeks or months. Who now would begrudge me a crumb of solitude?

'Who's there?' I yelled.

There was silence: just the wind hissing through the thrift. The pink flowers nodded at me, possibly in sympathy.

I sat down again, but it was no good. The spell was broken. I felt my happiness trickling away. I loved it up here, and someone had taken the trouble to ruin it for me. Someone . . . who? Who could possibly be up here, save for me? And then the hairs on the back of my neck stood up. I felt eyes upon me, but when I whipped about, the moor was empty. Below me, very far away, were the only other folk on this island. All at once the terror that can come upon one in waste places washed over me, raising my skin into cold gooseflesh. I was a stranger here, and alone. What spirits had I disturbed? What manner of ghost might lurk in such a place? Lonely, answered the wind. Hungry.

In a blind horror I took to my heels, tripped on a sedge tussock and went flying. Face-down in a bilberry bush, laughter rippled over me. Ahead, the crag faded into the gentle eastern slope and not far away the granite reared up again through the heather and one of the ruined stone walls led away from it down the hill. It was the perfect hiding place. Perhaps I might have considered the folly of hiding from that which cannot be seen, but I did not: leaping up again, I dashed towards the wall. The watcher laughed once more.

And in the same breath the laugh became a shriek that was abruptly silenced, extinguished like a pinched-out candle flame. I stopped dead in my tracks. I was alone again, and the quiet was stifling. The shriek still rang in my ears. That had not been a ghost, nor any sprite. It had been made by flesh and blood, and it had sounded like a child. What had happened? My mind raced. What was a child doing here? Perhaps there were folk dwelling here after all. I tugged at my hair in confusion. Such a shriek could only mean dire hurt or worse, and so against my better judgement I started off again, haste making me sure-footed this time. Reaching the end of the wall, where it collapsed in a heap at the foot of the granite outcrop, I scrambled over. There was no one there, but to my left the crag jutted out, and I wondered if my tormentor had fallen from the top and now lay on the other side of that corner of the rock. I dashed around, and ran full tilt into someone.

'No!' I grunted in terror, for the collision had almost winded me. All of a sudden I found myself flung against the granite, and saw that I had crashed, not into a ghost, but into a stranger: a tall, starved man. I had a glimpse of a cadaverous face, a sparse white-streaked beard and two great blue eyes, totally devoid of reason and quite utterly mad, before the man whirled his coat of rags about him and rammed me into the rock wall again. The back of my head met stone and I blacked out for an instant. I came to almost at once and saw the man rearing above a dark shape – the hurt child! – lying stretched out on the ground. He was howling like a beast, but I could make out words among the enraged screeching:

'Christ help me! Foul stench! Filth!'

The gabble was a chant, like a half-remembered holy office soured with unimaginable hate. 'Devils, O God! Devils! Christ Jesus, help your servant . . .'

As I stood, the scene swimming before me, the man groped for a huge stone and raised it with a mighty effort above his head. Without thinking I covered the ground between us with two quick strides and kicked him hard in the ballocks. It was the only bit of fighting I had ever learned, chiefly from having had it done to me during football games, and as the top of my foot landed solidly between his legs, I knew exactly what it would feel like. As I staggered backwards, off balance and trying not to step on the child, the man let out a strangled bleat. His arms went limp and the stone dropped, bounced off the side of his head and landed on his shoulder before crashing harmlessly to the ground. There was a nasty, dry cracking sound. Retching, the man twisted around and collapsed sideways, blood spraying from his head. He rolled away through the heather before scrambling to his feet. Then he was off, running away across the moor, wailing like a banished spirit until his voice was lost on the wind.

I could hear nothing except my own rasping breath, and the blood humming in my ears. The body lay face down. I could see the soles of bare feet, white and sorrowful. I dropped to my knees. Reluctantly, I reached out and rolled the child over. The cloak was wrapped tight and tangled, and I struggled to get my hand in amongst its folds to feel for a heartbeat. But I felt nothing save an odd, yielding softness.

A hand shot out and gripped my wrist. A slim hand whose fingers bore many rings of heavy gold and bright stones. I was staring into a pair of large, dark eyes under curved brows. Female eyes.

As if from very far away, I heard a soft, amused voice. I had heard it before, laughing at me. The grip on my wrist tightened.

'I am the Princess Anna Doukaina Komnena,' said the Laughing One. 'And if you don't get your meat-hooks off my tits right now, you'll be very, very sorry.'

Chapter Thirteen

'I . . . beg your pardon?' I squawked.

'I say again: stop your pawing, and let me up.'

But my fingers seemed to be trapped in the folds of the cloak. I tugged desperately. A knuckle popped: I was free. All the while, the Princess Anna Doukaina Komnena regarded me, one black eyebrow arched. She grinned suddenly, and I saw the gap between her front teeth. I find it strange to relate now, but at that moment I had no doubt that this strange creature was exactly who she said she was. She sat up. Two thick coils of heavy, midnight-dark hair fell from the cloak. In an agony of shamed confusion, I cast down my eyes and shuffled backwards on my arse. My insides had turned to frogspawn.

'Forgive me,' I mumbled. Oh, sweet blood of martyrs! Could I set my feet nowhere without a chasm of hell opening beneath them? My mind, a little more nimble than hands or tongue, whirled. How did one address a lady of royal birth? Fragments of rhymes and songs beat around my skull. Bright shards of paintings, borders from ancient tomes in dusty libraries, knights with their lady-loves . . . Suddenly, light burst in. I rose to one knee and, carefully pulling Thorn from her sheath, held the knife out, hilt first, to the Princess. Risking a look, I saw that she still wore a wide, bemused smile.

'My life is yours,' I began. Somehow this sounded right and proper. 'I am your servant. I fear I have given you great offence, so take my blade and do with me what you will.'

'Oh, bloody hell!' the princess was laughing now. 'You are English! You . . . you really are very English, aren't you?'

'Madam—' I held Thorn out a little further. The princess waved her hand, which I could not help noticing was slender and pale, an imperious hand, a fine hand . . .

'Do not call me madam! I don't want your knife – your *blade.* You seem to know how to use it: keep it. Who *are* you, anyway?'

'Petroc of Auneford, Your Majesty.'

'Petroc. From Cornwall?' she asked, and her eyes came alive with interest.

'Devonshire, Your Majesty.' I stood up and brushed heather twigs from my clothing.

'Devonshire! How far we both are from our homes. You have saved me from a demon, Petroc of Auneford. It is I who am your servant. And now, perhaps you can escort me back to the ship.' The princess tried to stand, but winced and held her hand out to me. She was very pale.

'Who was he, the madman?' I asked, gently.

'I don't know – obviously. *What* was he? Some manner of hermit, I think. I stumbled across him at prayer. There's a little shrine of some sort back there, a cross carved into a stone in a little dip. I actually fell over him. Like a demon from the fiery caverns, I suppose, poor old bastard. He seems to have had an aversion to the gentler sex – I thought he was going to rape me, but he was more keen on bashing my head in.'

'I hurt him badly,' I said. To myself, I was beginning to wonder how badly.

'Good. I hope you killed him.' Her eyes gleamed in their dark hollows.

I did not reply. I could still hear the stone landing on his shoulder. I thought I rembered that it had all but torn his ear off as well. He would most likely die if it festered. What a dreadful irony – that a holy man should seek out such utter desolation only to fall foul of another monk, albeit a retired one. And to save . . . whom? How did she know of the ship? Or of Devonshire, for that matter?

'So you came here on the *Cormaran*?' I said at last, feeling like a mooncalf.

'Don't look so bewildered,' she said, as if reading my thoughts. 'Pavlos will be quite frantic by now, so let us make haste. Here, take my hand. I think my leg is hurt.'

So I grasped her cool hand in my own hot paw and steadied her as she tested one leg and then the other.

'It's not so bad,' she decided. 'I will lean upon your shoulder.' And she flung an arm about my neck and drew herself to me. I flinched, and yet again she was laughing at me.

'*Gama to Theo!* Petroc, I am not a basilisk! Grab, hold here—' and she took my left hand and guided it around her shoulders until it lodged beneath her armpit. 'Now don't let go.'

She started walking briskly towards the east, and nearly pulled me over. I stopped her, and turned us in the opposite direction. 'This way, Your Majesty,' I said. 'The ship is this way, and I'm afraid we have to climb down this great crag.'

'Are you sure?' she said, and fixed me with those eyes. I nodded furiously, feeling like a trained ape.

'Oh, yes,' I burbled. 'I ran down this slope, and the crag is up there behind us, so we . . .' The Princess stopped me with a gentle squeeze.

'Indeed, O Petroc,' she said gently. 'But your crag is quite small. I walked around it. There is a path . . . that way.'

We set off through the heather, and it was as she said. A well-worn sheep-track skirted the granite, an easy walk. That was fortunate: it was getting very hot as the sun rose towards its zenith, and sweat was beginning to soak my tunic, especially where the Princess held herself against me. I could smell myself, and her as well. My mouth was very dry.

The track began to slope steeply as we came under the lee of the cliffs. It was hard to keep hold of the limping girl and to keep my pace steady. We were perhaps a third of the way down the hill when she misjudged a step, tripped on a root and fell forward, pulling me down with her. For one moment I felt our bodies lying upon the air, and then we struck sheep-trimmed turf and were rolling. We were still grasping each other tightly, and I rolled beneath her, my one thought being to save her leg from more pain. As we began to tumble through bilberries, bracken, heather, I flailed with my own legs to keep her on top, and so we came to a halt against a wind-blasted rowan tree, I with my head all but buried in bracken, eyes tight shut, the Princess lying full-stretch upon my body. I could feel her chest heave, and worse, the decided fullness of her breasts. I tried to wriggle free, but she held me fast. Then I felt fingertips upon my face, gently brushing dirt away from my eyelids and lips. Looking up, I saw she was staring at me intently, her brow furrowed with concern. Then, seeing my open eyes, she grinned.

'My goodness! Holy *Panayia*! I thought I had smothered you, my Petroc!'

'Not one whit, Your Majesty,' I rasped. (Oh! gallant, I thought to myself, ruefully).

'Then if you would just release my arm . . .'

Lord, it was true: I had her pinned. I rolled one way, and she grimaced, so I tried to rise a little. She wriggled, I jerked, and in a few moments she began to chuckle. I imagined how we must appear to some watcher high above us, and began to smile. Then we were both laughing, desperate joy rising up, in me at least, like bubbles in ale. Somehow we undid the tangle of our limbs and rose shakily to our feet, still laughing, bent over like an old gaffer and his crone until the fit left us.

No sooner had I come to my right mind than I stiffened in shame. What a brute I had made myself before this great lady!

But she stretched out her hand once more, and silently we went on down the slope. We had reached the boulder-field where I had first heard her laughter when I felt the Princess holding me back. She sank to the ground behind a stone and drew me down with her.

'We are too near the beach,' she muttered. It was true that I had all but forgotten the *Cormaran*, but peering over the stone I saw that the beach was perhaps half a mile distant, the boat lying at an absurd angle on the wet sand, a fine commotion of sailors all around its hull.

'Petroc, I cannot return like this, in daylight. I am . . . Only de Montalhac, Gilles de Peyrolles, Pavlos and the Cretan boys know I am aboard.'

'How long have you been on the ship?' I interrupted, my own mind racing. 'Since we left England?' She shook her head, a tiny movement. 'The Faeroes? No – Gardar!' I snapped my fingers. 'You were in a bundle of whalebone. And kept secret ever since. How?'

'It has been hard – no, it has been a foretaste of hell,' she whispered. 'I have not stirred from that stinking little hole for – I cannot say.'

'Mary's sweet – I mean, God's blood . . .'

'By the by, Petroc, how do your teeth feel?'

'Loose as nails in rotten wood,' I admitted, then looked at her more closely. How strange – I saw now how thin she was, and how deeply ringed with shadow were her eyes. She had suffered whatever I and my fellows had, and perhaps much more, imprisoned in the dark. Without thinking, I reached out and took her hand. She smiled, a little sadly, and I noticed a tooth was missing, up near the corner of her mouth. Now I smelled the familiar sour reek on her breath. 'It is the scorbutus, Isaac says,' I offered.

'And he has no cure. Isaac is an angel, isn't he? But he couldn't keep his own teeth in his head.' She sighed. 'Petroc, I do not wish my presence to be known. I am fleeing for my life—'

'As we all are,' I put in.

'Just so, just so. But, if I can be truthful with you, the crew frighten me out of my wits, what I have spied of them from behind that bloody curtain. Christ upon the cross! Those men would eat me up, vomit, and eat me all over again . . .'

'Princess!' I yelped, shocked. This was no way for a lady of royal birth to be talking.

'But it's true! Oh my, have I upset you?'

'You . . . you are a great lady! You should not speak in this way, Your Majesty!'

'Please do not call me Majesty, or Princess, or Highness, or any of that worthless chatter!' she spat, suddenly taut with fury, or perhaps pain. 'You find me harsh, I think? Not very royal? Well, you are right. I have no throne. To the world I am a dead woman. But look, doubting boy!' And she thrust her hand into my face. 'See this ring. *This* one!'

It was by no means the brightest trinket on that hand. A drab brown stone, with the lighter outline of a head in profile standing out upon it. The band, heavy and golden, was more impressive.

'A queen wore this in Rome in the ancient times, when my forefathers ruled the whole world. That was my birthright. And then . . . I was thrown away.' Her voice had faded to a bitter whisper, and her eyes were hidden. 'So do not call me Princess, or Majesty, or Lady. I have nothing but the blood in my veins.' She fell silent. 'And I do not wish to let that be spilled, Petroc. It runs hot, and I covet the heat.' She looked up and caught my eyes in her own gaze. I saw that tears ran down like tiny rivulets through the sand that dusted her cheeks. 'You saved my life, and that is all I have that can be saved. So, I suppose you had better call me Anna.'

*

165

Before I had even come within a hundred paces of the ship, Pavlos hailed me and ran out from the shadows under the hull. He reached me in a state of clear agitation, and I knew that it was not on my account. He grabbed my shoulders and shook me gently.

'Where . . .' He swallowed. 'Where have you been?'

'Up there.' I waved behind me.

'And did you see anything – any*one* "up there"?' Pavlos was a tall man, with dark curly hair that he kept shorn so that it hung a little above his shoulders. He cut a fine figure, and his bright green eyes and broken nose lent him the air of a fierce warrior, which was indeed the truth of the matter. But now he was sweating and trembling like a blown horse. He had run towards me as soon as I had jumped down onto the beach. I had planned to taunt him a little with the secret he could not know we shared, but now I did not have the heart.

'She is safe, and watches us from up there.' I jerked my thumb over my shoulder. Pavlos grabbed my hand and brought his face close to mine.

'Who?' He breathed, the sour stench of failing gums too close for comfort.

'Anna, of course. The Princess Anna.' I grasped his hand in turn. 'She is unhurt.'

To my horror, Pavlos dropped to his knees and began crossing himself like a madman, in the backwards fashion of his religion. I made sure that no one else planned to join us, and knelt down myself.

'Be calm, Pavlos,' I whispered. 'She has come to no great harm. There was a man—'

'A *man*?' Pavlos's head jerked up as if pulled by an invisible string. '*M'efayen ta jiyerya!*' A stream of Greek curses followed, more plaintive than angry.

'—But I rescued her,' I broke in, impatient. 'Nothing happened. She has pulled a muscle in her leg, I think. But she does not wish to come back to the ship in daylight – she fears the men.'

'Fear? That one fears nothing,' said Pavlos. He seemed to be recovering. Rubbing his jaw, he stood up. 'She ran away from me before dawn. I managed to get her off the ship without anyone seeing, and she bolted, laughing. Laughing! I have heard nothing but that laughter since.' He spat. 'The Captain is in an ill humour about this, I can assure you.'

'Did you all think you could keep her hidden for the whole voyage?' I shook my head in disbelief. 'She would have faded away to nothing in that pit.'

'By all the saints and their pox-rotten mothers, Petroc! Do I not know that? She is a princess-royal of Byzantium! I have taken oaths to lay down my life for her kind. The man I served in Epiros, the Despot, is her cousin. None of us wished to confine her, but what else could be done? The crew would never allow a woman aboard – there are some among them, and you know who they are – who would use her like a common whore of the bath-houses before they pitched her over the side.' A new thought seemed suddenly to bite him like a gadfly. 'You did not . . . lay hands upon her?'

'Yes, indeed!' This was too much. 'I had my hands all over her! I all but carried her down a fucking mountain, after, *after* I saved her life—'

'Peace, Petroc! Peace. Forgive me. The girl was in my care, and I failed her. I am overwrought. I owe you a debt of thanks, not vulgar suspicion. But now, if you please, take me to her.'

So we clambered back up the hill, Pavlos striding far ahead of me in his haste. Anna waited for us behind her rock. She lay on her belly, covered by her cloak, with only a slender crescent of her pale face showing beneath the cowl. At our approach she sat up, the cloth falling from her hair, which sent forth a bluish glint in the sunlight. She watched us for a moment, then grinned broadly and clapped her hands.

'My rescuers! Brave Pavlos, and my knight of Devonshire.'

Pavlos hurried to her and, to my astonishment – but what, today, was not astonishing? – knelt before her and took one of her bare feet in his hand.

'*Vassileia*,' he moaned. He writhed like a fish in air, gasping what I took to be the most abject apologies in his tongue, until Anna tapped him on the head with a finger, like a baker testing a loaf of bread.

'Get up, Pavlos,' she said in Occitan. 'I ran away from you, if you remember. I am very sorry, my dear guardsman.'

'Why, *Vassileia*? How could you do such a thing?' The poor man was wringing his hands now.

'I wanted to stretch my limbs, to breathe fresh air. I wanted to be alone! I have not stirred from that . . . that charnel house for a lifetime. You saw me, Pavlos. I could hardly stand upright! And when I felt my legs begin to work again, I had to use them. So of course I ran.'

'And the lunatic? Petroc told me, dear Highness. Did he . . . ?'

'I was wandering about up there, picking heather flowers—' and here she darted me a look, swift as quicksilver, '—simply gathering flowers, and he crept up behind me. I thought I'd had it, I can tell you! God, how he stank. He gave me a good pinching and pawing, I screamed, and then my brave Petroc drove him away, bloody and weeping.' She clapped her hands joyfully once more, like a little girl at play. I blushed at the look of admiration that Pavlos turned upon me.

'I don't know about weeping,' I muttered.

'Nonsense! You bold warriors, always so very modest. Drove him away, I say, drove him off to die,' Anna insisted, her face all but twitching with mischief. I held up both hands, hoping to change the subject.

'And your leg, how does it feel?' I asked.

'It is serviceable,' she replied. 'Sore when I lean upon it. It will be stiff tomorrow.'

'We must get you back to the *Cormaran*,' broke in Pavlos. 'The Captain is in a mighty rage – although I believe his anger is a disguise for concern. But . . .'

'I will not go back while the sun shines,' Anna snapped.

'But, *Vassileia* . . .'

'I will not, I say!'

'*Aghia Panayia* . . . Come, *Vassileia*, you must.'

'Here I stay,' Anna repeated, kicking her feet into the grass so that she indeed appeared rooted in place.

'I will stay here while you warn de Montalhac,' I ventured. 'It is not far to the ship.' I threw a warning look at Anna, who had turned her stubborn glare on me. 'If all is well, we shall come in at nightfall, on any signal you choose.'

'Did you hurt him to death, Petroc?' Pavlos turned to me. I shrugged, feeling horrible.

'No!' I said. 'I only kicked his ballocks for him. But he was holding aloft a great boulder, and he dropped it on his own shoulder. I heard it break, like piece of kindling.'

'Exactly where was it?'

I showed him on my own shoulder. 'I think the stone carried away his ear, too,' I added. He wanted to know how much blood I had seen. For a minute he paced in a tight circle, staring at us through narrowed eyes. Finally he stopped, and dragged his hands across his face.

'So be it,' he sighed. 'You will stay here. I do not think your lunatic will be back, and it seems unlikely that there are more of his like about. But, Petroc, I shall bring you something more useful than that,' and he waved a finger at Thorn. 'Can you use a bow?' I nodded – it was true, I had been a fair shot at the abbey, shooting at the butts set up by the river for sport and preparation, for it was not unknown for the monks to go forth armed to drive folk off abbey land. 'Good,' said Pavlos doubtfully. 'I will arrange a signal with the Captain. But if you see one hair of a stranger's head, you will shoot to kill, then run for your lives. Do you swear it?'

'I swear it,' I agreed.

'I swear nothing,' said Anna stiffly. 'But I will do as Petroc advises me, as he has guided me well thus far.' And she stared at Pavlos down her fine, narrow nose.

'Thanks be to God,' said the Greek, fervently, and crossed himself once more. 'I shall return with all speed.'

And he turned and all but ran down the hill. I felt Anna at my side, and heard her laughter, the same laughter that had disturbed my morning bath.

'Pavlos is a good man,' she said finally, 'but he does fuss over me like an old hen. He has the habits of a palace guard, you see – he can no more break them than . . . than I can resist making sport of him. I have the habits of the palace too.'

'Where is your palace – your home?' I asked her, hearing the sadness in her voice.

'In Nicea, which is in Asia Minor, in that part we call Anatolia,' she replied. She looked at me quizzically. 'Do you know where that is?'

'It is on the eastern shore of the Mare Mediterraneum,' I said, 'above the lands of Outremer, and east of Byzantium.'

'Well, well! A scholar! My Devonshire boy, you are deeper than the Sea of Darkness,' she said. 'You did not come by such map-learning amongst that band of cutthroats, I think.'

'No, you are right,' I said, still watching the small figure of Pavlos as it hurried across the beach. Now he had reached the ship, and disappeared behind the hull. 'But, my lady, very little aboard the *Cormaran* is what it seems – like bundles of whalebone, for instance,' I added.

She snorted disparagingly – a most unladylike sound – and, taking my hand, drew me down to the heather. She sat back and crossed her legs like a tailor. Feeling awkward, I knelt before her, as if at prayer.

'You at least are not who you seem to be,' she said. 'You are too gentle. Oh, I know . . .' and she held up a hand as if to silence my protest. 'You are fearless, I have the proof of it. But you do not seem like one of them . . . like a pirate, for that is what they are, isn't that true?'

'They are traders,' I mumbled.

'Oh, rubbish! That de Montalhac is a rogue through and through – a wolf. But a gentleman,' she admitted.

'And more,' I said. 'They are all . . . *most* of them are good men. They saved my life, and took me in like a long-lost brother.'

'Lord! That ship is manned by a veritable guild of life-savers! And from what did they save yours?'

'From a man . . .' I began reluctantly. 'From being hanged for a thing I had no part in.' I hung my head, still sickened at the memory of it all.

'Peace, Petroc. I have a mocking tongue, but a loving heart. Listen. It is but a little past noon, and we shall be sitting on this great dry mountain for hours to come. As I have fallen amongst *traders*,' and she reached out one leg and prodded me in the thigh with a dirty toe, 'I will *trade* you my history for yours. And I wager that you get the better bargain, although we shall see. So, is it yes? Do you agree?'

I considered. I had no great wish to pick over my dark time. The long sea-voyage had healed much, though I could sense Sir Hugh somewhere in the background, lurking like unclean smoke. But looking at this girl, who regarded me so coolly from under those arching brows, and past her at the strange shore upon which we had been thrown together, I realised that I longed to tell my story to someone – all of it, not just the fragments I had let fall in conversation aboard the *Cormaran*. Only the Captain knew it all, and confiding in the Captain was like consigning a secret to a deep, black pool in which count-less other sorrows lay sleeping.

'Well, where should I begin?' I asked.

'At the beginning, of course,' said she.

So I told her everything, from my boyhood on the moors, to the abbey, to gloomy Balecester and all the blood that had flowed there, to Dartmouth and, finally, to this place, this little rock in the ocean. I found I could tell of Will's murder, although my hands began to tremble, and I was glad when Pavlos interrupted me, loping up to drop a longbow and quiver of good, goose-fletched arrows beside me. I saw him appraise the situation, hands on hips, measuring in his mind the distance between his *Vassileia* and my common self. Apparently satisfied, he left us in peace. Then my tale flowed untrammelled to its ending on this island, hearing Anna's laugh on the wind. When I had finished, I looked up, for I had been gazing at my feet as I spoke, caught up despite myself in the tale I had not wished to drag forth. Anna was staring at me, hugging herself as if to ward off a chill, although the sun was scorching us. Her eyes were red.

'How great is the misery of this world,' she murmured. 'And how little it seems that the Almighty cares for his creations.'

I opened my mouth to reply, but no words came. She had touched upon the darkest shadow within me; the empty niche that had once held my faith. I wondered if that secret were written on my skin like leprosy, but then Anna grabbed my hand and squeezed it.

'I have wronged you, Petroc,' she said. 'I took you for yet another pirate, although, granted, with a gentle demeanour. But it seems that we are more alike than I thought, you and I. We are both clerics, for a start . . .' And she laughed, mirthlessly.

'Clerics?' I was startled.

'Renegade clerics, to be sure,' she agreed. 'Both plucked from the life that fate intended for us and cast adrift. Don't I look like a nun? I assure you that I am one.'

I nodded, confused. 'But be of good cheer, Your Holiness!' she continued. 'Now you must hear my tale, and a good one it is, to all who have not lived it for themselves. I too will start at the very beginning, very far away from your sweet land of Devon.'

'How do you know of Devon?' I burst out, my curiosity smothering good manners.

'From the palace guards, the Varangians. There are many English lads among them, and always have been. And that is how I speak your tongue.'

'I had a suspicion you did not learn it from a nun,' I ventured. She snorted.

'No, indeed not. But you interrupted. Do you know anything of Byzantium?'

I shook my head. 'Very little, apart from where it is and the nature of – forgive me – its Schismatic faith.'

She clicked her tongue in disapproval. 'But do you know how the crusade of the Franks was seduced by the blind serpent Doge Dandolo and took our city from us?' Her breast was heaving, and she had flushed dark pink. I noticed with a disquieting thrill how the glow crept down her neck and beneath her cloak.

'But, peace on us both,' she sighed, and seemed to compose herself with great effort. She swallowed and began again.

'Give me an arrow,' she demanded. She used the point to scratch a map into a patch of granite dust between us.

'This is Greece,' she said, 'And here Anatolia and the Holy Land. Here is Serbia and the lands of the Bulgars. All this—' and she waved a wide circle over the map, '—was the Empire of Byzantium, and the city is here.' She jabbed the arrow point-down into the ground. 'The Franks took all this,' she went on, scratching away at most of Greece and some of Anatolia, 'and the city itself. And Venice helped herself to our islands.' The arrow was waving alarmingly close to my feet now.

'The Romans set up an Empire in exile here, at Nicea.' She stabbed again, this time at a spot in Anatolia, near to her left knee. 'Do you follow? Now.' The arrow flickered. 'The Despot of Epiros, the Roman prince whose house Pavlos served, held out here, in the west of Greece. I was born in Nicea, *here*, for I was cheated by the Franks out of my birthright, which was to be born in the Palace of Constantine.' She waved the arrow at me. The sun glinted nastily from the tip. Then she lowered it.

'I am sorry, Petroc – truly I am. How could you be to blame? But you will find me ill-disposed towards Franks of any sort, I am afraid. With you as the exception . . . and the Captain, and Gilles. There is something most un-Frankish about those men.'

'There you are right,' I said. Then, catching her eye, I risked all. 'Will you get to it, then?'

'As you wish,' she said, looking daggers at me. Then she grinned, and I saw once more where she had lost a tooth.

'You will be spared the full horror,' she said. She pointed behind me with the arrow, then stuck it in the ground between us. 'The Captain is here. But I will not cheat you out of my tale, for I had yours in good faith. So, quickly then. As I said, I was born in Nicea. I am the third child of the Emperor's brother – the Emperor John Doukas Vatatzes. As is the fate of royal girls, I was destined to be . . . to find an *expedient* husband. I was only three years old when the King of Norway, Haakon, whom his subjects called The Old, decided that I would make a fine match for his second son. I was betrothed to a surrogate, and as I grew older I hardly thought about my husband – whom I knew only from his image on a medal: a handsome boy ten years my elder – until my thirteenth year when the Norse ambassador came for me.

'The journey . . . I am sure you can imagine it. And when I came to Trondheim castle, a great mossy kennel, I found that my handsome princeling had died of the pox six months before and now, waste not want not, I would marry the next son in line, Stefan, a pallid, holy worm. He had been intended for the Church and the finest bishopric in Norway, and I had spoiled everything. Oh Christ, Petroc, there is so much to tell, yet there is no time.'

Her eyes were beginning to redden, so without thinking I took her hand. She squeezed it gratefully.

'So I was married to this . . . this cold, slimy . . .'

'Toad?' I suggested, helpfully.

'No! Toads are wise, they carry a jewel in their heads. My *husband* . . . he hated me. He would not share our bed. He lay on the stone floor and prayed and cursed me by turns, and when at last I tried to reason with him he struck me on the ear and left. I never saw him again. Good. But the ladies of the court found my blood on the bed-linen the next day, and they declared the marriage consummated. Then . . .' she looked up, and now I could hear footsteps crunching through the heather.

'When it was clear I was not with child, they exiled me,' she said, 'to a nunnery in Greenland. Worse than death − and that was why. But I escaped. I made friends with the Bishop, and . . . Anyway, he has a thread of kindness in him, and he is an exile too, of course. He told me of the Seigneur de Montalhac, and after I had survived another winter your ship arrived. The Captain agreed to carry me to Venice, where many of my people dwell in exile. Then I slipped from the nunnery, met Pavlos, who kissed my feet! Dear God! They bundled me up in a load of whalebone − most uncomfortable − and here I am.'

We were holding hands, our fingers wound tightly together so that the hot sand scratched. She looked into my eyes.

'Two dead children, fallen off the edge of the world,' she murmured, and bit her lip. I saw that she was about to cry.

'I would say that you are a woman and a princess, and very much alive,' I said. 'And for a poor drowned monk, I feel quite cheerful as well.'

And so we sat, hand in hand, until the Captain and Pavlos strode up between the boulders. I slid a seemly distance from

Anna and picked up the bow, hoping that I looked diligent and dangerous. I could tell by the way the skin between her eyebrows puckered that I was convincing no one. We were both choking down laughter by the time the two men came up to us.

'No demons to report,' I told them.

'Good, good,' said the Captain. 'So, Petroc, it seems we owe you for the life of our royal guest. But now we have difficulties. How do we get *Kyria* Anna back on board? We have a rowdy crew and no whalebone handy.'

'Captain de Montalhac, I will not be smuggled or hidden any more. I would rather take my chances with your crew.' Anna's face was set once more in its imperial mask.

'My God, *Vassileia*, do you know what you are saying?' gasped Pavlos.

'Pavlos is right,' the Captain agreed. 'The men are in a vile temper. I have kept them too close to heel these past months. They have had no proper shore leave—'

'What about Gardar?' Anna broke in. The Captain winced.

'Gardar can hardly keep its own people alive, let alone entertain a company of villains like mine. No, they are apt to take very badly to the arrival of a lady on board, no matter how high-born or needy. I will not risk it.' And he folded his arms across his chest and regarded Anna down the length of his nose.

'Seigneur de Montalhac, if I am shut away in that corpse-hole again I shall die anyway. Unless you want to crack my skull and keep me insensible, you must announce a new crew member. How long until we reach Venice?'

'Weeks, *Kyria* Anna, long weeks, even if the winds are kind to us,' said the Captain.

'Well, I am sure I can tie knots or whatever it is you do to sail a ship, good Monsieur de Montalhac.' She spoke flippantly, but from the jut of her chin it was clear that she meant every word. The Captain saw it too. He sat down beside her.

'Let me see your hands,' he said gently. She held them out to him and he took each one and turned it over. I saw his expression change from amusement to surprise.

'Not the ivory hands of a princess, I'm afraid,' said Anna. 'At the convent we washed clothes for the poor, even if we had to break the ice with an axe to do so.'

The Captain stared at her for a long moment, then at me. 'You don't, by any chance, speak Basque?' he asked hopefully.

So it was that Mikal joined the *Cormaran*. He was a poor, half-starved Basque fisherman's son, only survivor of a ship that had foundered in a storm. For three months he had lived on gull's eggs, and had all but abandoned hope when our sail came into sight.

'The Basques have plied the ocean for generations,' the Captain told us. 'They tell no one where they go – it is the greatest secret in the wide world. So if a shipwrecked sailor appears among them, the crew will not be so surprised. You must have a disguise, and you must have a reason for being here. This is the only way I can see that solves both problems. And this mummery need only last until we leave Dublin. I believe the men will be more cheerful after a few nights of hard-earned riot, and I will re-introduce you as a wealthy passenger.'

'I cannot speak a word of Basque, however,' said Anna. It was plain she was already enthralled by the idea. 'But are there any Basques aboard?'

'That's the point,' said the Captain. 'There are none – dare I say it, the only language of the world not represented. I believe that Gilles speaks a little Euskadi, but that is all. You will be respected, believed – the Basques keep their own counsel, that is well known – and can retreat into silence whenever you wish. On the other hand, you will have to speak something.'

'I am speaking your Occitan now,' she answered. 'Will that do?'

'Indeed it will,' said the Captain with a little bow that was part mockery and part undeniable respect. 'Well, you have a man's clothes already. But you will have to cut your hair.'

'Certainly not!' she snapped. 'The silent sisters could not cut it, and nor shall you or anyone else. I shall plait it. My teeth may drop out, but my hair stays put.' And she wound a black, defiant rope around her neck.

'A female Samson, no less,' laughed de Montalhac. 'Very well. Here is what we shall do.'

After the Captain left, Pavlos stayed with us until it grew dark. Then we crept down to the ship and slipped inside the Captain's tent. The next morning I would make a pretence of climbing back to the high point, something none of the other crewmen were likely to want to join in, and come back with Mikal. I hoped the plan would work. I could not see Anna as anything but intensely, wonderfully female, as I discovered when I tried to picture her as a boy. It was as if a strand of that ink-black hair had begun to wind itself about my heart. As I watched her sup with the Captain and Gilles I remembered my hands under her tunic and nearly choked on the succulent morsel of fresh mutton I was mumbling at with my rickety teeth.

Later, as the Captain, Gilles and I left the tent to sleep by the fire outside, she was stretching out on the bright rugs that covered the sand. 'Good night, Petroc of Devonshire,' she said. 'Sweet dreams – if the dead can dream.'

'I believe this is a dream, and I am only afraid that I will wake from it,' I said, without knowing where the words had sprung from.

'Am I in yours, or you in mine?' She spoke softly behind me. 'Death in life, life in death. We are the same, you and I.'

I looked back, but she had blown out the lamp and I could

not tell where she ended and the night began. Then, soft as a moth's wings, her lips brushed mine and cool fingers rested for an instant on my cheek. Another instant passed and I felt her leave me.

I stepped outside. Under the great sky the fire seemed like a little spark. The stars danced their old, solemn dance above me, far, far away.

Chapter Fourteen

So it was that Mikal came aboard the *Cormaran*. It was as the Captain had predicted: the castaway boy was welcomed like a long-lost mate. He set to with a will, and if he wasn't the most expert seaman, he was excused – after all, it was his first voyage, and he hadn't got very far into the bargain. He had to endure the usual filth about sheep-shagging, and endless seagull jokes, but after a few days he blended, unsuspected, into the general mêlée.

As the two new boys, it was natural that we should be friends, especially as I had found Mikal somewhere on the other side of the Godforsaken island and brought him back to the world. And the truth is that we were inseparable. Although I was the more experienced seaman – a strange thought, this, to one whose only experience of water had been paddling in mountain streams – then Mikal's ferocious energy more than made up for his lack of skills. I taught him what little I knew, but he was precocious, and soon the crew found they had an insatiable student on their hands. By the time we passed the isle of Rathlin, off the north-east tip of Ireland, he was prattling about knots and broad reaches with all the joy of the newly converted.

Anna had folded and twisted her black mane into three short ropes, which she plaited at the nape of her neck. It was a little strange, but she passed it off as the fashion in her village and that seemed to suffice. Mikal was too young to shave, fortunately, and as Anna had starved with the rest of us her face was gaunt and quite mannish. As I have said, we were inseparable, but in ways that the rest of the crew could never know about. There are precious few private moments on a ship at sea, but Anna and I sought them out like gold dust in the bed of a river. Since that first, night-hidden kiss on the island – the first of my young and so far celibate life – my mind and flesh had been consumed by Anna. We would brush past each other, her touch striking sparks from me that I half-imagined were visible to the crew. Sometimes we could hold hands for minutes at a time, the desperate lock of our fingers the only outlet for passion. Often she would whisper such things to me in her dark voice – she took an endless delight in shocking my hopelessly innocent self – that I felt the deck lurch beneath me even though the sea was calm. And three times – no more – we kissed, hesitant with fear of discovery but full of heat and urgency, only to fly apart at the smallest hint of an approaching footstep. It was torture, but of the most wonderful kind. In truth I thought that, if this was to be the height of my earthly pleasure, it would almost be enough. But once the flesh has awakened, only death can still it, and Anna had awakened me as the sun awakens the earth in springtime.

As an odd counterpoint to all this – salt to temper the honey – Pavlos got it into his head that I would have to be schooled in those warlike arts which I had never so much as considered. It was sheer luck, he told me sternly, that I had bested the island madman, and my clumsy attack could just as easily have brought about the death of Anna or – and he emphasised that this, under the circumstances, would have been the preferable outcome – my own demise. So I found myself being tutored, every morning, by a terrifying college of teachers: Horst, Dimitri and Pavlos himself. Dimitri was the ship's unofficial fencing master and held his classes – I saw them as such, but they were both less and more than that: vicious games that honed skills and headed off any ill-feeling or rage that might otherwise have festered into real bloodshed – as soon as the sun had risen and the day was fair. In time I would join in these mêlées, but, as the first lesson proved, at my present level of accomplishment I would lose a duel with Fafner the cat. I faced Horst, both of us armed with a blunt sword and a round wooden buckler shield. Copying my opponent, I dropped into a crouch, shield before me, sword up. Then, in the blinking of an eye, Horst dropped his sword, knocked mine from my hand with the edge of his shield and felled me with his shoulder. Before I had even squawked in surprise he was sitting on my chest, the rim of his buckler pressing into my throat.

'Now you are dead,' he told me, smiling icily. And for the better part of an hour he showed me the many ways I could expect to die in the short moments between drawing my blade and deciding what on earth I should do with it next. It was not a cheering experience, but the next day I was a little quicker, and the day after that, faced with Dimitri – who had already tripped me three times and pretended to skewer my cods with his knife – I felt myself vanish – that is to say, the bumbling, anxious, flinching Petroc vanished – and when I came to my senses again, Dimitri was howling with laughter as blood poured in a torrent from his nose.

'Yes, yes! Magnificent, O Petroc! You have it! Again!'

This time I did not lose myself, but it was as if the scared, inept Petroc was trapped in the same skin as a man who could act on nothing more than brute instinct. In time I would lose this sense of division and realise that I was simply allowing myself to be free, to use my body as freely as I had when I was a child. But at first, although I learned fast and faster still, I was uneasy, and worried, for a while, that I was being posessed by some maleficent, violent spirit.

Off the mouth of the Liffey the Captain ordered the *Cormaran* hove to. He took Gilles off in the gig, and the little boat went bobbing off over an agitated grey sea. It was late in the day when they returned, and several large bundles wrapped in well-greased hides followed them on board. To our surprise we were ordered to make sail on a southerly course. We would not be stopping in Dublin after all. The crew muttered darkly but stuck, white-lipped, to their work.

On a muggy, grey morning a week later, we entered the mouth of the Gironde and, after a pleasant enough sail up-stream past low hills stitched with the coarse green lines of vineyards, drew near to the wharves of Bordeaux. It had been an uneventful passage, save for a hail-filled squall that lashed at us as we coasted past the Ile d'Oleron. Now the walls and spires of the city danced against the sky, which had cleared as if in welcome.

The port was full. Ships of all shapes and sizes jostled against one another all along the great length of the quay and at anchorages further out into the river, and we drifted past them under a wisp of sail. Big cogs bumped tarry hulls with fishing smacks and barges. Pilot boats and gigs bustled to and fro, ferrying people and goods from ship to shore. Many vessels flew warlike pennants and gonfalons, and bright shields hung on their sides. Between the swaying masts, the quayside was swarming, not just with the loading, unloading and portering of trade but with groups of armed men standing, sitting or running about with no seeming purpose. Pikes and halberds bristled in clumps, and the sound of drums and shouting came over the water.

I stood beside the Captain on the bridge. The crew, those who were not handling the sail, lined the sides and the forecastle. They saw the soldiers on the quay, and like hounds they scented blood. I glanced at the Captain, and saw that a wolfish look had settled there as well.

'What is happening over there?' I asked Gilles.

He shrugged. 'The English King and the French King, going at it like scorpions. When has it been different? But—' he paused, and I saw a look of sour disdain pass over his face, '—the English scorpion seems to be annoyed. An army is landing – a real one. It'll be battles this time, not skirmishes.'

Nizam wove us through the tangle of ships and anchor-lines until, at a signal from de Montalhac, the sail dropped and we weighed our own anchor between two fat-bellied cobs that bobbed and rolled like huge pitch-caulked barrels. Soon the gig was pulling away towards the wharf, the Captain sitting alert in the prow. I watched the men ply their oars, and wished myself among them. Here was life again as I knew it: the smell of real food drifting from good stone houses, bells chiming from proud steeples, the yelling and bantering of Englishmen. Anna had slipped to my side and was gripping the rail tightly as she gazed hungrily at the shore. She was quivering like a hound on a leash.

'If I could swim, I would be on dry land by now,' she muttered.

'I can swim,' I told her, 'and I would gladly pull you along, Mikal. But much as I would love a mug of beer and some good red meat, our balls would shrivel and drop off in that water.'

'Well, I agree we wouldn't want anything to happen to those balls of yours,' she breathed, leaning in close. I felt a familiar quickening below. 'But it is *summer*, you oaf – the water is warm. They have beds over there, you know,' she added. 'And doors. With locks.' I cleared my throat somewhat dramatically. 'Well, what do you say, brother?' she added loudly in her croaky man-voice. 'Will we see what trouble there is to find? I fancy a fight, a fuck and . . .' she waved her hand, as if to pluck words from the seagull-loud air, '. . . and a fried . . . a fried fowl,' she finished, and glanced at me, pleased with herself.

'Don't overdo it, *brother*,' I hissed. Nizam was chatting to Dimitri right behind us, after all. But they seemed unaware of our presence.

In truth, this might be Mikal's last day on earth. Mikal the luckless Basque boy would disappear into the stews of Bordeaux. The crew would think he had slipped away homewards, or that his purse and gizzard had been cut and his body flung into the harbour. Sad, but such things happened. Either way he would be gone, and soon afterwards I would introduce Anna Doukaina, mysterious adventurer in need of our protection. The masquerade would be over, and not before time. Anna had been wearing her Mikal disguise ever lighter, and I had begun to feel a constant knot of anxiety lest she give herself away.

I felt her frustration, of course. It came off her in waves, like heat from coals. Her bound breasts were a constant torment. She was in a state of permanent fury about the fuss involved in a simple thing like pissing – having to wait until no one was looking, so that the crew would not notice how hard it was for her to make water standing up with her back to the boat like the rest of us. Neither of us could believe that Mikal's secret had not come to light, but, I believe now, that was due to the intense focus of a long sea journey, when everyone's world shrinks, through boredom or discomfort, to the task in hand, and to one's own tormented body. Although I would not have dared to think such a thing then, I suspect that, if Anna had climbed the mast and stripped stark naked, as she had often threatened to do, not one of the scorbutic, half-starved, salt-burned wretches below her on the deck would have turned so much as an eyelash. They would have spit a little more blood over the side and gone back, grumbling, to their mindless work. But that picture – Anna standing bare amidst a snarl of wild-eyed men, her skin glimmering white through the half-light of an approaching squall – floated through my dreams and woke me more than once as we made our way south from Scotland.

The Captain had urgent business ashore. There were deliveries to be made, and cargo taken on, as in every port. But further, there was a man in Bordeaux who had availed himself of de Montalhac's special services, and who, the Captain assured me, was waiting most anxiously for the *Cormaran*'s arrival. A prince of the Church, a man of power. No seedy, passed-over failure like the Bishop of Gardar, but a person of rank and wealth, who was expecting an item that befitted that rank. The Captain was happy to oblige, as ever, but this was not the matter, I was sure, that had stirred him up and lit the eerie fox-fire which had been flickering in his eyes since we left Dublin. It was not just war he had scented as we made our way up the great water-road of the Gironde. I had no proof, but something about his mood had put me in mind of the night we had passed in Greenland.

Thus I was not surprised when the gig returned without him, to collect Gilles and Rassoul. Before he swung himself over the rail, Gilles gathered the crew around him.

'There will be shore-leave when I return,' he announced. The men were silent, but I could feel their taut excitement. 'Pavlos will organise a roster for the watch. I will be back shortly.' And with that he was gone.

The crew burst into life. We had felt the scorbutus lift its foulness from the ship as soon as the fresh meat and good kale of the island was inside us, and our gums were beginning to heal. Not so stiff and agued now, the men almost danced about the deck. Good clothing appeared magically from sea-chests, satchels, even parcels of oil-cloth that had been wedged God knew where for the past months. Beards were trimmed or shaved. Men stood in little clusters, untangling each other's hair with combs of whale-bone. Sword-belts were greased until they shone, weapons polished and, I noticed, given a new edge. Although not one of us had more on his mind than the taverns and bath-houses that awaited us on shore, the men of the *Cormaran* were preparing as if for a fine tournament.

I was no exception. The blue tunic that Gilles had given me that night at the White Swan, and which had come off worst from my last meeting with Sir Hugh, emerged from Dimitri's sea-chest, miraculously restored. 'A little sea-water,' he grunted, 'and a deal of scrubbing. Too good to throw away,' he added, watching with a flicker of pride as I fingered the place where Thorn had stabbed me, now all but invisible save for a faint spider's web of tiny stitches. I almost hugged the man in my joy, but did not dare. Instead I took his hand and wrung it while I poured forth a veritable fountain of thanks, and I swear that his butchered face almost blushed. So now I wore my tunic, a cloak of deep blue edged in red silk, a good long-caped hood of black wool, some fine black hose that Abu offered to lend me and my soft leather shoes, given to me by the Captain my first day aboard but never worn for fear the salt-spray would devour them. Thorn rode upon my hip, her hilt of green stone glimmering with a vaguely malign light.

'You look like a Rostock pimp,' Horst said, approvingly.

Anna was fretting. Poor doomed Mikal seemed fated to spend his last night on earth dressed in the same shabby sailor-rags he had worn to cross the Sea of Darkness.

'I will not go ashore in this shoddy,' she hissed to me. 'I am a princess – I wish to pass at least this one evening in the guise of a prince. Instead I will be spat upon and mocked by every whore in this pox-ridden village, kicked and sent upon errands. I will not do it, I say!' And she stamped her foot. I trod upon it, hard.

'Shut up!' I hissed in turn. 'In a few hours you will be rid of Mikal for good. You will be the precious Princess Anna again, never fear. Now put your tongue back in its scabbard and be easy. The trick is almost played.'

She harrumphed, and gave me a look sour as bad vinegar. Nevertheless she took my counsel and bit back the anger that was ready to master her. 'Be easy yourself,' she sniffed. Then she looked me up and down. 'For a monk and a sheep-worrying peasant, you look almost gentle-bred. Don't get too cosy with the wenches on shore, my fighting-cock. Tonight, you may meet a noblewoman down on her luck. And she might well be very, very grateful for your help.' With that, she pinched my behind, not gently, and slipped away towards the bridge.

Anna and I were in the party chosen to go ashore first, as we knew we would be. So were Elia and Pavlos, who had vowed not to let their princess out of their sight, although to myself I wondered how soon she would put that vow to the test. We stood in a gaggle waiting to climb into the boat, the other men, those who had to wait their turn, thronging around us and filling our ears with bad advice and filthy jokes. But they were not in good humour, and we lucky ones merely nodded and chuckled, knowing that men so long at sea might be glad to vent their frustrations then and there, a brawl in sight of land being almost as good as one on solid ground.

Once aboard the overloaded gig, it seemed we were running the keel up the river-beach in an instant, so frenzied were the oarsmen to escape the *Cormaran*. Anna was the first to scramble up onto the wharf, slinging her fat canvas satchel, which I knew held her woman's clothing, up ahead of her.

'Whoa, Mikal!' bellowed Snørri. 'Leave some trollops for us!'

'Make do with my leavings,' she laughed back, swinging the bag over her shoulder. I clambered up the weed-smothered sea-steps, feeling the bladder-wrack squish and pop beneath my feet. Then I was beside Anna. I looked around to get my bearings.

This Bordeaux was a comely city, built of yellow stone, with many proud buildings rising behind the wood and plaster warehouses that lined the river. Smoke rose from countless chimneys. Weathervanes of bright copper and brass flashed against the dimming sky. And everywhere, far and near, armed men were strolling, marching, running. Here came a band of foot-soldiers with long pikes across their shoulders and kettle helms upon their heads. They carried short-swords as well, and by the look on each hard face they would delight in close work with those swords when the time came. A couple of knights perched high on their great war-mounts cut across the pikemen's route, ignoring them. These men wore bright sur-coats and each had a long-sword at his side. Out of habit I noted their crests: a green oak-tree on one, three crows over a red arrow on the other. I did not recognise either device, of course, but to see English heraldry again after so long made my heart race a little. Now a bigger band of men-at-arms approached. They marched in step, and were led by a tall, proud-stepping man in a suit of bright steel mail. On his surcoat of pale blue shone a yellow bird. The same device fluttered gaily on a banner that whipped above the men. These were yeomen at least, not the murderous cutthroats who car-ried pikes. They were well armed and dressed. Some wore kettle-helms, others old-fashioned pointed helmets with nose-guards. Most of them seemed to possess at least one piece of chain-mail. They marched as proudly as their leader, and for a moment I thought that there must be worse occupations than that of man-at-arms.

Then a gnarled bowman carrying a heavy sack knocked into Anna.

'Out of the road, you little bloodworm,' he hissed in the flat voice of a Bristol-man. I saw that he carried his unstrung bow like a fighting stave, and my hand dropped to Thorn's hilt. Glancing about me, I saw that we all had weapons to hand, and the bowman saw it too, and backed off hurriedly.

'Foreign fucking bloodworms, all of you,' he growled. 'Fuck-ing cowards and sodomites.' He spat towards Elia's feet. 'Stick together with your thumbs up each other's arse-holes, don't you? If my mates were here . . .'

'But they are not here. So fuck off before I show you what your kidneys look like,' said Snørri calmly, for all the world like a man giving directions in the street.

To his credit, the ugly Bristol-man stood his ground for a moment, glaring. Then he shrugged his shoulders. 'I'll be looking out for you, boys,' he informed us, and walked away.

'Fucking English,' muttered Snørri. 'Begging your pardon, Petroc.'

'I liked him,' I said, nudging Anna. 'He had an honest face.'

That set us all laughing, and we forgot the scowling bowman. There were more interesting sights to entertain us as we left the teeming wharves and entered the narrow streets of the city itself, choosing a little opening some way to the left of the looming, crenellated jaws of the Great Gate, which dominated the wharves like a castle in its own right. Almost at once, Snørri and John of Metz disappeared into a tavern, the first one we passed. Before long I was left with Anna and the Greeks, the others having darted into bath-house and ale-house, cook-shop and knocking-shop. I had a mind to defer my pleasures a little longer, and I could not believe that sheer convenience would be a substitute for quality. I required the finest ale in Bordeaux. I had dreamed of it, rolled its ghost over my tongue and around my mouth day after thirsty day for months, and I determined to let nothing past my lips until I had the object of my quest before me.

Elia was silent, fretting over his brother, who had not felt strong enough to come ashore. Luckily Pavlos knew the town, and thought that the best ale might be found at the Red Angel, nearby in the Rue de la Rousselle. Anna, who had dropped all pretence now that she was alone with those who knew her secret, flounced and pouted. She did not want to drink reeking beer, she said. She wished us to escort her to a place where she might find courtesans of high price, a fine table and exquisite wines. And, she declared, she would go in as a man. Pavlos ran his hands through his hair in exasperation.

'How can we take you such a place, *Vassileia*? With all the filth of the world, all the sinners? And besides, you look like an urchin. Impossible, my lady.'

'Then leave me!' Her eyes flashed in the shadowy alley

where we stood. 'Petroc will see to it that I come to no harm.' She tugged at my sleeve. 'Come along now.'

But the Greeks would not allow the *Vassileia* out of their sight. Anna stood there fretting and baiting like a bored hawk. In the end it was I who broke the deadlock.

'Well, it is still daylight, and the fine courtesans are still abed, asleep. Let us continue our sulking at the Red Angel at least. For the love of God, Pavlos, lead on.'

This, at least, Pavlos could agree upon, and we set off down the alley. He was true to his word. The Red Angel – *L'Ange Rouge* – lay up a side street a little way from the Church of St Pierre. It looked a little drab from the outside, simply another building of plaster and timber that leaned far out over the street. But a wondrous carved angel, with wings outstretched and brandishing a flaming sword, painted all over in differing shades of red, hovered over the doorway, and I felt a strong tingle of excitement as I followed the three Greeks over the threshold.

The Red Angel's beer was a wonder indeed. As I took a deep swig of my second mug, I thought that St Michael himself must have stirred the wort with his fiery blade. The brew was almost smoky, dark and pungent. I would happily have drunk it until it flowed in my veins in place of blood. I barely noticed the other three. Pavlos and Elia were drinking the red wine of Bergerac, and expressing their satisfaction. Anna had sipped my beer, made a face, and called for the finest wine in the house, which proved to be golden, sweet and strong. She attacked it like a cat with a bird, biting, so it seemed, mouthfuls of wine from the goblet, chewing them murderously, and dipping straight back down for more. Glancing up from my mug, I saw her staring at the table with hooded eyes. She had closed herself off from the world around her.

I ordered another mug of beer, then another. I listened to my companions chatter away in their own tongue, then allowed the drink to carry me away down its dark current. I felt the floor beneath me shift, the remembered motion of the ship that my body could not forget. I saw clear green wave-tips; the terrible void of the Sea of Darkness. Then the golden waters of my own river Aune appeared to me. I followed a freckled trout as it flitted over the sand and between rocks overgrown with spongy moss. I was a little boy again, and I knelt down and picked up a stone, a jagged fistful of granite the colour of the sky before a snowstorm, and lobbed it into the pool. The ripples spread, out and out and ever out.

'See, *he* dreams. You bloody carpenters: your minds are full of wood-shavings. You should let them soar as high as the trees you cut to pieces. I will talk to one with loftier thoughts – so good day to you, gents.'

I felt a tug on my sleeve, and looked up, into a pair of kindly but red-rimmed eyes. A skinny man in a threadbare cleric's costume stood over me, his body working slightly as if not entirely under his control. He held an almost-empty goblet. His fingernails were long and dirty.

'Give me the pleasure of your company, good master,' he said in a pleasant enough voice, in which education and wine fought for mastery. He was speaking French. 'I can find no spark in those rude fellows.' I looked behind him. A pair of craggy-featured men sat talking earnestly to each other, relief on their faces. I glanced back at the skinny man and blinked, still half in my dream of home. Taking this for my agreement to his company, the man sat down beside me and called loudly for more wine.

'I should not disturb you, but I see you are a man who uses his head for more than battering a path through life. And by your garb I see you are from the city – the real city, not this backwater, yes?'

'I am from no city, sir. I am a travelling man. You are welcome to join me if you must, but you will find my French and my wits a trifle lacking, I am afraid.' In truth I had no wish to make the acquaintance of a stranger, but the man missed my hint, or in any event ignored it. I looked around for my companions, but the three Greeks were huddled close, talking fast and furiously in their own tongue. Before I could interrupt them, the man's rich, somewhat cracked voice started so close to my ear that I felt his spittle. I turned and met his red eyes.

'A travelling man, sir? And an educated one, by Jesus! Wonder of wonders. Allow me to introduce my humble self: Robert of Nogent – *Robertus Nogensis* – late of the great Universities of Paris and Bologna. A travelling man myself, you see, and my cargo is learning.'

I bit down to kill a smile. The man was clearly half-starved. I hoped he had packed something more edible than learning for his travels. Meanwhile, how was I to introduce myself? This was the first time I had been asked my name by a stranger since the inn at Dartmouth. I thought for an instant.

'Peter,' I replied at last. 'Peter Swan of Zennor.'

'Zennor, Zennor . . .' pondered Robertus. 'A Breton, then?'

'Cornish,' I replied hastily. 'Zennor is hard by Falmouth.'

'But educated, surely? You have drunk deeply at the fountain of learning, I can tell.'

'My family were wealthy. I had private masters. But tell me of Paris,' I said, to steer things away from my flimsy subterfuge.

Robertus threw up his hands. 'Paris!' he breathed. 'Greatest city in creation. And within it, another city, built on thought, walled around with wisdom, peopled by scholars: the city of Pierre Abelard. Words are its coin.' He sighed deeply and examined his empty goblet. I waved my arm for the serving girl, who was happy to serve me at least: she knew I had more than words in my purse.

'The greatest masters in Christendom are gathered there,' my companion went on after a goodly slurp of wine. 'A man may travel from one teacher to another as a bee travels from flower to flower, sipping the nectar of knowledge – a little here, a little there . . .'

Robertus rattled on in this vein, gulping wine to punctuate his utterances, which grew longer and more flowery until I felt I was being smothered by a vine of words, a twining ivy that threatened to send me off into oblivion.

I had ordered another mug of beer, then another. The effort of keeping myself courteous to Robertus, indeed of keeping myself awake, was growing ever more difficult. The Greeks had long since grown quiet. But Robertus burbled on implacably. His words seemed to drift away, faint and then loud again. Then he tapped my arm.

'You have seen the cathedral of St André, of course?' I shook my head. 'They have almost finished work on the great door. Beautiful craftsmanship, to be sure: a worthy offering to the Almighty. But as I was saying to those worthy carpenters—' I saw that Robertus' previous victims had long since slipped away, '—building in stone and wood is but one way to raise an edifice to the glory of God and the spirit of Man. I have written on the subject, a slim volume – you are interested, I see. Excellent! Worthy Peter, I make no claims to the mystic life, but such a vision came to me as I slept one night in Paris. So strange and wonderful a vision it was that I have been certain ever since that it came not from within but from *without*.' He lowered his voice and pointed a bony finger at the ceiling. 'As I say, I set it down, but the authorities frowned upon it – unsound, they said; seditious! I ask you. The vision was of a great cathedral that rose high above a fair, golden city. Angels flew about the spire, which touched the very clouds. But, and hark to me now, this great building was wrought not of stone, nor wood, nor brick, but . . . *food*!'

'Fancy that,' I said curtly. Robertus did not notice. His red eyes seemed to glow even redder as he leaned towards me. I smelled sour wine.

'Yes, yes . . . The floor was laid in wondrous patterns,

formed of blood sausage opposed with the finest white lard. The walls were great blocks of golden butter, raised between towering buttresses of bread. The windows seemed like the finest stained glass, fairer than those of Notre-Dame, but were composed of the thinnest slices of Basque ham that let the light of the sun through in rosy shades of red and pink. The leading was anchovies. The choir stalls . . .'

'Peace, good Robertus; enough, enough!' I cried. 'You are making me famished.'

'The choir stalls were of salted codfish, the cushions plump rounded cheeses,' he went on relentlessly. 'The rafters were honeycombs, the roof was tiled with cinnamon. Upon the altar, which was hewn from one enormous goose liver, stood golden reliquaries of spun Cyprus sugar. And in them, the relics themselves were *ossi di morti* . . . bones of the dead, do you see? But these *ossi di morti* are a sort of sweetmeat I dined upon in Bologna. Now where was I?' His eyes shone ever brighter. 'Ah, yes. The doors . . .'

But alas, I will never know of what delicacy the doors of the great cathedral of Robertus Nogensis were crafted, for at that moment I looked up and saw that Elia and Pavlos were snoring face-down on the table and that Anna, and her satchel, were gone. I leaped up, all but knocking Robertus off the bench. I shook the Greeks, but they did not stir. The serving girl was passing by. I grabbed her arm. She squeaked.

'Where is my other friend,' I demanded, 'the thin dark one? Drinking the sweet wine?'

'Sir, truly I do not know! Let me go! You are hurting me.'

I released her, fumbled in my purse for a gold bezant and held it out.

'There's for our drinks, and that mad drone there, his too – and the rest is for you if you take care of the sleeping ones. Good care: if one hair of their heads is missing, or one coin from their purses, I'll be back to burn this place down.'

She clutched at the gold, and I spun away and ran through

the tap-room, knocking shoulders and spilling beer and wine to left and right.

Furious curses followed me, but I was already through the door and into the street.

It was dark. Night had fallen as we drank. Christ alone knew how long that diabolical bore had been babbling. Anna could have slipped away hours ago. Out here, the cooler air rapidly draining the warmth of the beer from me, I felt no surprise at all, only rage. Damn her! Damn her, and damn her airs, her caprices, her hellish stubbornness. She could not play along, not for one hour. Now she was off somewhere, getting into deep water, probably looking to get herself killed, or worse. I shoved my knuckles into my eyes.

'How now – crying, sirrah?' said a strange voice from the shadows. I turned, and my hand went to Thorn.

'Lost your sheep?' said the voice. I eased Thorn out a little further. 'Flashing a fat purse in a strange town . . . you need someone to watch your back, shepherd.'

I could duck back into the sanctuary of the Red Angel, or I could make my stand. I stood. A slender figure drifted out of a dark archway. The light from the lantern over the inn door picked out silver and gold on a short sword, belt, doublet. There were rings on a hand that gripped the sword's hilt. I drew Thorn and let her hang down against my leg. The tip pressed into the side of my knee, and I felt the first shudders of the ague of battle. Into the light stepped a young nobleman. I saw silk and cloth of gold shimmer softly. The ringed hand stroked a silver pommel.

'Sheep-worrier.' The voice cracked.

'Anna . . . Anna.'

We stood in silence, looking up at the great door of St André's cathedral. Some wooden scaffolding was still in place, but it was easy to pick out the layers of carving, arcs of saints and kings piled one upon the other. Making a small concession to the insufferable Robertus, I had to admit that it did look a little like honey-cake.

Anna had revealed herself just in time. Afire with nerves and beer, I had been about to throw myself at the menacing stranger. My thumb had pressed down so hard on the flat top of Thorn's blade that I could still feel the channel in the hard skin. Anna had allowed me no time to compose myself, grabbing my hand and pulling me at a dead run down the street, laughing like a madwoman. Only the wall of St Pierre's church brought us to a halt. We leaned our backs to it and struggled to catch our breath. Finally Anna turned to me.

'Did I not tell you that I meant to make Mikal a prince for his last night on earth? Quite the *bravo*, am I not?'

'I nearly killed you.'

'Oh, yes. I was quite scared.' A grin belied her words.

'I mean it, Anna. I have a violent aversion to well-dressed lurkers. You know very well who I thought you were.'

'I do not.'

'You do: the devil who chased me across half of England.'

'Peace! Petroc, peace. I did not mean to scare you at all, just to have a little fun.'

'Fun! I would have killed you. I swear it: I would not have let you live, had you not . . .'

'Stop. Stop it.' No longer smiling, she took my right hand and held it to her heart, which knocked fast and steady against her ribs. I shuddered. My knife could have been buried in that heart. Would I have felt its dying twitches through the cool green hilt? I pulled her head down to my shoulder and buried my face in its spicy tresses. Then we hurriedly broke off our clinch, each realising at the same time that, to the watching eye, we were two men caught in a lover's embrace, and by the church wall, no less.

So we set off strolling, and wandered through the streets of the city, oblivious for the moment of the crowds that pressed about us. It was still early, and many soldiers and sailors were going about the serious business of pleasure. Before long we found ourselves before the cathedral. It was only then that I remembered our companions, whom I had abandoned, stupefied in a public tavern.

'Tincture of poppy,' Anna explained happily. 'I found it in Isaac's magical chest. A couple of drops each. I know my medicines,' she added, seeing me aghast. 'An ancient Arab gentleman taught me when I was a girl. I would have used henbane, but Pavlos fears it as a witch's poison and besides, the poppy is gentler. They are dreaming sweetly, I promise. And I used so little that they will wake very soon.'

'Pavlos will kill me,' I said.

'Nonsense. It is I he should kill, but I am his precious *Vassileia*. You are just keeping me out of mischief. Or are you?'

'Am I what?'

'Keeping me out of mischief.'

'That would depend on what mischief you were considering.'

'A fight, a fuck, and some food is what I said, and that is what I intend to have.' She rattled her sword in its sheath. 'I suppose we've had the fight, so that leaves . . .'

'Food,' I said quickly. 'I'm starving. I was listening to some old fool ramble on about a cathedral built of sausages and sweetmeats and the like. I've just remembered how ravenous he made me.'

'Oh, the drunkard! He was a lucky interruption. He saved you from the poppy, my dear.'

'You wouldn't have drugged me as well?'

'Why not? I haven't anything to lose. I'm a dying man.'

So we strolled a while more, following our noses until we found a street full of cook-shops and eating-houses. Here the crowds were thicker still, jostling and shouldering up and down. Knots of men-at-arms lingered here and there, tearing at meat and bread. We halted before an open shop-front in which a sheep and a pig turned on spits, throwing off clouds of steam spiked with pepper, thyme and fennel. Racks of trussed squab grilled slowly, oil dripping and exploding on glowing charcoal. It looked busy inside, but I could not resist the fennel-scented pork, and Anna agreed with a wolfish nod.

We forced ourselves inside, squeezed our behinds onto a packed bench before a long table, and feasted until I thought I would burst. The pork was hot, sweet and spicy, and fat dripped down our chins. We gulped down draughts of cool, sharp red wine. Our companions at table ignored us. They were mainly soldiers, and must have taken us for young gentlemen entertaining themselves with a night out amongst the poor folk. For Anna, I had to admit, looked magnificent. Her cloak was edged with golden thread, worked into swirls of grape-heavy vines. Her tunic fell to her knees in the soldier's manner and was made of the finest cloth I had ever seen. Over a field of emerald silk romped sinuous beasts the colour of flame, and yellow flowers sprang up between them. The fabric shimmered with its own light. It was outlandish, almost barbaric, and I noticed that the man sitting next to Anna edged away from her, as if the strange tunic scared him. Beneath it, she wore hose of lustrous green wool, caught below the knee with garters of a deep pink studded with gold. On her feet were pointed shoes of deep red leather. She had gathered her hair under a coif of green linen, over which she had donned a green felt hat, the brim pulled up all around.

'Where did you find such stuff?' I asked, at the same time marvelling how she seemed able to cram pig-meat and bread into her mouth and spill nothing on her clothes: my own were lamentably spotted with grease.

'There are enough clothes on the *Cormaran* to dress the court of Sicily,' she replied. 'The Virgin alone knows where they all came from – I suppose de Montalhac gives and takes them in trade. This silk is Syrian: rare stuff to you benighted Franks, but not to me. I've been rummaging, off and on, since we left Iceland, and there's all manner of strange costumes:

Saracen, Moor, Roman, some silks so rich and wonderful even I was afraid to touch them.'

When we could not force down one more melting, silky mouthful we drained our goblets, threw some coins to the host and ducked back into the crowd outside.

I was full, fuller than I had been for months. I felt a little dizzy and a little sick, but also buoyed up on a wave of excitement, a rushing of blood about my limbs. I was breathing hard. I turned to Anna, and she met my gaze with her own level stare. I felt myself redden to the roots of my hair, and sweat broke out on my upper lip. I brushed at it distractedly. Anna rubbed a hand lazily over her greasy lips.

'Let us find a bed,' she said.

I followed her out of the street of cook-shops and into another busy thoroughfare. I had no idea where we were. The food had, it seemed, destroyed my sense of direction for the time being. No landmarks showed themselves in the narrow strip of black sky above us. Where was the Red Angel? Where, for that matter, was the river and the ship? I was lost in a strange town that had the air of an armed camp, and now, it seemed, I had to find a room in which two men could lie with each other in privacy. I needed another drink. I needed, all of a sudden, to postpone what I had yearned for since . . . since I had first heard her voice, or seen the gap in her teeth, or felt her body on mine in the warm heather. Long days of furtive touches and whispered promises in corners of the ship had not prepared me. I wished that Will were here. He, of all people, would know what to do.

'Let us follow them,' said Anna at my side. She pointed to a group of well-appointed soldiers, gentlemen to judge by their clothes and weapons, who, very drunk, were stumbling along, arms around each other's waists and shoulders, singing a lewd song I recalled from the lower taverns of Balecester.

'Those are fellows in search of a bawdy-house, or I know nothing of men,' Anna said, tugging at my sleeve. I shrugged.

'Why a bawdy-house? I do not want a trollop.' I paused; there was a choice here, and I had to make the right decision. My mouth was dry as sand.

'I want you,' I told her.

I felt as if I had stepped off a high ledge with this admission, but Anna seemed oblivious.

'Perhaps I would like a trollop myself . . . a lusty young *bravo* has such desires, you know.'

I laughed dubiously. 'You are playing games again,' I said.

'I am not! Why should you men have all the fun? I have worn breeches and pissed standing up for weeks. I am half a man now, I think. Perhaps more. Do you want to check?'

I blushed and shuffled my feet, lost for words.

'Tra la! What would be the penance for that, Petroc, my priest?'

'For sodomy? Seven years,' I muttered.

She whistled. 'Seven years without Communion. How will we stand it?' She cocked a hip and winked. 'Come along, then.' I hesitated. 'Look,' she said. 'In a brothel flesh is paid for with money. If there is gold on the table, no questions are asked. If we pay, we will get a bed. If we pay a little more, we have never been seen.'

She was right, of course. I felt my blood rise despite myself. All I wanted was Anna, but the prospect of entering one of those places . . . All Will's stories flashed through my mind. I swallowed dryly.

'After you,' I said.

The men seemed to know where they were going – at least their leader did. A stocky man who wore a short-sword and a dagger, with a long pheasant feather in his hat, he bellowed out the coarse words in a strong North Country accent, turning now and again to urge his comrades on. We hung back, although I doubted any amongst this sorry crowd would notice were they being pursued by Beelzebub himself. Anna was muttering.

'Seven years. For two men doing it? How about for two women?'

I thought back to my lessons. The *Decretum* of Burchard of Worms, a terrifyingly detailed penitentiary full of sins I had never even dreamed existed, had been drummed into us in the Abbey. Now it came flooding back.

'Seven years for doing it with beasts,' I said.

'I don't want to do it with a beast, you odd man,' Anna said.

'Five years if a woman does it with another woman, I think. A year for wanking – for women. Less for men. That's lucky,' I added. 'Let me see. Two years for adultery—'

'Oh dear.'

'—seven years if a man gives it to his wife up the arse—'

'Petroc!'

'—and for dorsal – that's with you on top – it's three years.' It felt good to rattle on like this: I was beginning to feel a little hysterical. 'From behind is three years too. And that's if we were married. Did you learn none of this when you were in Holy Orders? Now if . . .'

'We may have to keep a tally,' Anna said. 'Now be quiet, O master of penances. They're turning.'

The street we now entered was crooked and barely wide enough for the men ahead of us to squeeze through three abreast. The houses all but met overhead, and from the shadowy eaves hung lamps whose flames shone through red glass. Our quarry had burst into a new song which extolled the praises of 'Rose Street', with much play on the plucking of roses, rosy petals and sweet nectar. The voices had a more urgent tone now. Then the group halted in front of a door. The leader knocked, exchanged words through a grille. Then the men filed in. The door clicked shut behind them.

'So here we are in Rose Street,' Anna said.

'Every city has one,' I said. Balecester's own Rose Street, street of the red lamps, had been down near the Crozier, and I had studiously avoided it, of course. I heard a rapping, and turned. Anna was knocking on another door.

'What are you doing?' I hissed.

'I think this one looks promising,' she replied, and knocked again. I tried to pull her away.

'Not yet,' I said desperately.

'No time for cold feet,' she sang. 'Or rather, let me warm those cold feet for you in a nice warm bed. How many years' penance is that, by the way?'

Then the door opened a crack and a bulbous nose appeared. A man's face followed, livid with burst veins. He looked us up and down through rheumy eyes.

'Yes, noble gents?' he said at last.

'I . . .' I began.

'We seek a little sport, my good fellow,' said Anna in her deepest voice. The man's eyes narrowed. Anna tapped the purse that hung from her belt. It clanked, the smug tone of gold upon gold.

'Oh, sport! That we have, that we have, dear lords,' said the man, his face lighting up. I was afraid more veins might burst. He threw open the door and ushered us inside.

A fire burned in a big fireplace, tables were scattered about, at which a few men sat with goblets before them. Women bustled about, fetching drinks and food. We might have been in an ordinary tavern, save that the women were all naked but for the elaborate headpieces that a few wore, and which made them look even more unclothed. Some were young, some not so young. I stood as if turned to stone. So many breasts, so many bums! And that patch of hair at the base of the belly: here thick, there sparse; dark on one, fair on another.

'What's the matter, brother, never seen a naked wench before?' said Anna from the corner of her mouth.

'*No,*' I hissed. It was true. And now here were . . . how many? Ten? Twelve? I almost crossed myself, such was my agitation.

A couple of women approached and took us by the hands, exclaiming over our youth and fine clothes, almost as if we were not present. They led us to a table. Anna ordered wine, and drew two bezants from her purse.

'Take these to your mistress,' she said, 'and say that we desire to speak to her.'

We sat back and sipped our wine. The fire was warm and its light danced over the bare flesh of the women. Anna and I slipped into a conversation that had nothing to do with anything, a comfortable chewing-over of some minor event back on the *Cormaran*. We would break off now and again to admire our hosts, and I found the sensation of Anna watching me watching the whores oddly arousing. I thought of Burchard, and how one of his strictures governed masturbation with the aid of a pierced wooden board. Twenty days on bread and water for that. It struck me with crystal certainty that Burchard must have had leanings, of a lewd nature, towards wood. To him a carpenter's shop had been a brothel. I burst out laughing, a lovely warm laugh that started deep within and seemed to swell my soul until it burst free of all the dark, dismal threads stitched into it by Burchard and all his grim, cheerless crew. I threw back my head and hooted at the ceiling.

'What's the matter, my love?' Anna asked, a flicker of worry in her face.

'Nothing. Nothing in the world, my love.'

When the madam arrived, a large, fully clothed personage with the apple cheeks of a farmer's wife and the gimlet eyes of a usurer, Anna came straight to business.

'My friend and I are here under false pretences, my good woman,' she said. 'I told your doorman we were after some sport. Indeed we are, but we play the Game, and fair as your girls undoubtedly are, we have other plans.'

'The Game, eh?' said the madam, crossing her arms and regarding us with pursed lips. Then understanding dawned. 'A couple of ganymedes! Boys, boys, what are you doing here?

There are plenty of bath-houses near the cathedral. You are wasting your money, and my time.'

'Not at all,' said Anna, leaning forward. 'We have money to waste. And this city is alive with men of war who might think it a great laugh to hunt a pair of ganymedes like us. You can provide a bed and a door that locks, and we will pay you over the odds for it. And who knows? Maybe we will feel the urge to convert, and you can send a brace of your fairest wenches up to us.'

The madam pondered. Then she smiled, almost warmly.

'Oh, well . . . and why not? I've always had a soft spot for your kind, after all. There's a couple of girls upstairs already. If you go up now, no one will bat an eyelash.'

She reached deep into her bodice and thrust a warm key into my hand. 'Fourth room off the second landing,' she whispered loudly, and winked. 'You naughty young things – and so handsome! What a waste, eh? I'll bring up some wine myself, shall I? Well, get along with you!'

We grabbed up our goblets and the flagon and picked our way through the whores to the stairs. Anna went up first. I lifted her tunic as she climbed. Her bottom swayed before me, wrapped tight in white breeches and framed by the dark hose. She reached up and undid her hair and it fell about her shoulders like a storm cloud.

The hallway was dim. Regular grunts and squeals came from behind the first door. A woman sang in the second room, a low, soft song, the words unclear. Silence behind the third door, and then our room. In a frenzy I grappled with the handle. A single candle burned inside. I kicked the door shut with my heel. The crash brought me to my senses: here we were at last. Here *I* was, after weeks of longing and a lifetime of confused and guilty lust. I stood, feeling like a lump of stone, as Anna skipped to the big, crudely carved bed, unbuckling her belt as she went. The sword clattered on the floor.

'Come to me, my love,' she said hoarsely, fingers nimble at the ties of her tunic. Then in one great swoop of her arms she threw it off and it collapsed slowly on the dusty floor. There she sat, her skin very white between the darkness of her hair and the green of her hose. Still whiter was the band of linen that wrapped her chest. She dropped her head to her shoulder and regarded me. All at once her face seemed not her own, suffused by a heat and a hunger that set my own face burning. I took a step back towards the door.

'What is it, Petroc?' she asked, her voice tight.

My stomach was clenched. My skin crawled and burned and I blushed so hard I felt heat crackle from my hair. Desire, it seemed, felt like plain terror. All at once I felt my hands rise and touch, palm to palm, a reflex forgotten all these long months. In confusion I pushed them against me and felt my heart beating itself against its cage.

'I do not know what to do,' I said at long last.

My eyes met hers and we stood, locked, my heart counting out the eternity of my shame. Then Anna's face softened and she began to smile. She reached out her hands to me.

'All you need do is come here to me, my lovely man.'

And so I did, almost tripping in the folds of Anna's tunic, and sat beside her on the bed. I was shivering as if with an ague, and she pulled me to her, holding me tight and tighter until the fit had passed. Then without words she unbuckled my belt and, as if undressing a child, pulled my tunic over my head.

'Now,' she murmured, taking my hands and guiding them back to where the linen was knotted behind her. I tugged and an end came free. Anna raised her arms and slowly I unwound the long band until it fell away and we embraced, warm skin against warm skin at last. Then I was myself again, and the dance of our hands, as we untied laces and garters and found the places hidden beneath, did not seem strange any more. We fell back on the raddled old bed and I let my world become

Anna: her hair, her scent, freckles that came and went in the candlelight, flesh that rose and puckered to my wondering touch. And so we drifted until we found where the heat of our two bodies and souls could safely burn, the refiner's fire of life and love.

Some time later, Anna stirred, her face still deep in a pillow.
  'How much was that worth, penance-wise, Brother Petroc?'
  'Three years, my child. At the very least.'

Chapter Fifteen

The candle had burned down until the wick floated in a pool of tallow, guttering. Anna and I lay and watched the mothy shadows flitter about the rafters. We had taken the trouble to strip, eventually, and now a scratchy, smelly coverlet kept the chill from our skin.

'If my uncle could see us now . . .' said Anna, wriggling against me.

'The Emperor? What would he do?' I replied, lazily.

'He would make you stare at a white-hot iron until you were blind. Then he would have you castrated. Then he would lock you away somewhere, blind and ball-less, and let you think about matters. Then he would have you strangled.'

'Oh.'

'He would do the same to me, minus the castration of course. If that makes you feel any better.'

'I can't say that it does.'

'Don't trouble yourself, my precious love. I am not going to tell him. Are you?'

'Just as long as it doesn't come up at my next audience with him.'

She cackled. 'He thinks I'm dead, of course.'

I stared at the struggling candlelight playing along a beam. Someone had tried to paint a lewd scene on it, but had given up half-way. I could make out the odd breast here and there in the scrawl of flaking pink paint, and a man's face, the eyes bulging in a ludicrous portrayal of ecstasy. I hoped I hadn't been making that face earlier.

Earlier, as I made love to the niece of the Emperor of Byzantium. And as she made love to me. The immensity of it hit me like a stone from a sling. I, Petroc of Auneford, renegade monk, outlaw and accused murderer, sheep-farmer's son from the peaty wastes of Dartmoor. How had this come to pass? The Emperor's niece! Somehow I had put that fact from my mind. The thin, hollow-eyed creature whom the crew knew as the boy Mikal had simply become my dearest friend.

And now we were sated, lying warm against each other. I turned and brushed my hand down her breast to her belly, feeling goose bumps start at my touch. I ran my fingers along the edge of the springy curls below her navel, which now I knew smelled of gillyflowers, Anna's true scent, but more powerful here. I pushed my nose into the softer hair on the pillow, and closed my eyes. Her lips found mine and we kissed, soft and quiet. I felt the heat of her skin seep into mine and found I cared nothing for Anna the Emperor's niece. It was this Anna, the girl of flesh and hot, wild blood, who lived inside me now, and she would never leave so long as I still drew breath.

'Your nose is cold,' I said.

She rose up on one elbow and looked down on me. A breast fell free of the coverlet, the nipple almost black in the shadows.

'Well, my ganymede, are you ready to kill Mikal?' she said.

We decided that it would be better to leave the brothel as men, if only to avoid more questions. Although Anna had said that her uncle believed her as good as dead, I noticed that a new caution – the merest tint, like a drop of dye in clear water – had entered her mood. Perhaps she had realised only now that she was back in the civilised world, and that someone as powerful as her uncle – let alone her erstwhile husband – could have ears and eyes in a big port like Bordeaux. A bold sodomite who suddenly became a noble lady would be something that was remembered, even in a place such as this.

So we dressed and made our way downstairs. It was the dead of the night, just after the watch had rung four bells, and the house was quiet, but not silent. The sounds of rut still came from the room by the landing. Downstairs only two women were still awake, and they had thrown on some clothes. A man sat slumped at one of the tables and tried to fondle one of them, but he was very drunk and could do no more than pluck pathetically at her rumpled shift. Only the bulbous-nosed doorman noticed us. He unlatched the door and accepted a small gold coin with a simper empty of sincerity. It was clear that we disgusted him. That a man who made his living in a place like this could allow himself the luxury of disgust made me smile, and I laid a hand, deliberately, on his shoulder.

'Thank you, good fellow. I look forward to seeing you again very soon.'

He tried to shake me off while still appearing obsequious, but it was an ugly performance. I was glad when the door closed and left us alone in the street. It was very cold and dark, and reeked of beery piss.

We needed to find some abandoned place where Anna could change into her woman's garb. Now that we were alone in the cold, I wanted it done and over with. We had to get back to the ship and face the wrath of Elia and Pavlos, if indeed they had yet woken. I wished we had changed in the brothel after all. That foul old goblin of a doorman wouldn't have noticed or cared, surely? Where would we go now?

'Could you not just slip whatever clothing you have over your tunic and hose?' I ventured. 'Who would know?'

'*I* would,' she said, firmly. 'Mikal is finished. I want no more of him. I feel my womanhood rushing through me, which is all your fault, by the way.'

'Well then, what now?'

'Let's find a nice church,' said Anna.

It wasn't a bad idea. There would be no one about in a small church at this hour, and the doors would not be locked. St

Pierre was close to the Great Gate, but was big enough to perhaps have a verger in attendance. But I remembered a smaller church in its own square a little further in to the heart of the town. That would have to do.

I thought I could remember how to get back to the cathedral, which I believed was at the opposite end of the town from the river. If we kept the west door of the cathedral to our backs and followed the inner wall of the town, we should arrive at the wharf before long. But we needed to hurry and to be cautious, for now we were breaking the curfew, and would have to keep a sharp eye out for the Watch. I told this to Anna, and she gave me a crooked grin and rattled her sword. I did not find this a comfort, but kept my thoughts to myself.

It was easy to find the street of the cook-shops from the trails of bread, bones and vomit that led to it from all points of the compass. We crept past the shuttered storefronts that had been so full of life and cheer just a little time past. From there I tried to remember the twists and turns we had taken. After finding a couple of dead ends and streets we had no recollection of, we burst into a square, from which we could see the cathedral spire looming off to our right. Soon we were back beneath the scaffolding around the door.

'Why not in here?' hissed Anna. I remembered the last time I had been inside a great cathedral such as this. Nothing, not the foulest demons of hell clacking red hot pincers, could drive me into such a place again. I shook my head and led the way to the west door. Sure enough, the old wall of the town stretched away before us. It would be easy to find our way from here. We set off once again, keeping to the thickest shadows and stepping lightly.

The church of St Projet was smaller than St Pierre, and the square it stood in was smaller too. We padded around the dark shell until we reached the door. I tried it: it was unlocked, and we stepped into the dim, candlelit nave. The place smelled like all churches: old stone, polished wood and incense. We listened, our ears pricking like hounds, but there was no one there. I noticed that some of the candles before the various altars had long since burned out. A verger would have relit them. We would be alone for another hour or so.

It was a grand place, in its way. Enough wealthy families had lavished money on altars and tombs and windows to fill the modest space with carved wood and stone, gleaming plate and brass. Nevertheless I felt the same hollowness within that had come to me first in Gardar, and I almost turned on my heel and walked out. Instead I muttered to Anna that we should be quick as lightning.

A door led up to the bell-tower, and it was not locked. We slipped through it and pulled it to behind us, leaving a narrow crack through which I could see the main entrance. Behind me, Anna unbuckled her sword-belt and sank down onto the steps that wound up into the spider-guarded shadows. I heard the sough and hiss of doffed clothing, and a faint Greek oath directed at an over-tight knot. Two clinks as her garters dropped onto stone.

She was leaning back on silk-draped steps, her body glimmering, pearl-like, in the faint candle-glow from beyond the door. I looked from her face to the darkness between her legs, sprawled wantonly. Into the cold air crept the scent of gillyflowers. And then for a timeless instant I was back in Balecester, in the church of Saints Sergius and Bacchus. The painted hell had blossomed into life. The pink, naked house-wives pranced as the devils jabbed away with their toasting-forks, but I saw that the points were soft and gave delight, not pain. All these jolly folk, ladies and devils, romped and laughed until all were entwined in a heaving, happy knot, and dissolved before my eyes.

Anna was rummaging in her satchel, pulling out pieces of clothing and strewing them on the stairs. I gathered up an armful of her nobleman's costume and began to fold it, running the fiery silk of Anna's tunic through my fingers. How immediate were the pleasures of the senses, but how real also. The church, I now realised, was a place of beauty. I could admit that much to myself. It had given delight to those who had built it and wrought its fine decorations, the delight of creation, the delight that the eyes and hands convey to the heart. That delight, it seemed to me now, was enough, all, perhaps, that we earthly beings had a right to expect. The glow of love was still upon me, and joy still flowed through my limbs. How many times had I knelt on cold stone in a place like this and waited in vain for some divine sensation to flood me? And now it had happened.

Anna had put on a long, tight-sleeved tunic of deep-blue silk and drawn a sleeveless surcoat of deep red over it. Her back was turned and when she turned back to me I gasped. I had never seen her attired as a woman, and I had never seen a woman attired as she was now. The fine ladies of Balecester had gone about like columns of drapery: elegant, modest sometimes, and often severe. But Anna was revealed as much as she was hid, at least from throat to waist. She was pushing her hair into a net of golden threads. Seeing me stare, she pouted fetchingly and twisted so that the loose folds of tunic and surcoat swirled around her legs.

'Do you like it?' she asked. I nodded. 'Venetian – the very latest style. So says de Montalhac, anyway. He picked it up in Dublin, I believe. It fits, doesn't it?' I nodded again. 'For heaven's sake, Petroc. You look thunderstruck. Have you never seen a lady before?'

'In truth, I never did see a lady before this moment,' I said at last.

She had thrown a green cloak around her shoulders and fastened the jewelled clasp across her breast, drawing it close. Now she picked up her sword-belt, buckled it and slung it over her left shoulder so that the point of the sword hung mid-way down her thigh. Then she swung her heavy man's cloak around her. The sword was hidden from sight.

'Can I wear your hood?' she asked. 'You can have my hat. And since I am, at long last, one of the gentler sex, you can carry my satchel as well.'

With the hood over her head, clasped tight beneath her chin, she was all but masked. I put on the green hat, feeling a little ridiculous. 'If you are ready, we had better go,' I said.

We crept back across the aisle and peered round the main door. There was no one in the square, so we slithered out and hurried into the shadows. There was no light yet in the sky, no false dawn. We still had time.

We walked as before, slipping from shadow to shadow, slinking over cross-streets, keeping silent. I calculated that we had only a little way to go. I saw St Pierre before us, and surely that must be the bulk of the Great Gate away in the distance? I took Anna's hand and quickened my pace.

We crossed over another street and heard loud voices and singing not so far away. Anna squeezed my hand. 'That's good,' I muttered. 'They will draw the Watch.'

We had reached the next line of buildings when Anna tripped over something and cursed softly. From the doorway of the shuttered house came a loud rasping and scuffling. I pulled Anna to me and was about to set off running, believing we had disturbed a dog or worse, a sleeping pig, when a voice, the slur of Bristol made thicker with drink, lashed out of the darkness.

'Bloodworm!'

The bowman from the wharf stepped out. The rasping had been the iron-bound haft of his axe scraping on the doorstep. Now he clasped it and half-drew it from his belt. His other hand was on his misericorde dagger. Whatever entertainment the night had held for him had not improved his visage. Behind him another form stepped out, and another.

'I've my mates with me now, little boy, and you have only your tart.'

'What is it, Benno?' The second man was a bowman too

from his leather wrist-guards. He wore a short-sword. The third man had a nail-studded cudgel already swinging in his hands.

'It's the little foreign sodomite who I was telling you about. And a whore. You little prick! Where are your lovely friends now, eh?'

'I don't know what you mean,' I said. My mouth was bone-dry. I felt Anna's hand slip from mine.

'You do. You know what I mean,' said the bowman. 'I mean this.' And he pulled axe and dagger from his belt with an ape-like jerk. The other man's sword scraped from its sheath. Not oiled for a spell, I thought, with a part of my mind that seemed already to be leaving my body. The other part had, it seemed, taken over, and I found I was holding Thorn against my leg as I had earlier, when Anna had played her game with me. Then I was entirely there again. I saw that Benno wore a thick old leather jerkin and some sort of padded under-tunic. His mate with the sword wore a sheepskin surcoat. The third man had a mailed hood pushed down around his neck.

'Come on then, you little shit,' croaked Benno.

'Anna, run for the boat,' I yelled, and, tearing my cloak from my shoulders, wrapped it around my left arm with a couple of flicks. But Anna did not run.

'Leave us be, filth,' she said, and her voice was as cold as the Sea of Darkness.

'Ho ho!' cackled the man with the sword. 'Hark to your mouth! When we're done with your precious little customer I'll put that mouth to use, darling.'

Benno rolled his shoulders and drew a deep breath. It was coming. I settled myself on my feet and brought Thorn up, loose at the end of a straight arm, as Rassoul had taught me.

'Run, Anna!'

But it was too late. The three stepped towards us in one movement. With a sudden shout, Benno swung his axe. I stepped back and stooped to get inside his reach. And then the axe was no longer in his hand, but jumping away down the cobblestones. Pale light seemed to shoot out of his throat, but it was Anna's sword, and she held him upright on its tip as the blood poured down the blade and onto her hand. Then she jerked it out and Benno's life hissed wetly out of the hole and away into the darkness above us. He tottered, and sat down suddenly on his arse. Then he was on his back, his eyes as blind as boiled eggs. His friends stopped. Everything stopped.

'The tart's killed Benno,' whined the cudgel-man.

'Fuck!' screamed the man with the sword, and leaped at us. Perhaps he was going for Anna, perhaps for me, but she stepped wide and he rammed me with his shoulder, spinning me round. He had his balance again, and the point of his sword was up and pointing at my chest. He stamped.

'Ha!' he yelled, and stamped again. He meant to back me against the wall and skewer me there. He lunged, and I brought up my cloak-wrapped arm like a shield. The blade caught in its folds and, twisting, I trapped it. He tried to tug it out, his eyes on Thorn, pointed now at his face, just out of my reach. With his free hand he tried to grab the blade, but I saw his move and lashed out. The blade bit between two fingers and parted his hand almost to the wrist-bone. He howled, and threw himself back, trying again to free his sword. He was strong, but the blade must have been notched, for it was held fast by the cloth. I felt the full weight of him through the sword lashed to my arm, and felt his balance go. I swung with all my might, and he staggered sideways and crashed into the wall. He let go his sword, but too late. I punched Thorn up under his breast-bone, and hit him with the length of my body. The breath burst from him, rotting teeth and rotten wine, and the stink of his sheepskin like a cloud around my face. I felt his chest convulse once, twice, and rammed the knife in harder. I wanted this to end. I wanted him to end. And with another heave he died, and slumped against me. I tugged on Thorn but the blade was stuck fast, so I stepped back and let him crash to the ground. As I stooped to take his sword I heard the scuffling of feet behind me, and a guttural curse.

Anna and the cudgel-man were circling each other in the middle of the street, some way away. She had thrown off her cloak. The man was scared, but fear was leaving him, and something like murderous amusement was taking over. I saw that he had picked up Benno's misericorde, and held it in his left hand. He seemed oblivious to me and to his friend. Anna's face was a blank. I dared not move, in case I distracted her attention. She held her sword stiff and steady. Every now and again she gave the end a flick. But I saw that her feet were in danger of being wound up in the hem of her tunic. She knew it too, for she kept her steps small and precise. The cudgel-man, though, was growing brave. He began feinting at her, now with the cudgel, now the knife, making her step back and risk a fall. All at once she seemed to decide that this must end. Waiting for a feint with the knife, she stepped to the side and flicked again with her blade. The knife-arm went limp and the man cursed and stepped backwards. Anna shifted her grip and lunged, but too far: her tunic caught at last and she sprawled.

But she still held the sword, and the man was hurt. He was not quick enough and she rose to one knee, the blade up again and pointing. And then another shape erupted from the dark side street and hurtled into the cudgel-man, who one instant was choosing his blow and the next was flat on his back. I was there in another instant, and Anna behind me, but by that time the rescuer from the shadows had stuck his thick, narrow knife through the cudgel-man's eye.

I stepped back. Anna's sword was up and ready for the stranger, who rose to his feet after working his knife back out of the dead man's skull. He wore a plain black surcoat and a hooded cape. The hood was up. He wiped the dagger on the cudgel-man's shirt.

'Turn around, if you please, friend,' said Anna, her voice as empty of friendship as the cudgel-man's body was of life.

'Certainly, my lady,' said the Northerner.

He straightened up and turned to face us, dagger carelessly dangled from loose fingers. Then he dropped it.

'For fuck's sake!' he said, and pushed back the hood with both hands.

'For . . .' he started to say again, but by that time I had him round the waist and was laughing and sobbing in turn.

When at last I was able to speak, it was to Anna.

'My love,' I said, 'Will has come back from the dead to save us: my dear friend Will.'

Will and I stood there, beyond speech, deaf to the sounds of the world. Not so Anna, to whom my friend was nothing more than a name from a long tale. She bent down and retrieved Will's dagger, pushing the hilt briskly back into his palm.

'Put your weapons away, boys,' she snapped.

I looked down at the corpse at my feet. Not much blood had flowed from his wound – the thrust had killed him outright – but the sight of one pale eye staring up beside a dark pool where its twin should be brought my own senses back. Will was staring at the other two corpses. I tottered over to the man I had killed. His lips were drawn back, and through a sheen of black blood his teeth glimmered yellow. I felt my gorge rise. Anna was looking around at the other two corpses. 'Drop that,' she ordered, pointing to the sword which dangled in my limp hand. Her own sword was already back in hiding beneath her cloak. 'There are three men dead, and we must not be here when they are discovered. Come now!' And she grabbed me by the elbows and shook hard.

'We'll drag this one into the doorway over there, next to his mate,' she said briskly. I didn't argue, and Will and I grabbed an ankle apiece. I could not help staring, a stupid grin on my face despite the horror all around, at my friend. Short minutes ago he had been as dead to me as the corpse we now hauled, skull bouncing on stone, over to where Benno lay. There was blood here, to be sure. We dumped the cudgel-man across Benno. I bent over the crumpled swordsman and pulled at Thorn. I had to put my foot on his chest and wrench the blade out. When I stood up again, Anna and Will were looking at the corpses as if they were cabbages on a market stand. 'If we hew at this fellow with the other's axe, it might seem as if they killed each other,' Will said, as if discussing a grammatical point in the Epistles. Anna was nodding thoughtfully. Then we heard footsteps and voices, and above us a rusty shutter was wrestled open.

'Leave them!' I had found my voice. 'Hurry, for God's sake – we'll be seen.'

She grabbed my hand. 'And you,' she said, turning to Will. 'Stay if you like or come with us to the river, but come now!'

I turned to Will. He cocked his head towards the fast-approaching voices. Then his face broke into the wolfish grin I remembered so well.

'The river? Let's run, then,' he said, and without another word took off down the street. Anna shoved her satchel at me. 'And there,' she hissed, pointing to where her absurd green hat lay next to the dead swordsman. I snatched it up and then we were chasing Will pell-mell along the cobbles. He ducked into another side street, still running, and we followed. Will knew his way through the maze of the city, and cut up and down three more alleys. Anna ran alongside me, her clothes hitched up around her knees. All too soon I felt my chest tighten and my limbs grow heavy. From Anna's tight grimace I knew she was flagging too. We had spent too long cramped aboard the *Cormaran*. Our limbs had all but withered on our bodies. I knew that, very soon, I would be able to run no further. Then Will ducked out of sight again, and following, we almost ran into him. He had stopped and was peering round a corner.

Looking over his shoulder, I saw we had reached a broad street at the end of which, and very near, a gate rose against the lightening sky.

'The Porte Saint Eloi,' whispered Will. 'It will be opening in a minute or so. We'll walk through nice and quietly. You two are the lord and lady, and I'm your bodyguard, just behind you with my head down. If they hail us, perhaps the lady—' and he nodded politely at Anna, '—should answer. And cover yourself up, Patch. You're a mite bloody.'

I had no idea how far we had just run, but there were no sounds of pursuit. The bodies had surely been discovered by now, though, and it would be to the gates that the Watch would first send word. We had to slip through before that happened. I looked down at myself. Dimitri would curse me for sure when he saw what I had done to my tunic. I wrapped myself in my cloak, shuddering as the blood-dampened clothing pressed against my skin. I still had Anna's hat scrunched in my fist. I hid it away in the satchel. Anna did not look like one who had just run for her life through strange alleyways. Her cheeks were alive with colour, but when she dropped the hem of her robe and drew herself up I almost gasped at the way the princess emerged from the panting fugitive. She unclasped her hood and pushed it back. Gold mesh shone against black hair. I doubted, all of a sudden, that if anyone had witnessed the fight, they would believe that this regal creature could have been within a mile of such vulgar goings-on. I hoped I looked like enough of a gentleman to be her escort. I doubted it. And Will: Will was the perfect cutthroat. I studied him for a moment. He wore a hood with a long, trailing point that hung far down his back. His black surcoat was unadorned. He wore it over a long, leather cuirass the colour of old blood that hung down to his knees. Muddy high-boots were drawn over undyed wool hose.

'What do you say, Patch?' he asked, feeling my eyes upon him.

I grabbed the front of his surcoat and shook it gently. 'You are a soldier,' I said, wondering.

'I am,' he said. 'And a sergeant-at-arms, no less. My company is the black boar, under Sir Andrew Hardie.'

'I thought you were dead, Will!' I blurted.

'Well, I *knew* you must be.' He reached out and prodded me in the stomach. 'Real enough, though,' he said. 'When Kervezey . . . But let's wait. I am a stranger to your lady, and that must be remedied.' He turned to Anna, and made a perfect courtier's bow that sent his hood flopping down over his eyes.

Anna looked at me over Will's back, her eyebrows high arches of bemused enquiry.

'Will,' I said, before he could open his mouth, 'This is Anna Doukaina Komnena, Princess Royal, niece of the Emperor John Doukas of Byzantium.'

He straightened up with a jerk and looked from Anna to me and back again, his face a study in bemusement.

'Oh, come on, Patch, I never . . .' he started, but a sound from the street behind us cut him off. There were shouts, a creaking and groaning, thuds.

Anna peeped around the corner. 'The gates are open,' she said.

'Right,' I said. They would hang us all three times over while we explained everything to each other. 'Anna, your cloak. Straighten your tunic. Can you see any blood on me? Good. Will, two paces behind, I think, don't you?'

'Right you are,' said Will. 'Give me that bag, Patch. Chin up, and act the nobleman, for Jesus' sake.'

I hooked my arm through Anna's and we stepped out into the wide street. It was decidedly lighter now, and the sky had cleared. The last stars were burning fiercely overhead, but a glow was creeping in from the east. I did raise my chin and tried to look regal. Beside me, Anna paced calmly. Her face was an utter blank. I could hear Will pad along behind us.

The gate was close. It was set in a slender tower in the city's curtain wall, a minor entryway but still guarded, I saw, by three or four helmeted men armed with halberds. A trickle of folk were already seeping in, pushing carts or staggering under sacks and bales, traders hoping to steal a march on the competition. There seemed to be no one leaving. There were four guards, I saw, sleepy and leaning on their halberds. They paid little heed to the traders, but they noticed us. The tallest straightened and nudged his fellows. I heard our shoes scrape, tap, scrape on the stones. Perhaps we could fight our way through . . . but these men were armoured. I saw mail shirts and leggings. I chewed on the inside of my cheek and prayed that I looked lordly.

As we reached the gate, the tallest guard, whom I took to be the sergeant, shouldered his halberd and stepped towards us.

'Good morrow to you, my lord, my lady,' he said. 'It is an early morning to be setting off, to be sure.'

'Early it is, but we are late,' I said, in the best French I could muster, looking at the soldier down my nose. I am decieving no one, I thought wildly to myself. And indeed the guard's look seemed to sharpen.

Just as I thought his fingers were tightening on his pikestaff, Anna swept off her hood, revealing her hair in its golden prison. In the half-dawn her skin was very white.

'Do they presume to bandy words with you, my lord?' she asked me, turning her head deliberately from the guards.

'So it seems,' I said. Anna's gaze was drilling into me. I understood what was required.

'We have no time to waste with fools,' I barked. 'You will bow down before the Princess Doukaina Komnena, and keep your eyes on the ground where they belong as we pass by.'

The sergeant stared, slack-jawed, at Anna. She did not flinch, but drew her right hand slowly from her cloak. For a horrible moment I thought she was drawing her sword. But instead she held out her hand to the man. On her third finger, huge and heavy, was a ring I had never seen before. The man gawped at it, and dropped to his knees with a crunch of chain-mail. The others, watching, followed suit.

'Your pardon, Highness,' he mumbled. 'My men are good boys, and this is only the Porte Saint Eloi – we don't get . . .' The poor man was almost wringing his hands. 'We beg your forgiveness.'

And so we passed through, killers, defilers of churches, fornicators and outlaws, as armed men grovelled in the dung. I felt their eyes on our backs as we paced on, turning to our right towards the grander turrets of the Porte de Cailhau. There was a wide open space before us, over which a few figures were moving. A little way ahead, tents had sprung up and men were milling about, lighting fires and coughing noisily. Beyond them the wharves began. I could barely keep my steps even as we strolled over the well-trodden marsh-grass, breathing in the soft air of morning and the salt of the Gironde. It seemed like a thousand years before we reached the clutch of tents and passed among them. Will was at my side at once.

'That was well done, my boy,' he said. I saw that he was as white as a sheet, but still grinning. 'It was lovely, the way those bastards got down in the stink.'

'We aren't safe yet,' I muttered.

'From them we are,' he replied. 'They won't say a solitary word about this to anyone. They're town men. If the town got wind that they'd shamed a great lady and her retinue, there would be whippings all round. No, they'll keep mum.'

'Not much of a retinue, though,' I said. 'They must have been suspicious of us on foot – Anna should have been aboard a snow-white palfrey at the very least.'

'And I on a mule, I suppose,' said Will. 'No, we fooled everyone. By the way, I forgot to tell you about the crossbow-men. Two at least, above the gate in the tower. I'll bet their eyes were out on stalks.'

'Crossbowmen?' Anna and I said together.

'They clean slipped my mind,' Will said happily. Then his face grew serious. 'Your Highness, you truly are . . . a princess?'

She fixed Will with her most imperious stare, the one that could reduce Pavlos to tears. Then she smiled. 'I am. And you, if my guess is right, are a Northumbrian. Alnwick?'

'Morpeth,' stammered Will, aghast. 'How on earth . . . ?'

'I am a princess,' she said, happily.

Will was still gawping, so I linked arms with him as I had done so many times in another life. 'She is indeed a princess,' I explained, 'But she had English guards – what do you call them, Anna? Valerians?'

'Varangians, idiot,' she laughed.

'Anyway, she speaks better English than . . . than you, certainly, you sheep-shagger.'

'Christ!' muttered Will, awestruck. I had never seen him so amazed and, feeling a great surge of joy, I grabbed Anna with my other arm and, three abreast, we tripped through the dewy grass like milkmaids on their way to the fair.

When we were beyond the tents and breathing a little more easily, Anna picked up her trailing hems and I pushed back my hood. The day was arriving, and the sun crept up behind us and flooded the river with gold. We were coming to a part of the wharf I recognised. There were the sea-steps where the long-boat had dropped us off yesterday. This was the spot where the bowman had run into Anna. A wave of nausea hit me suddenly, and I put my hand on Anna's shoulder. Beyond the nausea I felt a black cloud of guilt, of horror, crawling towards me. I looked out into the river. There was the *Cormaran*, radiant in the new light. And there, sitting on the sea-steps, were Pavlos and Elia, with the long-boat bobbing below them.

Pavlos saw us first. He leaped to his feet, almost lost his footing on the slimy weed, and staggered up onto the wharf. His face looked like a skull, so dark were the hollows around his eyes, put there by worry and, I had no doubt, the work of the poppy. Never taking his eyes from Anna, he reeled towards us and threw himself to the ground at her feet. He seemed to be trying to kiss her shoes. Anna tried to pull them away.

'*Vassileia*! Before the *Panayia* I beg you, forgive your servant Pavlos . . . I have abandoned you like a Judas! False friend and false servant! Holy mother and all the holy saints believe me, I . . .'

'Come now, Pavlos,' said Anna, in the tone that I had come to think of as her *Vassileia* voice – regal and a trifle exasperated. 'Let us put it from our minds. You must have been tired, dear man. But I was in good hands, and quite safe. You are quite forgiven. Let us put it from our minds and never speak of it again.' And she patted him on the head. He looked up adoringly and only then did he notice Will.

My friend was standing at my side, staring unconcernedly out to sea. He saw Pavlos jump to his feet and turned to face him with a look I had never seen before: blandly pleasant with an inner flickering of alertness, even menace. He gave Pavlos a curt nod.

'G'morrow,' he said.

Pavlos narrowed his eyes. The same dangerous flicker played over his face. 'Who are you, then, my friend?' he asked.

I hastily laid a hand on Will's shoulder, as if to claim him. 'Pavlos, it has been a night of horrors and wonders, but there has never been a wonder like this: my greatest friend in the world, whom I saw die, has returned to life. This is William of Morpeth, former scholar and cleric, now . . . what would you call yourself, Will?'

'Hungry!' he said, and the spell was broken. The Greek smiled a little, then held out his hand. To my enormous relief Will took it and gave it a good warm shake. 'To answer Patch's question properly, I would call myself a soldier, which is what I take you for, friend Pavlos.'

'Returned from the dead? Is this so?' Pavlos asked. Will

chuckled. The Greek was opening his satchel and offering Will a hunk of bread. I let out a deep sigh and looked about me. Elia peered sheepishly over the edge of the dock. Anna waved regally in his direction. It was rather dreadful to see his face light up. I walked carefully over to the sea-wall and sat down, dangling my legs over the edge. The memory of the swordsman's innards clenching and unclenching around my blade had come back to me unbidden, and for a moment I felt faint. What had I done? I looked at my hands and they were streaked and stained with red. My fingernails were black. I wanted to wash them, but the wall was too high, so I tucked them beneath my legs instead. The sharp brine-soaked air felt clean and reviving, and in a few moments I could look at the *Cormaran* in the distance without the urge to puke.

'You do not look well, my friend,' said Elia from the gig. I shook my head.

My mind was starting to turn again, slowly, and I forced myself to think. There must be witnesses to the fight, although would the deaths of three murderous rogues cause any great upset? I must talk to the Captain, and soon, I decided, and stood up.

'Pavlos,' I said, 'There is something you must know. Hardly an hour ago, the lady Anna and I were attacked by . . . three men, English archers. One of them was the fellow who had words with us last morning. They are dead. Anna – I mean the *Vassileia* – killed one, I another, Will the last. We ran, but we must, *must* have been seen. The gatemen did not suspect us and dared not obstruct the princess. But there will surely be a hue and cry. I think we should make our way back to the *Cormaran* now, if we can.'

As I said my piece, Pavlos' eyes had widened, then narrowed. Now he looked me up and down, and I believe I saw something like admiration in his stare.

'Killed, you say,' he snapped. 'You know this?'

'Yes,' I nodded.

'Where were they wounded? Tell me quick.'

'One in the throat, one in the chest, one in the eye.'

'The chest-wound – he died?'

'Yes . . . he died.'

'You are sure.'

'I am sure.'

'Why? Hard to be sure, with a chest-wound.'

'Because,' I said through clenched teeth, the sickness rising once again from my stomach, 'I cut him all to pieces inside. I felt him die.'

Pavlos nodded, all business. 'The eye – he was dead.'

'For certain,' said Will, cheerfully.

'You are sure?'

Will shrugged. 'I stirred his brains around a bit.'

'Good lad. And the throat?' Pavlos cocked his head at Anna.

'Oh, yes,' said Anna.

'I am sorry, *Vassileia*. But it is important that none of these creatures lived, even for a little while, to tell tales. And . . . Petroc said you killed him, this bowman?' It was plain he did not believe that such a thing might be possible.

'She did, Pavlos. One thrust. And fought the other like a . . .' I paused. I had been about to say 'like a man', but that seemed, I thought, inadequate. She had fought like a flame, like an archangel with a fiery sword. 'She is a warrior,' I said instead. 'Truly.'

'*Vassileia*?' asked Pavlos.

Anna shrugged. 'I was raised by our Varangians,' she said. 'You know that. They let me watch while they trained. I would join in. They thought I showed promise, I suppose, so they taught me.'

'I knew many Varangians,' said Pavlos, wistfully.

'My fencing master was a Hereford man,' said Anna. 'Fourth son of a knight. The best swordsman in Greece – his name was John de Couville.'

'Eh!' gasped Pavlos, crossing himself. 'Kovils! *He* taught

227

you? *Po po po . . .*' He ran a thumb back and forth across his mouth.

'The sun is getting high,' prompted Anna. Pavlos dragged his hand across his eyes, and looked up. He was smiling – faintly and with a certain lack of conviction, but smiling nonetheless.

'Well, my *Vassileia*,' he said, 'perhaps some fencing lessons? If, that is, you are taking on new pupils.' He blinked like an owl in the daylight, and we blinked back at him in surprised relief. 'Meanwhile, back to the ship with us all, before difficult questions are asked.' He paused and turned to Will, then jerked his chin up and regarded him down the length of his lordly nose. 'And you. What shall we do with you, O risen one?'

'He cannot stay here,' I said. 'He will be pursued along with us. They will kill him if he does not come with us on the *Cormaran*.'

'They?' Pavlos said, sharply. It was incredible that he could be so unbelievably, terrifyingly calm. I waved my hand frantically towards the walls. 'The Watch,' I almost yelled. Pavlos rubbed his red-rimmed eyes in exasperation, then pressed his hands to his forehead.

'I cannot . . . Come, then. You will talk to the Captain and he will decide. Now we will go. Now!' And he snapped his fingers at Elia, who began to pull the gig in towards the wharf. Will turned to me, his face slack with relief.

As the drug-fuddled Greeks dipped and pulled their oars, a great joy at being free and alive rushed over me. I glanced over at Anna and caught her eye, then Will's, and then we were laughing with sheer relief, as Bordeaux drew away from us and the sun warmed our faces.

The reckoning I feared never came. We were not even late back, I realised, and there were bloody, bruised faces aplenty amongst the crew who had returned before us. Mirko had his arm in a sling, and one of the Italians seemed to be missing an ear. I thought I would puke on the scrubbed deck as Pavlos reported to the Captain, who merely looked at us over the Greek's slumped shoulder. When he strolled over, it was merely to shake me by the arm in an almost fatherly way.

'Where did you find her, Pavlos?' There was a commotion behind me. Anna stood in a circle of crewmen, Pavlos at her side like the palace guard he was. She seemed to have grown – she rose above the men like a huntsman among a pack of hounds. How gnarled and villainous they seemed in comparison, jostling and nudging one another as they crowded round, uncertain what to make of this radiant apparition. I knew, though, that they could not be happy. Women aboard a ship: it was bad luck, it meant trouble. The men, ragged, mauled and hung-over from their night ashore, were not in the best of tempers. They were turning into a mob. Pavlos' knuckles were beginning to whiten around the pommel of his sword as I elbowed my way to his side, but then Anna's voice, clear and deep, froze us in place.

'Well, O Stefano, did you find your plump Spanish girl, your little Cabretta? By your sour face I would guess not. And Carlo, what happened to your ear? Did you hear Dimitri's confession?'

The bark from the back of the crowd was Dimitri's laugh. The one-eared master-at-arms was forever making as if to whisper secrets to us, then grabbing the proffered ear in his teeth and growling like, as he put it, a hungry Tartar. Stefano had a taste for a certain type of women he called his 'little goats'. And Carlo was a defrocked priest from Ancona who had killed his mistress's lover in a duel after fate had brought the man to his confessional.

'Who is she, Pavlos? She knows us,' said Horst.

'A sorceress!' hissed Guthlaf.

'Right enough – put her over the side,' called Latchna, the sailmaker from Galway.

'Oh, silence, Lak! You're still sour because you missed your cockfight in Dublin,' Anna shot back.

'You go over the side, Lak, you fucking seamstress,' growled Dimitri. 'Let the woman be.'

I saw that half the men were simply enthralled by Anna and gawped like netted carp. Others clearly wished to make her acquaintance in the usual ungentle ways, but a few, those like Guthlaf, who were born to the sea and knew it as their only home, were truly angry and frightened to the same degree. Superstition runs as deep as the dark ocean in the lives of sailors, and their worlds can be as small as the curved walls of their ship. To them, Anna might be a woman, but she might also be a thing from that place where the cold tide rolls drowned men's bones forever over black sand. It was clearly not something they felt like chancing.

'Who is she?' Horst demanded.

'The Princess Anna Doukaina Komnena of the house of Nicea, under the Captain's protection and mine,' said Pavlos, coolly.

'I am she,' said Anna, catching her hair and pulling it tight behind her head. 'But you know me already.'

The crowd went dead quiet. Guthlaf's jaw hung open like a broken shutter. Then Dimitri's harsh laughter grated over us.

'Mikal? My God, boy, what have they done to you?'

The tension broke in an instant as one by one, the crew caught on and began to smile, then laugh. Pavlos caught my eye and we grinned queasily. But it seemed that, although the joke was on them, the men were finding it hilariously funny. They swarmed around us, eagerly staring into Anna's face for a glimpse of their favourite Basque castaway.

'What a boy you made,' they cried. 'And what a sailor! Come back to us, princess, come back to us!'

Anna was laughing too. She held out her hands, and her rings flashed and sparkled. 'You taught me well, friends, and made me welcome – the warmest welcome I have had for . . . for many a year. I cannot be Mikal again, alas – I cannot bind my chest a day longer, for one thing. But I will be Anna, if our Captain doesn't object.'

'I have no objections,' said the Captain. 'You do us honour with your presence, *Vassileia*, and you, men of the *Cormaran*, should be glad of it: it seems this lady can swing a sword as well as she can reef in a sail. Now back to work, boys. We sail in an hour. There is too much trouble in this town for us, and we have trouble to make elsewhere.'

He turned and walked back towards his cabin, pausing at my shoulder.

'A word, if you please, Petroc.'

So I had not escaped after all. With a stricken glance at Will I dragged myself after him like a hog to the butchering table. He closed the door behind me and motioned me to a chair while he paced.

'Pavlos has told me what happened. Now I will hear it from you.'

So I told him. You could not lie to the Captain – that is to say, I could not. He wanted details about the men who had confronted us on the riverside, and who we had seen in the city. To my great relief he made me gloss over the night's revelries – 'your affair and yours only' – but I had the uncomfortable feeling that he knew everything. Meanwhile, he drew forth every last shred I could give him of the fight, and I forced the tale from me, shuddering and queasy with the telling of it.

'These were Englishmen, you say.'

'Yes, sir. Rough bowmen.'

'Did they bear any crest, any insignia?'

'None. Though one was from Bristol, I would swear.'

'Mercenaries, very likely. That would make sense. And none escaped you?' I shook my head. 'That is good. You did well. Are you worried about consequences? Do not be. There was more blood spilt last night than at your hand.'

'What do you mean?'

'Two other parties of my men were attacked by men such as you met, and . . .'

'I saw Mirko.'

'Mirko had his arm shattered by a stave. He was carousing with Jens and Hanno. You will not see Jens again, alas.'

'Jens . . .'

'They cut his throat. Mirko was lucky: Hanno did for the one with the stave. The others – English, all of them – got away. And Gilles had a small set-to also. An Englishman tried to stick him with a poignard. This was at midnight near the cathedral.'

'Is he hurt?'

'Gilles? No, no. The man with the knife . . . the city fathers will be scratching their beards today over a pile of dead Englishmen, it is certain.' He fell silent, and suddenly his gaze was eating into me like vitriol. 'This William, this miraculous, resurrected savior, is the friend you thought Kervezey had killed, yes?' I nodded, dumbly. 'Yet he is alive, and in Bordeaux, and at the right spot to be of service to you and the Princess Anna. Do you know how that might be possible?'

I shook my head. Looking up, I met the Captain's eyes.

'He was following us. So he says, and I believe him. He was roving – that is his nature – and thought he glimpsed me. Thinking he had seen a ghost, he trailed us through the streets, and . . . As he said, he was not the only rogue abroad that night.'

If anything, the Captain's stare grew more intense, and he leaned towards me like a great, hungry bird of prey. I felt like Saint Bartholomew, slowly flayed alive.

'In that great city of – what? Ten thousand souls, he found you?'

'He is a mercenary, sir! The city is full of them. The Company of the Boar's Head . . . no, the Black Boar – he serves with them. He's been here for weeks. And he's no respecter of curfews or nightwatchmen, and . . .' I swallowed.

'. . . He chases whores. I know Will as if he were my own brother, sir. Again, I swear that he saved us.'

'That at least is clear. But not much else is. It seems that none of this was accidental, does it not? Someone was having the riverside watched – by your bowman, among others. And then some – perhaps all – who came ashore from the *Cormaran* were followed.'

'But we met those men by chance. Anna actually stumbled over one of them.'

'There was nothing of chance about it. Think. Bordeaux is a big town, and full of soldiers. What kind of coincidence would it be to run into this same fellow, in the dead of night, and him with armed and willing friends?'

'A very ill-mannered one, to be sure.'

'So you begin to see. We were expected, and traps were set. Not for you in particular, Patch, but for anyone from the *Cormaran*. And there is more. The client I came to see could not receive me, and my other business . . . I was to meet a friend I had great need of talking to, and he was not there. Indeed he was long gone. And that is why we are leaving immediately.'

'Who is behind this, do you know?'

'I do not know; I suspect.'

'And Will? We cannot leave him here!'

The Captain sighed, mildly, as if someone had told him that his dinner would be a little late. 'I need to have a very long talk with Master Will,' he said. 'He was a scholar, like you. I would like to hear him discourse on the nature of coincidence.'

I dropped my head into my hands. Would I find peace ever again? I felt as if my skull was cracking like a clay pot filled with hot embers. I had killed a man. Anna and I . . . I could not think of that now. And Will. I wished the deck would open and let me drop down into the cold, deep darkness of the river. Then I felt the Captain's hand on my shoulder once more.

'Peace, Patch. I believe you. Your friend has an honest face. A very villainous face, to be sure, but honest. He will tell me his tale, and perhaps we will know a little more. But one thing I know: someone is trying to take over our business. I have been feeling it for a while now, more intuition than certainty. Then I had some news in Dublin: enquiries were being made about us. My contacts there were uncomfortable, and I decided then to press on for Bordeaux. Sometimes troubles like that disappear of their own accord, but now . . .'

He stood up suddenly and stretched, pressing his palms against the dark wood of the ceiling. Towering above me, he seemed to fill the cabin.

'Now cheer up, Petroc my friend,' he said, briskly. 'At least this time we are sailing towards the sun.'

Chapter Sixteen

I brushed shoulders with Will as I emerged, blinking like
Lazarus, from the Captain's lair. Gilles had him by the arm
and was leading him through the door. He had time to wink at
me, for all the world as if he were going for a tutorial with
some fat old Latin master. The door clicked shut ominously
behind them. Out here the sun was quite high, and the
Cormaran was slipping down the Gironde, Bordeaux dropping
away behind. The kites were already wheeling above the
towers. It looked a lovely place today, warm and golden in the
sunlight, and it was strange to think corpses lay in its alleys,
black clots fouling the stones. Anna was nowhere to be seen,
and I guessed she had taken refuge below. My innards were
not right and my skin prickled with a nasty, hot sweat. I hauled
up a bucket of river water and set to work scouring the blood
from my hands and arms. Then I stripped and found that even
my breechclout was bloody. I scrubbed every inch of naked
skin and put on my old sailing clothes. My beautiful silk tunic,
all stiff with dried gore, I gathered into a ball and dropped
overboard. No doubt Dimitri could resurrect it once again but
too much had soaked into its beautiful threads, first my blood
and now a man's whole life. It unravelled and found its shape
again on the surface, bleeding a dark stain that gathered
around it like a thundercloud. As I watched it drift away, I
heard a breath behind me.

It was Anna. She was still in her finery, but she had thrown
her cloak about her and held it close, although the day was
growing hot. Her face was ashen. Great shadows wreathed her

eyes, and her lips were dry and pale. I had a great desire to take her in my arms, but I imagined – imagined more than felt – the eyes of the crew upon me and so instead I attempted to look respectful, like the humble sailor I was, greeted by a great lady. I believe that Anna would have been quick to shake me from my stupidity had she not been somewhat stupefied herself by all that had happened, but instead she drew back a little.

'How does it go with you, Patch?' she asked, shyly: a voice I had not heard before.

'It goes better. Better, now that I have scoured every speck, every mote of last night from me,' I said, without thinking.

'Every trace of last night?'

'Everything,' I said passionately. It was true: I had been desperate to free myself from the blood that had drenched me, dry and flaking where it had dried on my face and hands, still horribly wet where it had run under my arms and even between my legs. Its salty fetor had kept me on the verge of retching as I sat before the Captain. Now all I could smell was the familiar mustiness of long-worn clothes and my own clean skin. But Anna had hung her head a little, and her eyes seemed to follow something across the deck at our feet.

'I took sand and rubbed myself raw,' I blabbed on. 'Mother of God! I feel clean, at least, but . . .' I trailed off, thinking yet again of the swordsman's last breath. 'I doubt I shall ever feel pure again.'

'Petroc, look at me!' Her voice was tight, almost desperate. Her cloak had fallen open and there was the blue tunic and red surcoat she had put on in the church. The sunlight glimmered over the magical complexities of the silk and picked out where the cloth was stiff and lifeless. Blood had stained it in gouts from neck to hem, and there was a black smear on the skin of her throat.

'Please help me, Patch.' She was pleading. 'I do not want to touch these clothes,' she whispered, and reached out for my arm. Her hand was bloody to the wrist. I flinched, meaning no more than to keep the gore from my skin, but she snatched her hand back and held it to herself as if it burned. Before I could reach for her in turn she whirled away from me and hurried off across the deck to the hatch, where Pavlos happened to be standing. He began to help her down the ladder. I shrugged, not at all sure what had just occurred. I was going to help her. I wanted more than anything to talk, to take both her hands in mine and hold my cheek against hers. But the ghastly sheen of the crimson silk and those dark clots in the fine hair of her arm had unbalanced me for a moment. I thought I remembered that her eyes had widened with shock, almost terror, in the instant before she had turned from me. All at once everything – every taste, pleasure, pain, sound, sight and smell – from the past day and night came back to me, whirling about my head like rooks around a ruined tower, and I barely groped for the rail before I was sicker than I had ever been. I emptied myself into the river until my throat bled. I had no thought of Anna, and whether she watched me before ducking down into the peaceful gloom of the hold I do not know.

When I was done I picked my way aft and pissed into the wake, watching the city blend into the haze. Although there was no wind and the river was flat as a counter-pane I nearly lost my footing and found myself hugging a rope, forehead rasping on the bristly hemp. I realised that, on top of the bane afflicting my soul, I had a ghastly hangover made worse by a sleepless night. So I staggered off in search of Isaac, who gave me a revolting tincture thoughtfully diluted in a little cup of wine. The wine, at least, helped, and in a little while I was dipping into a pot of beans and pork fat that Dimitri had thrown together for all who had returned from last night's bloody carouse.

Mirko was there, pallid and drained, his arm in a splint. By the slow, stunned look on his face I guessed that Isaac's poppy was working in him, for he did not seem in pain. The same was not true for Hanno, who had a ragged cut down one thigh and was cursing hot enough to boil the river beneath us. Others were bruised from other, less ominous brawls, the kind that can kill a man any night of any week with no reason or meaning at all. We all were sick from drink and sleeplessness, and Dimitri fussed over us like a great ugly hen, giving us swigs from a goatskin full of harsh wine laced with some bitter herb and feeding Mirko with a horn spoon as tenderly as any nursemaid. I had no chores and no watch for a while and so, soon enough, my belly full of beans and warmed by the wine, I curled up behind a coil of rope and fell asleep.

Time passed, measured by the slow rocking of the deck. I slept, drifting in soft, empty darkness, until a foot prodded me awake and I looked up blearily from my tar-scented nest. Will peered down at me.

'I was worried about you,' I croaked.

'Indeed. The suffering is plain to see in your face. Now move over.' He dropped down next to me and we sat, leaning on the rope and each other, watching the gulls. We shared the silence of old friends, and for a brief while it seemed as if it might at least be possible that the horrors and wonders of the past few months had never happened, and that we were two careless students stealing an afternoon away from our books. But then Will stretched out a lazy hand, pointing something out to me on shore, and I saw the blood staining his fingernails. There was no escape, then. Time could not be made to retreat, the shadows chased backwards around the dial until we regained our innocence. I sighed and wished for another swallow of Dimitri's wine.

'So what did you make of the Captain?' I said at last.

Will stared at the distant riverbank. After a long silence, he said, 'It would be a foolish man who tried to hide anything from him.'

'What do you mean?'

He paused again, then laughed a little hollowly. 'I only meant that he is like a great owl and you are a rat scuttling

238

across the floor of his barn. Does it not seem as if he sees where you are, where you have been and where you will go?' He shook his head. 'I . . . I like him, I think. He scared my guts near out of my breech, but I like him very much.'

'Is that the right word? "Like?"'

'Well, "fear" would be another word. And, I think, "trust". Do you trust him, Patch?'

'I have done. I do. With my life.'

'And I have done the same, gladly.'

'He had your story from you, then?'

'He did.'

'Then so will I – and you will have mine in return.'

'Done. But does that great ugly man yonder not have a wineskin about him? I am feeling quite in need, now that you have reminded me of my audience with the owl.'

Dimitri was happy to make Will's acquaintance and to share his wine. There were some scrapings of fatty stew left and he doled them out, searching my friend's face with approval.

'You are a fighter, eh? Good, good. One is lost – poor Jens, may he find peace – and another is found.'

'What is in this wine, friend Dimitri? It is tanning my throat as it goes down,' Will enquired through a mouthful of beans.

'Yarrow, melissa, rue, dandelion, and—' he made some harsh sound in his own tongue, '—for to thicken up the blood. Drink more. It will make you piss like a warhorse, boy, and carry off the bad spirits.'

And indeed we spent a good part of the afternoon hanging off the stern, voiding our bad spirits into the Gironde. But I told Will all that had happened since Sir Hugh de Kervezey had ambushed us that quiet morning. My flight from the abbey, the fight on the wharves of Dartmouth and Greenland, and Anna's rescue: I ran through it all as quickly as I could, far more eager to hear Will's adventures than to retell my own, although he was forever stopping me to hear something in greater detail, and those details were not what I wished to linger upon. But after my jaw ached with talking, and we had found a jar of wine free of herbs, I placed my finger firmly on his breastbone.

'That is my sorry life, up to this very instant. You have had it all, every last drop. Very gruesome, is it not?'

'No! Not at all. You have lived, man. Christ! But you have left out everything important: the lady Anna. How . . . Patch, have you . . .'

I held up a too-hasty hand. 'The *Vassileia* Anna is under the protection of Captain de Montalhac, and – could we, please, not talk about her just now? She is the niece of the Emperor of Byzantium, for God's sake!'

'Brother, I feel I have tumbled into quite a different world. My old friend Patch, the great Captain and an imperial princess! But what were you doing in the dead hours of the night with her in the city, eh?' His eyes were twinkling. I shook my head grimly. The last thing I wished to do was besmirch Anna's name any more than it surely was already.

'Nothing. Escorting her back to the ship. I don't know. For fuck's sake, Will, tell me your story, or must I beg you?'

I knew him well, and he was desperate with curiosity. But he saw my unease and rolled his eyes. 'You wish to hear it so badly? You will find it very thin gruel in comparison to yours,' he said, resignedly.

'I doubt that, brother.'

'But I swear it!' He held up both hands in his old familiar protest of innocence. It had always made him seem more roguish and guilty, and it did now. I told him so. But he shook his head. 'Truly, Patch. You will see.' He took a long swig from the jar and cleared his throat like a mountebank at a village fair.

'Kervezey's flail – it was Kervezey, wasn't it? I have never been completely certain . . .' I nodded. 'The flail caught me a good whack—'

'I thought I heard your skull shatter,' I put in. He winced.

'Not quite, brother. It caught me high on the shoulders, in the main, although it laid me open from here to here.' He leaned forward and parted his hair to show a tangle of thick scars like pink twine that ran at a slant from his left shoulder-blade up his neck and almost to the crown of his head. 'You heard bone break, sure enough, but that was my shoulder. I lay like a dead man in the mud, and it was the mud that stopped the bleeding, I think. When I woke up there was no one to be seen. You were gone, and I remember a horse in the water, thrashing. I dragged myself into the hedge and left the world again for a while. I heard people pass by, and I think they were searching, but they did not find me. I would hear things from a long way off, then the world would be dark again. I may have slept for days, I don't know. When I finally came to myself, though, I was as hungry as a wolf and every inch of me burned or ached or stung. I had been raked over by a fever, it seems, as my clothes were salty with old sweat and – Christ's stones! – I stank. There was nothing for it but to set out up the road, although I found myself to be quite safe, for everyone I chanced to meet could not so much as glance at me, foul and stinking as I was. To make things worse I could not move my head or neck – for weeks, in fact, which made me seem even more lunatic, I suppose. Finally, towards night, as I was staggering along all giddy with pain and starvation, some fine church-prince on a grey horse came up with his companions and saw fit to throw me a fistful of coin to demonstrate his Christianity. Very Christian it was to take his amusement as I grovelled, all crippled, in the dust for his charity, but no matter. I bought food and drink at the next village, stole some clothes, cleaned myself as best as I could in the river, and set out for London a new man – a man without the use of his neck, true enough, but at least there was a head still upon it, brother!'

'Indeed. And next?' I said, all impatience.

'Next I thieved my way to London, found my father's

business acquaintances, and set off to Flanders, where I took up with a mercenary company. It was the plan I made for you, Patch, do you remember? But I knew that it would not be safe to go home, and I am afraid I did not relish explaining matters to my old papa. It was the right choice, though, was it not? The path that should have been yours led me back to you!' He shook his head in wonder.

'You are not done, brother,' I said, exasperated.

'Nothing else to tell. I found Sir Andrew Hardie's company, the Black Boar, in Antwerp, and they took a shine to me – I could move my head again by then, which was a help. I . . . truly, nothing has happened since then, Patch. The soldier's lot I have found to be an exceedingly dull one. We lazed about in Flanders, growing fat and poxy; we made our slow and easy way south at the first sniff of war, and we have been lolling around Bordeaux for a good month, doing nothing but eat, drink and feel fat French rumps.' He sighed and looked at his hands. 'These soft things are about to get a shock, by the looks of it,' he said wistfully. 'I understand I may be required to do what they call—' he made a ridiculously foppish motion and twisted his face into a mockery of noble horror, '—*work*.'

'Oh aye, work you shall, boy! Work you shall!' I grabbed the wine from him. 'No more of this, for a start.' We grappled for it as I tried to drain it dry, choking and coughing wine all over the deck and myself, then we were laughing until the tears came. As we were drying our eyes I had a thought and asked: 'But hold up, brother. You know how to fight well enough. You skewered that man's eyeball like a matron threading a darning-needle. You didn't learn that in Balecester. I never knew you to carry a blade.'

'Well, they taught me. And they found I had a natural . . . aptitude. The thing about mercenaries is that they fight for money. And they fight over money. There are all sorts of little wars, Patch, flaring up like grass fires anywhere that mercenaries come together. The Black Boar had it out with a band of

Catalans who had been thrown out of Greece and thought we'd slighted them over some contract or other. It . . . it wasn't like Balecester, right enough. No drunken scholars dodging fat watchmen. My company wanted me blooded. They started a fight at a little Flemish market fair and pushed me into the thick of it. My choice was kill or be a corpse, and here I am. It happened again, more than once. I have been blooded, all right. But you know what it is like, too. I am . . .' He looked at me and smiled: rueful, bitter, the most honest look he had given me all day. 'I am good at it, Patch. I do not enjoy the killing. I enjoy the *fight*, but to kill . . .' he shook his head. 'More wine, if you please. Last night, brother – that was the first time for you?'

For a ghastly moment I did not know what he meant. How could he possibly know about the bawdy-house? Then I realised.

'Not my first fight, but the first . . .' I put my hands to my temples. 'I never killed a man before last night. I wish with all my heart I had not done it. I wish he lived and it was I lying dead . . .'

'But you live. You are here drinking wine under the great blue roof of heaven. And is it not sweet? Kill, Patch, or be a corpse. I would rather be alive, brother. And from the many rough miles you have travelled, I think you would, too.'

'It cannot be as simple as you put it.'

'But it is, brother. It truly is.' And he put his arms behind his head, lay back and closed his eyes. The sun shone down on us both, but as I too stretched out to bask in its warmth a chill whispered through me, although the day held no shadows.

I went on watch at five bells and Dimitri put Will to cleaning the blades that had found so much work on shore. There was still no sign of Anna, but there was plenty to be done as the *Cormaran* sailed out of the Gironde and into a perfect sea, and I was glad to empty my mind of anything but the wind and the ropes. We rounded the Pointe de Grave and turned south, gliding past the long dune of Arcachon towards Bayonne. The sun fell slowly towards the forests away to the west and at last, as the brazier was lit to heat our dinner, Anna appeared on deck. We were about to put the ship about, and I could not leave my station, but she saw me and raised her hand. She wore a simple tunic of some dark, rich-looking stuff, and her black hair was pulled back and hidden under a simple white coif. She looked both pure and alluring and my blood began to whisper softly in my ears. 'That is your woman,' it said. I shook my head in happy disbelief, then as the sail cracked and bellied there was a minute of wild activity, and when I made fast my rope and turned to her again, she was stepping into the cabin and did not look back. Gilles followed and closed the door behind them. It was no more than I had expected. Mikal had eaten with the crew, but the Princess Anna Doukaina Komnena could hardly be expected to squat around a cauldron and bandy words with the likes of us, although I knew she would probably prefer to. But all the same my dark humours crept over me again, and when someone tapped me on the shoulder to relieve me of the watch I could hardly bring myself to make the few paces over to the brazier.

Tonight there were stories to be told and I did not want to tell mine, but knew it would be dragged from me anyway. I took no pleasure in the memory of what I had done, but I obliged when my turn came, and discovered, as the demijohns of good Bordeaux wine went around, why soldiers tell their war stories. The telling and retelling began to ease some hurt deep within me. I am not one of those men to whom each killing is a mark of pride, and in truth I believe I carry each cut I have inflicted on others in some scarred quarter of my soul. That night, though, as we danced every murderous step again, I became part of the *Cormaran* for good. I had fought and I had killed, and tonight I brought currency of my own to the circle of men, and as I stood and showed for the third time how I had stuck my knife up under a man's ribs and held him until he breathed his soul into my face I found I was among friends, and home at last.

Later I slept like a thing of stone, to be awakened at dawn by the tossing of the ship beneath me. We had run into a storm off San Sebastian, and it chased us down to the Pillars of Hercules, green water a never-ending torrent across the decks and lightning playing about the mast-top. Will, whom the crew had taken to with a vengeance, did his best to learn sailcraft in between hours spent puking off the stern. He was wan company at best but it gave me a simple, boyish pleasure to teach what I knew of this strange new world to my friend. He must have found my ease and enthusiasm a little wearing, and began to tire of my assurances that the sickness would soon pass, I who had never suffered it. But unlike many I have known, who have begged to be put ashore, or even weakly tried to put an end to themselves, Will tottered about his work doggedly, and the crew, and I, loved him all the more.

The Pillars were a gateway indeed, and sailing through we left the dismal weather behind. I must have made a fool of myself, running from one side of the ship to the other, straining my eyes this time towards Spain and the great bulwark of the Gibr-al-Tariq, this time over to the distant brown shores of Africa. We were in a different world entirely, it seemed, a place of hot breezes and warm nights. Will's sea-legs found him at last, and we marvelled at how lean he had grown. 'I have puked my old life away,' he said in wonder. For the first time in my life I went about shirtless and my skin turned from its waxen English white to livid, smarting red and then to a deep brown. Even my teeth were feeling better. The only thing missing was Anna.

Since revealing herself to the crew she had kept her distance. I understood why, of course. She could not throw on her sailcloth tunic and go back to being Mikal, and I knew that when she had first come aboard she had feared the men – not without reason, although she had won over most hearts, I believed. She would be safe amongst them, though perhaps no longer comfortable. But it was me she was taking pains to avoid, and fool that I was I could not fathom the reason for it. She spent her days with the Captain and with Gilles, or with Nizam up on the steering deck, my own favourite place on the *Cormaran*, which I no longer had time to visit. Even Will, whose roguish spark had well and truly kindled itself again, would find time to lean on the rail and tell her things that made her laugh. When we did talk she was distant or distracted, and the one night when we shared the Captain's table she barely said a word to me. I missed her horribly, although she was there before my eyes every day. Then I began to worry, and worry tumbled with guilt and confusion until I had convinced myself that everything was my fault. She had never wanted to share my bed: I had forced her. Then I had led her fecklessly into danger and forced her to kill. Now she undoubtedly hated me as much as I was beginning to hate myself.

These were becoming black days, despite the glory of the weather and the friendly sea, and we were no more than two days' sail from the Pillars when I began my rapid fall into a despair deeper than I had ever imagined man could suffer in this life. The humours of melancholy filled me as smoke from a guttering candle fills and blackens a closed lantern. The fight returned to me again and again, sometimes as a blur, sometimes in horrible detail, far clearer than it had been at the time. I felt again and again the resistance and then the give of the man's innards against my knife. I remembered that I had smelled shit as he died, and that his bowels must have let go. And then the face of Deacon Jean would return to me full of terrified outrage at what was happening to him. I heard, again and again, the hot splash of his blood on the floor of the cathedral, and it mingled with the screams of the mad hermit of the island after I had wounded him. So much death, so much pain; and all at my hand, all on my account. And Anna . . . Perhaps because our night together had been so violently changed from love to bloody riot, I could hardly think of what we had done together without it seeming a defilement, and I the defiler. I began to have dismal, churning dreams, and then sleep itself came less and less often, which was a blessing. I took to avoiding company – even that of Will – when I was not needed, and would sit behind a water butt, my arms clutching my knees, silent and still as the hours passed by.

I had all but forgotten the miraculous chance that had bought Will back, so much so that sometimes, as my afflicted conscience gnawed me, I would see him struck down by Sir Hugh's flail and add his death to my burden of guilt, even though he walked the deck a few yards away. Mostly I took his presence for granted, and he had the good sense to leave me to myself. He seemed to know when the shadows were not so thick around me, and then we would be easy with each other once more. One night, after the sun had set with its usual magnificence behind the hills of Spain, the stars had appeared and the *Cormaran*'s wake glowed and sparkled faintly, I felt so overwhelmed by the beauty of it all that I felt a sudden need to blot out this lovely world on which I was but a stain. So I sought out a full wineskin and set about emptying it into myself. Had the ocean been wine I would have gladly jumped overboard with mouth open, but although no wineskin could hold enough to dull my torment I found myself, at some later point in the evening – the intervening parts having vanished from memory – leaning heavily on the forward rail and regarding the blade of the new moon which was sinking, yellow as a sheaf of ripe corn, below the invisible horizon.

The stars blazed here in the south, as bright as a winter's night in Devon. With the fixation, the false clarity of mind that comes with drink, I tried to fathom the unimaginable distances between my little self bobbing on the sea and the moon, set in its crystal sphere, and beyond it past the planetary spheres to the sphere upon which the stars were fixed, and even further, to the Primum Mobile itself. Brother Adric had given me Ptolemy's *Almagest* to read at the Abbey, and, although I had understood what was written therein as an ant understands a pachyderm, the vast machinery of equants and deferants, the wonderful, logical complexity of it all had never ceased to fill me with joy and wonder. Tonight, however, I was thinking of distances, endless tracts of emptiness and the lonely music of the spheres as they turned in their immutable orbits. The moon was waxing and there was the faintest hint of the old moon caught in the calliper-grasp of her arms.

Will came to lean beside me and we passed a wineskin back and forth and watched the strange glow of the wake. I wanted to be alone and so said nothing, but after a while he cleared his throat.

'I am intruding on your . . . solitude, Patch,' he said. I shrugged and kept silent, but he went on.

'I know what melancholy feels like, brother,' he murmured. I turned to him in surprise despite myself.

'You?'

'Yes, why not? It was early in my time with . . . the company. I was brought very low, low enough to wonder how quick a rope around my neck would get the job done. I didn't get very far, but I thought about it very carefully. Probably thought about it too much, actually, because while I was agonising and debating I began to feel better, and little by little the life came back into me.'

'But why? What made you?'

'There is much I cannot . . .' he paused, and gave me the most haunted look I had ever seen upon his face. 'I do not know. The shock of being cast out of my familiar world, perhaps. The knock on the head. Many things can stir up the black bile. It is done, though. That's what I wanted to tell you:

it passes. Time is as good as any potion, of that I am convinced.'

'I have thought about it too,' I admitted, unwillingly. 'But it seems too easy an escape.'

'And what of the comforts of Mother Church?' he asked. 'It was no help to me, but you . . .'

'No comfort there, Will.' I told him a little of my epiphany in the cathedral at Gardar.

'There has been a burden on you for a long time, then,' he said. 'Loss of faith . . . I am no theologian, no Albertus Magnus, God forbid! And I never really had faith like you did, Patch – horrible confession, is it not? Do not tell me that you did not suspect! But when the faithful are stripped of all they believe, they are like a stone house gutted by fire: the walls stand, but all within is gone: rooms, stairs, decorations, beds, tables, everything familiar, gone. If the walls are sound the house may be rebuilt inside – in time. But it will not be familiar, Patch – it will not be home.'

'No Albertus Magnus? You are right there. Hardly even a hedge-scholar, brother!' But Will had found me out. My faith was gone, and although I did not wish to regain it – strange how fast a lifetime's habits of thought can come to seem like childish superstition – the hollow it had left had yet to be filled with anything as sustaining.

'I live like a beast,' I told him. 'I breathe, I eat, sleep, work . . . I have no purpose other than to remain alive. And I am less and less sure why I bother even to do that.'

'But life itself – what more is there? You have the *Cormaran*, and the brotherhood of this fine crew of villains, myself included. You have two arms, two legs, two eyes, you are strong . . . and what of all you have learned? Does that not fill you up?'

I raised my arms hopelessly. 'I am filled, brother: up to the brim with guilt,' I said. 'What good is it to keep yourself alive if you must do it at the cost of others? I live like a beast, but I am no beast. I am a man, and if God or his son Jesus Christ will not judge me, then I must judge myself.'

'Aha!' cried Will. 'I have found you out! You are like that snake who eats his own tail, the . . .the . . .' he snapped his fingers in frustration.

'Ouroboros,' I muttered.

'Exactly. But instead of your tail, you have rammed your head up your own fundament and are gnawing away at your tripes. You are blind to anything but yourself – any*one* but yourself. Pull your head out, Patch. It must be very dark up there.'

'It isn't like that,' I whimpered.

'Then how is it? Have you learned nothing since we left home? You must seize hold of life and squeeze it until the juice comes. Patch, you were doing a fine job until I came along. What about Lady Anna? How do you think . . .'

'I will not talk about the Princess Anna!' I snapped, jumping up in a rage that caught us both by surprise.

'Peace, peace – I meant nothing and you know it. Now sit down and take another drink.'

And so I did, but only stayed for another minute. Then with a civil 'goodnight' I took myself off to my berth. I lay sleepless that whole night until at last my anger melted into self-pity. Who or what I raged against I did not know, for I was no more the master of my moods than a bee caught in a hurricane can choose which way to fly. I longed for someone – it was too hard even to name that someone to myself – to come to me and wash away my sins, as I knew was in her power. But no sacrament would be given that night, and instead the stars were my company, mocking me with their cold distance.

We were hurrying across this beautiful sea. Land lay always to port, but far away: no more than a low purple bruise on the horizon. We were following a course towards the coast of Italy and a rendezvous in the great city of Pisa: that at least I knew from the Captain, but if he confided more I do not remember, so wrapped in misery was I. I say wrapped: it did indeed feel as if I were caught up in a winding-sheet but still walked, my limbs alive, my insides dead. Isaac began to watch me closely and ply me with potions and pills – dill, rue, hyssop, bee-balm and other wonders from his store which I had never heard of but which tasted as bitter as any roadside weed. Under his ministrations the melancholy would ebb sometimes, long enough to marvel at the clever porpoises and dolphins who came to visit the *Cormaran*, weaving in and out of our wake and racing with us, a race they always won with ease. On such days Will and I would find our old delight in each other's company, although I sensed that he treated me carefully, as if I might break suddenly. One day I saw a shoal of fish leap out of the water all at once and spread wings. Like silver swifts they glided stiffly for a distance, then plunged back into the deeps. Soon this miracle – miracle for me, although the other men hardly paid it any mind – became a commonplace, and when a brace of the magical fish missed their aim and crashed to the deck, I hardly noticed when they were added to the night's meal. I became a zealous fisherman, as it was the best excuse for spending my free hours leaning over the side, staring into the sea. I was not interested in what I caught, but the crew were: strange, lovely and occasionally hideous creatures that all tasted good enough. Once, I think the day after we raised the island of Formentera and were creeping past the mountains of Mallorca, I dropped my line unknowingly into a great shoal of mackerel and, as I hauled them up, frantically tying more and more hooks to my line, every man with a free hand rushed to the side with their own lines and soon the deck was carpeted with a writhing, stranded shoal that gleamed and rippled like living chain-mail. Everyone – even the Captain and Gilles, even Anna – waded in to gather them up, stun them and throw them into one of the salting barrels that Guthlaf had pulled from the hold. It was as I bent to this task that I heard a squeal and saw Anna fending off a mackerel that flapped and jerked in her arms. She flung it away, stooped and picked up another struggling fish which, with a triumphant laugh, she threw at one of the crew. Her aim was good: the mackerel hit Will square on his crooked nose.

Like all those who suffer a surfeit of melancholy I was drawn more and more inside myself, studying as if with an inner eye the sooty and damaged rubric of what I took to be my soul. It is hard to look back on those days with any great sympathy for myself, for the humours made me selfish, sour and unfriendly, and those traits are not easily borne in a community as tight-knit as a ship. It says much for the good nature of the crew that they did not heave me overboard, but it must have been a great temptation for them at times. But I was oblivious to the feelings of others, indeed I barely noticed them, so intent on anatomising my worthlessness had I become. But looking up at that moment to see the look of pure happiness on Anna's face, and finding it mirrored in Will's, brought me to my senses like a whiff of sal ammoniac. While I had brooded – how many days had it been? Weeks, perhaps? – life had been going on without me. Things had been happening under my nose. I had turned my feelings for Anna over and over like meat on a spit, watching them become shrivelled and burnt. Out here in the sunshine, though, Anna was happy and quite unconcerned.

Or so it seemed. Now it is easy to see that I was not looking directly at the world. Instead I was peering into the mirror held up for me by melancholy, which distorted and corrupted all that appeared in it. So I did not see Anna's happiness for what it was: the proof that my fears for her were groundless. Instead I searched the mirror for a more sinister meaning, and it was not long in revealing itself. For there stood Will, my worldly, wicked friend, and the look he was giving Anna was one I had seen a thousand times before in the low houses of Balecester.

*

The unwholesome epiphany I was granted from Anna and Will's mackerel-fight worked a miraculous cure, as epiphanies are wont to do. From that moment on I found my senses clear and life once again humming within me. I was mistaken, though, if I believed that my melancholy humour had been cast out. It had instead transmuted itself from the base matter of despair to the harder, brighter metal of jealousy. But like any good poison, this one did its work slowly and insidiously, although I would not understand this until it was too late. At that moment, standing bare-chested in the hot sun with my arms full of slimy, writhing fish, I was suddenly feeling something like my old self. Without thinking, I lobbed the mackerel in my hand at Will who, faced with scaly assault from two quarters, ducked behind the mast and aimed another fish at me. It went wide and hit Carlo in the stomach and he, thinking Dimitri behind the wicked deed, launched an attack of his own that signalled out-and-out war on deck. If a flying-fish had chanced to peer over the rail as he glided past he would have been treated to the marine version of hell itself: a writhing bedlam of half-naked men hurling fish, beating one another about the head with fish and treading live fish underfoot, hooting and screeching the while like a legion of Beelzebub's fiends. It had been long months since the men of the *Cormaran* had been allowed their heads in this way – they had missed a true shore-leave in Dublin and Bordeaux – and the Captain let the mêlée run its course, even permitting Istvan to belabour him with a fast-disintegrating dog-fish that had thrown in its lot with the wrong shoal.

Once some sort of order had returned to the *Cormaran* it became clear that we would have to pay for our jollity. In many ways life aboard a ship resembles that of a monastery, and that perhaps was one reason why I felt so at home on the sea. It is a self-sufficient community of men in which a life of labour is regulated by bells. There is always much to be done, but on ship as in monastery, idle hands are the greatest danger to order and work must be found for them. I spent my boyhood scrubbing floors and polishing wood at the abbey, and now I found that my days passed in much the same way. So it was with mounting panic that we stood, fouled with scales and blood, and regarded the chaos we had wrought.

The deck was creamy with the trodden guts and mashed corpses of fish. Many survived to be pickled, and the rest went overboard. Fafner emerged from below, his whiskers fairly trembling with excitement. A cloud of seabirds appeared as if from nowhere to feast on the oily, stinking trail that the *Cormaran* dragged like a slug across the pristine sea. We set to work sluicing everything down with sea-water, then scouring the deck with sand and stones. It was somewhat purgatorial, as the sun heated everything to the rotting point almost straight away, and we laboured in a rich fetor of putrescence. Black slime had to be scraped from almost every surface. In the end we had to scatter lye, which made our eyes water, and wash ourselves down with sour wine, but it was days before the ship – and its cat – lost its pungency.

Meanwhile, fish had come to feed on the debris in our wake, and greater fish to feed upon the smaller ones. A shout from the steering deck brought me running, grateful for a respite from my scouring-stone. Nizam was pointing down into the water, and Anna, who had wisely taken refuge up here after starting the mêlée, was bouncing on her bare toes with excitement – or perhaps fear, for when I followed Nizam's finger I saw a strange and wonderful sight. Great silver-grey fish, the size of dolphins, were roiling and thrashing on the surface, seemingly driven mad by the mackerel blood. 'Sharks,' someone beside me said, awe in his voice. Now I understood why sailors fear that beast above all others. I saw little fish disappearing into wide, toothy maws; pointed heads lash at water, at other sharks, even at the seagulls who hovered just overhead. Then Anna let out a scream of real terror and a couple of the crew stepped back abruptly from the rail. A monstrous grey shape had scythed into the churning pack. It seemed as big as two oxen stood nose to tail, and its jaws gaped wide as a door, all studded about with a thicket of curved, needle-pointed teeth. But the monster's eyes were the worst: two black sockets that seemed to open onto night itself. No expression was there, no glimmer, no sign that any spark of life dwelt inside that merciless head. Instead it seemed driven by remorseless hatred for all that moved. It fought briefly with the other sharks, turning the water into a red ferment, and when they had fled or died it turned its appalling eye on us and drove straight for the rudder. There was a thud, the deck shook and Nizam went sprawling. The tiller juddered. Then the monster was gone, sunk to whatever bleak depth it claimed as its kingdom. I turned to find reassurance in a human face, to wipe away the memory of those empty eyes, and saw that Anna, in her fear, had pressed herself close against Will.

I could not get the memory of it out of my head. All the rest of that long day I scrubbed the deck like a madman, until my hands were numb with the constant grating. But my mind was anything but numbed. So recently dead within my skull, it had awakened and was buzzing like a nest of wasps, yellow as the gall of jealousy I could all but taste upon my tongue. Had I troubled to consult Isaac, he could have told me that the melancholic black bile that had devilled me had been driven out by an excess of yellow bile – so out of balance had my body become that I had begun to swing, like a pendulum, from one extremity to another – and this choleric humour was now driving me helplessly before it. I think he saw us all as a collection of vessels more or less full of foul or fair liquids, to be topped up or drained at his discretion. But foolishly I did not seek him out, and instead allowed the image that had painted clear upon my inner eye – Anna leaning into Will's side – to grow and grow until it became first a glowing Veronica, then a gigantic thing that filled my world as if it were painted on the sail itself. In truth, what had I seen?

Nothing more than the simplest urge for protection against an all-devouring fear, and had I not felt the same thing myself? But the grand Veronica of my jealous fancy was my work and mine alone, and like any painter I began to add details: had Anna's hand reached for Will's? In my mind's eye it had. Anna's face: had she turned it to Will, helpless, beseeching? Certainly. Had a look passed between them, secret, complicit? Yes, hell's shark-toothed mouth swallow them both, yes.

I laboured through another white-hot day, then another, and dreamed bitter dreams each night. Finally I woke to cooler weather with a steady wind out of the west, and caught my first sight of Corsica to starboard. As we drew closer, the island seemed a great wall of stone topped by a head of white cloud. By midday it had resolved itself into a jagged collection of mountain peaks, among which the vaporous clouds seethed and twined. Towns lay under those peaks, apparently, although the thought of living in such a forbidding place made me shudder. Nizam pointed out Calvi and the Red Isle, and with some difficulty we turned our course north-north-east.

'The wind is fickle in this sea,' Zianni told me. Like many of the crew, Zianni had lived the life of a pirate before chance brought him aboard the *Cormaran*. He came from a noble Venetian family but had killed a magistrate in a brawl and had fled from the Doge's executioner. He had robbed his way up and down the Italian coast with a gang of Istrian corsairs, fought with the Catalan mercenaries in the islands we had sailed past a few days before and cast in his lot with the *Cormaran* after dabbling with honesty in Valencia had reduced him to beggardom.

'The wind at our backs is the *libeccio*,' he said now. 'It blows through here like a bastard this time of year. See those clouds over the island? We'll have thunder tonight, for certain, and then enough wind to blow us to Pisa and half-way over the mountains beyond.'

He was right. As we coasted up towards Cap Corse, the sea grew darker and the clouds seemed to boil over and fill the whole sky. It was after midnight when we rounded the cape, the whole crew on deck, and a few minutes later the sky caught fire. I had never seen such lightning. It spun across the sky like the spokes of an infernal cartwheel and stabbed the sea all around us. I felt the thunder from the soles of my feet to the teeth that rattled in my head. The wind hit us so hard that the *Cormaran* heeled over to starboard, and those who did not have a tight hold on rope or spar were sent flying into the bilges. We scrambled in the deep darkness – lit every few seconds by light that seemed brighter and fiercer than the sun – to reef the sail, and soon we were flying on a broad reach across the seething waters. The lightning flailed above us, bursts of light freezing us in the midst of our frenzied work, branding fleeting impressions onto my eyes so that, whether they were open or closed, I saw wild faces, pale madmen bathed in blazing quicksilver.

There was no sleep that night, nor the next morning. We had only twenty or so leagues to cover from Cap Corse to the mouth of the Arno, and again Zianni's prediction came true. On our broad reach, the *libeccio* screeching onto our port side, we raised the Italian coast soon after ten bells. But soon after that, the wind dropped and the storm pulled its rags from the sky. By this time we were near enough to land to see the reedy mouths of the Arno and, beyond it, the distant outline of the city itself. We were not alone on the sea: ships of all description were plying in and out of the river, and I could not help noticing a new, tense vigilance in the faces of the Captain and Gilles. I was just wondering if I could snatch a few minutes of sleep when Gilles beckoned me to his side on the steering deck.

'Do you wish to see Pisa? Good, for you are coming ashore with us,' he said, leaving me no time to protest. 'Find your friend and make the gig ready.' He must have caught sight of something in my eyes, for he went on: 'Your friend Will. He will be coming as well.'

I did not care whether I saw Pisa or no, but I keenly did not want Will's company. Nevertheless I gritted my teeth and dragged myself over to where he sat, helping Dimitri in his endless task of keeping the salt sea from devouring our weapons. It did not improve my mood to see the look of almost doggy pleasure he gave me at the news.

'Let's get to it, then,' I said briskly, in case he tried to talk to me. Turning on my heel I stalked off aft climbing up on the rail to skirt the stern castle. The gig would be full of water from the storm and heavy, I thought, angrily. I already had hold of the painter and was pulling at it, watching the gig bob happily in the *Cormaran*'s wake and noting that it was, indeed, much heavier than usual, when Will dropped down beside me and clapped his hands over mine. We gave an experimental heave.

'She's a heavy one,' said Will brightly.

'How surprising,' I returned, so coldly I wondered I could not see my breath.

'So lay on, Patch!' he chattered. 'Lay on! It is a beautiful day – God's nails, that storm! – and we are going ashore in sinful Pisa. Is Pisa sinful? I hope so. All cities are sinful, somewhat, eh, Patch?'

'For fuck's sake stop your prating and pull the sodding rope!' I snapped.

'What's wrong with you?'

'Nothing's wrong. We need to shut up and work. I don't want to do this, so let us get it over with.'

'No, wait, Patch. You have been acting like a basket of bad eggs since we came through the Pillars. What is going on?'

Will had both hands on my shoulders. I cringed, and loosened my hold on the rope. It shot through my hand, burning it, before I snatched it away with a curse and turned back to my torturer.

'I do not understand why you had to come back at all,' I yelled at him, spittle forming on my lips. 'Why did you? You have . . . you have pushed me aside!'

'How? How have I pushed you aside, Patch, and from what, pray?'

'From the life I had made for myself here. From my friends. I feel like a corpse – no, no, I feel like your bloody shadow, you bastard!'

'Shadow be fucked. I ask again: pushed you aside from what? No, let us rather say, from *whom*?'

'From the Captain,' I muttered.

'No, that is not it. Try again.'

'I don't know. Gilles. Dimitri. My friends – everyone!'

'Everyone? Is there anyone in particular whom you feel I have . . .'

I slammed my hand down on the rail, and turned to him, teeth clenched in fury. 'Look, Will, you know who I mean. You certainly know. Don't make me fucking say it!'

'I'll say it for you. Anna.'

I believe my hand would have gone to Thorn at that moment, but Will knew my mind better than I knew it myself, and laid his hand gently over mine on the rail. If I had expected to see triumph in his face I was disappointed. He was watching me soberly, carefully. Then he held up a finger and kept it there between our two faces.

'Anna – yes? I am right, and please don't say anything. You think too much, brother. You always did. Back at college you were always thinking, while I was out fucking or brawling. You envied me, and I confess I envied you somewhat too. Patch, we both should have fucked and thought in equal measure, but we did not, alas: look where it's got us. And yes, you know my ways and suspect the worst. But you are wrong. Wenches . . . wenches like me because, mostly, they don't do too much thinking and they like a lad who tends to put his dick before his brains. And that's always served me well. But I am not the fool you imagine me to be. Not quite. Your Princess Anna . . . I *like* her very well, boy. But she is not, Brother Petroc, what I would call a wench. She thinks all the time! And although she likes me well enough – I make her laugh, fiddlededee! I make her blush, for shame! – it is something of a sisterly affection.'

He laughed with no trace of humour. We were staring into each other's eyes like two tomcats ill-met on a roof. Still his finger did not waver before my face.

'Do you understand what I am telling you?' he said, finally.

'She won't let you fuck her,' I answered, every word soaked in livid yellow bile.

Will took a deep breath and bit his lip.

'She doesn't want me to fuck her, you little shit. She wants—' and suddenly his finger was stabbing into me below my breastbone. 'You. She wants you. Is that clear enough?'

'She doesn't! She does not!' I heard my voice rise to an unpleasant shout. 'She dodges me like a leper! I might as well be ringing a fucking bell! But you, she's all over you, isn't she?'

'Yes, and do you know what she talks to me about? Day in, day out? You. Bloody Patch this, that and the fucking other. I am so happy that you are miserable, brother, for I am just as miserable as you, and Anna, sweet Anna, is more miserable than the two of us put together. I am going off my head, Patch! My life . . . I am living under a great grey rain cloud that drenches me day in, day out with its pitiful bloody sorrow.'

My head was spinning, and I could feel the wine I had drunk and how it was weighing me down. I did not want to listen to Will any more. I could not bear to listen to what he was telling me. For if he was right, then my own actions . . . I tried to clear my head. Will's face came into focus as if for the first time in weeks. He looked dreadfully tired and old. I felt ancient myself. All at once the bitter humours that had been choking me drained away like vinegar leaving a broken keg. I was myself again, feeling my skin like a long-abandoned set of clothes. I felt a bit sick, and worse, much worse, I knew I had made a complete, unforgivable and unredeemable idiot of myself. My burnt hand stung, but I grabbed the painter and tugged at it feebly. I could not bring myself to look at Will, so instead I began to mumble, watching the gig merrily defy me.

'She can't possibly want me, brother,' I began. 'But thank you for saying she does. It . . . anyway, a noble attempt, and I am in your debt for it.'

Will sighed heavily. He leaned far out over the rail so that I was forced to meet his eyes again.

'Listen to me,' he said. 'I do not know – much less care, you understand – what has passed between you two sour creatures. But I do know women a little, and it is plain that there has been a misunderstanding. Or rather more than that, I'll grant you. The truth of it is, she does not hate you, but she is certain – deathly certain – that you loath her, and that is the canker that gnaws at her. How fitting that it should gnaw you as well.'

'Oh, Christ,' I moaned.

'You have been cold towards her since the fight in Bordeaux.'

'No, no, she has been cold to me! Since she came to me, all bloody when I was trying to wash myself . . .' Suddenly everything was horribly clear. I beat the rail with both fists, and the gig sped backwards through the wake yet again.

'Ah, ha. She disgusted you.'

'No!'

'Understandable, all stinking and covered with blood like that. But that—' and he was smiling now, '—that is the only thing that I do understand. She is . . . she's a fucking princess, Patch, and she is arse over tit in love with you, you worthless Dartmoor sheep-shagger. That, my brother, is the greatest mystery of all.'

I fear I overwhelmed Will with the force of my embrace and the hot tears that soaked into his tunic, but he was good enough not to say anything, except to stifle my litany of contrition. I believe it was then that he truly returned to life for me, and as we finally mastered the gig and made it fast alongside the *Cormaran* we were both cackling and chattering like tannery sparrows.

Chapter Seventeen

I barely noticed as we tied up among the grey marble buildings of Pisa, and Zianni slipped ashore to disappear into the crowd. Gilles had to grab us both to break into our merriment, telling us to arm ourselves and put on our best clothes. It was time to find out what awaited us on shore. There was some great and mysterious scheme afoot, it was plainly written in the tension with which the Captain and Gilles held themselves. They paced the deck like two great coursing hounds waiting for the off, and remained distracted and close-lipped as we rowed towards the bustling quays of the Republic. I was a little surprised when the Captain clapped a filthy old travelling hat on Will's head and sent him off ahead of us.

I should have been swept away by the noise and the energy of this city and these people, who chattered away like starlings as they bought and sold, strutted and embraced. As we hurried across the Campo dei Miracoli I should have gawped at the marble cathedral and the odd, half-collapsed building shrouded in scaffolding which was either being shored up or knocked down. But I was far too happy – I who had not felt happiness for an eternity of bitter, angry days – and Gilles and the Captain strode so quickly through the midst of these wonders that we were soon into the narrow streets beyond. Night was falling and the lamps were being lit when we ducked under an arch of flowering vines and made our way up a blind alley to the house at the end. It was an inn, the Taverna dei Tre Corvi, and three carved ravens brooded over the door, which opened to reveal Zianni, who nodded in response to a whispered word from Gilles, slipped past us and made off down the alley. We paused on the threshold, Gilles staring at the alley's mouth until he was satisfied. He nodded to the Captain, who led Will inside.

'Wait out here, Petroc. The inn is closed tonight to all but us. If anyone seeks to enter, draw your sword and call out. We will not be long.'

I was left looking at the closed door and wondering why they had chosen me of all people as their bodyguard. Perhaps it was because I had become such a killer, I thought wryly. It was getting very dark now and the torch that burned at the mouth of the alley did nothing but throw weird shadows through the leaves of the vine. It was silent too, although we were in the midst of a swarming city. I curled my hand around the hilt of my sword, leaned casually against the door post and tried to feel brave. Now and again, footsteps would clip up or down the narrow street beyond the vine and I would see a figure pass by the entrance. Despite my mood, I began to wonder who the footsteps belonged to. A workman? A lady, or a nun? Now and then there were flurries of activity and the street would be full of passers-by. Then, for long minutes, no one at all.

It was during one of these lulls that I heard another set of footfalls approaching. They were hard and confident: a soldier for certain, I thought, but now they softened. A lawyer, perhaps? I had no idea, of course, whether a lawyer walked any differently from a costermonger, but I liked the idea and was amusing myself idly thus when the footsteps stopped. I looked up, surprised, and thought I saw a figure under the torch. As I watched, it stepped across the alley and seemed to press itself into the wall. I strained my eyes and thought I could see a shadow there. Perhaps there was someone watching me, perhaps there was no one. I carefully loosened my sword in its sheath. The more I stared the less I could see, and the more convinced I became that eyes were on me. Finally, when I could see nothing at all, I took a step into the alley.

Immediately there was a flickering in the shadows and someone took off up the street. The footsteps faded and I let go of the hilt of my sword. My hand came away damp with sweat. I wondered for the hundredth time what was happening behind me. Over my head the wooden ravens creaked on their iron perch.

It was some time after that when the door opened and Will stepped out. He wiped greasy lips and treated me to a spectacular belch. 'You are wanted inside,' he informed me, and indeed the Captain leaned through the doorway and beckoned me inside. Will took my place in the alley. I left him picking his teeth and stepped gratefully into firelight and the smell of good roast meat. I was in a big, square room with ochre walls and a ceiling of painted rafters. There were two long tables, and at one of them sat the Captain. A plump, long-haired man was busy taking a suckling pig from a spit and he beamed at me and beckoned. In no time I had a trencher full of steaming pig-meat and a full beaker of wine and was seated opposite the Captain, who was cleaning his own plate with a hunk of bread.

'Someone was watching from the street,' I told him.

'Did you see them?'

'Not really, but I heard him.' And I told him of the lawyer-ish footsteps. He laughed, but looked serious.

'They didn't sound like the footsteps of English mercenaries, then, I take it?'

'Not at all.' I paused and grinned. 'Genteel feet.'

'Hmm. Excuse me for a moment.' He went over and opened the door, leaned out and whispered something to Will. Then he returned.

'You should be full of questions,' he said, cocking his head at me.

I was, full to brimming, and after being alone with my thoughts for so long the floodgates were opening.

'I've been talking to Will, but you have spent the most time with her of late: does Anna hate me?' I blurted.

The Captain looked genuinely surprised, then threw back his head and laughed long and hard. He took a gulp of wine that trickled into his beard and chuckled some more. Finally he lifted his chin and regarded me down the length of his eagle's nose.

'No,' he said.

'No? Are you sure?'

'No, she does not hate you. What other questions do you have?'

'Why is she ignoring me, then?'

The Captain seemed to be having a hard time swallowing back more laughter.

'I can assure you that the *Vassileia* Anna does not hate you. She . . . she is very fond of you, Petroc. But she is having difficulties of her own.'

'Like what?'

'She is finding it hard to be herself again – to be a great lady on a ship of fools such as we are. And other things that I have surmised but would not tell you even if I knew them to be true. Now for God's sake, Petroc, ask me something else.'

I picked up my pig bone and gnawed, almost melting into the bench with relief. Then I remembered where I was.

'If you will allow me to guess, I would say we are here to meet the man you missed in Bordeaux.'

'You are right.'

'And he is here in Pisa?'

'Right again.'

'And the others from Bordeaux, the Englishmen – they are here too. They followed us.'

'Not exactly. Someone has followed us, though, or rather they have followed our friend. But he is safe. Would you like to meet him? He will be able to answer more of your questions.' And he got up and pointed to a door I had not noticed at the other end of the room.

'Through here,' he said, beckoning with a crooked finger.

He looked almost devilish, with the firelight flickering on his dark face and picking out the sweep of his brows. 'He is waiting for you.'

I felt a sudden reluctance, but picked up my beaker and walked over to the door. The Captain knocked twice and opened it. Gilles must have been standing on the other side, for he slipped out with an unreadable look on his face and, with a gentle hand between my shoulder blades, pushed me inside. I found myself in a smaller room with a smaller fire and one square table, on which stood a wine jug. A tall, stooped figure sat with his back to me, hooded and swathed in a black travelling cloak despite the warmth. I took a step back but the door closed behind me with a soft click. The man at the table reached out and tapped the table opposite him. Starting to shiver a little myself, but not wishing to be rude, I made my way slowly to the high-backed chair and pulled it back.

'Sir, may I sit down?' I croaked. The man rose to his feet, cloak billowing, and threw back his hood. I staggered back and would have fallen into the fire had a long hand not shot out and grabbed my sleeve. We stood, the table between us, and then I had leaped around it and wrapped my arms around him.

'Adric!' I gasped.

'Dear boy!'

He was all bones, hardly more than a skeleton in a black cloak. But he returned my hug, hands fluttering like bats at my back.

'I never thought to see you again,' I said finally, when we were seated by the fire.

'I must confess that I was a little less sure of that,' said Adric.

I sat back and let out a great gasp, as if I had been holding some part of my breath all these months. Speechless and overcome with joy, I raised his fingers to my lips and kissed them. He harrumphed, embarrassed.

'The Captain seems to think you are full of questions,' he said at last. I held up my hands in resignation.

'Where to begin?' I said.

'Well.' He filled our beakers. 'Do you know how we both come to be here?'

'Yes, of course. Sir Hugh de Kervezey.' I spat into the flames.

'You've learned a sailor's habits, I see. You are right – Kervezey it was who hurled us out into the world. But he, like the rest of us – you, me, the Captain included – are caught up in a game, or rather a maze. And at the centre of the maze is something small and simple, oddly enough.'

He had not changed, despite having wasted away almost to nothing. I waited, knowing from long experience that he expected my query but would answer his own riddle whether or not I spoke. In any case, what could he mean?

'What was Kervezey after?' he prodded.

'The hand.'

'Ah. No. Well, not exactly. He was after the Captain. I will tell you why in a moment. And what did that have to do with you? Simply that he had discovered that you had been my – what is the right word? Helper? No, protégé, as the French say.'

'And friend, I hope,' I said.

'Always that. In any case he had an informant at the abbey from whom he learned of my occasional meetings with the Captain. Purely by accident, I suppose, I happen to be one of the only people in England who knows de Montalhac's true identity and business. No. Actually that is not quite true. I have known him for years, and we have met often. I do not need to be deceitful with you. I do so hate deception in any case, but it has been forced upon me. No, the truth is that I am an associate of Seigneur de Montalhac, as he says.'

'Adric! You work for the Captain? You have *always* worked for him?'

'In an academic capacity, dear Petroc. I am his bookworm, you might say. I research the esoteric questions he brings me, and hunt on paper what he hunts out here in the world. This, or something like it, Kervezey learned, although I don't think he realised the depth of our connection until much later. Meanwhile I was to be the unwitting snare, and you the bait, that he set for the Captain.'

'But what about the deacon?'

'Aha. He was going to kill the deacon anyway. You just provided a handy scapegoat. Serendipity, I suppose you might say.'

I slumped against the high back of the bench. My head was beginning to buzz with confusion. First my old friend had appeared as if from the dead, and now he felt the need to tell me my own story in a way that made no sense whatsoever.

'Serendipity, Adric? It's hard to think of serendipity involving so much blood.'

'No, no, you don't see it. Well, how could you? But it was so. The hand was a lucky accident for him, which he exploited. I think he was hoping that making you a fugitive would send you back to Devon and the abbey, and give him some advantage over me.'

'Wait, wait. He tried to kill me by the river. He did kill my best friend.' I could see Will spinning away, his head lost in a cloud of blood. 'He wanted me dead then.'

'No, that was an accident, I think. Or rather he meant to kill your friend but not you. He wanted you alone and frightened so he could drive you. He miscalculated you, boy, and he lost you for a while. I am afraid I took a dreadful risk sending you to Dartmouth – risked both your safety and the Captain's – but it was the only path I could see. But you did escape with the hand, and that was a wonderful development, the perfect bait for a relic merchant. Anyway, Kervezey couldn't approach me in person, as he'd already done so and I had seen through his scheme . . .'

'Stop, Adric, for God's sake!' I raised both hands. 'Kervezey had already been to Buckfast? Why, when?'

Adric sighed. 'I am getting ahead of my tale. Let me start at the beginning. Have you heard of Saint Cordula?'

Now my head was spinning in earnest. I pressed my fingers to my temples and mouthed a 'no'.

'But Saint Ursula and her eleven thousand virgins? Every schoolboy knows Ursula.' He waited for my baffled nod. 'Good. For a start, there were eleven virgins, not eleven thousand: Sencia, Saturia, Saturnina – tricky – Saula, Rabacia, Palladia, Pinnosa, Martha, Britula and Gregoria.'

'That's ten virgins, Adric.' I took a long gulp of wine.

'Exactly so. Cordula was hiding on her boat.' He beamed.

'What bloody boat?' My teeth were beginning to grind together.

'The boat that brought Ursula and virgins to Cologne, where they were massacred by Attila. Pay attention, Patch. Cordula sensibly didn't want to be massacred, so she hid on the boat, only to be winkled out by her conscience the next morning, when the Huns sent her off to join Ursula and her friends. Thus making up the eleven. Or, if we assume that Ursula was herself a virgin, which we must, the twelve. She missed out on sainthood for a century or two, but she made it onto the heavenly roster in the end, which is the important part to us.'

'In what possible way could she be important to us?'

'Because she's turned up.'

'But surely most learned people don't believe any part of the Ursula story. I've always heard that the Holy See has been trying to get rid of her for years.'

'Most *learned* people, yes. And what a tiny number that is, I don't have to tell you. To the rest of humanity she's as real as this wine jug – pass it over, would you?'

'What I meant was that, if Ursula is a myth, how can one of her companions' bodies exist?'

'How indeed? But it seems that Cordula, at least, was real.'

'Saint Cordula has turned up. And how about the other ten – excuse, me Adric, *eleven* virgins? That, I will admit, is a powerful lot of virgins, dead or not.'

'Oh, come on, Petroc. You used to like nosing around after old bones – remember? And remember what business the Captain – and you, nowadays – are in. I say again: the body of Saint Cordula has been found, or its whereabouts learned. A long-dead girl forgotten on an island – that is the centre of our maze.'

Adric paused again, and I grinned. He had me, as he always did in the end.

'Well then, dear friend, please tell me about poor Cordula and her part in our downfall.'

He grinned in turn, and Ælfsige of Frome's bony visage flashed in my mind. Waving for more wine, he settled down to tell his tale.

'In a land far away – England, dear boy – there was a bishop whose luck it was to land a rich, fat diocese in a city full of scholars. He had a palace, soldiers, servants and, best of all, a great cathedral, many years in the building and newly finished. What more could he want?

'But this was a greedy man. He saw that his fine cathedral, although it gloried God with every stone and crumb of mortar, was not bringing enough glory to him. Or money. For although it had many wonders, it lacked one important thing: a relic powerful enough to draw pilgrims. Its saint, a local martyr, had local affection but no draw outside the county. The Bishop looked towards Chartres and Canterbury and felt nothing but the grimmest envy.

'The Bishop had a right-hand man, a crusader knight returned from Outremer who was a little headstrong but willing and able to do whatever the Bishop needed doing, in return for money and, better, power over others. The Bishop enlisted this man in his quest for a great relic. This had to be small but important – an apostle's finger, a tooth of the Baptist – or less important but big: enough to fill a coffin, enough to parade through the streets.

'All familiar enough so far? Good. Now, the problem with relics is that entire saints are hard to come by – most of them are in little bits and pieces these days. There are holy corpses by the bushel in the East, but here in the Holy See, those schismatic Greek saints aren't worth more than the price of their winding cloths, and then only to the oakum man. The really big prizes went centuries ago – you'll know all about Saint Mark.

'But then all of a sudden, a scholar in Germany – a pupil of Albert of Cologne, in fact, Albertus Magnus, a charming fellow I had the good fortune to meet a few weeks ago . . . your pardon, Petroc. This scholar – who happened to be an Englishman studying abroad – while working on the life of Saint Ursula, discovered a clue buried far down in the archives of a monastery outside Cologne – that the body of Cordula had been carried away from the place of execution by a mercenary of the Huns, a Greek soldier who saw the martyrdom and saved the remains from the barbarians, who seem to have disposed very efficiently of most of the other eleven virgins – or perhaps the eleven thousand. This soldier made his way back to his home on an island in Greece, where he set up a church in Cordula's honour. As I'm sure you know, the Greeks have always done things very differently to us, and in their Schismatic way they made Cordula a Greek saint. I would imagine that, on a small island, the local folk forgot her origins very quickly and made her a daughter of the village. Her name was lost in a foreign tongue, and so she disappeared for perhaps a thousand years.'

'But she is not very important, is she, Adric? A very minor saint, surely?'

'Ah – there you have it – the small, simple thing at the

centre of it all: a long-dead girl. You would seem to be right. But Ursula's cult is not minor in the least. It brings a great deal of gold to Cologne – virgins come from all over Christendom to seek her protection. She has her own order of nuns. And around a century ago someone conveniently turned up a great cache of bones – apparently those of the virgin army – which Cologne has been busily selling off ever since. No, a complete virgin of Ursula would be a find indeed. There are always virgins in need of protection, dear boy . . .' And he shot me a look.

'So I've heard,' I answered carefully.

'Quite.' He coughed discreetly into his fist. 'And then this fellow found Cordula, or at least picked up her trail. Our world – the scholarly world – is very, very small, Petroc, and word gets around. It reached the Bishop of Cologne, and very soon your very own Bishop of Balecester was hatching schemes. With all those scholars at his beck and call, he started some research himself, and dug up some facts, so called, of his own. Most people know that Ursula came from Britain, and so did her virgins. But imagine his surprised delight – so very *surprised* he was, Petroc, and delighted – when his scholars uncovered the name of Cordula in the Balecester city records! Imagine . . . Pure serendipity. Ours is a tale of serendipity, is it not?

'Now the Bishop must have Cordula for himself. But he doesn't know exactly where she is. The Cologne trail goes cold in the Ionian Islands – a small enough area, but a lot of islands, and many, many churches and saints. For in Greece, so I've been told, a village may have a church to Saint John, but it won't necessarily honour the Baptist. More likely it is some local man, a holy Yanni who performed some small miracle or renounced the world and lived in an olive tree or some such. It doesn't take an army of virgins to impress a Greek peasant.

'There is one man in the world who can find a lost saint, and the Bishop needs him. The legendary dealer in holy relics, known to some as Jean de Sol, to many as the Frenchman, and to a very few as Captain de Montalhac. The problem is that this man is almost as mythical as the relics he procures – did I say mythical? I meant elusive. He appears when needed, and is invisible otherwise. The princes and church-lords who are his customers never question his integrity – they need his wares too badly. He has the gratitude of kings and popes and, it is whispered, the ear of the Stupor Mundi, wonder of the world, the Emperor Frederick. The Bishop is no fool. He knows that Cordula will be in demand, and that the Frenchman is most probably on her trail on someone else's – without a doubt, the Bishop of Cologne's – behalf. But Sir Hugh believes he can find him and by fair means or foul, lay hands on Cordula for Balecester cathedral.'

'But what did this have to do with Deacon Jean? You said Kervezey meant to kill him.'

'The Deacon was recently returned from Cologne, where he had been studying under the great Albert, whom I believe I've mentioned. Yes. And . . .'

'. . . He was the scholar who found Cordula. Oh, God.'

'Exactly. Sought out for special advancement by his lordship the Bishop to keep him close. But Balecester found that the Deacon had promised the relic to Cologne, and decided to get rid of him. Now, I think I'm allowed to tell you – this is going to sound rather alarming – that a little while before you became involved, the Captain was approached, through his system of intermediaries, by the Bishop. Only a very few of his most powerful clients, and by that I mean emperors and even popes, ever meet him in person. The intermediaries ensure that his identity remains a secret from all lesser mortals, and the Bishop of Balecester certainly counts as one of those. Anyway . . .'

'Wait, wait! The Captain is working for the Bishop? How can that possibly be?'

'Dear boy, the Bishop is exactly the kind of person who

requires the Captain's services: someone whose dignity and importance are in inverse proportion to their wealth and self-regard. In any case, he is hardly working for him. He has agreed to provide him with something.'

'Cordula.'

'In fact he had quite a shopping list. Cordula was at the top, of course, together with a certain Saint Exuperius, one of the Theban Legion,' and he gave me his teacher's look.

'Saint Maurice and the martyred Roman soldiers. Victor, etcetera. They didn't exist either, did they?'

'Well, probably not. But a rumour is going around that Exuperius is – I was going to say alive and well! No, that he is available, or at least somewhere for the finding. Balecester is almost as excited about Exuperius as he is about Cordula.'

'But if there is already a business arrangement, why . . .' and I waved my arm helplessly.

'Greed, pure and simple greed. Balecester hatched a plan with his lieutenant, Sir Hugh de Kervezey, to cheat the Captain. They want him to find Cordula, and then they will . . . kill him and take Cordula *gratis*, and everything else in the Captain's very considerable horde. They would then be in a position to control the greater part of the entire trade in holy relics, and I don't need to tell you what that means.'

'And so Kervezey – well, I know the rest of it. So I was merely to be set up as the Deacon's killer, but instead I became the bait to catch de Montalhac, just because I took the hand? So the hand had nothing to do with it.'

'Oh, no. Sir Hugh wanted the hand – he sent you to get it. He was going to use it himself, of course, but you saved him the bother. I suppose he was going to offer it on the clandes-tine market and see who bit. And he was going to use you – your apostasy, really – as a way to gain power over me – threaten me, as your teacher, with an enquiry or some such – if I refused to betray the Captain. Quite a tangle, eh? Anyway, it half-worked: in fact it worked so much better than he could ever have dreamed. You actually joined the Captain's company, and I had to leave the abbey in a hurry. You were there to see how he lorded it over us. Well, he finally roused the Abbot – it was the day you left. He mustered the brothers with bow and arrow and we greeted the bugger with drawn strings. I don't think he believed that monks could be so angry. So he left, calling down fire and brimstone and the wrath of mother Church on our heads. Alas, he had made the abbey a little too hot for me. The Abbot regretfully suggested I take an indefinite sabbatical abroad – he was kind enough to write me some nice references – and here I am.'

'And this isn't serendipity either, is it, Adric?'

'Not quite. I've been doing a little sniffing around for the Captain while tramping around Christendom like a poor friar – what a wonderful time I'm having, Patch! – hence my time with Albertus, who is wandering like me. We met in Utrecht, and I was able to find out a few more crumbs, little clues to Cordula's resting place.'

'Has it all been wonderful, though? You had to leave Bordeaux in a hurry.'

'They found me, yes. When Kervezey lost you he decided to follow me – old and slow, you know. But I have learned a few tricks, especially in this last year. I got away just in time, but that too was lucky as it hurried me to Rome, where I found the last piece of our mystery.'

Silently I poured us more wine, then hurried him along. He had me again.

'Rome, Petroc, Rome! I intend to spend the rest of my days there, God willing, rooting like an old hog in the Vatican libraries. It was fortunate that I had a particular task, or I would be there yet. You would not believe it, Patch. Everything is there! The answer to every question, and a million more questions and the answers to those as well . . .'

'And our particular answer?'

'A letter!' he said, banging the table. 'Very easy to find. A

276

letter from Pope Leo the Great to a certain Eudorius, a Greek consul who had evidently written seeking clarification about something: a question of beatification. Old Leo was a master of linguistic economy, you might say, but this particular letter – remember, we have only the answer, not the question – mentions the words Cologne, martyr and a place, Koskino, an island in the Ionian Sea. By the way, Leo is most discouraging to poor old Eudorius, urging caution and suggesting further investigation. The Captain has been doing a little digging of his own, and his own researches have discovered that on Koskino there is a local cult of fertility centred on the shrine of a Saint Tula.' He looked at me expectantly.

'Cordula, Tula. Perhaps.'

'More than that. You are bound for Koskino, boy.'

'And you, Adric?'

'I think Brother Adric deserves a rest. I am sending him back down to Rome in the morning.' It was the Captain. I wondered how long he had been standing in the open doorway.

'Will you sell Cordula to the Bishop?' I asked him.

'Great God, no. I ceased to do anything on that man's behalf the day you came aboard in Dartmouth. But I would like to have Cordula, and now, unfortunately, I have to find her before the secret gets out: for it will, it will.'

'He is a monster,' I said.

'The Bishop? No, Balecester himself is no great monster. He has a monstrous ambition, though. He would like to be Archbishop of Canterbury, a kingmaker, probably even Pope. It is common enough. But the true monster is his son.' He stopped, and rubbed his beard.

'The Bishop has a son?' I looked blankly from one to the other.

'Kervezey is the bishop's bastard, Petroc,' the Captain said.

'Oh,' I said. I examined the pitcher of wine in front of me:

empty. Four eyes – two hawk-like, two owlish, studied me intently.

'So what will happen now?' I asked finally.

'We will find our relic and convey her to her new resting place in the cathedral at Cologne,' the Captain told me. 'The Bishop was almost apoplectic with joy when I offered her for sale. She will add some lustre to his Ursula collection.'

'And Balecester?'

'Bugger Balecester,' said the Captain.

Will had seen no more suspicious shadows in the alley, but we kept our hands on our swords as we walked Adric the short way to the little monastery where he had his lodgings. Before leaving the inn he had passed a small scroll to the Captain, who tucked it away carefully among his clothing. It was the letter, I assumed: the key to everything that Adric had told me. I was still dizzy with all I had heard. I was just a poor lad from Dartmoor, and yet a woman who had died when an emperor still sat in Rome had reached out and plucked me from my cosy little life. And just as strange, I had learned that I was part of a game and had been one of its pieces long before I had stumbled upon Sir Hugh in the Crozier. So I was not paying attention when Gilles grabbed my arm and pointed up the street to where a crowd had gathered. The Captain had already pulled Adric against the nearest wall.

'Look there, Patch. That is the monastery, I think! Quick, go and see what has happened, but keep in the shadows. Will, hand on hilts, if you please.'

I nodded and slipped into the stream of people hurrying to get a look at whatever excitement was up ahead. The crowd had blocked the whole street and I had to jostle my way to the front. There was an angry murmur around me. I craned my neck over a feather-crowned hat.

The monastery door was open, and in the doorway a body lay sprawled among the folds of a brown Benedictine robe, a rivulet of blood welling from the cloth and into the gutter. Another body lay just inside the courtyard, lit by flames that, as I watched, burst from an open casement and began to lick the low eaves of the building. More monks were dashing about, and one of them limped into the street and spread bloodied hands to the crowd in dumb entreaty. That was enough. I squeezed back through the press and into the shadows to where my three companions waited. The Captain pulled me close.

'Fire and murder,' I panted, and saw Adric's face turn white as ash.

'Fire? Where?' he demanded, and I told him.

'My cell!' he stammered. 'They have killed my hosts and burned my cell – oh, good Christ, my papers!'

'Calm yourself, brother: we have the letter,' hissed the Captain, looking about us anxiously. 'Now we must all get back to the ship.'

'There was another copy! A copy, damn my foolishness – and now I have killed those good brothers of mine! I must go to them . . .'

And with a force that took us unawares he threw himself between us and began to run on faltering legs back towards the crowd. Will and I stared at each other slack-mouthed, then took off after him. We were two or three strides from the edge of the crowd when we caught up. I almost had hold of his flapping cloak when a man broke free from the mob and met Adric as he careened heedlessly on. The two seemed to bump shoulders by accident, but Adric gave a high yelp of surprise and pain and stood swaying, bony hands raised before him as if in benediction.

'Knife!' Will shouted as Adric collapsed against him. My hand was on my sword but the man was drawing back his hand for another blow – now I saw the long, slender blade – and so I slammed my right shoulder into him, drawing my sword as I brought my elbow up under his ribs. He stumbled back –

perhaps he would have attacked, or maybe he was about to hide himself in the crowd – as I swung backhanded. The sword jarred as it struck him full in the neck. His head bounced forward onto his chest and bobbed there, held by the windpipe as he tottered, gouts of blood pumping from the void between his shoulders. Full of rage and disgust, I kicked him over. Then I looked down and saw the man I had killed. A pale eye goggled fishily at an impossible angle. I felt my gorge rise.

'Adric is hurt – quick, Patch,' said Will, from a great distance. At that moment Gilles and the Captain came running up. Will was on his feet, sword out, and the two of us faced the crowd which, torn between two entertainments, was beginning to edge towards us. Adric sat hunched over, rocking in pain and clutching his left side.

'Help me lift him,' Gilles said to no one in particular.

'No, let me up – I can stand,' wheezed the librarian, unfolding himself like a rusty clasp-knife. Gilles grabbed him under one arm, and I made to take the other, but Adric winced and waved me off.

'It is not bad: the fool hit my pectoral and scraped my ribs. I can make my own way, boy,' he said, his voice weak but determined. 'Let me away to my brothers . . .'

'No! Do you want to die? I will not let you. Back to the ship with us all, now!' It was the Captain. 'Don't let him go.' He tapped Will and me on the shoulders. 'Fine work, lads. Do you know him, Will?'

He nodded curtly at the dead man. 'Aye,' my friend said tersely. I began to wonder what he meant, but then the corpse gave a horrible, mechanical kick and the crowd gasped as if with one breath and surged forward. We turned and ran for it, Gilles with Adric slung over his shoulder as if the old man were nothing more than a bundle of dry twigs. We had taken no more than a dozen strides when we were brought up short by a knot of latecomers to the grisly spectacle behind us. They paid us no heed, but gave no leeway either. One of them, a paunchy burgher, halted directly in front of Gilles, craning his neck impatiently, seemingly oblivious of our burden or our haste. Will and I made ready to apply rough shoulders to this obstruction, but as we approached, and the man's arms came up in remonstration and his fleshy mouth opened to protest or scold, I heard an odd sound like two wet hands clapped together and the man staggered backwards and began to pluck at the front of his tunic. Still frowning indignantly, he dropped to the ground. His companions began screaming at one another, and at us: appeals for help, for explanation. A tall woman, her face caught between horror and tears, grabbed me by the elbows and began to shake me. I brushed her aside, and as she reeled past Will her coif seemed to leap from her head and I caught a vision of rent cloth, grey hair and hot blood that spattered my cheek before she sat down hard, mouth open in a silent, perfect O. That was enough for us and we leaped forward. As we did so, Will stumbled and fell heavily against me, his arms tangling in my scissoring legs. I fell in my turn and hit the cobbles hard, but in a moment I was up again, reaching for my friend, who I assumed had tripped over the woman. But even in the dim light I could see that something was wrong. Will's face was a gargoyle's mask of agony and he was whining through bared teeth.

'Come on!' The Captain had paused, looking back.

I bent down, trying to haul Will upright, and as my hands sought a hold on his clothes they touched something hard and Will gave a choked, animal shriek. I realised I had hold of the shaft of an arrow, in up to the feathers in the centre of Will's back. Looking up, I saw that the woman, bent over now, her head between the knees, was bleeding hard from a deep, long gash in her scalp. Her companion, a younger man in foppish headgear, was in the act of drawing his dagger, his eyes fixed on me, teeth bared in fury. At that moment another arrow struck the wood of a nearby door with a hollow whack, and the man dropped to the ground and covered his ridiculous hat with quivering hands.

'Captain!' I yelled. 'Will's down! He's been shot!'

There was a whirring in my ear, then a clatter. Then another whirr, and Gilles cursed.

'Away, boys! The swine has the light behind him!'

'I have had my cloak shot through,' said the Captain, matter-of-factly. 'Will: can he walk? No? Petroc, take his legs – be quick about it!'

What happened next is not very clear. Gilles and the Captain grabbed Will by the arms and I seized his legs and between us we ran, Adric following close behind, the body of my friend face down between us, limp and leaden. There may have been more arrows, but I had no thought but for the man I carried. The tumult grew dim behind us. Then we were back inside the Taverna, laying Will down on the table where – an hour ago? More? – I had dined on roast pig.

'It was a crossbow,' said Gilles, cutting away Will's tunic. He slid his hand under Will's body and shook his head. The bolt, thick as my finger, had struck where Will's shoulder blade met his backbone. The feathers – no, not feathers: strange ribs of leather – were red with blood, which welled strongly around the shaft. 'A quadrello: a mankiller. And it is buried. If it was out the other side . . .' He tugged gingerly on the bolt and Will convulsed. 'No, no . . . It is barbed.'

'For the love of God, turn me over.' Will's voice was like the wind blowing through a field of corn. Gilles looked at me. He had bitten through his lower lip. He leaned close and whispered in my ear.

'Your friend is going to die, Patch, whatever we do. I cannot pull the bolt out. He is bleeding fast, and probably much faster inside. He will not last out the night. I am . . . I am sorry.'

'Can we do nothing?'

'We can make him comfortable.' He looked up, and saw the innkeeper watching us anxiously. He went over to the man and whispered urgently to him. The innkeeper hurried from the room and returned a minute later with something that he handed to Gilles. After consulting the Captain, who was seated in front of the fire with a pan of hot water, treating Adric's wound, he returned to the table.

'Farrier's shears,' he said, holding up a pair of enormous, crude black scissors. 'Hold your friend still.'

I went to the head of the table and grabbed Will's arms above the elbow, pinning him down. I leaned close.

'Don't worry, my brother,' I said, sounding as calm as I could. Gilles had taken the shears in both hands and now, with one motion, cut through the bolt where it met Will's flesh. There was a sharp crack and Will screamed, high and lonely like a fox on a winter's night.

'It is done, it is done, my brave lad,' I soothed. We rolled him over as carefully as we could, Gilles taking care to bunch Will's cloak under his back so that his weight would not force the bolt in further. When we were finished, he lay, eyes wide and staring at the shadows on the ceiling, breathing like a spent horse. Sweat had soaked his hair, and his feet twitched and beat gently against the table and each other.

'Does it hurt very much, Will?'

He closed his eyes as if thinking, then opened them again.

'There's something on my feet. Get it off, would you?' I made to look, but of course there was nothing there.

'Is it gone now?'

'I think so. It must be. Is there a cat in here? Felt like a big cat pinning me down.' He winced. 'Listen to me, Patch. I have something to confess.'

'I will not hear your confession, Will!' I said. 'I am no priest, and besides, you will be fine.'

He chuckled weakly. 'I don't think so, brother. Don't worry, I'm not going to unburden myself of the sins of my flesh. I'll take those with me, thank you very much. Besides, you wouldn't appreciate them.' He tried to wink, but I saw he had lost the mastery of his face. His cheek twitched dismally, then went slack.

'Lean close, brother. I don't have very much puff . . . Is one of you sitting on my legs?' I shook my head. 'Fancy that. There's a weight . . . now it's gone. That's better. Now listen well. You heard the Captain ask whether I knew that lad whose head you lopped off, yes? All right. I did know him. Rufus, his name was. I knew him because he was an old comrade of mine.'

'From Morpeth?' I asked, stupidly.

Will sighed and closed his eyes. I leaned forward sharply, but they fluttered and opened again.

'Still here, brother. They're sitting on my legs again, aren't they? Listen. When I told you I served under . . . who did I say? Sir Ranulf?'

'Sir Andrew Hardie,' I said. 'The company of the Black Boar.'

'I never could remember a lie. No. My company was the Cross of Bone, under Sir Hugh de Kervezey.'

I shrank back as if he had struck me. 'How, Will?' I said at long last.

He let out a long, ragged sigh. 'I was taken,' he said at last. 'I told you that lovely tale, and some was true, at least. But I did not quite make it to London. They found me in the road, beat me half to death again, and I woke up in the Bishop's dungeon. I . . . There is no time, is there? I must be brief. Yes – by some odd chance, Kervezey took a shine to me and the Bishop gave me to him as his slave. I am – I *was* bound to him by every law written and still unwritten. He made me one of his band, those who do his bidding on the Bishop's behalf. We came to Bordeaux a month and more before you with orders to wait for a ship, the *Cormaran*. When it came in, we were sent to spy out the crew as they came ashore and kill as many as we could. It was not my lot to ask questions.'

'And you followed Anna and me?'

He grinned mirthlessly. 'No. And if I had known you were alive, let alone in Bordeaux, I would never . . .' He widened his eyes at me, pleading. 'You believe me, brother?' I nodded helplessly. 'Thank God. But that night . . . I had given that night up for lost. Those drunken, raddled fools I was with made me watch while they stuffed themselves all night and felt up girls. You stumbled upon us, brother. Benno was trying to sleep it off and you woke him up. I didn't know it was you – how could I have? I just didn't want those pigs to hurt anyone.'

'I thought you were dead!' I blurted.

'Well, I *knew* you must be.' He drew his breath in and with a huge effort reached out his hand and grasped mine. It was cold as stone, but the grip was tight. 'Real enough, though,' he said.

'Why didn't you tell me, Will?'

'I told the Captain. And he . . . he said keep it quiet for a while. And I said I must tell my friend Patch. And he said . . . he said tell him when you are ready. And. Now I am ready.'

'Oh Christ, Will!'

'Why don't you forget I came back? Perhaps that would be best.'

'No! That is not what I meant. I was thinking about all this time on the ship . . . I wasted everything.'

He squeezed my hand. 'Despite your behaviour, brother, I have never been happier than in the past couple of weeks.'

'Will? I'm so sorry about the things I said. About Anna.'

He tried to laugh, but a spasm passed through him and I saw that blood was seeping from his nose and the corners of his mouth.

'I would have been offended if you had not said them, dear brother. But the princess loves you with all her heart, I'm afraid. I never stood a chance. Do not . . .' and he gripped my hand again, '. . . do not hurt her, Patch. Do not let her go. Swear to me.'

'Of course. I swear.'

'Good, good . . . how strange, Patch, are you still there?'

'Yes, brother.'

'I cannot see you. Shoo that cat away, and cover me up, Patch. Later on, shall we go out, to the Crozier?'

'I would like that, Will.'

'So would I.'

He sighed and lay still. Only then did I notice that Adric had come and knelt at the head of the table. One arm was in a sling, but he had covered his face with the other hand and I knew he was saying the prayers for a departing soul.

We had to leave him lying there. He had not moved again, and his breathing had grown fainter until with one deep gasp he had come to his end. The innkeeper had brought candles, and Adric set one at his head and one at his foot. I stood and stared into his face. His lips had drawn back a little from his teeth, and I wiped the blood away. I told myself it was a smile, but it was not. Thin slivers of white shone beneath his eyelids. I would not leave until at last Gilles and the Captain prised my hand loose.

'We must be gone before sunrise, Petroc,' said the Captain gently.

'I won't leave him,' I rasped. I had not cried. Instead I seemed to have dried up from the inside out. My eyes stung and my mouth was parched.

'The master of the inn will take care of him. He will get a proper burial. I wish we could take him back to the ship . . . to his home. But we cannot. If we do not leave now we are all dead men, and he would not wish that.'

'And Adric?' I said finally.

'Adric is fine,' said the librarian. 'My wounds are not worth dwelling upon, now,' and he crossed himself with a glance at Will. 'He must have been a good man, Petroc, for he made a good death.' He shivered, and drew his cloak about him. 'And he died with the blessing of friendship. Now, my friend the

Captain is right: we must leave here this instant, and I am coming with you.'

They pulled me to my feet and out of the taverna, and dragged me until I started running with them. The others feared meeting the Watch, but there was no one much about, although the streets near the Taverna were still full of the stench of burning. We did not stop until the Campo, and when we had crossed it we ran again. The jarring of the cobbles beneath my feet helped keep my head empty, but as soon as we were back on the *Cormaran* I could not escape and stumbled away to crouch against the rail, hugging my knees, stupefied with grief. Adric was sent to lie down in the cabin. The Captain was giving orders and the ship was springing to life, another shore leave cancelled, angry men taking out their frustrations on rope and wood. When everything was to his satisfaction he beckoned Adric from the cabin, and the two men came and knelt down next to me.

'He was a good man – I had so little time to get to know him, but he had his own . . . his own honour, and it was very strong,' the Captain said. 'You called each other brother, but that is truly what he was to you, I think? It is hard to see a brother die.' He paused. 'That I do know.' He passed his hands across his face. 'Now forgive us – this is the last time we will invade your sorrow – but we must make you understand one more thing about last night.'

Adric nodded. 'Do you remember Saint Ælfsige of Frome?' he asked, and I looked up in surprise. 'Quite a story that made.'

'But you were working for me that day,' continued the Captain. 'Ælfsige ended up as someone else entirely, you know. He made a Flemish abbot very happy. I have known of you since you went to Buckfast, Petroc. But you will wonder, one day if not sooner, whether Adric meant for you to . . . to end up in this life. I can assure you that he did not. His heart was quite broken by your troubles.'

'But they were not of your making, Adric,' I said quietly.

'Not directly,' said the librarian, 'But you were chosen by Balecester and his son because you were my student. That alone has filled me with guilt.' He studied my face. 'But you are alive. And now, it seems, we are of the same company.' He stood up leaned on the rail. 'Now we must end this, must we not?'

'We must,' said the Captain. He took me by the shoulders. 'Your brother Will would want us to claim the prize. And that we shall do. We are putting out this minute for the Ionian.'

I felt as cold and lonely as the great ice-fields of Greenland. I hardly cared what these two had been saying to me. At that moment, what cared I for Adric's guilt, or the Captain's sympathy? But, like an iceberg bobbing alone on the Sea of Darkness, a thought formed itself in my mind.

'It was Kervezey, wasn't it?' I said.

'That is my guess.'

There was nothing more to say. Adric limped off to the cabin. The Captain went back to directing the crew: a fight had broken out on the deck and the mutterings were getting louder. There would be many promises made and ruffled feathers smoothed before the men were happy again. I wanted no part of it. Feeling utterly alone, I went and stood in the bow as the *Cormaran* drifted out into the main channel and began to slip away down the Arno to the sea. The lights of Pisa were dimming behind us when I felt an arm slip through mine. It was Anna, and we stood like that, silent, until the sun rose and the flying fishes came out to dance back and forth across our path.

Chapter Eighteen

Koskino was a mountain, a slab of white rock thrust straight up out of the sea. Lush lower down, the trees thinned as the slopes became cliffs, with here and there a slash of dark green where a company of cypresses had taken hold, and then the island ended in an abrupt, stark line, seemingly flat as a table on top. It was getting dark as we drew near, and the clouds had formed out of a clear sky and were rolling slowly over the top of the cliff wall. It had seemed tiny from a distance, this place, another speck among specks in the ruffled, inky sea. We were sailing into its shadow now, and the day's heat reached us, a parching breath, along with the mad choir of insects.

Anna was with me in the bow. We were friends again, although we had not spoken of what it was that had come between us since leaving Bordeaux. Indeed I did not want to dwell on it, for it seemed a time of sickness, as if I had been suffering from a long fever and a wandering of the mind and now was well again. That is a strange thing to say, perhaps, by one who had just seen his greatest friend suffer a bloody and untimely death. But now what troubled me most was not the manner of Will's passing – for that was pure pain and could be treated almost like a wound – but the knowledge that his life had been poisoned by Sir Hugh de Kervezey, long before Kervezey – and I did not doubt it had been his hand on the trigger – had put an end to it. The sense that Will's life had been doomed long before our last night in Balecester, in fact from the moment we had met, came back to haunt me. I found

I could not even remember our first meeting – the refectory at the cathedral school, perhaps? – and this troubled me even more. Kervezey had cursed us – not just in the trials we had suffered in our flesh, but in our souls, for whatever else I believe about the soul, I know it is there that love, and friendship, grow like bright flowers. Kervezey had blighted us, both outside and in.

And now the anger that had so afflicted me while my friend was at my side returned in earnest. But this time, with a potent fuel, it burned like a pyre. It is strange how rage can drive away sadness, but it was as if my tears were dried up inside me by the heat of my anger. Sometimes it burned hot, like a fistful of coals aglow within my belly, and at other times it was utterly cold, and my soul felt enveloped in hoarfrost. But although I was full up to the brim with this anger, so that I feared I might at any moment vomit live cinders onto the deck, in my outward self I was calm. My mind was clear, and indeed I seemed to see everything with a clarity and a brightness that would probably have frightened me at any other time. I saw that there had been no chance in our reunion and took an obscure comfort from it. The thought that everything might have been arbitrary, that we had met and been torn apart again by some heartless, random coincidence, was more frightening than the knowledge that we had both been struggling in the same net. It is a habit of men, that we search for meaning in the deaths of those we love, and here was meaning aplenty, however cruel.

That first morning, Anna had stood with me, silently – for hours, perhaps. The sun had risen in earnest when she reached out a cool, careful finger and touched me, feather-like, below one eye, then another.

'They are dry,' she said, puzzled.

'There is nothing there,' I answered, my voice raspy. 'Nothing. But . . . I loved him, you know.'

'I know,' she said. We stood quiet again. Then she said, 'May I weep for him, then?'

I took her in my arms and let her offer up her tears. My own face grew wet with them, and I thought, how strange that I must have a surrogate to mourn Will for me.

'He made a good end,' I told her after a while, when we were both sitting on the deck, our backs to the rail. How insufficient my words had become. 'He was clear in his mind, and he went with love . . . with love in his heart,' I finished, which was true in its way.

'Did he suffer?' asked Anna, tremulously. I winced, and took her hand.

'If I told you no, would you believe me?' She searched my face with her salt-red eyes, then shook her head, a tiny shiver.

'No,' she whispered.

'Yes, he suffered very much, but less towards the end. He was brave and strong, and death had to wait his turn. We talked of many things, of . . .' I paused. I found I did not wish to tell Anna how I had sworn to Will that I would never let her go. Perhaps I worried she would be horrified, to be bound by an oath made to a dead man. But in truth that oath was the last thing that tied me to my friend, a secret shared with no one but him and so an invisible thread that connected us, stretching from the land of the living to wherever Will now dwelt. It had its beginning deep within my heart, and there was a tension in it, a thrum of motion sent through this lonely, fragile thread across empty worlds where the winds of loss blow coldly and without cease, that told of some presence holding fast to the other end. I felt it then, and it brought me solace. I feel it now.

'Do you still not weep?' she persisted.

'Will would not have approved,' I said, gruffly. 'Not of me blubbering, in any case. You, however . . . Besides, I wept a veritable Nile for the man, in error, while he still lived.'

'Oh! My God, Patch, you are a miser of grief!'

I shook my head and took her hands between both of mine. 'I was wrong to grieve then: I should have raged! Well, now I shall. There will be no tears, my love, not one tear until . . .' My voice began to shake, and I pressed Anna's fingers to my lips until I had mastered myself. 'Sir Hugh de Kervezey . . .' I grimaced at the name, bitter as gall. 'I will have that man's life, I swear it. That will be the Mass I say for my brother. When I have stopped his breath, then I shall weep.'

'Patch, I . . .'

'No, my love. I am burning up like a barrel of pitch! I must let the fire burn, and so must you.' I would have added, if I had known what words to use, that it was too wild a fire for me to control, although I knew that, as it burned through, I would see its form and know, from the embers, what my course would be.

Soon, too soon, it was time for Adric to take his leave. With him, at least, we did not have to conceal our feelings with great care. The old man had never been one to bother himself with how others lived, so long as nothing interrupted his gathering of knowledge, but I was a little surprised how his cadaverous features took on a certain glow after first making Anna's acquaintance. He became positively courtly, although Anna assured me that he was only interested in the manuscripts that lay in her uncle's library.

With me he seemed almost frightened, until I sat him down in the bows and convinced him that I did not blame him for Will's murder, for my flight from England or for any of the other dolorous strands of the web that held us both. After that we were as we had always been, although we both knew that nothing was really the same. I was no longer his pupil but a blooded outlaw, and he was no longer an abbey librarian with an appetite for esoteric wonders but an intriguer at large in a world that did not appear to frighten him in the slightest. I had never really thought of Adric as a brave man, only heedless of his safety in the way that eccentric people sometimes are. But after the events in Pisa, and remembering our adventure in Vennor long ago, I realised that not only was he fearless but that he was in possession of a very cool head indeed. We spent a happy two days running down the coast to Ostia. He was going back to Rome after all and there was no concealing his excitement.

'I have unfinished business in the Vatican libraries,' he said dreamily, and I knew that he was understating the case more than a little. Had Adric the nine lives of a cat – indeed, had he the gift of life eternal, his business with libraries would never be done.

'What are you digging for this time?' I asked.

'Hmm.' He treated me to an inscrutable look. 'A small investigation here, a few loose ends tied there. I will tell you everything when we meet again.'

'Do you think there's a chance of that, Adric?'

'A chance? My dear boy, I believe we now serve under the same captain,' he said. 'There's every chance that we shall be heartily sick at the sight of one another before too long. No, no – you go to Koskino, and I to Rome, and we shall all meet up before the winter's here . . . Venice, perhaps? I rather wish I were coming with you, of course.'

That cheered me, as I had feared this would be our last parting. So while I was terribly sorry to see him clamber, in his long, spidery fashion, down into the fishing barque that would take him up the Tiber to Rome, I drew some comfort from the knowledge that he would be the happiest man in that city as he burrowed ever deeper into its endless libraries. 'We will see each other soon, then,' I had said as I helped him over the side, and although he only nodded in reply, his mind on the shaky rope-ladder and the waiting books, I felt it might be true, and when he struggled upright in the fishing boat – to the evident concern of the fishermen – and waved back to the *Cormaran*, I understood that if Adric said we would meet again, we likely would.

In the days that followed it was almost impossible to be alone with Anna, and so we made do with hasty caresses and now and then a kiss, separated by long spans of time in which the blue waters sped by, mile after mile, beneath the hull. Although the knowledge that, sooner or later, she would be put ashore in Venice cast a faint shadow, we chose, I think, to put it from our minds, there being much else – and worse – near at hand about which to fret. But one night Anna had woken me from a deep sleep and led me through a maze of slumbering men to her lair in the hold. We had spent an hour of agony and pleasure there in the dark, brazenly alive to every fingertip, every touch of skin upon hot skin, while keeping as silent as the dead. It was torture, but exquisite. By some miracle we were not discovered, and afterwards we sat together on deck, watching the stars. Anna's head was on my shoulder, and she traced a slow circle with her fingernail on the back of my hand. I heard her sigh, then she turned and spoke softly in my ear: 'I never did tell you about my time in the Norse lands, did I?'

'You did not finish – or you did, but we were interrupted,' I said. It seemed a very long time ago.

'I told you they locked me up?' I nodded. 'They kept me locked away for two years,' she went on. 'Two endless years, in a plain white room with no glass in the window.'

'You didn't . . . it must have seemed a lifetime,' I said, taking her hand.

'And I was only a child, really, at least at the beginning.'

'How did you – you know, how did you manage?' I asked carefully.

'There was a kind priest. Father Jago,' she said. 'He was a good man, for a Frank – no, by any measure. He did not try to cram his doctrines down my gullet. Instead he bought me flowers for my windowledge, and found my belongings where they had been thrown in the cellars, so I could hang my tapestries. And he bought me my books. He was amazed, quite amazed, that a woman could read, and we spent hours together. He gave me hope.'

'So you were not very lonely?' I asked.

'I have never been so alone,' she said. 'Jago would read with me – Virgil, Aristotle, even Augustine – and I would see my home. Bees would come to sup at my flowers, and I would mourn, for they would never taste the rosemary or the lavender of our palace gardens. The mind plays cruel games.'

'Terrible games,' I agreed.

'Petroc, can I tell you something?' I nodded absently, looking up at the peaceful river of the Milky Way.

'Do you remember when we . . . back in Bordeaux? The first time?' I nodded again, and kissed her hand.

'It was not the first time. Not for me,' she said. I dropped her hand.

'Really?' I said, my voice reedy with surprise.

'No. You are shocked,' she insisted. I paused, considering. Then I picked up her hand again.

'I have no right to be shocked by anything,' I said. 'The greatest shock I ever had was discovering that you desired me. I have never judged you, Anna.'

'That is not true,' she protested. 'The day after Bordeaux, you acted as if I were Eve and Salome rolled into one.'

'No, no!' I shook my head furiously. 'No, it was the blood! I was sickened to my very soul by what I had done. And you had blood on your hands – I mean just that: your hands were all bloody, and I did not want more blood on me. That was all, Anna! I swear it!'

'I thought that you were revolted by me, by who – *what* – I was, what we had done. No, listen! In Trondheim, I was so lonely that I took one of my guards for a lover. He was a boy – big, blond, a peasant – and I was a girl. We did it exactly twice, then he boasted to his mates, there was a fight, and he lost the use of his arm. The whole castle found out. They put me in the cells, Patch! They would have tortured me were it not for my imperial blood.' She spat the words out distainfully. 'Then they decreed I should go to the stake. To burn. They would have done it, but Jago, my old priest, saved me. That was how I ended up in Greenland.'

'What about the guard?'

'Oh, I'm sure they killed *him*,' she replied. There was mockery in her voice, but it did not conceal the pain.

'Anna, you are neither Eve nor Salome. You did not kill that boy. Yes, there are many who would say otherwise – your husband, for one, and those pious murderers who administer the noose and the pyre as if those were Christ's sacrament. It is they who are damned, Anna. I judge them, not you.'

'Oh, what nonsense, Petroc!' she cried. I hushed her with my finger.

'Listen to me,' I said. 'That morning, after the fight, I was recoiling from what I had done to that man, not from what we had . . . There has never been anything finer than that in my mean little life. What you did in Trondheim, whose affair is it but yours? My God, Anna, how long were you in Gardar – two years? Well then, you have even done your penance as it is written down by the Church itself. But do not ask absolution of me. In my sight you are spotless. You are as pure as the whitest lily, my love.'

'Do you really mean all that?' she asked, quietly.

'With all my heart.'

'Then you are a fool,' she said. Her words were harsh, but her lips on mine were not.

The saint who watches over lovers and fools – and over foolish lovers most of all – was guarding us that night, for no one saw us, or if they did, chose not to make it their business. We were not so reckless again, but that night had battered down every last vestige of the reserve that had come between us for so long. If we were not so bold, then at least we spent our idle hours, be they night or day, together. And if my terrible rage was not quenched, it was tempered, and I saw, at last, that although I had come to know death, I had also found out life's store of sweetness, and how to share it with another.

Thus we had passed the great Bay of Naples and the great smouldering peak of Vesuvius, of which I had read in Pliny, and then down past the flames of Stromboli and the smoke of Etna – I remember these sights more than any other, as they were the strangest and filled me with wondering dread. We passed Stromboli at night, and Anna's lips found mine for a moment as we stood at the rail and watched the flames from the mountaintop cast ghastly pink and orange shadows on the black cloud that lowered overhead.

Then, as we passed the Straits of Messina and left Italy at Cape Spartivento, setting off into the Ionian Sea – I loved to hear these names, and pestered Nizam all I could to learn them – I felt a change in Anna. She was quivering like a courser about to be slipped free, and grew silent, although she seemed to seek my presence more. But most days she spent in her station at the bows, wedged in the angle between the rail and the bowsprit, watching the dolphins and flying fish that kept us company and gazing endlessly at the blue distance which hid Greece. She had taken her place there early on the morning we reached the island, as soon as land showed itself as the merest sliver on the horizon. Now her hair was stiff with salt spray, and her eyes were distant and slightly fevered.

'Do you hear it?' she asked. 'The land is singing to us. That is the song of my home.'

We were making for a gap in the lower cliffs that seemed to ring the island. Smaller breaks in the rock gave onto little beaches, each with a grove of trees clinging to whatever level ground there was. But Nizam had pointed the *Cormaran* at a stone gateway, where the cliffs dipped down into tapering spits and finally broke, letting the sea flow in towards the base of the greater mountain. At the end of each arm of rock stood two small stone turrets from the top of which spun four triangles of pure white cloth. They were windmills, childlike compared to the creaking giants of home but strangely festive amid all this water and arid rock.

We passed close enough to the starboard spit to hear the swish of the mills and to see the rock drop sheer into the deeps, white stone gleaming through the air-clear water. Thick red weed grew there, with fat sea anemones and clusters of black, spiky orbs.

'*Echinoos*,' said Pavlos, licking his lips. 'You would say "urchins".'

I told him we had no such barbaric creatures in Devon, and that I wasn't going to have them anywhere near my mouth. 'No, no: *you* are the barbarian here, Patch,' Anna reminded me. 'You will eat *echinoos*, I insist. They are sublime. They taste like . . . you'll see.' I huffed. But in truth I was strangely drawn to this place already. We had made only one other landfall in the Mediterranean Sea, at Pisa, a place of man's artistry and artifice, and the filth that always accompanies man had turned the water a sickly, opaque grey. We had skirted the arid coasts at a distance, close enough to smell the herb-laced breeze but too distant to make out details. Now it was close enough to touch, and I felt a sudden shiver of excitement. Then we were past the point, and the Bay of Limonohori opened before us.

It was a gigantic cove, a giant's stone basin tipped towards the sea, the lip just submerged, the walls rising on all sides until they fused with the mountain that towered high over everything. Straight ahead, a white village on a strip of white beach shimmered through the heat. Suddenly we were out of the wind and the air was still and hot and filled with the shrieks and rasps of unnumbered legions of insects. I smelled pine resin and thyme, and herbs that I could not name; stone dust, and a faint, pungent stink that was not unpleasant. The place was soaked in scent and noise and dry heat, as if the bay were an alchemist's alembic and we had intruded on some miraculous operation.

As we moved on, I could see houses on either side of us, small whitewashed cubes with roofs of red pan tile standing out from the dark grey-green trees. On the beaches, men sat mending nets while their brightly painted boats skipped at anchor in the clear, silver-blue shallows. I waved – something not done aboard the *Cormaran*, but I could not help myself – and a few waved back. At my side the Greeks were visibly shaking with joy. They whispered back and forth, their hands drawing urgent signs in the air between them.

'Have you been here before?' I asked them.

'I have,' said Pavlos. His face fell for a moment. 'They were not so pleased to see me then. It was when I sailed with . . . when I was with the pirates. I think we raided every village on these islands, but we didn't see the people. They would hide in the mountains, and besides, they had nothing to steal. But Venice is strong now, and the pirates are all dead or fat and old. Or respectable—' and he dug Panayoti in the ribs.

'They don't seem to be afraid of us at all.'

'Because we bring trade, not ruin. In any case, this time our brand of piracy will be more – what shall I say? – delicate.'

'He means that we aren't going to land, collar the first old man we see and tell him we've come to pinch their Saint Tula.' It was Gilles. 'The Captain is very, very good at his work.'

The truth, of course, was that we were here to steal these people's most precious possession. Tula's body was the beating heart of Limonohori and of Koskino itself. Although I did not believe that – nor did any of us – I had not forgotten that I had once been one of the faithful, the credulous. I missed it, that feeling of certainty. When you lose faith you never quite fill the emptiness left behind. And so I was not yet so estranged from my past to wave away the import of what we had come here to do.

But then I thought, as the cypresses and those strangely gnarled, grey-leaved trees slipped by, if no one knows that Tula has gone, has she really left? It is faith that has the true power, not the object, and provided we left their faith intact, maybe we would have done no great wrong. I spat over the side. Well, I had solved that problem, I thought, bitterly.

I am a little ashamed to report that these dark thoughts slipped away as soon as I heard the rattle and hiss of the anchor cable and felt the *Cormaran* stall beneath my feet. We were perhaps four rods' length from shore, but the cable paid out twenty fathoms before the anchor struck. It was deep below us, and the sun's rays, very low now, made darts of speckled gold that dived and vanished. The village was there before us, a scatter of houses and a strange little church, with a merry chaos of painted boats at anchor in the shallows and drawn up onto the glaring white pebbles. A crowd was gathering at the edge of the water. They certainly were not afraid of the *Cormaran*, I thought, as I watched men wade out to their boats and begin to row out to us. They rowed standing up and facing forward, pushing their whole bodies into the task, sunburned men with curly black hair and beards, wearing simple tunics as white as the stones of the beach.

Pavlos, with Elia and Panayoti at his heels, was clambering into the gig. Anna made to follow, but Gilles held her back gently. 'Not yet, *Vassileia*,' he murmured. 'We will do this properly, with a little style.' Meanwhile the three Greeks were rowing madly towards the villagers. They met in open water, and the villager in the lead boat grabbed the gunwales of the gig and pulled it alongside him. I saw Pavlos put out his hand and felt a certain relief when it was taken warmly. There was much hand waving in the Greek style, and then the flotilla pulled towards us again.

'So they trust us for now,' said the Captain behind us. 'That is good.'

*

300

The village headman had ordered a feast in our honour, and despite the short notice, pigs and goats were already sizzling on their spits by the time Anna and I waded ashore. Trestles had been set up in the square beneath two great trees whose bark was smooth and peeling, showing the creamy skin of the trunk beneath.

'*Platanos*,' Anna told me. 'I don't know what you call them in your country. Here every village has one in the square for shade. Often they are older than the village itself. And those other trees you are gawping at are lemons. *Limoni* – how this place got its name.'

She sat beside me at the head of the table – that is to say, she sat at the head of the table, the Captain on one side, myself on the other. It seemed unfair to me that Gilles or another, more senior crewman should be placed below me, but Gilles himself insisted, waving away my protests. Anna, he explained, had been presented to the village as Eleni, the daughter of a Macedonian duke. She was being married off to a Flemish lord living in Venice – myself, as it turned out – who had come to fetch his bride and carry her back to the Serenissima. The Lady Eleni had heard of the shrine of Saint Tula from her old nursemaid, and had come to make an offering and pray for many sons. That had overjoyed the folk of Limonohori. They loved their saint, they told us, and everyone who came to visit her was sent by God to bring joy to the island. But of course, few had come while the pirates (may their intestines be chewed by wild pigs) had held sway. Now pilgrims were coming again, thanks be to the Frankish lords, but never often enough.

The food was wonderful. Chargers of red earthenware piled high with the hacked-apart meat passed from hand to hand. There were bitter greens, little grilled fish, strange and rich stews of vegetables, some of which I recognised, some not. '*Melitzana*,' Anna would explain. '*Bamyes; fasolyes.*' I finally tasted a lemon, squeezing a half into my mouth and almost choking on the knife-like sourness while the villagers roared.

A boorish Frank, but at least he's trying, they seemed to think, and that was fine. Anna and I were at the very centre of a constant swirl of bustle and noise: we, the noble lovers, were the guests of honour. Every new dish came to us for a first taste, every speech – and there were many, each one more eloquent and wine-loosened than the last – began with a toast to us. I took a guilty joy in the thought that these poor people, so profligate with their hospitality, had no idea just how lowly one of us was, and how truly imperial the other. We did not have to play-act very much, there being small likelihood of anyone in Limonohori knowing much about the social life of Antwerp – not that I knew much more than them. I kept my chin up and my manner as lordly as I could under the determined siege of the strange pine-soaked wine. Anna, meanwhile, seemed to be in paradise. They brought her babies to bless, and I blanched at first when she spat on the little swaddled things until she explained that it warded off evil. She pinched children's cheeks and had her own pinched beet-red by an endless line of old women who would have loved to get their claws on my own jowls had they dared. Rank evidently had its advantages.

The wine flowed as if from a fountain. It was honey-coloured and tasted strongly of freshly cut pine wood, a flavour so unexpected that I forgot to be repelled. By the second cup I hardly noticed it, by the third I welcomed it, and then I ceased keeping count. How Will would have loved this, I thought: the wine, the laughter, the proud dark women. Gradually the rumpus of the party faded and I sat staring up at the glowing night sky, the most sublime, unearthly blue I had ever seen. Big bats flitted about up there, and the sharp edge of the mountain shone faintly, a silver thread below the stars.

Someone was nudging me. It was Anna, and she was drawing my attention to a big red bowl brimming with spiny black balls held by a grinning, toothless village woman. 'At last, the *echinoos*,' she said, picking one of the terrible things out with a light touch. She laid it on the table and with her knife jabbed vigorously at the centre, loosening the vicious spines and opening a hole in what I saw was a fragile, bony shell. She poured water into the hole and with a swirl and a flourish tipped the urchin's guts out onto the ground. Another flick of the knife, and there on its point was a bright orange slug.

'This is the bit you eat,' she said. 'Go on, then.'

'It's a slug,' I protested, my tongue suddenly thick with wine.

'No it isn't. It's the eggs. Go on – the village is watching, my lord.'

Head reeling, I bent and licked the ghastly morsel from the steel. There was a burst of salty, fishy, bloody pleasure on my tongue. I took a long swallow of the pungent wine.

'So that's the secret of the *echinoos*,' I heard myself say, as the table rose up fast to meet me. 'They taste just like . . .'

I awoke the next morning to the realisation that every bat in Limonohori was roosting in my head. Many of them seemed to have relieved themselves in my mouth. I was back on the *Cormaran*, under the Captain's table, wrapped in the Egyptian carpet. It was early, and only Fafner saw me as I crawled to the water butt and ladled merciful, brackish water down my throat. After a few rough swallows I had the energy to pull myself up on the rail. Beneath me the sea was a dark mirror. The stars were just beginning to fade before the sun, still far below the horizon, and the trees and edges of the island were sharp purple outlines. My clothes felt clinging and stale, so without thinking I stripped and swung myself over the side. For a moment I was hanging in the lambent air and heard a single note of birdsong before the shock of the cold water swallowed me. I let myself sink, knowing I would not touch bottom, then opened my eyes to the sting of salt and looked up. The false sky of the surface trembled like disturbed quicksilver. I kicked and rose slowly, letting the air bubble from my mouth, more quicksilver streaming around me. The bats were leaving their roost in my skull.

'To work, drunken lord!'

A coil of rope dropped around me, and grabbing it, I found myself being hauled back aboard, until I stood, naked, dripping and sheepish, before the Captain.

'Feeling full of life? Humours all in agreement?'

'Oh, Christ, sir. I am so sorry. I must . . .'

'Nonsense. Greek wine, my boy, is one of the world's great deceivers. Goes down like water, and waits for you with a giant's club. You were almost the soberest there: you passed out early enough. Very good thinking on your part.'

'Yes, well, I had everything carefully planned. So dare I ask where everyone else is?'

'Mostly in a heap under the trees of Limonohori. The *Vassileia* is below – she has an armoured gut, that one. No, after you went down – you just missed ramming your face into that bowl of sea urchins, by the by – things got a good deal more spirited. God alone knows how they have such an endless supply of retsina. Anyway, there were no fights, no angry words – a miracle, you might say. The Greeks are very, very good at being hospitable, though. They had us under control.'

'And how . . .'

'Gilles and I lugged you back in the gig. We were going to leave you in it, and the *Vassileia* agreed, but you came to life enough to climb the ladder.'

'Thank you,' I said.

'You are entirely welcome. And now, shall we step into my cabin? I think the fumes have dissipated a little.'

Gilles sat at the Captain's table, and I was happy to note the green tinge to his cheeks.

'How do you fare, Master de Peyrolles?' I enquired, all innocence.

'I am as fresh as a little foal, dear Master Auneford.'

'And that is exactly how you appear.'

'Enough, lads: you can compare hangovers later. Meanwhile, drink this.' And he poured us all a cup of some dark wine from an old clay jar. 'This is the good stuff,' he assured us. 'Choke it down. We have much work to do, and I need your heads clear.'

The wine was good indeed, and once the wave of nausea had passed I began to feel quite alive.

'We cannot draw out our time here, pleasant as it is,' the Captain began. 'The village loves us now, and we will trade today, so they will love us more. But the moment one of us gets too drunk and pinches the wrong bottom, let alone tups the wrong daughter, they will drive us off. These are kind folk, but they are as hard as the rock of this land and have suffered many lifetimes under people like us. So we will do what we came to do and leave, today if possible, tomorrow more likely. However.' And he poured himself another finger of wine and drank it off. 'There is a complication.'

'Ah, yes,' said Gilles. 'Tell him.'

'While you were napping in your dinner, Petroc, the village headman came over to pay his respects to the Lady Eleni. Amid the obsequies he let drop that he had heard of another Frankish lord – how Koskino is blessed! – who had arrived a day or so earlier on the other side of the island and taken lodgings in the big town. We asked politely if this lord had a name. He did not know, but told us that the town children had christened him "Polyphemus". Now we looked at each other then, you can be sure. And why, we enquired, was that? Well, he was rather frightening, apparently, and – Petroc, you have an educated mind. Who was Polyphemus?'

I paused to think. I had read bits and pieces of the ancient writers, and Adric had been particularly fond of an ancient copy of Homer, a ragged and neglected old thing that only he and I ever opened. I had dipped here and there – the walls of Troy, Achilles' unseemly friendship with another fellow, various murders, and a long voyage. Odysseus. All sorts of adventures with whirlpools, witches, nymphs and a giant called Polyphemus, who lived in a cave, and . . .

'This man has only one eye?'

They nodded gravely. The bright morning had become grim in the cabin. I felt cold drops of sweat start under my tunic, but then the furnace of my anger began to glow.

'Well then.'

'Indeed,' said Gilles. 'It means he has a ship, and a fast one, to beat us here − he must have killed horses beneath him to cross Italy. He is confident now. He will show his hand.'

'Let him,' I said. Gilles and the Captain cocked their heads towards me in surprise.

Anna was sharpening her sword. Dimitri turned the wheel, but she would let no one else touch the blade. It was small and double-edged and tapered slowly to a wickedly sharp point. I had not seen it since that night in Bordeaux, when she had spitted the mercenary Benno with it.

'She is Circassian, a *kama*,' Anna said. 'A gift from my fencing master. I can use a long-sword, but I've never found one light enough for me. The Circassians still make their swords in the Roman style, and so I feel close to my ancestors when I wear her.'

Satisfied at last with the edge, she rubbed the grooved blade to life with a greasy rag, and the wavy lines of damask seemed to ripple like clear water. No perfectionist, I handed my own sword to Dimitri.

'Let me,' said Anna, and waited until the armourer handed it over. 'This is a good blade.'

I nodded. Gilles had picked it out for me from one of the mysterious corners of the hold one morning after we had left Bordeaux. The blade was a little shorter than usual, wide at the base and pointed, not blunt. 'This is a new style,' Gilles had told me. 'See: you can stab and thrust, as well as slash. You are used to a knife, so this will suit you better than one of those crude hackers. I have one, so does the Captain. May it serve you well.' I liked how it felt in my hand. The hilt was an upturned half-moon, the grip was a tight braid of some woven metal, and best of all, the pommel was a smooth, eight-sided ball of steel, pointed like a filbert and inlaid on each facet with a little flower of silver. I had liked wearing it last night. It was pretty, but it had a purpose. It had helped me kill one man and more than likely I would soon be needing its services again.

'It is French,' I shrugged. 'Apparently it's the latest thing.'

'And *apparently*,' she mocked, eyebrows cocked, 'you can use it.'

In fact I could, after a fashion. By now, I had long been part of the fencing games that Dimitri insisted upon every fine day. Some of the men were skilled indeed, others just very vicious. There was much to learn from all of them. Pavlos, who with his Varangian schooling could probably have cut the whiskers from a flying moth, had shown me many subtleties of wrist and posture. From Horst, on the other hand, I had learned how to smash the pommel into the enemy's face while mashing his stones with your knee. And I already knew how it felt to kill a man. In that baleful way at least, I was the equal of any man aboard, and even of the woman who now stroked sparks from the edge of my sword.

'We'll see,' I answered.

In a half-hour we would go ashore and make our procession to the shrine of the saint. It would be our scouting trip. Then later we would go back and do what we had come to do. Now we were dressed in our finest. Anna's hair was caged in its golden net, and she wore the gown I had seen first in Bordeaux. And I was draped in the finest Venetian silks. I hoped I did them justice: Dimitri had been busy with his needle and thread, and whoever they had once belonged to, they now fitted me as if cut by the Emperor's own tailor. I retrieved my sword, now sharp enough to shave with. It hissed into its sheath. Anna's own blade was well hidden: why would a lady go armed to a shrine? Why would any of us? I felt a little hollow inside, and not with fear.

Anna had been watching me. 'You have moped around since I woke up,' she told me. 'Why?'

I muttered something about my guilty conscience.

'This is our work now,' she shot back. 'So do you believe in this Saint Tula all of a sudden?'

'No, but . . .'

'But habits die hard, is that it? Well, let them die. These people . . . they are *my* people, Petroc! These people are full of life: they brim with it. And yet you worry about stealing something dead from them. I will tell you something. When they told me how the Franks sacked Byzantium and stole the holy relics, I was happy. I have always hated priests and their spells and mumbles, and their old bones most of all. They keep us in the shadows. We are not doing an evil thing. We are delivering these folk from being in thrall to an old corpse.'

'Well, if everything goes properly, they won't actually know the old corpse is gone, so I don't think that is true.'

Anna waved her hand as she always did, swatting away annoying words. 'But . . . but *we* know, and their precious Saint Tula will *actually* be gone, and that's all that counts.' There was no point in arguing. She was an armed princess, and as such was under no obligation to make sense. And at least she was talking to me.

As the honoured guests, we rode up to Tula's shrine on two knobbly, fly-bitten donkeys, the finest the village could supply. The saddles were wooden and fitted on the beasts like little roofs. I had to straddle the ridge, which was only slightly less than sharp, as if the maker, proudly introducing a note of luxury, had given it the once-over with his bluntest file. The path was long, twisting and steep, and before we had even left the village I felt like Saint Simon the Zealot, sawed in two up the middle. Christ alone knew how Anna managed to keep such composure perched side-saddle. But the donkeys were an honour it would have been suspicious of us to refuse, so we toiled up and up, led by the jovial priest with his cross-crowned staff and followed by ten of the most presentable of our crew and what seemed to be the entire village of Limonohori done up in their finest.

The day was beautiful, and infernally hot. The track ran between high stone walls that hid orchards and gardens, and many vineyards. Vines heavy with unripe grapes hung over the grey stone. We stumbled over rough cobbles and up wide steps cut – who knew how long ago? – into the mountain itself. The insect noise blazed. Often we were bombarded by grasshoppers, bigger than any I had ever seen, whose dull brown armour hid wings of vivid red or blue. Flies had laid siege to our donkeys' ears, and soon turned their attentions to us, nipping at our sweat-beaded flesh. I had drained my water flask too early, and watching Anna sip sparingly at hers piled on the torture. More than once it occurred to me that by the time we made it to the shrine I would be well and truly martyred myself. Perhaps they would accept my donkey-mangled corpse as a substitute for Tula.

The track was steeper now, and the donkeys' hooves rang on stone. For the first time that morning I was glad I was not on foot. Up ahead, the priest looked on the point of apoplexy as he floundered in his long black robe. And then the walls on either side opened out and we were in a wide open space, circled by more walls. In the centre, surrounded by a grove of cypresses whose narrow trunks were contorted with age, was a tiny domed chapel hardly bigger than the cabin on the *Cormaran*. So old that it seemed to have sunk into the ground, it had been freshly whitewashed so that, like most buildings on Koskino, it hurt to look at in the bright sunshine. Two steps led down to the blue-painted door. The priest signalled for us to wait, staggered down the steps and opened the door. I noticed it was not locked. He disappeared into darkness. Around us the villagers were spreading rugs on the hard earth and laying out food and drink. How had they managed to lug all that up here, I wondered as I swung my bruised carcass down from the diabolical saddle. It was agony bringing my legs together and I prayed my stones had not been pounded flat, as I could no longer feel them.

I was just hobbling over to Anna with as much Flemish nobility as I could muster when the priest emerged from the chapel, planted his staff in front of him and began to sing. It was a liturgy of some sort, swooping, quavering, echoing from the walls around us. The man had a voice that seemed to flow up through him from the roots of the mountain. The villagers left their picnics and began to gather around us, crossing themselves in the backwards Greek manner. The song paused, and a murmur of *ameen* drifted up. The priest was beckoning us. It was time.

I took Anna's hand and we made our way on stiff legs towards the door of the chapel, which gaped like the mouth of a cave behind the priest. Gathering his robes about him, he stepped down and went in. I hesitated for a moment. The doorway was black as the darkest night, and framed by the sun-blasted white of the chapel wall it seemed to me like a hole cut in the day itself. Then a gentle tug of Anna's hand and I was inside.

It took an instant or two for my eyes to accustom themselves to the gloom. All around me was a glimmering, and as my eyes came into focus I realised we were surrounded by hundreds of candles, narrow tapers that each gave out a minute flame of light. There was more space in here than seemed possible from the outside. We stood on a well-worn floor of black and white checkerboard tiles. Around the walls, pews of dark wood flowed with carved vines and snakelike dragons. I looked up. There was a skylight, but the glass was so smoked from centuries of guttering candles that it let in only a dull amber glow. There were faces up there, angels amid a wreath of entwined wings. And ahead, in a halo of candlelight, lay the coffin of Saint Tula. I sucked in my breath with surprise.

Tula lay in a reliquary as rich as any in the great cathedrals of Christendom. It was a rectangular casket clad in hammered silver, into which a skilful hand had inlaid a tracery of leafy branches where birds perched and little animals played. In the centre was a Greek cross in relief, four arms tipped with emeralds radiating from an immense garnet. It was the work of the old Romans, so much finer and lighter than anything of our age. And surely this was the coffin of a Roman noble-woman, not some hedgerow saint. So Adric had been right. The scholars in Cologne had been right. Someone of im-portance had fetched up here in this out-of-the-way place, and instead of a great cathedral and a cult that brought pilgrims from all corners of the world, she had sunk into obscurity: just another village guardian. And Will had died for her.

As our chaperones, Gilles and the Captain, had followed us into the shrine. I turned and caught Gilles, eyes like saucers, taking everything in. He looked a little like a fox in a henhouse and paced slowly and carefully back and forth across the narrow room. I could read nothing in the Captain's face. Meanwhile the priest was busy with the ornate catches at the head and foot of the casket. He bowed his head and half-sung, half-mumbled a prayer, his palms flat on the lid. Then, with a distinct flourish, he opened it, swinging it back on its hinges until a silver chain held it upright, and beckoned us forward. There was a coverlet of new green silk, which the priest drew to one side. Another loose shroud of linen was parted, and we were looking down on the face of Saint Cordula.

It was still a face, even after nine centuries. The years had turned her skin to the colour and shine of jet. Closed eyelids had fallen in to the sockets, but her eyebrows still arched haughtily. A straight, pinched nose led down to thin lips whose rictus barely hid a flash of shockingly white teeth. Perhaps her hair had been brown. Now it was a dusty bronze, and clung in loose, brittle curls to the black dome of her skull. She wore a tunic of yellowed, stained linen richly worked at collar and cuffs with threads of precious metal, and over it the body was wrapped from neck to ankles in transparent muslin, perhaps to keep the fragile clothing from crumbling. Beneath the cloth the ribcage reared up over the void of the belly. Her hands, rings on three of the black fingers, were crossed below her vanished breasts where a rich pectoral cross nestled. Her feet were encased in new slippers of incongruously bright red leather. The priest removed these with another conjuror's flourish and signalled Anna to approach. He whispered into her ear, and she nodded. Crossing herself slowly, gathered fingers to forehead, heart, right shoulder, left shoulder, she bent and touched the saint's withered lips with her own, then laid her hands on Cordula's chest, then the empty bowl of her stomach, before coming to rest on her groin. Then another motion from the priest, and Anna bent again and kissed Cordula's feet. Then the priest kissed her, one cheek and then the other.

To my intense relief, I was not required to lay lips or even hands on the dead saint. We were ushered out, blinking like moles, into the searing outer world. The people of Limonohori were waiting with flowers, which they threw at our feet as we passed by. So we were drawn, through a lane of grinning, flower-strewing, spitting villagers ('remember – the Evil Eye,' hissed Anna), to the shade of the cypresses, where a trestle table laid with fruit, cakes and a mound of roast fowl awaited us. There were big earthenware pitchers beaded with condensation, which surely held more of that strange island wine. Suddenly I was in powerful need of a drink, and well-water was not going to be enough.

I need not have worried. There was wine in abundance, and although I knew better than to repeat my mistake of the night before, I soon had my thirst satisfied. The balance of things was being restored. Anna taught me how to eat a pomegranate, which I thought an odd kind of food, and an orange. It was sour and refreshing, nothing like anything in my experience. I could find nothing to compare it to: perhaps the juice of a plum with the tang of sorrel – but no. The orange was something else that belonged to this place alone. It would make no sense at home.

Neither the priest nor the village headman spoke anything but Greek and a smattering of Venetian, so we were safe talking in English. I hoped the Greeks would mistake it for Flemish. I did not want to be too obvious, but my impatience was driving me mad.

'So?' I finally asked the Captain, who was to my left, absently spearing grapes with the point of his knife and popping them into his mouth.

'You know as well as I do.'

'We've found her.'

'I really think we have.'

'I *know* we have,' said Anna, reaching out for a grilled quail.

'So sure?' The Captain had an eyebrow cocked in her direction.

'Oh, yes. There's evidence. Did you see the cross on her chest? It had a gold coin set into it, a Roman solidus. Thank your good fortune that I have eyes like an owl. The emperor on the coin was Valentinian the Third. I'm happy to tell you that Valentinian ruled the West from 425 to 455, and Attila sacked Cologne in . . . 453, wasn't it?'

'I have no idea. Lady Eleni, you are a prodigy,' said the Captain.

'I simply have a basic education,' she grinned.

'So that really is . . .' I swallowed. 'It is who we hoped it would be, I mean.'

'So it seems,' said Gilles.

'But – and perhaps I'm a little slow, so make allowances, please – I thought Saint Ursula and her virgins were a myth. I mean, that's what most educated people think.'

'And what about Adric's paper trail?'

'Superstitious fabrications, surely.'

'So what are we doing here, then?' asked Gilles through a mouthful of spice cake.

'I thought – I *assumed* – we were taking advantage of some ancient nonsense and giving our client what he expected, an old body with some sort of shady provenance. Our proof for him would be the fact that we took her from this particular place. But the lady in there really could be you-know-who. And I don't understand how.'

'I can try to answer that,' said the Captain. 'Have a little more wine. Now, it is as Adric suspected. In these cases, where there is a popular legend that seems exactly that, a legend, there is no smoke without some kind of fire. Eleven thousand virgins? Ridiculous, of course. Eleven virgins? Not impossible, but too neat, too pious. A girl called Ursula who got killed along with a friend or two? Now that happens all the time, particularly when the Huns are around. Remember that Adric's letter said nothing about virgins, or even mentions the name of Ursula. I believe, as Adric did, that you-know-who, as you call her, was the daughter, or niece, or cousin – even lover, perhaps – of the soldier who brought her body back here. He was an important man, probably a senator or a consul – we can tell that from the coffin in there. Given the effort he took to bring the body all the way back here, does it seem unlikely that he left a monument back in Cologne as well? Something – a stone tablet, perhaps, with a name, a date and perhaps how she died – that was found later and tied in with Ursula, who meanwhile had become celebrated. I would guess that Cor – *you-know-who* – is the only real thing in the whole Ursula myth, and perhaps what started it all in the first place. So. Are you answered?'

'I have to admit that it makes perfect sense.'

And it did, incredible as it was. I did have some more wine, and munched my way through a number of small birds, delicious and crunchy and doused in olive oil and spicy herbs. Stripping a minute leg of its meat, I realised that this was probably why I had heard almost no birdsong on Koskino. I was just reaching for another blackbird, or possibly a lark, when the happy chatter around us went quiet. I turned to see three men walk into the walled circle. And one of them I recognised.

By their dress they were plainly Franks: loose tunics and leggings in the style of Outremer, and long surcoats belted at the waist. Surcoats of blue cloth, upon which reared white hounds. Two of the men wore wide-brimmed straw hats, like pilgrims. But the third, who seemed to be the leader, was bareheaded, and as if in a dream I saw a face from my past. As I struggled to make the connection I felt as if I were being pulled down a whirlpool of bad memories. And then I had him. It was Tom, page to the Bishop of Balecester. I stared, dumfounded, at a man who could not possibly be here. But he was. My companions had seen the strangers too, and I saw Gilles drop his hand gently to his lap, where no weapon lay. All of us − except Anna, whose blade remained our secret − had unbuckled our swords in deference to the saint and they were piled, guarded by the village children, under the trees. So it was with a glimmer of relief I noticed that the Frankish apparitions had no arms in sight. But for the first time in my life I felt utterly naked without even Thorn at my belt. The three men had stopped and were looking about them, dazed no doubt from their climb up here. But they had come from up the mountain. They must have crossed from the other side of the island. Meanwhile, they had not yet seen us over in the shadow of the chapel. As casually as I could, I leaned over to the Captain.

'I know that man,' I murmured. 'His name is Tom. The bishop of Balecester's page. They all wear the Bishop's livery. What the fuck are they doing here?'

'Will he know you?' he replied, smiling as if I had told him a joke.

I wondered. He had seen me once, and he had seen a young monk in a dark hallway. I was much changed – perhaps I was a completely different person. In any event I had a full head of hair and the sun had beaten every vestige of boyhood from my face.

'I think probably not,' I said, carefully.

'But you know him.'

'I met him once only, but I have forgotten nothing about that night. He was a nervous boy hiding in the shadows. Sir Hugh made him jump, that I know.'

'And Kervezey must be on the island – this proves it. But why come here now? Play this very close, Patch. Very close indeed. This lad will not recognise us. Maybe he will believe we are who we say we are.'

Anna gripped my knee beneath the table. 'Who are they?' she hissed.

'They have something to do with Kervezey,' I told her. 'Be very calm.'

Even as we spoke, the three men saw us and began striding through the crowd. I had gone rigid with anticipation, planning the fight to come, but when Tom reached our table he bowed low to Anna in what I had to admit was a very courtly manner.

'I am truly surprised to find such a fair lady in this rough isle,' he began. I noted that his voice had sunk an octave since I had last heard it. But now Tom was bowing to each of us in turn.

'Forgive me,' he went on. 'I had no intention of causing any disruption. I see you are people of quality, and from the north and west, by your dress. I am Thomas of Trobridge, and my fellows and I are bound for Cyprus. We stopped in this Godforsaken place to take on water, and took it into our heads to climb the mountain. I am glad we found you, as we are a little low on water ourselves. Again, please forgive me, but I am so happy to have met some fellow – what do these people call us? – Franks.'

'The pleasure is ours, dear sir.' It was the Captain, at his most charming. His English was near perfect. 'We are feasting in honour of my lady Eleni's visit to this shrine of Saint Tula. My lady is the Duchess of Grammos, and this is her betrothed, my lord of Arenberg, currently residing in Venice. We are returning to the Serenissima for the wedding, but my lady heard a charming native tradition that this Saint Tula has a virtue of fertility and . . .' He waved his hand discreetly.

'And I have the pleasure of addressing?'

'I am Zianni Maschiagi, young sir. I keep a squadron of ships at the Doge's disposal, but my current passion is my vineyards at Monemvasia. My lord and lady's ship stove in her keel in a storm off Cape Lérax and put in at my port. I was bound for Venice on business and . . . a jolly accident, in any event. And yourself? Cyprus is very far from England.'

'Cyprus, sir, and then Jerusalem. I made a vow to my lord the Bishop of Balecester, in whose service I am – this is his emblem,' and he tugged at his surcoat. 'I will fight the Infidel for three years.'

'And return to serve your bishop?'

'Indeed. He let it be known that I might find my fortune in such a way.' Tom paused, almost panting, and looked about him. 'So this is Tula's shrine? What incredible luck. I mean, we've trudged . . .'

'My young companion had heard of some stupid Greek superstition and wanted to take a look. We're sorry to trouble you, my lords – we'll be on our way.'

It was another of the Franks. He had come up behind Tom and now stood with a not altogether companionable hand on his shoulder. If I did not recognise him, I knew his sort: a Balecester thug, the kind we students would fight with on Saturday nights. They became tannery hands or men-at-arms.

The third man was the same. Now I could see that Tom was quite guileless compared to these two. The man who had spoken had pig's eyes that roamed across our faces, intent and angry. The third was sullen, breathing listlessly through a slack mouth. They had round Balecester heads and the sun had scorched their faces nearly raw.

Anna's clear voice cut through the tension-heavy air. She was hiding her English behind a thick Greek accent that I had never heard before, but her words were clipped and as cold as hailstones.

'Is this how knaves deport themselves in the lands of the Barbarians?'

'If . . .' The pig-eyed one was swelling with belligerence, but it was his turn to be cut off by Tom, who whispered urgently into his red ear. 'Your pardon, Highness,' he began again. 'I did not know who I stood before.'

Much to my horror, Anna turned to me. 'My lord, I am going into exile for your sake – will you allow me to be insulted on my own soil? Or is my people's stupidity legendary in your country?'

My eyes had somehow become locked with those of the angry pig. An appalling calm settled on me, a white-hot, almost joyful clarity. I reached out, carefully selected a bird from the dish, and pulled off a leg. Sucking off the meat, I laid the tiny bone on the table in front of me. Now the whole gathering was staring at me.

'My love, are you insulted by the stench of the pigsty? The pig cannot help the stink of his shit: it is his nature to live out his days with a muddy snout and a shitten arse. So with these creatures: the low-born Englishman is a creature whose ignorance clothes him like the pig is clothed in his own dung. Do not be insulted, dear one. One cannot be insulted by beasts.'

I took the other leg, dragged it between my teeth, and laid it cross-wise over its fellow. I took a long swallow of wine, draining my cup, and ran my thumb once across my lips.

'Give these thirsty hogs some water, and cry them on their way,' I said.

'You were quite good, Patch,' said Gilles. 'Every inch a lord.' The three of us had wandered off from the shrine under the pretence of relieving ourselves. Now we sat on an outcrop of rock overlooking the sea. We could still hear the festivities behind us, and below us one of the mountain's many spurs swooped, a knife-edged ridge, down to the blue water a half-mile below. One of those miniature coves glimmered there, and a flock of goats was ambling across it, black dots against white stone. 'Kervezey is here, and that settles it, I suppose. We'll sail in the morning.'

'No, no,' said the Captain. He had been in an unusually good mood since the Franks had been sent packing up the mountain.

'But this is business,' said Gilles, surprised. 'We have no obligations, we have received no advances. Kervezey was using those oafs to scout for the prize. Now he has found it, and he will fight for it, the island will be raised against all Franks, and that will be the end. It is over.'

'It will be over tomorrow,' the Captain replied. 'We will take the saint tonight. No, dear friend . . .' and he raised a hand. 'We can. You know that we can.'

'We *could*,' said Gilles. 'It is possible. I can see as well as you that the *Cormaran* could anchor down there and that a party could scramble up. But in the dark, over unfamiliar ground? We need preparation.'

'I could do it,' I said.

'You?'

'Why not I?'

'What has got into you?' It was the Captain, and he was grinning. I was not.

'Death,' I muttered. 'You know what I have had festering inside me since . . .' The two men nodded. 'Well, then: if this is to be a chance to hurt Kervezey, even in his . . . his *purse*, then that will do for me.'

'You are strong of heart, Patch – no one doubts it,' said the Captain, gently. 'But for such a task, there are a few more . . .' he pinched the bridge of his nose, as he did when searching for the right word, '. . . experienced men on the *Cormaran*. This time, perhaps—'

'Sir, with the greatest respect, there is no one aboard with more experience of Kervezey. My own . . . think, Captain, of that boy Tom. Kervezey is like a bot-fly, laying his eggs in innocent flesh and watching as the maggots hatch and feed, on the Toms, the Wills . . .' I fell silent. From the moment Tom had spoken, the horror of my last night in Balecester had wrapped itself around me like corpse-breath. I looked up. The Captain was studying me through narrowed eyes.

'How did it feel to face those swine, Kervezey's beasts?' he asked.

'I felt nothing,' I said. 'Save pity for Tom.' I stood up and walked to the edge of the cliff. 'I grew up scrambling,' I said. 'And I am not afraid any more. Do you think I can manage Tula on my own, though?'

'Tula will be light as a feather, my lad,' the Captain said. I turned and found the two of them on their feet, studying me. 'The job is yours if you wish.' They both reached out to me and laid hands on my shoulders. 'Now let us get back – your betrothed will be getting worried.'

Anna was not the least bit worried, though. She was learning a folk song from the headman's wife, and by the blush on that good woman's face it was clear that the noble lady had wheedled out something ribald.

'It's a good one,' she confirmed. 'About goats. I swapped for one I know about an old couple and a giant melon. They use it as a privy: brilliant song.'

So I listened to dirty Greek songs as the cicadas thrummed along, and sipped astringent retsina. As the cypress shadows lengthened and turned our walled circle into a giant sundial, as the village packed up and said farewell to their saint, and as I jogged back down the mountain on the fiendish donkey, all I could think about was the long, dark climb to come, and opening the old blue door on a blackness that would be deeper than any moonless night.

Chapter Nineteen

We made our excuses and weighed anchor as soon as we got back to Limonohori. I was happy to leave. My conscience was troubling me with a vengeance, and the warmth of our send-off felt like a knife twisting in my soul. The villagers seemed to want to keep us there forever, and when we finally tore ourselves away they loaded us with food and wine, gifts they certainly could not afford. And so I kept my back turned as we crossed the bay and swept out past the guardian windmills that were turning madly in the evening breeze which filled our own sails.

The plan was to sail north and west to a small rocky island we had seen from the mountainside. A casual question to the headman had revealed it to be deserted save for goats. We would hide until nightfall, and until the fishermen of Limonohori had put out. They fished at night in these parts, using flaming torches to lure the fish up from the deep and into their nets. Fortunately for us, the evening wind was sharp this time of year, and the men would use it to run south along the coast, rowing back in the early hours when the air would be still again. Meanwhile, we would make our way to the cove below the shrine. I would climb up, Tula's replacement strapped to my back, make the switch and scramble down again. It was nothing if not simple. The only thing I had to remember was not to break the relic. My own neck felt far less important.

Gilles called me down to the hold. A number of chests and bundles had been moved and a coffin of rough deal planks had been dug out from the bowels of the cargo. Gilles handed me the lamp he was carrying and pried off the lid with a claw hammer.

'The eighteenth woman,' he intoned as the contents were revealed. It was indeed a body, and I suddenly wondered how many other corpses I had been sailing with these past months. It was not a pleasant thought. I could see several more coffin-shaped chests now that the covers were disturbed, and although I had seen at least one of them before it had never occurred to me that they held anything like this. Eighteen women? How many more were there? I must have said something aloud, because Gilles seemed to guess what I was thinking.

'This is our stock-in-trade, Patch. Our inventory. We try to keep them from piling up down here, but . . .' He shrugged. 'And there is much else besides, all of which you will learn about soon. Now come and help me. Don't worry: they won't hurt you.'

The occupant of the open box was swaddled in soft white sheeting, which Gilles unwound from the head. A soft, dry scent crept into the air, not altogether unpleasant and some-how familiar.

'Well, that's not going to work,' I muttered as a face came into the light.

The eighteenth woman looked nothing like Cordula. She had short, dark curls lying close about her scalp, through which yellow skull-bone showed where the skin had peeled back. Her eyes were half open, but the sockets were filled with what looked like pitch. The nose was perfect but the corpse had no lips. Black skin opened onto a hedge of snaggled brown teeth set in a piteous, hopeless snarl.

Gilles swore. 'You are right,' he admitted. 'Never mind. Help me.'

There was obviously some system governing the cargo. Gilles clambered into the heart of it, moved a large rolled carpet and tugged out another crude coffin. He set it down next to the open one and pried the lid off.

'The nineteenth woman?' I guessed.

'No, twenty-third,' Gilles replied, absently.

She was a far better prospect, but still not perfect. The hair would pass in bad light. The face was battered but intact and in proportion. She was also the right height. While Gilles had paced nervously in Tula's shrine he had measured out the reliquary and guessed the size of her body, and this cadaver would fit.

'We can work on the face,' Gilles explained. 'That is not so hard. The priest and probably some of the older women will have spent time with Tula and will notice details, but the truth is that most people do not like to study dead people. Who can blame them? But it makes this sort of thing a little easier. Anyway, this is just to cover our tracks until we have put a good few sea leagues between us and Koskino.'

'Is this easy, then?'

'For me, you mean? Yes, I think it is. I have seen a legion of corpses in my life, many of them people I loved. The body is simply a shell made by the Evil One, but still Death's work is never easy to contemplate. This one, poor dear, left this life many, many years ago. Her soul . . . that is not right. Her *essence* is long gone. She is merely a thing.'

And then I remembered the smell. It brought me back to the night in Gardar when the Captain had shown me the heart of St Cosmas.

'She is from Egypt,' I said.

Gilles looked surprised. 'That she is. How did you know?'

I told him of my evening in the Gardar tavern. 'So you know all our secrets, then,' he said when I was finished.

'I greatly doubt that,' I said, and he smiled.

'But Egypt is our greatest secret,' he said. 'It is where we hunt for our stock-in-trade. We can make a relic if need be: it

324

is not hard. But for quality and true age, the tombs of Egypt are where you must look.'

'So are they all counterfeit, the relics that we deal in?' It was a question I had wanted to ask the Captain, but I had never had the chance after we sailed from Gardar.

'The answer is twofold. No is one of them. Many genuine relics pass through our hands. You are sitting on the shroud of Saint Lazarus' wife.' He laughed as I jumped to my feet. 'There is a great trade, a *legitimate* trade as it were, in relics, and we are at the very heart of it. But the second answer is, what is counterfeit? That shroud, for instance. It is indeed genuine. We found it last year in a monastery in the Sinai desert, where it has laid for generations. Another monastery in Alsace is awaiting its delivery. The monks of Sinai were glad of the money from Alsace to redig their failing well. A business transaction, all above board. The shroud is really a Coptic burial tunic in good condition, but several centuries younger than Madame Lazarus. I know that. No one outside this boat does, though. It is my business, and I have studied long. But most people do not care for history, or the study of ancient things. They require easy answers. For perhaps eight centuries folk have believed that the wife of Lazarus wore this shroud, and that makes it a fact. We are certainly not going to be scrupulous about it: no one would welcome the truth. Faith is more powerful than truth, and that is how we can earn our living from the dead.'

'I think Cordula is real, though. You do too.'

'Yes, you are right; that is most unusual. But it makes our job easier – a straightforward sale, no deception needed.'

I left Gilles with the Egyptian corpse. He had fetched an inlaid box such as women use for their beautifying and was busy working on the face with a pallet knife and a pot of some sinister black paste. It felt like resurrection just to walk on deck again. The immediate problem in hand was whether I could climb that almost sheer spur up to the shrine with the substitute Tula strapped, as Gilles had explained, to my back in some sort of wooden frame that was at this moment being built. There would be no moon tonight, and yet again I realised that I was the one who knew least about this plan – and probably about anything at all – out of the whole crew of the *Cormaran*.

The island – it was called Hrinos, Pig Island, as it took the vague shape of a boar's back – was coming up ahead. It would be dark in three hours, and then we would sail back, beating across the channel to Koskino. With a bit of sailor's luck, the night wind would still be strong and would carry us north with Cordula. I was trying not to think about the hours in between, so I climbed up to where Nizam stood at the tiller.

'I will be sorry to leave this sea,' I said, as we watched Hrinos slide towards us.

'And I,' said the Moor. 'It is my sea too. Sometimes I believe that every ocean is a mere road to bring me back here.'

'But I will not be sorry to have this night's work over and done,' I muttered.

'Oh, my friend: it is in your blood.'

I had the same answer from Rassoul, from Pavlos, from Isaac. According to them, I had nerves of iron and this would be easy. But I was beginning to feel less sanguine about volunteering for this endeavour. It was less the mechanics of the thing: the climb, the theft. Rather, it was Kervezey in the shadows. But when I closed my eyes I could see Will's lips pulled back in his death-smile. I would not back down now.

I think I wanted Anna to make a fuss. But she did not. She had tucked herself into her favourite spot alongside the bowsprit and was letting the salt spray stiffen her hair again. When I leaned beside her she put an affectionate hand on my chest.

'Brave boy,' she said. 'The Captain wants you.'

That was all. She went back to studying Hrinos, coming up

fast now. I could only shrug and take a lonely walk back to the Captain's cabin.

'I should think you are ready to soil yourself with terror,' he said as I ducked through the door. They were the sweetest words I had heard all day.

'Something akin to that,' I admitted.

'Good lad. Only the lunatics feel no fear. It is a good thing: it keeps your mind sharp and open. Now, here is my plan.'

We would anchor off Hrinos, out of sight of any watchers on Koskino. The shore party would row across in the gig. There would be six of us: four to row, one to steer, and me, saving my strength. The five would wait on the beach until I returned, and we would row back. Very simple.

'But what will I do in the shrine?' I asked. 'How careful should I be about making the switch?'

'As careful as you can be, which might not mean very much in the dark. Gilles will have our stand-in looking as much like Tula as he can. It will be good, I can tell you that. He has a phenomenal memory, that one. Our own relic will be wrapped like Tula. You will simply replace those ghastly red slippers, the pectoral and the rings – do not worry. They will come off easily enough. Now, you will need this.'

He pulled a small, cloth-wrapped bundle from under his seat. It held a tinderbox, a stubby, thick-bladed chisel and the smallest lantern I had ever seen. Blind on three sides, it had one window of thick yellowish glass. 'You'll use it with these,' said the Captain, showing me two squat candles. 'Smell them: beeswax,' he said. 'That way you won't leave any odd smoke odour. It is the kind of detail which someone like that priest might notice.'

'I should take my sword.'

'No, just your knife. That way you won't spit yourself if you lose your footing. I do not think you will need it. Your mind is on Kervezey, but he is on the other side of Koskino. His men will hardly have got back to the town, and even if Kervezey cared to, he could not reach the shrine before morning. No, I am more worried that you will meet a shepherd or a hunter. If you do, run. Make your way back to the sea, and keep signalling towards the *Cormaran* with your light. We will find you.' He patted my arm. 'It is a simple task, Petroc. But I am proud of you, and we will all be very grateful. Now prepare yourself.'

As the gig sliced its way towards the dark bulk of Koskino, I sat in the bows, wrapped in my cloak. Gilles had bound Thorn to my left arm just below the shoulder, and rubbed my face with lamp-black. I could not get used to the feel of it. For the thousandth time I wrinkled my nose and grimaced. It was driving me mad, but at least my mind was not dwelling on the job at hand. Behind me, Pavlos steered, while Istvan, Zianni, Kilij the Turk and Horst bent over the oars. I was grateful to the Captain for such companions. They were, I thought, the most terrifying fighters aboard the *Cormaran*. Granted, they would be skipping stones on the beach while I did the hard work alone, but it felt good to be in their company.

Between the rowers lay the long dark shape of the False Cordula, as I had dubbed her. She was bound tight with oilcloth and splinted between three boards, to which straps had been fastened. The lamp was strapped across her chest. She weighed almost nothing. I had climbed up and down the ladder to the steering deck with her, and she was more a presence than a burden. But I was trying not to dwell on her presence. I glanced back. Hrinos was a black shape against a field of deeper blackness. We were almost there.

The gig ran up onto the white cobbles of the beach, and I jumped ashore with the painter. There was nothing to make fast to, so I tied it around a large boulder. Stones crunched behind me. It was Zianni with my pack. 'I hate to touch this thing,' he shuddered.

'Thank you, my friend,' I told him, acidly. 'It's fortunate that you don't have to lug it up a mountain in the dark, then. Now help me put it on.'

We huddled at the head of the cove, where a goat path showed palely through the scrub. 'Be very careful, Petroc,' said Pavlos. 'And remember, if you slip, try to land on your front. Your ladies are fragile.' I looked at the circle of faces around me. Five pairs of eyes gleamed wolfishly. I shrugged the straps into place and patted Thorn.

'Well, I'll be on my way,' I muttered. There was nothing more to say, and I had run out of bravado, so I stepped onto the path and began to climb.

It was steep at first, a dusty scramble up loose pebbles, but then the path levelled and I looked back to find that I was already more than a mast's height above the beach. Above me, the sharp ridge of the mountain spur was another few minute's climb, then I judged the going would be easier until just under the shrine, where I would come to a crag. It had not looked too difficult that afternoon, but now I would be searching for handholds in the dark. I followed the path until it began to veer off to the side. Cursing the goats for taking the easy route, I plunged into the scrub. Straight away I was enfolded in a cloud of scent as the herbs of the mountain, which Anna had named one by one as we rode to the shrine and I had not listened, were crushed beneath my boots. It was hard going. Many of the low bushes were spiny or so dense that they tripped me. Soon enough, though, I came upon another goat path, which I followed until it too began to head off in the wrong direction. And so it went: a wade through scrub, an easy stretch on a goat way, then back into the scrub. I was hot and scratched but not much out of breath by the time I came out onto the ridge.

In my memory I had pictured a stony knife-edge, but in fact I was on a wide neck of land that had once been terraced for farming. There was an olive grove ahead of me, and to my disbelieving joy a real, man-made track. I adjusted the dead woman on my back and set off at a fast stroll.

Now that I was not surrounded by the scrape of twigs and the clatter of stones, I could hear the sounds of the night. The cicadas were quieter, but they had been joined by other things that peeped and chirped. Somewhere above, an owl was hunting, and nightingales were awake in the olive trees. I remembered the last time I had been alone in the countryside at night: my dark journey to Dartmouth. For months – in truth I did not know how long it had been – I had lived on the *Cormaran*, where solitude meant nothing. It was strange to be alone under the stars again. The air was warm, and sweat was gathering on my back where the false saint clung to me. I had given her almost no thought. Gilles had been right: she was just a thing, empty of the last presence of her existence, and I was thankful for it. Up ahead, the olives stood like a gnarled coven. But it felt safe, and I picked my way past the ancient, latticed trunks, the nightingales stilling, dry leaves crunching underfoot.

The faint silver light of the stars was enough to light my way. The going was easy up here. It had looked fierce, but I found that the spur rose in a series of gigantic steps and the steep parts were mercifully short. Here and there I had to climb over a tumbledown wall that must have marked old boundaries, but as far as I could tell I was making good time. I could already see the shape of the crag above and to my left. I would have to pick my way through a patch of huge boulders, which as I came up to them proved to be even more gargantuan than I had thought. They threw great shadows of pitch blackness, and for the first time since I had left the beach I felt a stab of disquiet. I reached out and touched the nearest stone; it still had a ghostly warmth to it, a last vestige of the day, and that made me feel less uneasy.

It was not particularly hard climbing the crag, which was

deeply fissured and furrowed, as if more monstrous boulders were struggling to birth themselves from the living rock. I had to be careful not to use my back as I squeezed up one long gutter, and once a root which I had stupidly grabbed came away in my hand and I had a second of panicked scrabbling before my fingers found another hold. But before I realised it, I was pulling myself up onto the rocky platform where I had sat with Gilles and the Captain mere hours before. There was a big old fig-tree, I remembered, at the entrance to the walled track that would bring me to Tula's shrine. There it was, and that must be the shrine, a pale daub at the far end of the passageway. I plucked a plump fruit and turned it inside out into my mouth. I was parched, and the seed-filled pulp felt good as it slipped down my dry throat. I picked another. A bat flitted past me and dived between the walls. Suddenly there was a great clattering, and two black shapes were rushing me from the mouth of the track. Before thought could form I hurled the fig at my attackers and had Thorn half-unsheathed. But they rattled past me and I saw four sickle horns against the sky before the goats hurled themselves down some secret path in the cliff. Only then did I hear the hollow clank of their copper bells.

My heart was beating itself out from between my ribs. I shoved my knife back and cursed silently, viciously. By some miracle I had not had time to lurch backwards, or my passenger would have surely been smashed to dust against the trunk of the fig-tree. And what fucking good, I thought, would that fig have done? Somehow the futility of trying to defend myself with a fruit had shaken me more than the goats. I stood and quivered for a good few minutes until I had mastered myself enough to set off again. And I also wondered whether something – someone – had scared the beasts, or if this was just what Greek goats got up to after dark. But at last I bit my lip and started towards the shrine.

*

331

It seemed lighter in the stone circle. The little shrine appeared to give off a glow of its own, the whitewash shimmering between the black brushstrokes of the cypresses, or perhaps the starlight reflected more brightly from the pale stone walls and the white gravel. There were no goats about, and everything was still except for the rattle of the cicadas. To make sure, I walked slowly around the outer walls, peering around each opening in turn, but there was no one. Only then did I strike out across the gravel to where the shrine waited for me.

Stepping down into the sunken area before the door, I slipped the False Cordula from my back and propped her against the earth wall. I ducked down and untied the bundle that held the lamp. The tinder struck first time, and I fitted the lit candle into the tiny steel box. To my surprise, it threw a strong, thin beam of yellow light. I reached out and gingerly tried the door: it was unlocked, as before. I would not be needing the chisel, so I tucked it into my boot. It was time. I took a deep, diver's breath and opened the door.

As I had feared, the darkness inside was absolute. It seemed to pour out over the threshold like spilled ink. But the beam from my lantern cut through and broke the spell. I stepped inside and closed the door gently behind me. I had rehearsed the next move in my mind over the last endless hours of waiting. Laying my pack down, I untied the knots that held it together. The splints fell away easily, and I unfolded the oilcloth to reveal the dead woman inside. I did not care to look at her: the blackness of her skin seemed to have some affinity with the shadows around me, and I felt my flesh begin to prickle. Rubbing the sweat from my hands, I padded over to the reliquary, from which the lantern beam was striking shards of metallic brilliance. I propped the lantern on the nearest pew so that it threw its light lengthwise across the lid, searched out the catches with my fingers and opened them. Then, with my flesh crawling in earnest now, I slowly raised the lid itself and let it settle back on its chain.

In the dim light, Cordula had lost even the vestige of benign peace she had seemed to possess that afternoon. Now she lay rigid and clenched, her hands like talons. I could hardly bring myself to touch them. They were hard as wood and very smooth, but at least the rings came off, clicking faintly but horribly over the knuckles. I lifted off the pectoral cross and laid it, with the rings, on the oilcloth behind me. Then the slippers. That was worse: the feet were more dead than the rest of the body, somehow; at once pathetic and threatening. I bent over the coffin and slipped my hands around the body. As I lifted, I inadvertently looked into the saint's face. It was strange how Cordula had retained so much more of life's vestige – essence, as Gilles had said – than had the stacked bodies on the ship. I could sense disapproval in the raised eyebrows, and a warning in the curled, desiccated lips. A warning . . .

And then I heard it, a faint chink chik! chink chik! not much louder than the cicadas but out of place in the choir of the night. Metal against metal. I let go of the body in my arms, and it sank back into its nest of linen with a faint whisper. On my haunches now, I laid my forehead for a moment against the cold silver of the coffin. The worst had come to pass, as it had to. I was dead. This would teach me to volunteer. I would never see Anna again. All these thoughts and a hundred more hurtled around my mind like sparrows trapped in a room. Then I noticed that the sound had not come any nearer, and was quite unhurried. Perhaps there was time . . . for what? Quivering, I reached up, grabbed the lantern and set it on the floor, glass against the stone of the altar. Instantly the shrine was plunged into complete darkness. I did not wish to crush the other body or trip over some hidden thing, so as quickly as I could I crawled on my belly to the door. Prying it open, I slipped outside into the little sunken space.

The noise was indeed some way off. It seemed to come from further up the mountain, not from the direction of the village, which gave me a crumb of hope. With infinite slowness I peered over the edge of the hollow. There it was: a light, a red light, swaying with the gait of the invisible person who carried it. A mere spark of fire, the bearer must be a quarter-mile off, but walking fast. Then, as I watched, it flickered out, then reappeared, then vanished again. The bearer, or bearers, of course – it had to be Tom and the two piggish Franks. God of grave-robbers protect me, could Kervezey be with them? How had they managed to make it back so soon? The Captain had been wrong: Kervezey must have been nearer. Or perhaps it was just a goatherd. But goatherds did not carry lanterns, did they? That red spark was an English watchman's lamp, or I had never seen one. So it was Tom and his friends at best, and the worst did not bear thinking about. They were after Cordula. They would not expect to find me. I could probably get away – they would be here in a few minutes, but if I ran now . . .

I would have to make the switch, or Kervezey would get the relic. I knew I did not have time. But perhaps . . . Suddenly I had the notion of a plan. I would let Kervezey or whoever was out there believe that they had surprised me in the act. I wanted them to see me drop the prize and run. Surely they would believe that they had the real saint, who would be back in her coffin, waiting, with any luck, for one of us to come back for her. Meanwhile I would have to pray that the Franks would make off with the False Cordula in a hurry, and not chase me. I could not think why they would do that, but enough had gone wrong tonight already. At least I would have the advantage of knowing the path, though that was little comfort, and I would be able to outrun those two fat fools.

Slithering back into the shrine, I found the lantern, singeing my fingers on the hot steel. I fumbled Cordula's rings onto the Egyptian corpse, worked the slippers over the knotted toes until they were secure, and stuck the pectoral cross into the folds of muslin that Gilles had swaddled her with. Only now did I see what a good job he had done with the face: only a serious inspection would show the fraud. But his work would not be wasted. I had the advantage there: I had seen the real relic, and they had not. I wrapped the false saint loosely in the oilcloth so that her face showed, bound the splints back roughly into place. I gathered her up under my arm – strange to carry what once had been a living person as easily as a bundle of dry twigs. I reached for the lid of the coffin, pausing to take a last look at the face of Saint Cordula. She would be Tula now for a while longer. Again I felt her essence creep over me, caressing gooseflesh. I had not forgotten her warning.

'You might be safe after all, my lady,' I murmured, and brought down the lid. Then, grabbing my lantern, I made my way outside. This time I did not bother to hide the light. I could not see the other lantern, but the clinking noise was nearer, and I thought I could hear the crunch of footsteps. Now I needed to wait. I could definitely hear footsteps now, and I began to count them. How many men where there? I judged that they would enter the circle from the same opening they had used that afternoon, as they must be following the same path. That would allow me to show myself, drop the bundle and then put the shrine between me and them as I ran. For the first time I felt grateful for the lamp-black on my face. Thorn was secure in her sheath.

They were coming. I could see red light playing along the passageway I was watching. I steeled myself. I wanted to scream as the energy of fear flooded through me. Grabbing the ring of the door I slammed it hard and ran up the steps, light in one hand, False Cordula under the other arm. I made myself stand in the open, hearing nothing but the pounding of my heart. Then, much quicker than I had expected, the lantern was through the opening, washing the circle with red, and one, three, four outlines followed. They had been running, and stopped awkwardly. If they hadn't seen me, they were blind. Then another two men stepped into the light, and then one more. Seven men. They weren't leaving much to chance, I thought bitterly. I had to move right now, so I cursed loudly in French, flung my lantern in their direction and took off. Swearing again, I dropped the body. Then I was sprinting for the wall and the alley beyond.

I made it to the fig-tree and paused to look back. They were not subtle, I thought, as I watched the distant figures bent over something on the ground, red light held above them. It was too far to make out details, but I thought that one figure stood up briefly and squatted down again. Then I saw another of the men stand and begin to walk with the lantern towards the shrine. The swine were going to check the coffin. I had failed. Then for the second time that night I heard a goat bell. First one, then another, then a hollow, distant chorus of them. A high whistle whipped through the air. A goatherd must be driving his flock along one of the alleyways that led to the shrine – by the sound of it, he was coming from the village. The man with the lantern stopped and ran back to his fellows. That was more like it: at least they were moving now. One of them picked up the bundle, took the lantern and loped out of my view.

'Go on then, you bastards, go on,' I hissed under my breath. I could just see them in the fading red glow. Two more shapes left, but the other four stood their ground. I was about to slip away when the two reappeared with my little lantern. They played the beam around and then, to my horror but not my great surprise, it shone full up the passage towards me, and all seven men were following. That was enough. I took off at a crouching run.

Without the False Cordula it was much easier to climb down the crag. I had perhaps a furlong on my pursuers. I knew the ground, but they had a light. I had to reach the slope above the beach. Pavlos and the others would hear me yell from there. And then? I shrugged to myself. And then I would grow wings and glide back to the *Cormaran*. There probably would be no 'and then'. I dropped into the long gutter and slid down on my front, feet first into the dark. My foot caught on a jut at the bottom and I barked a shin. Then I was in another crevice which I did not remember. It was easy at first, a stone ladder, but then it narrowed and before long I was hanging on by fingers and toes. I had come the wrong way. I couldn't climb back – no time. Between my legs I could just see the smooth top of one of the cyclopean boulders right below me. Without thinking I let go. I dropped for bone-tingling moments and struck, bending my knees and rolling. But I rolled too far and before I could stop myself I was in the air again. I crashed through the canopy of a tree, grabbing vainly at the dry branches, and hit the ground hard. This time I was winded badly, but staggered to my feet, felt no broken limbs and set off again at a wounded lope.

There were voices above me.

'I can't see him!' said someone: a voice full of ugly Balecester menace. 'Bring the fucking light.'

'Follow Tom, then. Christ, it's a fucking cliff – thinks we'll break our necks, does he?'

'I'll break his fucking neck for him.'

That was the pig-eyed one. So Tom was already on his way down. Where was Kervezey? I was sure he was there. Tom and his two friends were after me, with Kervezey and the rest of his company. More Balecester thugs, probably. Them I didn't care about. They would be big and slow. If I could stay ahead of them they wouldn't be dangerous. Tom was not a killer, I was sure: Christ knew what he was doing in this. But . . . I cut that thought off. Just keep running.

It was probably half a mile to the olive grove, and I would be out in the open once I left the field of boulders. The great smooth rocks were a maze here, and I had to work my way through. Worse, shepherds had built walls between them in places, and twice I had to climb over them. As I jumped down behind the second one, I looked back. The pre-dawn glow was just beginning to suffuse the sky, and it was a little easier to see. Four figures were clambering painfully down the face of the crag. Two were almost at a standstill, one of them waving my lantern aimlessly. No sign of Kervezey. He must be on the ground. Squeezing between two more boulders I was clear. There was nothing for it. I sprinted.

The air had cooled, and it was good against my face, but I felt hideously exposed. It was not dawn yet, but it was not exactly night. I could see the horizon, and Hrinos, a shadow on the empty sea, hanging as if skewered on the end of the spur down which I raced. I seemed to be running to the island. I took the first steep place in two jumps that jarred my bruised legs. I looked behind but no one followed yet.

The grove was getting closer. I could not understand why I was not being pursued. Perhaps one of the oafs had fallen off the crag? I had come to one of the old walls that occasionally wandered across the track, and leaped up through the tumbled stones. I steadied myself to jump down. I heard, very clearly, a soft thud and a split second later I was lying, open-mouthed, face-down on the track beyond. My mouth was full of sand. The cicadas were making an odd, scattered clattering. I must have slipped, I thought, and picked myself up. Instantly I keeled over hard on my side. I could not seem to move my left leg. Whining with fury I tried to roll over. How perfect, to get this far and break my own leg. A gut-churning slash of pain ripped through the inside of my thigh. I clapped my hand down and knocked something hard, which set off another landslide of agony. Panicked, I fumbled, and looked down. Christ! An arrow – no, too short: a bolt – had gone through the muscle of my thigh behind the bone and was sticking out of my britches. It doesn't hurt that much! I thought queasily, and then I saw the bolt was a leather-winged quadrello. I had been shot by the same crossbow that had murdered Will. What I had thought were cicadas were more bolts ticking into the wall every few seconds. One hit the top and cart-wheeled off into the sky over my head.

I sat up and instantly my mouth was full of puke. Spitting and gagging, I had an odd moment of clarity. I saw very clearly in my mind's eye that I had been hit by the first shot, an absurdly lucky one in this light. The crossbowman was not incredibly skilful, if his wild shooting now was any indication. If I could get away, at least I probably wouldn't be shot again. But I would have to do something right now. Right now. And all I wanted to do was lie back and go to sleep. No. I stuffed the neck of my tunic into my mouth and bit down. Grabbing the leather fletching I jammed the bolt further into my leg until I could feel the iron head break the skin on the other side. Shouting silently into my gag I snapped off the fletched end and yanked the rest of the shaft through and out. Suddenly there was blood: a lot of blood. I would have to bind it, but not now. I staggered up and found I could stand and put a little weight on the wounded leg. The bolt had cut the meat but not the tendons, thank Christ, and I began to hop away. As I picked up speed I found I could use the leg somewhat. The feeling had come back and while that made it a pillar of agony I could at least make it do my bidding.

I squeaked as a bolt hissed past me. Another clattered on the track behind. I picked up speed, arms out like a child playing at birds. Now I could hear their voices, and I wondered if I had been unconscious back there, and for how long.

'I see him! Look, there!' That sounded like Tom. They must be nearly at the wall. Yes, there was the lantern, bobbing along, much too near.

I had almost reached the olive grove. I stumbled once, and heard a scrap of high, cruel laughter, like a buzzard calling over the moor. Kervezey. I wondered if he had shot me. But here was the first tree. I threw myself into its shadow and looked back again. They were over the wall and coming fast. I wondered if they had used up all their bolts. The crossbow wouldn't be much use among the trees anyway. I limped on into the heart of the grove and dropped behind the roots of a vast old tree. I had to think now. I had another furlong to go beyond here before I could start to drop down to the beach, in the open again the whole time. Once I was on the steep slope, though, it would be roll and tumble the whole way down, and at the bottom at least there were men to even up the odds. I stood up to run again, but sank back to my knees. I was very, very sleepy all of a sudden, and a livid mist was creeping over my eyes. I was tired, oh God how tired! The rough bark of the olive felt so good against my forehead. No! I had to stop this. But I knew that I was losing too much blood. I did not know any more if I could make it out of this wood. And now it was too late in any case. The lantern was entering the grove.

'There's blood, sir!'

'Bleeding like a fucking hog, boy!'

The Balecester voices did not belong in here. I wondered where the nightingales had gone. All in all, this wasn't a bad place to die, I thought suddenly, but if only I could smell Anna's hair once more.

'Wynn and James: go on ahead. Find him, and flush him if he's still moving. Don't kill him, boys, remember. He's de Sol's man and I want him alive. But be quick. The ship will be putting in below us as soon as the sun rises.'

So it really was Kervezey, calling down my doom once more. And what about a ship? They must be trying to take the *Cormaran*. Well, my noble lord, I thought, you can be damned. I'll slow you down and make your creatures kill me so you won't have the pleasure: that at least I can do. I tugged Thorn out of her sheath and laid her on the tangle of roots before me. Then I remembered that she had been bound to my arm with a cloth band. The knot opened easily and as fast and as tightly as I could I tied the band around my thigh above the wound. It was too little, I supposed, and far too late, but I did not wish to be helpless when they found me. Then I pulled the chisel from my boot, replacing it with Thorn's sheath. The chisel fitted nicely into my left hand. Heavy feet were crunching through the dead leaves towards me. Then they stopped.

'I can't see the blood any more,' complained the pig-eyed one. Was he Wynn or James? I wondered. And who had the lantern?

'Fuck. He must be right ahead somewhere. You creep round. I'll go straight.'

Crunch, crunch. He was going to walk right past me. Crunch, crunch, crunch. Here he comes, I thought. I peeped over the root and saw him step past the nearest tree, short-sword in hand. I did not know his face. He was four strides away. Crunch, crunch, crunch, crunch.

I jumped to my feet, but my leg screeched beneath me and I staggered. There he was, right in front of me, frozen in surprise, but as I got my balance he recovered and yelled, swinging at me backhanded with his sword. It whispered past my face, weight carrying it wide. There was a dull twang and the sword flew off and thudded against a tree. The man was looking at me with deep concern in his eyes. The head of a crossbow bolt stood out just above his Adam's apple. Then he gave a whistling sigh and collapsed at my feet.

'Got the cunt! Didn'I?' One of the Balecester boys had the crossbow, then. He was a good shot after all.

Kervezey's voice, tight with rage, gave the man his answer, but I was not listening. I was a bit dizzy with elation and horror. Where had his sword gone? I could use his sword. Then I heard a crashing. I staggered round to see another white figure charging from the shadow of a thicket, sword raised. My first instinct was to lurch towards him, both arms out, and in two trance-like strides we met, both wrong-footed. I missed him with Thorn and just before we rammed faces I saw it was the pig-eyed man. I felt my eyebrow and lip split, and the pommel of his sword come down between my shoulders. I kneed him but missed and lost my balance as my bad leg

341

gave way. I was sliding down his body as he flailed at me with the pommel. Before he could smash my skull I hugged him around the thighs and threw my weight sideways. Now he was off balance too and we crashed to the ground, my right arm pinned beneath him. I tried to turn Thorn in to stab, but he felt it and headbutted me, missing my nose but bludgeoning my split eyebrow. Blood burst over us and through one blurred eye I saw him rear up, pull back his sword and drive it down. I jerked my head away as it sliced my ear, but now he was cursing, trying to pull the long blade back out of the earth. I struck with my right hand and felt Thorn slide through cloth and air. I pulled back and the knife's hilt caught in the torn surcoat and held me fast. He felt it and, still cursing, pushed his left hand over my nose and mouth and bore down with all his weight as he worked the sword loose. In blind terror I kicked my legs and he pushed harder. I was suffocating and choking on my own blood. The sword came out with a jerk. Now my left arm was free, and I felt the haft of the chisel in my hand. As he pulled back with his sword I punched the blunt blade into the side of his head as hard as I could. He went rigid and fell backwards onto my legs, Thorn ripping out of his surcoat. I lay there sucking great racking breaths into me until I had the strength to drag myself free. As I did, one of his legs shot out and kicked convulsively. I scrambled back against the tree. The other leg jerked and, like something from the very farthest corner of a nightmare, he sat up and stared full at me. His once piggy eyes were bulging and glassy. Blood welled from them like tears and ran in thick cords from his nose. His mouth drooped as if pulled down on one side by an invisible finger. The haft of the chisel stuck out from the side of his head like the handle of a chafing pot. I cried out, but no sound came. He lurched to his feet and tottered, on stiff legs, to stand a few feet away, hands hanging uselessly, head slightly raised, as if he heard something in the trees.

'James! By the Baptist's wrinkled balls, what are you doing?'

Kervezey's voice shook me free of numbness. I dimly thought to shove Thorn into my boot before I was off, running – half hopping, half flailing like a madman – through the grove and onto the hillside beyond. I was well past caring who followed.

'There he goes!' It was Tom this time.

A bolt sighed past, and floated out into space over the sea. It was dawn now, and Hrinos was glowing pink. There was the place where I had climbed up onto the ridge. Another bolt rattled at my feet and made me glance down. Instantly I lost my balance and sprawled. I tried to stand but this time the wounded leg had stopped working. I could see the edge of the slope. I began to crawl, arm over arm, dragging the useless leg. Voices and footfalls were coming up fast. I was almost there. It was too late. There was turmoil all about. Someone kicked me hard in the stomach and rolled me over.

There was a ring of faces above me. Tom and the other man from last afternoon. Two others, shaven-headed Balecester men. And a slight man, with dark hair and a jutting beard, and one slate-grey eye.

'What have we here?' drawled Sir Hugh de Kervezey.

'It's a bloody blackamoor!' spat one of the men.

'Wipe his face,' ordered Kervezey.

Hard hands grabbed my hair, and Tom's companion spat in my face and rubbed, cursing as his palms came away black. He spat again and ground the warm spittle into my cheek.

'Fuck me, it's the lord from yesterday,' he croaked, drawing back in shock. Kervezey squatted down at my head and cocked his good eye at me like a great falcon.

'This is Lord Arenberg? I do not think so. Get him up.'

The man who had wiped my face caught me under the shoulders and dragged me to my feet. I felt like a dead bird in his grip. Kervezey pulled out a silk kerchief and rubbed off the last of the lamp-black.

'Well met, Petroc of Auneford,' said Kervezey.

343

Now I could see his face properly. His right eye, where Saint Euphemia had stuck her finger, was sewn shut. But the left one had me pinned.

'Sir Hugh,' I said.

'It seems I taught you well,' he went on. 'If I had but realised you had such talent as a thief I would have kept you on. But now you lift coffin lids for Monsieur Jean de Sol. And you did a very nice job for us back there.'

'Thank you.'

'Ah, yes, and thank *you*, Petroc, for doing the truly blasphemous work for me, just like before. I don't really like pinching things from off the altar, you know. But you, on the other hand: no such qualms. I have the relic. But I also have business with Jean de Sol.'

'Of what nature?'

'You *have* changed, Petroc. The nature of my business with Monsieur de Sol does not concern you.'

'But I know your business. I know who you are. I know what you want.'

'You know who I am?'

'You are the Bishop's bastard. And you are as greedy as that fat pig your father. You schemed to catch the man you call Jean de Sol for his wealth and for his business. You meant to trap him at Dartmouth, with me as bait. Now it seems you have failed to do so here.'

He had flinched at the word 'bastard', and I could see he was mastering his anger with difficulty.

'Not at all. The trap is already sprung. You played your hand early, but meanwhile we were watching you from the mountain top. Now I have the saint, and I am about to take your ship. Show him.'

I was yanked around to face the sea. There was the *Cormaran*, far below. She had put out from Hrinos and was half-way across the channel. And there, coming up fast from the south, a narrow craft like a giant water-boatman scurried on long banks of oars towards her.

'A galley. Very fast. Built in Venice and better in these waters than de Sol's barge. And a good English crew.'

I was too tired for this nonsense, and I was not scared any more. There was nothing left of me save hatred and contempt for the man who was making sport of the last minutes of my life. Perhaps if I taunted him back he would finish this.

'Yes, they've served you well so far. Your crossbowman made a miraculous shot in the wood.'

The man who held me jerked my arms almost out of their sockets. Kervezey winced. 'Poor Wynn. We had to finish James off too, you know. He was a standing corpse – still breathing. I made Tom do it. He needed some blood on his hands, that boy. But you are right. When I take the good monsieur's ship I will have his secrets, and his cargo, and his expert crew. I had even hoped to have his best thief, but that seems to be you and unfortunately I have long had other plans for Master Petroc.'

'I'm sure I can guess what they are. Please make it quick.'

'Oh no, I wouldn't dream of it. You have led me a merry dance, monklet. First Dartmouth, then Bordeaux, then Pisa. Did your friend – it *was* William of Morpeth I struck, was it not? I am a tolerably better shot than Fulke here – did he live? No matter. You are the one with the debt to pay. You owe me an eye, first and foremost. I will take it, and then its fellow. Then, I think, you will come with me to where I can winkle all the useful knowledge from you. If there is anything left of you after that, well yes, I might make it quick then. But for now, watch.'

'You did not have to kill William.'

'No, I did not *have* to.' He sounded peevish. 'I could have shot you instead. Or old brother skin-and-bones, or indeed the Frenchman. But I was angry with William. I gave him his life, and he turned on me. Not a hard choice, in the end . . . And a killing shot, I gather! Now shut your mouth and watch.'

He put his arm around my shoulder and whispered in my ear. 'See how my ship is gaining on de Sol? We will ram him and board him, and then we shall stroll down to the beach and deal with your friends. I would like you to watch with one eye at least.'

It was quite beautiful, the two boats like toys on the perfect water. Kervezey was right: his galley was faster than the *Cormaran*. It would catch them amidships any second. The men around me were craning their necks, and the thug's grip on my arms went slack for a moment. His hot breath played on my neck and I felt a sudden burst of hot anger. Every nasty trick I had reluctantly learned from Horst and Dimitri unfurled before my mind's eye like illuminations on a page, and surrendering myself to them I slammed my head back into his face. He gasped and let go. From the corner of my eye I saw Kervezey reaching for something, a knife surely, and with all my might I threw myself at him. We hovered for a long moment above the sea and then went over the edge together.

For an instant we were weightless, and then my bum hit gravel and we were sliding feet first down the almost sheer hillside, crashing through scrub. I could see a goat path below. We reached it, and the impact stood me upright for a moment. Kervezey had broken free but we were plunging down again, rolling this time. Then another path, and a big bush caught me. I lay on my back, the sky impossibly lovely overhead, and saw that Tom and the other men were dropping towards me like angels cast out of heaven, wreathed in dust and flying pebbles. I couldn't see Kervezey. Forcing myself through the thorny twigs I set off again, leaping down the scree, trying to land on my good leg. I could see the white of the cove down there, so near. Another goat path. I landed wrong on my wounded leg and it crumpled. I could hear clattering just above me and hurled myself over the edge. I tumbled, out of all control. Then an arm caught me round the neck and there were two dead weights hurtling through space, through a chaos of whirling sky, sea, rocks and leaves. I tried to fend the man off and caught hold of his collar. His face came round and it was Kervezey. Then we were lost again. I heard voices above and below us, muffled and lurching like music heard from a distant room. My head banged against something firm. A man's leg: I saw red garters crossed over white cloth flash past, then another pair of legs in green boots. Zianni was proud of his boots. We bounced, flew and crashed down again. I felt myself fly clear of Kervezey's grip. The sky flared silver and went out.

It was a scent that brought me back, sweet but stinging and distantly familiar. I opened my eyes. I was lying under a big bush with grey leaves. Small pink flowers with yellow throats shone about me. I could not place the smell, but it made me happy and I smiled, split lips leaking blood into my dry mouth. Then I felt round cobbles beneath me. I was on the beach. I sat up. My head was ringing and one ear was plugged with blood, but above me I could hear shouting and the peal of sword against sword. I looked up: a body was rolling wildly towards me. Slack limbs flailing, it fetched up against a boulder and lay still, shaven head at a grotesque angle. The duelling men were wreathed in dust and too far away to make out faces, but as I watched two of them crashed together and fell, and only one rose. I could not lie here and watch my friends fight for their lives, so I began to crawl back up the path. Then I remembered the ships and looked back. Between me and the water a ragged shape limped towards me. I saw the delicate, bloodied lips and one grey eye gleaming through a mask of white dust.

Kervezey reached behind his back and drew a dagger, a long, thin poignard. He held it loosely in front of him, hefting it as though guessing its weight. He was favouring his right leg, but he could still smile.

'Come here, Petroc,' he said. 'Come here! You can't get away. Time to pay up.'

I fumbled in my boot and pulled out Thorn. Kervezey's eye widened.

'Shauk! So you stole my knife as well, you little shit. Give her back.'

Blood from my nose was leaking into my mouth. The saltiness was reviving. I spat and wiped my face with the back of my knife hand.

'This is my knife. If you want her, take her!'

I hurled the words at him, and he lunged. I was barely upright, leaning against the sheer side of the path, and rolled out of his way. I pushed off and staggered down the pebbles. At least my leg was locked straight. Kervezey had spun round and the poignard was pointing at my face.

'Your eye, boy, your eye,' he chanted. His knife, thin as a spear of grass, was dancing in the light. He lunged again and I caught the blade with my own and turned it, tottering backwards and slashing at him as he went past. Thorn cut a dark swathe through dust-pale cloth.

'You've kept her sharp for me,' Kervezey croaked. His blade was cutting little circles in the air between us. 'Ha!' He feinted, and as I flinched he laughed. 'You've given me good sport and led me to my prize. Should I forgive you my eye, Petroc? Forgiveness! What did your priestly studies tell you about that, eh? Eh?'

He feinted again, and again I flinched. Quick as a snake he darted at me. I tried to parry but his hand slid up the underside of my arm and the blade caught me in the web of my armpit. Thorn was caught under his arm and I kicked out and swung him off me. It was his turn to stagger and I slashed him across the chest, catching the base of his neck and opening another rent in his tunic. He shouted in pain and I stabbed again. As I lunged he ducked, butted me in the stomach with his head and threw me over his back. I rolled down the cobbles and into the water, the brine flooding every rip and rent in my body and setting me alight with pain. I writhed, weighed down by my clothes and trying to escape the torment, as Kervezey picked his way towards. I had made it onto hands and knees when he reached down and grabbed me by the front of my tunic, pulling me up until I knelt at his feet.

'It was just a game, monklet. You were never meant to win. Now keep still.'

His grip moved to my throat and he forced my face up to meet his gaze. His finger was on the blade of the poignard as he sighted along it. All I could see was a glittering shaft of steel and at its apex, Kervezey's grey eye. A red spark flashed there and suddenly he let go.

'Oh, my lord God.'

He still stooped over me, but he was transfixed by something over my shoulder. The poignard wavered. I brought my hand up to grab it and found that I still held Thorn. Taking her in both fists I rammed her up under Kervezey's ribs. He gave an odd little hiccup and I stabbed him again. I felt the poignard blade brush my neck, and then it fell into the water and Sir Hugh turned his head back to me. Something that could have been a smile worked at the corner of his white lips.

'I think you have killed me, Petroc,' he gasped, and a bubble of blood welled up and speckled us both. 'With my own little knife. I never thought it . . .'

He began to shudder, and his eye roved as if in urgent quest of something hidden in my face. I felt his hands pluck feebly at my chest and as I flinched he leaned his forehead gently against mine, took a shuddering breath and died. I pushed him off and he fell back, arms outstretched on the white pebbles.

I turned slowly to see what had saved me. There, not three furlongs away across the mirrored calm, a long-boat flowered from stem to stern with a great blossom of orange fire. The great dark shape of the *Cormaran* was pulling slowly, calmly towards me. I could see the water as it dripped from the oars. Someone was calling me. I couldn't even turn my head as Pavlos stepped into the ripples and sat down beside me. He laid a cloak across my shoulders and pulled me against him, and I began to cry, deep, wrenching sobs that would not stop. I cried for Will, for Cordula, for James among the olives, for all the blood that seemed to be flowing from me into the endless salty sea.

Chapter Twenty

'Greek fire!' Anna was beside herself with joy. 'It was Greek fire, do you see?'

'I don't even know what that means,' I rasped.

'The most terrible weapon of the Romans,' she explained, bouncing on her heels. 'It is a secret known only to us. Trust the Captain to have some to hand. He won't tell me how he came by it. Not very surprising, really: my uncle would have his guts as bootlaces for even knowing the recipe.'

I was lying on a pallet on top of the stern castle. We were two days out from Koskino and sailing among the little islands of Dalmatia. Isaac had patched me up while I slept, and I had been asleep since Pavlos carried me aboard the *Cormaran*. Nizam had kept watch over me through the days and the warm nights, and had been the first to bring me cold water when I woke. I had not wanted to talk at first, so he waved away anyone who started up the ladder. Now and then he would name one of the islands that floated by: Lastovo, Susak, Vis. Finally the Captain had come to sit beside me.

'I owe you a great debt of gratitude,' he said.

'How so?'

'For ridding me of Sir Hugh. And I also owe you my abject apology. I did not think they would attempt to steal our relic from the shrine, and I certainly did not believe that Kervezey would be with them when they did.'

'As I was foolish enough to volunteer for the task, no apologies are needed,' I reminded him. He looked rueful.

'But what about Kervezey's ship?' I asked suddenly. 'You knew about that?'

'No. That is, I knew he must have a fast ship, because he beat us to Koskino, but not an armed galley. His father has deeper pockets than I ever suspected. No, we saw Kervezey's red lantern on the mountain, then your light, and we realised something was amiss. I put out from Hrinos to take you off the island or to reinforce Pavlos, and it was lucky I did, for we saw the galley coming down the channel towards us. It would have surprised us at anchor otherwise, and we might not be taking our ease now if that had happened.'

'I am sorry about Cordula. I failed you after all.'

He smiled and shook his head. 'No, no. The outcome . . . I could not have wished for a better one. We are rid – *you* have rid us – of a dangerous enemy. And we at least have the false saint.' He noted my look of surprise. 'We had a fair wind, so after we took you off the beach we sailed around to the town, just in time to catch three very surprised Franks, standing on the dock with a long bundle. They took one look at Dimitri and handed it over with great haste.'

It was then that Anna, who had crept up the ladder in fine disregard for Nizam's warnings, added her information about the fire of the Greeks.

'But what is it?' I asked, despite myself. I still did not want to dwell on what had happened.

'I am not giving up any more secrets,' laughed the Captain. 'But very broadly speaking, it is a fire that, once lit, burns even on water and will destroy anything that it touches. Two pots of it, dropped on their deck just as they were about to ram us, and they were lost. And so were we, almost. The men had to row like devils in hell to pull us away in time.'

'It was incredible,' Anna broke in. 'The whole deck went up in flames. The—' She stopped. 'Really, it was horrible,' she went on, sober now. 'The men at the oars couldn't get out. I think most of the deck crew got off, but the oarsmen . . . only a few got free. They screamed and screamed. But it was over quickly. She burned to the waterline in minutes.'

She had taken my hand and was gripping it. Our knuckles were white.

'What about the others on the island?' I asked. It was the question I had dreaded, but since the mood had turned to horror . . .

'Kilij will limp until his dying day – may it be far off. Zianni is a little cut about, but he will be strutting in a week. The others are fine.' He shrugged. 'Kervezey's men died, except for your friend.'

'I met him only once, under bad circumstances,' I protested weakly. 'But I'm glad. What happened to him?'

'He proved himself an honourable man. He would only defend himself, not attack, and when they disarmed him he revealed that he had been indentured to Sir Hugh by the Bishop and had been planning to escape. He did not know of Kervezey's tomb-robbing plans, it seems. In any case he satisfied me. He came aboard for a while, you know. We talked for a long time. He will do us a service, and in return will get his freedom and a nice purseful.'

I raised the eyebrow that could move. 'Go on.'

'We put him ashore at Ragusa. He will travel on to Jerusalem, which he genuinely wanted to see, poor fellow, and send word from there to Balecester, a letter that will tell the Bishop that his son perished of a quartain fever on Samos. Or did we say Samothrace? It doesn't matter.'

'But why bother?'

'Because,' trilled Anna, 'We still have business with my lord the Bishop.'

Later that day, Nizam steered the *Cormaran* with great care between the rocky walls of a bay on a tiny nameless islet, a hump of rock lost amongst the tangle of islands off Zadar. It was a remote place out of the sea lanes and populated only by cicadas. Not even fishermen came there. It was crowned with a thatch of stunted pine-trees, and there was one building, a stone dwelling that had been empty for years but which still had a roof of sorts. Inside there was nothing, Anna told me, save a flaking icon painted on the wall and a big stone trough.

'Perfect: I told you,' said Gilles, when he saw it. The Captain chuckled and nodded. 'We'll start at once,' he said.

The men went to work hauling sacks up from the hold and over to the hut. I practised walking on the little beach with Anna, who never left my side, and sometimes with Zianni, whose left arm had been 'filleted like a mullet', as he never tired of telling me. Isaac's needlework had saved it, and the physician had been to work on my leg as well, and under my arm. It was he who had insisted on my stay on the steering deck: he had a strange idea that fresh air was good for recovery, but I never saw fit to question his judgement after I had healed. The salt water must have done me some good, too, he said. I told him that if I had been at home I would have been daubed with white mercury and cat shit and left to die in a sealed room. Isaac had nodded soberly, and offered to collect some of Fafner's droppings if it would make me feel better. I decided to trust him from then on.

We passed an idle month on our islet. The sun shone every day and I could feel it soaking into me, knitting me back together and lifting my spirits. One morning I felt strong enough to go for a longer walk, and so Anna and I set out from the beach and into the carpet of herbal scrub that blanketed the island. We held each other around the waist and I leaned on a carved stick that Dimitri had found for me.

'Where are we going?' asked Anna, as if there was any choice in this Spartan place.

'To the hut, of course. I want to see what they are doing there.'

Anna paused. 'How strong do you feel?' she asked me gravely, searching my face with her great brown eyes.

'Strong as an ox,' I told her. I met her gaze. I was definitely feeling better. A tremor of desire flickered, then another. It had been a long time since we had even kissed. I felt another stirring, and realised it was not lust I felt.

'Anna, I love you,' I told her.

'Do you, my little shepherd? My brave little shepherd?'

She was mocking me again. I opened my mouth to answer, but she closed it with a cool finger.

'I've been waiting rather a long time for you to confess that, Petroc. I love you too.'

'Since Bordeaux?' She nodded. 'Since the hermit? I've loved you since then.'

'Since the hermit, my Petroc. Since the beginning.' She was crying. We were both crying like little children. She sniffled and wiped her nose with a sleeve.

'There,' she whispered. 'That wasn't so hard, was it?'

After that, it was a while before we reached the hut. A fresh, well-beaten path led through the tangle of head-high trees to the remains of a wooden gate. One olive tree and one fig grew in the yard before the hut, a squat cube of stone with a roof of shattered pantile patched with furze. Anna knocked and put her head around the door, then beckoned me inside.

It was gloomy in there, and at first I could make out nothing at all. The room was filled with an intense, astringent mineral smell. I wrinkled my nose. A beam of light from the one tiny window angled down and sparkled on what lay heaped the length of a long wooden table in the middle of the room. Someone stepped out of the shadows.

'Step over to the table, Petroc,' said the Captain. 'There is something I wish you to see.'

Moving closer, I could see that the table carried a vast burden of what looked like coarse salt.

'It is natron,' the Captain told me. 'Useful stuff. We carry a few tons as ballast. It is a salt from the lake called El Kab, in Egypt.'

'Useful for what?' I asked.

The Captain crooked his finger at me and, leaning on Anna, I joined him, a little reluctantly, at the far end of the table.

'For this,' he said, and pushed aside a portion of the natron. It trickled onto the table with a faint susurrus. I leaned forward to look.

Sir Hugh de Kervezey was asleep under the salt. I choked with shock and pulled away, and Anna barely held me upright.

'I am sorry, Petroc. I did not mean to terrify you. But I wanted you to see. I want you to cast him out of you. He is gone from this body, and from your life.'

'But what are you doing? Why is he here?'

'I will tell you everything,' said the Captain. 'But first, come.'

I steeled myself and shuffled back to the table. At first I could not look, and stared instead at the salt crystals and the way they gleamed listlessly through the gloom. But, like a child, I could not help myself, and my eyes travelled slowly upwards until they rested on the dead face.

He looked peaceful, Sir Hugh, indeed he barely looked like himself any longer. His skin, which had changed to a dull, translucent alabaster yellow, had stretched tight across his skull, and the nose and ears had shrunk in on themselves. His eyes were shut, thankfully. I could not see the crude stitching that had sealed the eye I had taken. I looked up at the Captain, and he nodded gravely. I turned back to the man on the table, and this time saw that Sir Hugh, the man who had scarred my life so deeply, who had lurked in my sleep and idle wakefulness like a flame of evil, always ready to trip me into blind panic, was not here. I had felt his presence in Greenland, out in the midst of the Sea of Darkness. He had been everywhere, but I could not feel him now. He was gone from this body, this room, and from me. I felt a crushing weight rising from my soul, and for the second time that day I sobbed into the living mantle of Anna's hair.

Gilles was right: it was not hard to make a relic. After I had sat down outside and drunk a good draught of wine, they explained it to me. Gilles had been busy in the trees, and he staggered into the yard, arms full of freshly cut pine that drove out the reek of natron from my nostrils.

'It takes a month,' said the Captain.

'Closer to five weeks,' Gilles corrected. 'By that time your body – *the* body – is completely pickled. The natron has the power to draw every drop of moisture from whatever it touches – we had Kervezey down in the hold with natron on him while we sailed, in case you wondered. If he had started to rot, it would not have worked. You need a fresh corpse . . .' I waved at him to stop. 'My apologies, Petroc. In any case, Herodotos – we learned of this method from him – says seventy-odd days, but that is unnecessary and the old Greek is a horrible exaggerator.'

'And then what?' said Anna. She was free of any squeamishness, I knew: if anything, she found the whole thing delightfully fascinating.

'At the end of the month, or five weeks, or whenever the corpse is ready, it is, as I said, completely pickled. But it looks like wax, as you saw, like the skin of a salted prosciutto. That is what it is, really – cured ham. So you need to make it look old. The ancients bandaged their dead and poured tars and resins over them to preserve them that way. We don't have time for that. Think of hams again, Patch. Do you see? We smoke our corpse over pine and various other things – frankincense, myrrh, spices – that darken it and give it that nice smell: the odour of sanctity, yes? We give our clients what they want, you know. And so: a perfect relic.'

'Do you do this a lot?' I asked. I was finding it hard to digest

357

this information, and I hoped I would be able to eat ham again.

'Only in an emergency. Occasionally for other reasons,' said the Captain. 'The reason now is that we need a Saint Exuperius, and, if you remember, no such fellow ever lived.'

'We do not have Cordula,' said Gilles, seeing my bafflement. 'So we need Exuperius. And because we could rifle every grave in Christendom and never find him, we are at liberty to conjure him into existence.'

'And he is going to smell lovely,' Anna said, and raised her cup towards the hut where the natron was going about its slow, careful work.

It took thirty-three days in the natron before Exuperius was hung, with little ceremony, from the rafters of the hut. The table was carried out and the natron, all 600 pounds of it, dumped into the sea. Then Gilles sealed the window and lit a fire in the stone trough. He fussed over it until it burned with a low smoulder and then arranged the green pine wood and a scattering of the aromatics. One of those I recognised: the grey-leaved plant with pink flowers that had broken my fall to the beach on Koskino. It was myrrh.

Then we watched as the white smoke began to seep, and then billow, through the holes in the roof. A week went by, and we all smelled of the fragrant smoke before the fire was allowed to die and the body carried out, as black as the ancient corpses of Egypt. Gilles rinsed the soot away with retsina, and I took one end of the stretcher that carried our new saint aboard the *Cormaran*. We were ready to sail, and Nizam had plotted our course: we would postpone Venice, and head back across the warm Mediterranean to the Pillars of Hercules and further, past the Bay of Biscay, past Bordeaux and up to the misty Channel, where one day I would see Start Point rear out of the furrowed green ocean and know it pointed the way to my home. Perhaps I would even see the gentle rounded shoulders of the moor, fading to blue in the far distance. And for a while longer, Anna would be by my side.

Before the relic was wrapped in old, stained muslin and packed into the hold, Anna arranged the stiff bronze hair and carefully slipped a Roman ring onto one shrivelled finger. I knelt beside her and stared at the hand that had once thrown gold coins at the feet of a young monk. The face of Sir Hugh de Kervezey did not belong to him any longer. It was old now, older than the knight would ever have been. It had a sheen of sanctity, of power imagined by vanished armies of the loving, credulous faithful.

'He looks like a saint at last,' I said.

'Yes,' said Anna, smoothing down a brittle curl with a spit-moistened finger. 'His own father wouldn't know him now.'